WHITEOUT

WHITEOUT

BRIAN DUREN

BEAVER'S
POND
PRESS

ISBN 10: 1-59298-287-5
ISBN 13: 978-1-59298-287-5

Library of Congress Catalog Number: 2009926092

Printed in the United States of America

First Printing: 2009

13 12 11 10 09   5 4 3 2 1

Cover and interior design by James Monroe Design, LLC.

Beaver's Pond Press, Inc.
7104 Ohms Lane, Suite 101
Edina, MN 55439–2129
(952) 829-8818
www.BeaversPondPress.com

To order, visit www.BookHouseFulfillment.com
or call (800) 901-3480. Reseller discounts available.

For Neil, Michael, Daniel, and Jane

This hard, forgotten lake that haunts beneath the frost
The transparent glacier of wings that didn't fly away.

—*Mallarmé*

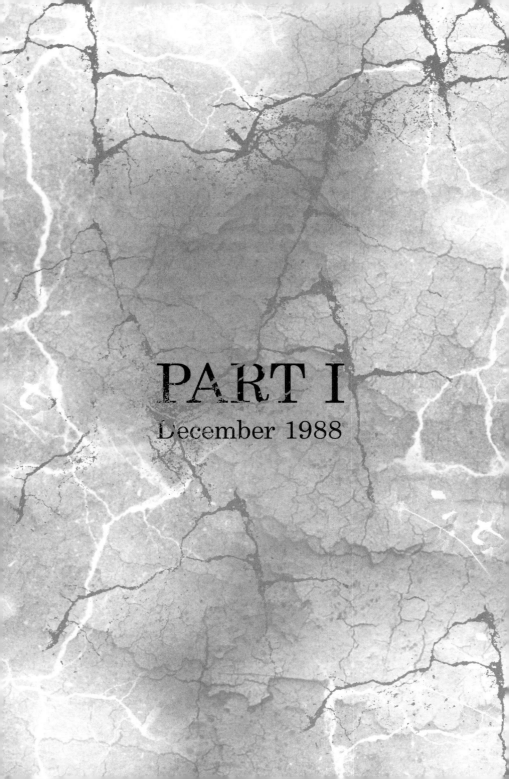

PART I

December 1988

1

PAUL WALKS OVER TO THE WINDOW TO LOOK AT the mail in the gray winter light of late afternoon. Bills, junk mail, and a square white envelope addressed to him in his mother's handwriting. He opens the envelope. Instead of a Christmas greeting, he finds an old card with print in an ornate serif script.

Mr. and Mrs. Herman Joseph Larsen
request the honor of your presence at the
marriage of their daughter
Joyce
to
Mr. William Francis Bauer
on Saturday morning, December nineteen
nineteen hundred and thirty-nine
at ten o'clock
at the Church of the Holy Spirit
Mirer, Minnesota

Accompanying the wedding invitation is a worn, frayed, and creased black-and-white photograph of three little girls carrying parasols and wearing white summer dresses that balloon around their knees. The two girls on either side turn their heads slightly, probably to avoid the sun, while the small blond girl with a Dutch cut in the center gazes upward, smiling at someone outside the frame, to her right. Her head cocked to the side, she has a smile—not just a smile but a plump, impish grin, full of the dickens, as his grandmother might say—that makes her stand out from the other two girls.

He stares at the picture and the invitation, as if by looking long enough he could make them reveal his mother's intention.

The apartment door closes. Keys clank on the table. Claire's footsteps move through the rooms.

"Oh, here you are. What are you doing?"

"Just looking at the mail."

"In the dark?"

"There's enough light." He nods his head in the direction of the window. "It's always a little lighter when it snows."

Claire takes a quick look at the slowly falling snowflakes. "And tomorrow it'll be gone. Snow never lasts more than a day in Paris." She kisses him, looking into his eyes to see how he is. "Anything for me?"

"Just the usual—bills and junk mail." He lays the envelope with the card and the picture on the desk beneath the other mail.

She hesitates, glances at him. "Are you okay?"

He smiles, nods his head. "I'm fine."

A few hours later, having left Claire asleep in bed, he sits at his desk and gazes at the picture. This little blond in the middle has captured the energy of the sun in her smile.

She's a cute kid. Or was. If this is Mother, then the picture's got to be at least sixty-five years old.

Paul looks at the invitation, the names, the date of the wedding, and suddenly it dawns on him that today would be the couple's forty-ninth wedding anniversary, if his father still lived. But he doesn't. He died long ago, without leaving a trace. Like he'd never existed. But, Paul reflects, she doesn't either. Not for him.

He's returned home to the lodge just three times in the last fourteen years. That's been enough. If they didn't exchange Christmas cards every year—cards with generic, sentimental messages that spare them the need to say anything personal—he'd forget her entirely. Oh, she adds little notes about the weather, her health, his brother, sister, and nephews, but he forgets them as quickly as he reads them, if he reads them at all.

His cards, he just signs, "Sincerely, Paul," and drops them off at the post office, duty done. Sometimes he forgets to send her a card until he's received one from her, and then … why bother, it's too late anyhow.

Now it's too late for any kind of communication, even in response to something as puzzling as a picture nearly seventy years old, or a wedding invitation one year shy of a fiftieth anniversary.

Paul turns off the light and looks out the window. Amorphous, milky clouds churn above the seven-story apartment buildings and mansard roofs whose windows turn a blind eye to the parachuting snowflakes. Snow crystals capture the diminished light and create a strange luminosity. The white stone buildings, with their closed shutters and portes cochères, form a single, continuous wall, like cliffs overlooking a ravine. And down below, the sidewalks and street remind him of a frozen stream covered with snow. He remembers the frozen lakes and forest buried beneath thick layers of snow and feels the silence; the shadows in the lodge fold over him like the gray wings of a monstrous bird of prey.

No, he will never return. That part of his life is dead.

PART II

Autumn 1989

"PAUL, YOU'VE GOT TO COME HOME. IF YOU HAVEN'T
left yet, call the lodge. Please, call."

He rolls over on his side, his body responding to his
mother's plea, opens his eyes and blinks, trying to focus,
trying to find her in the dark. The strange forms before his
eyes finally take on the familiar shapes of the lamp and
alarm clock on his night table. Thank God he's still in Paris.
No need to worry, no need to think about this demand she's
making in the middle of the night. He'll talk to her in the
morning. He collapses onto his back, touches Claire's thigh,
his outstretched fingers grazing across her skin, and tries
to sleep. But now he's awake, wondering how his mother's
voice could have been so clear, as if she were there.

Standing in the doorway to the study, he sees the
flashing red light in the dark. He rewinds the tape and
plays it back. "Paul, I just talked with the doctor. He said
Mother could go at any time. I know it's going to end soon."
The hollow, raspy voice pauses. That's not Mother talking;
it's Christine, his sister. "Paul, you've got to come home.
If you haven't left yet, call the lodge. Please, call." He

will, of course, but not now. Not in the middle of the night. There's time to call, time to sort out his feelings, brace himself, think of what he'll say. He needs that time. Has to be prepared. Has to know exactly what he's going to tell Christine. Will he leave right away? Is there work he needs to get done? He has to finish an article. He can't just up and leave. It took him years to get where he is. And if he does return right away, what will he say to her, to Mother? His mind goes blank. Nothing. That nothing feels like a precipice. He needs to think about this. He needs time.

Paul stares at a map of the world. Above his desk. Above the arc of light from the lamp. In the dark. He drinks the last of the red wine in his glass, leans forward, pours the bottle empty, sets it down, and stares at the article in draft form, spread out in the pool of light, covered with markups in blue and red ink. "Speculative journalism is a contradiction in terms," he remembers his editor saying to him sarcastically. Bullshit! The Berlin Wall's coming down in weeks, even if it seems impossible to nearly everyone he knows. If he could just get a final draft done! He picks up a sheaf of pages, looks at them, tosses them back on the desk. His eyes burn from a lack of sleep; he closes them; the tears wash the burn away. His brain feels like dry cotton. Nothing's working. He can't think, can't write, can't finish anything. Ever since the calls from Christine.

Fingers slide across his shoulders, and he nearly jumps. *"Te voilà. Viens te coucher. T'as besoin de dormir."*

Claire's voice encircles him with its warmth, promises him rest, if only he'll come to bed. He sets the glass on the desk and reaches back to take her hands in his. *"Je ne peux pas dormir.* I can't sleep. I just can't."

"You had that dream again?"

"Yes." It's there, still gripping him. "I don't know why it makes me so ... so anxious. Maybe it's the darkness. Maybe it's just that it keeps on coming back."

"Why don't you see someone about it?"

"I don't want to think about it."

She moves closer to him, laces her fingers over his forehead, and gently pulls his head back against her abdomen. "Maybe you should take something."

"I always feel drugged in the morning. And then I can't write. I'm not worth anything."

After a pause she says, "I don't understand why you don't return Christine's calls. Your mother's dying, Paul."

"I told you. That part of my life is dead."

"It's your mother."

He just shakes his head.

"She's your mother, Paul. Call home."

"No. I told you. There's nothing there for me. Nothing. I decided years ago I'd never go back."

She sighs, pulls back, releases her hands, and firmly grasps his shoulders. "You know, during all the time we've been together, you've never talked about your family. It's as if you were miraculously born an adult in Paris and had no childhood."

"That's right. It was a miracle." He stares at the map, then down at his article, in French. "With every new language, you become a new person."

Her hands gently massage his shoulders. "I'd like to know who you are in your mother's tongue."

*
* *

Snow funnels twist one after another to the crest where they blow to nothing. Tornadoes of wild, white dust abruptly vanish. He can't hear the wind, but he can see it howl in the snow, as if he were watching a silent movie. And he can see a boy walking on a plane of snow—a huge drift, maybe ten feet deep. Walking toward the crest of the drift where the white funnels vanish. Bundled in a black wool jacket, a black stocking cap pulled down over his forehead and ears, and a red and black plaid scarf drawn over his face and knotted behind his head, like the bandanna of a bank robber in a Western, the boy steps gingerly from one foot to the next, the thick crust sometimes collapsing just as he springs forward.

Once he reaches the crest, he turns to the right and follows it toward the summit of the wind-swept slope. Leaping and lunging forward with each step, sending clouds of fine snow flying in the silent wind, he reaches the summit, takes a few more steps on the shallow snow, and with secure ground firmly beneath his feet, stops to gaze down the steep hill at the valley that lies before him. Snow, deep, like down. A thick comforter of snow. Snow that glistens in the absolute stillness. Innumerable crystals of snow. Infinite whiteness.

He can see for miles ... see the woods in the distance ... and beyond the woods the white hill that merges with the pale winter sky. He soars on wings that span the valley far below, delighting in the sensation of air currents buffeting his wings and flowing against his chest. He swoops down over the valley, flying effortlessly with extraordinary strength, veering to the left or the right as he follows the contours of the land while feeling the broad bosom of snow gliding beneath his chest. His shadow continues flying without him, following the same trajectory as a crow flying deeper and deeper into the ambiguity of the horizon.

Gasping for air, as if something has been sucked out of him and now he's trying to suck it back in with each breath, Paul opens his eyes, blinking, staring into the darkness. It's there again, the fear, unnamable, that always follows the dream. He can't stop thinking about the boy who struggles to reach the crest of the hill, soars and dives like a bird, feeling so powerful, then disappears in the darkening horizon. Each time, the boy takes a little more of him, leaves a little less of him to go on living. Oh, Paul thinks, he'd give anything to forget him, but fat chance, he can't forget him anymore than a man with an amputated leg can forget the limb he no longer has. And to make sure he can't forget, the dream returns, as if it were on a mission, insistent. But insistent on what?

"Jesus, what a mess I've become."

Claire's arm around his shoulder draws him close to her, and then still closer, until his body begins to fold into hers. "Let's try to get some sleep," she whispers, pulling him with her as she lies down.

He rests his head on her shoulder. "It was the boy in the snow again."

"Shhh! Let's go to sleep."

"It was all so clear, like a film, as if it had really happened."

"Sleep, Paul. Sleep," she whispers.

"Why do I dream about something that makes me so unhappy?" He rolls away from her and stares into the darkness, wondering why the dream returns if it leaves him with such a horrible sense of loss, as if he has died and gone on living knowing he's dead.

Later, his left hand travels across the crest of her hip and down the slope of her belly, and he slips in behind her, takes the form of her body, and draws as close to her as water on a beach. He listens to her breathe, inhaling the perfume on her neck that tastes like sweet ash and salt on his tongue, until the waves of his breath join the same current as hers and draw him deep into dreamless sleep.

He lies in bed reading *Le Monde* late into the night, hoping to forget his resistance and sink into sleep. Sink as easily as a swimmer too fatigued to care he's slipping beneath the surface. Just let go. Like Claire. Holding on to nothing but her pillow. Look how beautifully she sleeps. Her shoulders rise and fall—almost imperceptibly—on whatever current has carried her off. She sleeps like a child, like innocence itself. He places his hand on her shoulder, gently, so as not to wake her, and feels the rise and fall as she breathes. He has been lying awake the last few nights, reading the newspaper, anticipating the next call from home, and fearing the vulnerability to dreams that comes with sleep. Never has he desired sleep so much ... the sweet balm of sleep ... sleep that knits up the raveled sleeve of care. Sleep that only the innocent can find. He closes his eyes again. If only ... and for a moment he does let go, sleep slowly pulling him under. Panicked, he opens his eyes. He shivers. Leans forward, finds the sheet he has kicked to the bottom of the bed with his tossing and turning, and pulls it up over his shoulders. Grazing on her skin he works his way up her bare legs, rubs his face against the silk stretched across her bottom, and then pulls the sheet over her back. His fingers glide up her neck, across her hair to the top of her left ear and the tiny piece of cartilage that forms a point, the little point that is so quintessentially hers. He kisses that point, barely touching it, whispers, *"Petit elfe de mon coeur,"* and draws back. He must not wake her. He returns to his newspaper and reads, passing time, until his eyes close, the paper slips from his hand, and he sinks beneath the surface, his fingers reaching for Claire's thigh, for his life in Paris.

The next day he feels particularly happy, in spite of his fatigue, until he sees the flashing red light of the telephone recorder. Christine's voice, hoarse, exhausted, monotone. "Mother died ... about an hour ago. Around four this morning." A pause. Then the voice continues. "I hope you're coming home. I thought I could handle this ... If you haven't left yet, call the lodge ... or call me at home. One of us will pick you up at the airport." His mother's face flits through his mind and disappears, a blur in the peripheral vision of his memory. He replays the tape. A sliver of ice penetrates his heart.

3

THE PLANE GLIDES SILENTLY ABOVE THE TOWER-
ing peaks of clouds white as snow. If only this were a dream,
he would wake up and find he wasn't flying home for his
mother's funeral, for a last encounter with his brother and
sister, for a final return to the lodge. He shivers, feeling the
cold shadows of the lodge close around him, and remembers
his determination to get out of there. Start a new life, a real
life, in Paris. Everything was going so well until the calls
from Christine. Mother's sick; she's dying; she's dead. All
the nights he lay in bed next to Claire, anticipating another
call—when are you coming home? These calls that pursued
him like Greek furies, making him feel guilty, refusing to
let him sleep. Oh, my God, he thinks, shaking his head, get
hold of yourself, bring the hyperbole down a few decibels.
You're going through what people go through all the time:
returning home for a funeral.

Instead of dwelling on those emotions, he gives himself
a pep talk, a victory rally. He remembers his toughness and
courage in moving from Minnesota to France, creating a
life for himself as a freelance writer in Paris, writing and

publishing in French. And even if he had loftier aspirations growing up—because one always does, that's just life—he has proven himself, earning a good living, enjoying great friends (the family, he affectionately calls them), and he has Claire, a brilliant woman, a professor, the daughter of a publisher. This is the life he's made for himself, the life to which he will return—and none of it was handed to him—after the funeral, so why should he worry? He's made himself what he is. He leans back in his seat, flying high above any turbulence, and presses the call button for the flight attendant to order a drink.

The alcohol flows through his veins, slackens the tension in every limb. He feels he might like to read, pulls out the books he quickly crammed into a tote bag, stares at the cover of one, *Arctic Dreams*, that he started several months before, and sets the book on his lap.

He leans back in his seat and looks out the window at the brilliant field of clouds extending as far as the eye can see; he remembers the view from his bedroom window, of snow covering the slope in front of the lodge, the frozen lake, and the hill beyond with its pine forest dwarfed by the distance. On a sunny day he'd set off on skis, gliding across the lake on the thick crust of snow that had been burnished by the wind. Sometimes he'd let the wind carry him along, his body his only sail, and fly across the ice. The frozen lakes and portages formed continuous, snow-covered freeways, unbroken by borders of land and water, that opened the wilderness to his curiosity and enticed him to go further and deeper, crossing lakes he didn't know, seeing how far he could go, reckoning a path to circle back to familiar landmarks (a small peninsula, a huge boulder, a particularly tall white pine with an abandoned osprey nest) that would guide him home before dark. He'd stop to rest in the middle of a lake, watching his hot breath form clouds in the cold air, feeling each bead of sweat trickle down the small of his back. He might spot a pack of wolves standing stone still a hundred yards off, staring at him for what seemed several minutes, before drifting into the woods as if carried by a gust of wind, never disturbing the absolute stillness and silence, so that he'd wonder if he'd really seen the wolves or if they were a hallucination. He remembers how snow muffles sound, creating a world of silence in which things appear and disappear, as if by magic, as if in a dream.

With the breakup of the ice in the spring, he'd set out canoeing, the water almost black, rippling between the still-receding shores of ice. The loons would mate in May, and by June he'd see one of them swimming with a pair of gray chicks while the other plunged beneath the shimmering surface, resurfacing where he'd least expect it. In the late afternoon his eyes would wander from a wall of granite boulders, from the birch and pine along the shores, to their reflection on the still water over which the canoe glided like a ghost as it passed through a channel or followed the lazy, meandering current of the Kawishiwi River through the maze of lakes. Once out in the open lake, he could see the entire shoreline reflected perfectly on the black surface. The real world, which seemed at some indefinable point to rise from its own reflection, lost its primacy for him as his gaze followed the landscape on the lake.

Spirit Lake was one of the principal entries to the Boundary Waters Wilderness; he'd spend his summers outfitting campers and watching them paddle across the lake, their canoes, with backpacks standing in the middle, riding low in the water. In late August, when the nights turned cooler, a mist would rise from the lake like a spirit army, and in the morning, when he walked down to the boathouse, he'd stop on the main dock, trembling in the damp air, and gaze at the thick, gray clouds of fog that hovered above the lake. Wisps of fog would ascend like gray-haired ghosts and glide away. An island would rise from the water, slowly emerging from the mist. It seemed at once real and an apparition. Then the sun would begin its visible ascent, slowly hemorrhaging along the horizon, tinting the ghosts with a blood-red glow. Eventually the red blaze would burn the spirits of their wispy filaments, dissolving them in the clear morning light. Finally the island would stand stout as a British empiricist, a no-nonsense mass of rock slabs, boulders, scrub pine, and a few reeds in the shallows at either end.

As the days became shorter and colder, ice would slowly lock up the lakes, layers of snow would blanket the forest and the lodge, and the eerie silence of winter would become an echo chamber for thoughts. He would look out his window at the snow-covered slope and lake and hear the wailing of the wind, the creaking of timbers, the thoughts whispering in his head.

He never left this place. He carries it inside him. It's the stuff of which he's made.

A crackling voice over the loudspeaker startles Paul with the announcement that the plane will be landing in Minneapolis in an hour. He looks down through the deep, clear chasms among the mountainous clouds at the ground below where the shadows of the clouds and of the airplane glide across the land. Soon he will find himself face-to-face with Christine. He remembers her disembodied voice, coming to him from another world. "Mother could go at any time." And then, a few weeks later, her voice again, hoarse, cracking with emotional static: "Mother died about an hour ago. I hope you're coming home."

He walks out of the ramp, enters the airport gate, a little unsteady after so many hours in flight, and looks around for Christine. Not seeing her, he feels almost relieved. And then there she is, looking in his direction, smiling as if it hurt. Crisply ironed khaki pants and a white blouse, dark glasses, short waves of sandy brown hair. He walks over to her, puts his arms limply around her, and as they hug the stale smell of cigarettes and coffee evokes long, harrowing nights and the voice that spoke to him from the recorder. She is tall and big-boned, but as he holds her in his arms she seems fragile and frail. She releases him, bows her head and sighs as she runs her fingers across the surface of her hair, then looks up at him and apologizes in a raspy voice. "I'm a real mess. I've hardly slept the last three nights." But she's not a mess. She looks as she always has: so proper in her preppy clothes, perfectly pressed and pleated; so pretty, with the smooth skin—like a white rose, with barely a blush—of a young woman. Only the raspy voice and the smell of coffee and cigarettes hint at the suffering behind the mask and the sunglasses.

She is grieving; he is not. How can he mourn the death of someone he doesn't know? He should leave, but it's too late. He can only go forward into the past.

4

PAUL STANDS IN THE ALCOVE OF THE LIVING ROOM in Christine's house, staring down the long slope of the front yard at the lake. Christine's new house looks out upon a lake, just as the lodge does.

He notices a teenage boy in jeans and a black hoodie down by the lakeshore, in the neighbor's yard. Holding a rope strung from the limb of a cottonwood tree, his foot in a ring tied like a stirrup to the end of the rope, the boy leans back as he swings over the yard, then stretches his body taut as he flies out over the dark water. He swings back and forth, pumping and stretching, trying to gain speed and reach the rope's limit, flying as far as the rope will allow him to go.

Paul touches the window. Fly away, kid. Anywhere out of this world.

"He's a runner."

"What?" Paul looks at Christine standing next to him, her eyes still concealed by dark glasses.

"The boy." She nods at the teenager. "He's run away from home two or three times. They're at their wit's end …

trying to figure out what to do with him."

She hands him a bottle of beer and takes a sip of coffee from a mug.

"Thanks." His gaze lingers a while on the boy before he looks to see what she has served him. He recognizes the label with the German name *Leinenkugel's* printed in large gold script, and above the name, the head of a woman in profile, a feather rising from her headdress, and the words "Chippewa Falls, Wisconsin" circling the image. She looks very European for a Chippewa maiden.

"It's been eons since I've had one of these."

He takes a sip, then looks at the label again, remembering the men of the baling and threshing crews, in bib overalls, blue sweat-soaked shirts, and white t-shirts, standing in a circle under the cottonwood tree near the machine shed at his grandfather's farm, drinking Leinenkugel's, telling stories. He always stood a little behind, on the outer edge of the circle, quiet so no one would notice him. They'd listen intently to the storyteller, nodding their heads in recognition, spitting on the gravel, with the toe of their boots nudging the sandy dirt over the spittle, tipping their bottles up and taking long draws, each man's Adam's apple bobbing up and down as if metering the flow of beer. When the punch line came, men smiled and nodded and took another swig, while the storyteller kept a straight face, deadpanning to the end.

"Why don't we sit down," Christine orders.

She turns away. He follows her to the couch. She's silent. He sits next to her, feeling her grief, wishing he could grieve. He takes a short drink, sets the bottle on the coffee table. Stares at the Indian-head label. Begins scraping it with his thumbnail. Busying himself. Feeling useless and out of place.

Finally Christine speaks, in a slow, trancelike monotone. "I couldn't tell if she was asleep ... unconscious ... or awake with her eyes shut. Too occupied with dying to care about anything. It took her so long to die. Maybe if she'd been older, and weaker, the cancer wouldn't have had to fight so hard to kill her."

He continues staring at the bottle, slowly scraping off the German name and the image of the European Chippewa maiden.

"Tim was there part of the time. And Fran. Sometimes we talked about her as if she'd already gone, but she was still breathing. That's terrible, isn't it?"

"No," he murmurs, wondering if his mother had heard the three of them talking about her as if she were dead. He imagines her entombed within her own body, no longer able to respond to the voices she could still hear.

"I can't forget she died all alone, in the middle of the night. One of the few times in those two days I slept." She pauses. "I should've been with her. Someone should've." With a tissue wadded into a ball, she wipes away tears that flow from beneath her sunglasses.

He says, "That's probably the way most people go— alone, in the middle of the night." He fingers the spindles of gray label paper lying on the table.

"Sometimes she'd stop breathing. I'd wonder. And then she'd start again. One of the nurses whispered she probably wouldn't make it through the night." Christine slowly shakes her head. "All of a sudden it hit." She looks down at her coffee, then back up at him. "I'm sure you're right ... most people die alone, probably in the middle of the night. Death is for the dead and life is for the living."

"I don't think it's quite that neat a separation."

The long nail of her tobacco-stained index finger glides along the rim of the coffee mug. "She'll probably live with us for a long time." Christine smiles. "Maybe even a lot longer than we'd like." She gives a little laugh and shakes her head.

He is about to ask what she finds so amusing when she looks at him and says, "I'm so glad you've come, Paul. This has been too much for Tim and me, and of course, Fran ..." She shakes her head. "I'm sure you'll be happy to get this over and go back home. We all will."

"When do we leave?" Paul feels relieved to be able to talk about practical matters.

"Tomorrow morning. Soon as we can get on the road."

"Are the boys coming?"

"The boys?" She laughs. "The boys are men now. And no, they're not coming. Mother never got close to them, and they complained every time we took them to the lodge. Nothing to do, and Grandma just stared at people, like they're weird. When she was the one who was weird."

Paul smiles. "They've got a point."

"All she inspired in them was some nasty names— the Weird Witch of the North, old Miss Havisham, the Mummy—still alive and walking in her rags. And Arsenic and Old Lace. That one stuck. Sometimes Rick just calls her Arse and Steve calls her Nic."

Paul bursts into laughter, takes a couple of deep breaths, and finishes his beer, still smiling.

"I've been so upset, I didn't even think to ask you how things are going."

"I'm fine." He slowly nods his head. "Really. I have my own byline twice a week; write about whatever interests me; finally bought an apartment. I even take vacations, like everyone else."

"Are you married? I know that sounds funny, but you say so little in your Christmas cards."

"No, but I have a girlfriend. We've been together for nearly four years." He thinks of Claire and adds, "She's very special."

"I'd like to meet her sometime."

He nods his head, so that he doesn't have to lie, or tell

the truth—that he'll never again return.

"Well, I've got to get dinner ready. Tim will be home any time now." She picks up the empty bottle and mug. Paul notices the little rolls and coils of label-paper; feels embarrassed, as if he'd somehow sullied her world; and brushes the trash into his hand to carry to the kitchen.

"I'll show you your room."

He looks around the bedroom. Posters of the Rolling Stones, Led Zeppelin, *Apocalypse Now*, *Platoon*, Walter Payton, and Fran Tarkenton decorate the walls, and two framed pictures of football teams (high school boys in rows three deep, their jerseys resting on huge shoulder pads that make them look as if they've costumed themselves in clothes for older and bigger people) stand on the top of a book shelf. He scans the titles of science fiction and adventure novels and videotapes. Several of the tapes bear the handwritten title "Chaplin."

He turns on a television and puts one of the tapes, which has been stopped well before the end, in the VCR. Charlie strolling down a sidewalk sees a huge man seated in a restaurant window eating a large roast chicken all by himself. Charlie stops, looks at the food, devouring it with his eyes—black eyes dilated with hunger and sadness. He senses something, looks up, his eyes and those of the fat man lock onto one another. The fat man, dressed in a white shirt and a faded black tuxedo coat (so tight it looks ready to burst at the seams), has a round face, the stubble of a heavy black beard, and short, cropped hair. The second he notices Charlie's saucers staring at the feast, he draws a mean, villainous scowl. Charlie strikes a pose of indifference, looks away, adjusts his hat, takes it off, brushes it, puts it back on, strolls about in front of the window, twirls his cane, stops, pretends to gaze at something in the distance, adjusts the handkerchief in his coat pocket, removes his hat, brushes it, puts it back on, whistles a tune, and while he's performing all of his antics he casts furtive glances at the feast on the other side of the window. The fat man protects his dinner with a furled, black, burly scowl.

Sitting in the living room with time to kill, Paul looks at a coffee-table book of photographs of wolves in the Boundary Waters. He remembers the howling of wolves, a pack of wolves, three or four, maybe more, each howling in a different key, each starting at a different moment, one howl trailing off, replaced by another. Standing in front of his tent, the morning air cold and heavy with dew, fog still thick on the lake, he listened to the eerily high-pitched, discordant sound and he shivered with cold and fear; he understood how settlers could be so terrified of wolves and so convinced that their howls were the expression of a demonic force, of pure evil, that they would kill them to the edge of extinction. After what seemed an extremely long time, the howling finally stopped, but his body continued to shiver. For a few minutes he believed evil existed— somewhere other than in the minds of men. He had been camping on an island in the Boundary Waters when he was a boy, about fifteen, and the wolves had awakened him with their howling. Even now, as he looks down at the book, the hair on his forearms stands straight up.

"Well, you finally made it."

Paul springs up. Tim is moving toward him like the linebacker he was in college closing in on a running back, and Paul, trapped, instinctively extends his hand as much to stiff-arm the tackler as to take Tim's hand.

"Hey, how are you, stranger?" Tim beams a smile at him.

Paul tightens his grip to hold his own in this contest of strength, and is just about to answer when Tim blurts out, "You look great. Just great."

After having been sardined in a plane for twelve hours,

and trapped for another hour in the car with Christine, Paul wonders how he could possibly look great. But the ingratiating tone in Tim's voice makes it clear that the comment means nothing more than that Tim wants to please him. His idea perhaps of being a good host.

"When did you get in?"

"Just a couple hours ..."

"Tim, is that you?" Christine hollers from the kitchen.

"Who else would it be?" He grins as if it were a joke. "I'd better see what she wants." He gives Paul a quick lookover, as if measuring him for a new suit with his eye. "You really look great. Back in a minute."

Paul wonders, what's with the camaraderie? I've only seen him a few times in the last twenty-five years.

On his way to the kitchen Tim tosses his blue pinstripe suit coat over the back of a chair in the dining room, takes a dark green liquor bottle out of the buffet, holds it up and mouths, "Scotch?" Paul nods his head yes. He sits down again. He hears a refrigerator door slam shut, ice cubes click against glass, muffled voices. Finally, after a long silence, Tim returns with two tumblers of scotch.

"Here's to your arrival." Tim takes a deep breath and adds, "Wish the circumstances were different."

Paul finds the scotch smooth, heady, expensive—top shelf. He inhales the perfume and remembers evenings in jazz clubs in Paris, sipping scotch served by bartenders with dark cocaine eyes.

"We were wondering if you were going to come. Since we didn't hear from you until yesterday, we didn't even know if you were getting Chris's messages."

"I got them."

Tim nods his head in response, the smile still on his face. "Well, we're really happy you're here." He gazes at Paul for a few seconds, then comments, as if making a discovery. "You look great. You really do." Tim salutes him with his glass and takes another sip.

That makes how many times you've told me I look great? Paul thinks, as he sips his scotch.

"How was your flight?"

"Long. Luckily we had good weather. Blue skies. Clouds white as snow."

"Clouds." Tim shakes his head. "I'm strictly a feet-on-the-ground guy. Hate flying. That's one of the advantages of my promotion. Oh, did Chris tell you?"

"Tell me what?"

"I've been promoted to vice president."

"Congratulations."

"Thanks. It sure as hell has been a long time coming. The good thing is now I can send other people up. I've flown enough in my life."

Tim shifts his weight and settles more deeply into the thick-cushioned armchair. "Living in hotels. That gets old real fast. No, I'd much rather be here with Chris ... in this house ..." He nods his head and his gaze travels across the living room and settles on the picture window and the view of the lake. A contented smile creases his deeply tanned face. He looks like a mannequin, Paul thinks as he studies Tim's face, his blond hair (it has to be dyed) against the beach-boy tan, the nearly permanent smile, and the fine hands with their long, beautifully manicured fingers—no longer the hands of a football player. Paul imagines the linebacker who used to fix on a ball carrier like a heat-seeking missile metamorphosing into a corporate player targeting success in an organization with the same relent-less, programmed pursuit.

Tim turns his gaze toward him, catching him staring. "Well ... I hope Chris hasn't left you alone all this time."

"She doesn't have to worry about me. Actually I, ah ... noticed the boys have a collection of Charlie Chaplin films on video, and I was just looking ..."

"Oh, you found them!" Tim smiles and nods his head. "I was just looking at one the other day. I taped those years ago, when one of the channels ran them on Sunday mornings. The boys and I would watch them over and over. They'd laugh … " He shakes his head, amazed in retrospect at their laughter. "Sometimes, when I miss them, I go into their room and look at the tapes, and remember how they used to laugh."

"What a great memory! Shared happiness." Paul adds, "Oh, I also looked at this book on wolves." He touches the book cover.

"That photographer lived in the wilderness for nearly a year. He got so friendly with the wolves, he said by the end he felt like he'd almost become one of em." Tim pauses, then adds, "Of course, in the boonies, it's not all that unusual for people to kind of … revert." He chuckles.

Paul nods his head, still smiling. Growing up he heard countless wilderness legends about people who'd lived alone too long in the "boonies" and who'd ended up "reverting." Howling at the moon. Having incestuous and bestial relationships that produced strange-looking offspring. Human predators that stalked, killed, and ate raw meat. An ounce of truth, a pound of lies.

Later that evening, after dinner, Paul stands again in the alcove looking out at the lake, wondering what was eating Christine. She seemed withdrawn and angry all the way through dinner, oblivious to the praise Tim heaped on her for the way she'd handled such a difficult situation or to any compliments he offered about her cooking.

"It's almost dark." Tim stood next to Paul. "The houses on the other side are beginning to merge with their surroundings."

"*L'heure entre chien et loup,*" Paul murmurs.

"What?"

"It's the time of day when you can't tell the difference between a dog and a wolf." And you don't know whether to get closer or move away, Paul thinks. "Well, Tim, I need to get to bed. I'm asleep on my feet. Where's Christine?"

"She wanted to give your brother Fran a call and let him know when we'd be coming."

"How's he holding up?"

"You'll see."

"I told Fran we'd be arriving around two." Christine's voice surprises Paul. She's standing just behind them.

"Good," Tim responds. "I'm off to bed." He puts his arm around Christine's shoulder and kisses her on the forehead. "I'm taking the paper, but I might be asleep by the time you come."

"I won't be long," she answers.

"Christine, good night. I can't stay awake any longer." Paul yawns, more to make his case than out of fatigue.

"Paul, keep me company for just a few minutes. I want to talk with you."

Her voice has a hard edge; this isn't a request, it's a command. *Aussi aimable qu'une porte de prison*, he thinks. As lovable as a prison door. As if he were still a little kid, taking orders.

He sits down next to her on the couch. She takes her glasses off, sets them on the coffee table next to the book about wolves, leans back, and covers her eyes with her long fingers.

"I suppose you couldn't be bothered to take time out of your precious Paris life to return my calls."

"That's what this is about?"

She snaps back, "I've called you four times in the last five days, I don't know how many times over the last month. I didn't even know if you were getting my messages. And you waited until yesterday to tell me you were coming! Why?"

"I don't know."

"How can you not know?"

"I didn't want to think about it."

"About what?"

"About Mother dying."

"Do you think any of us did? You're just like Fran."

"No, I'm quite different from Fran, thank you. I didn't want to think about her, I didn't want to think about you, I didn't want to think about any of you." He feels her stare burning a hole right through the side of his head. "I've made a new life for myself. A good life."

"And?"

"I don't need you. I don't need any of you." He spits out the words as he turns toward her. "I'm no longer the kid who ... " The torrent of words—the kid who lives on the outside looking in, wondering who these strange people I call sister, brother, mother are; the kid who no longer lives in a world without love—runs underground the second he sees Christine's face, her bloodshot eyes like open wounds surrounded by black rings. He turns away. Tears well up.

They remain silent for a long time, gazing at the lake, a black expanse surrounded by dark, ambiguous forms. He finally reaches to turn on a floor lamp; she interrupts him.

"Please, leave it off. My eyes are burning."

She lights a candle and then, holding a match to it until the sulphur bursts blue and yellow, lights a cigarette, the flame briefly illuminating the pale skin of her face and hands in a red glow. She blows a stream of smoke above the aura surrounding the candle. A few seconds later the cigarette glows again in the dark, the sound of paper and tobacco burning so intensely Paul wonders if she might not scorch her lungs with the smoke. She exhales with a long sigh. "I didn't smoke for years. Then about three or four weeks ago, I started in. Maybe when this is all over, I'll quit." The cigarette glows, but this time she starts coughing as she exhales, a dry, hacking cough that rattles her lungs for several seconds before dislodging some phlegm. "This is disgusting!" She spits the words through clenched teeth, then crushes the cigarette in the ash tray while shaking her head and exclaiming, "Oh, that hurt!"

Paul grimaces, as if the cough stabbed his chest and lungs as well. He feels like a voyeur, witnessing the revelation of something too private for anyone to see.

Christine remains silent until her breathing has lost its rasp. "It would've made her so happy if you'd have come home."

"All she had to do was ask."

"Is that true?"

Paul doesn't answer. Would he have come home? Of course he would've. Wouldn't he have? Maybe. How can he know?

They stare into the darkness for a few seconds before Christine speaks. "Pain probably doesn't bind people together in a very healthy way. There's something ugly about it. Embarrassing."

He nods his head, even as he wonders exactly what and whom she's talking about.

After a long silence, she begins speaking again. "It's strange, what holds us ... what brings us back. There were times, the last couple days, I wondered why I stayed with her. She didn't open her eyes. Just breathed, like a machine that sucked in air and pumped it out, for no reason. I got up once and started walking out the door, and then I turned around and came back. I knew she was dead. I leaned over and put my mouth close to her ear and said, 'I love you,' and she whispered, 'I love you too.'"

She wipes her eyes and blows her nose. "I've become a real crybaby the last few days. Look at this!" She laughs, pulling balls of tissue out of the pockets of her blouse and pants and tossing them on the table, her laughter ending in another dry cough that reverberates in her chest. She leans back and remains silent for a few minutes before continuing in her raspy voice. "That was the last thing she said—'I love you too.' And a few hours later, when I was asleep, she died."

Paul extends his hand, and is about to take her hand in his, when she murmurs, "You should've called."

He folds his fingers into a loose fist and draws it back, angry with himself.

"I never felt part of this family. I always felt I was being punished for something, and didn't know what."

"When were you ever punished?"

"When? One example among many: each time I was sent to the farm, when I was just a kid."

"That far back! She wasn't punishing you."

"Well then, what was she doing?"

"She was sick."

"I don't buy that."

"She'd get depressed."

"So? She'd send me off to stay with Grandma and Grandpa because she got depressed? That's bullshit!"

"She didn't want you to see her. She'd have me pack your things, Stone would take you to the station ..."

"Stone ..."

"... put you on the train, and you wouldn't come back until she was feeling better."

"So why didn't she send you and Fran off to stay with Grandma and Grandpa?"

"Because you were special. You were her 'little sweetheart,' her 'little man,' her little this, her little that. Meanwhile, I ran the lodge, and Fran fetched."

He shakes his head. "I felt like a yoyo. She'd throw me out when I least expected it, I'd get to the farm, after a while I'd be happy there, and then she'd yank me back."

After a long silence Christine reaches for another cigarette, lights a match again from the candle, then shakes the flame dead and tosses the match and the cigarette on the table. "I should go to bed." She leans her head back on the couch, closes her eyes, and splays her fingers across her eyelids.

After a long silence, Paul says, "You spent a lot of time with her when she could still talk. What did she talk about?"

"Memories. The farm. Her father. She went on and on about how handsome he was, how he favored her above everyone else, how jealous her mother was of the attention she received." The happiness his mother must have felt at the memories colors the tone of Christine's voice. "A childhood friend by the name of Ruth came to visit. Do you remember her?"

"No."

"Fran didn't know her either. He said they spent most of an afternoon talking like a couple of young girls—whatever that means, coming from Fran."

"Did she ever talk about our father?"

"Look at the moonlight on the lake. It's sparkling, like sequins."

"Did she talk about him?"

"The lake is so beautiful. Sometimes, when I can't sleep, I sit here and look at it. It's like a stage. Anything can appear on it."

"Christine, did Mother talk about our father?"

After a long silence she finally answers, "No. Not when I was with her."

"That's strange. If she was reliving her past, you'd think she'd relive her marriage."

"She might've talked about him when I wasn't with her."

"Do you remember him?"

"I was much too young when he died."

What? She must've been nine or ten, plenty old enough to have memories. He glances in her direction. Still staring at the lake, she touches her cheek and the area around her eye with her fingertips, as if wishing to cover her face. Something about the way she holds herself makes him feel she's on the verge of bursting into tears. Maybe he should leave the questions alone, let her be.

"In a blizzard, right?"

Silence.

"Christine."

"Yes."

"He died in a blizzard, right?"

"Right."

"And how old were you?"

"I don't even remember." She sounds angry and defensive. "Why are you so interested? This is beginning to feel like some kind of an interrogation."

"No, it's ... I'm just curious. I have no memory of him at all. It's like our past is dying without leaving a trace."

"Maybe that's just as well."

He glances at her again. "Why?"

She rests her elbow on her wrist, covers her cheek with her right hand, and talks almost in a whisper. "I think when you lose someone, it's best to try to forget. I've forgotten everything."

How could she possibly forget everything? He's about to ask her, when he turns toward her; she seems so fragile, hiding behind those fingers, like she might just break into a thousand pieces. He sighs. "I should probably go to bed."

Christine bows her head, her fingers digging into her hair. "Mother talked about snow. She talked about how beautiful everything is after a heavy snowfall, how snow covers and conceals all that is dirty and ugly and transforms the world into something magical. It's so pure, she'd say, it's like a new baby, like starting a new life. And she'd talk about how babies smell, and once you've smelled your own baby's skin, then you know it's possible to create something pure and innocent."

Paul gazes at the lake, trying to make sense of what she's just said. The silver moonlight sparkles on the still, black surface and illuminates the night just enough to silhouette dark, ambiguous forms. Why would Mother talk about snow that way? he wonders as he looks at Christine; he thinks he sees a smile. "What's so funny?"

"Funny? Probably not funny. Ironic, I guess. That someone who wanted so much to be alone should end up dying alone. Kind of serves her right, doesn't it?"

"There's perhaps justice in that."

"Perhaps too much." She shakes her head. "Sometimes I feel I'm coming apart at the seams. I thought I had myself all sewn up tight." Pausing, she adds, "It's been years since we've talked like this, Paul."

"We've never talked like this."

"You might be right. But maybe we can, now that Mother's gone."

"Maybe."

Fragments of the day return in his sleep: moonlight sparkling like sequins in a black mirror; a woman he can see only in profile sitting next to him; Chaplin's tramp with his big dark eyes and the moonlight concentrated in his face, walking on the mirror; the raw, open wounds of Christine's bloodshot eyes. Even in his sleep he can feel his body twist the bedclothes into knots.

He awakes, turns on the light. It's after four; he can't sleep. He gets up, takes a book from his suitcase, and heads for the living room. He'll read for a while, then try to get back to sleep.

But when he arrives, Christine's already there. He sees her—a dark form in the moonlight. He stops, watches. She takes a deep drag off a cigarette. He hears the paper and tobacco burning, sees the stream of smoke flow into a nebulous pool floating above her head. She's all alone with her mourning. He stays for a while. The ember at the end of the cigarette grows red again, then disappears. She coughs. Her chest rattles. She's hurting herself. He wonders what she cannot forgive. He finally turns around and goes back to bed.

In the morning, on his way to the car, Paul notices the boy in cutoffs swinging again from the tree. The "runner" who wants to fly. Paul stops to watch him. The leaves swirl in the wind, then fall still. Paul can almost hear the sound of the branch creaking as the rope, taut with the boy's weight, swings back and forth. A gust of wind troubles the surface of the water and blows the leaves into chaos. The boy's gaze wanders until he sees Paul watching him. Their eyes lock for a few seconds, and then the boy pushes off again. And again. Swinging further and higher, stretching the rope to its limit.

It's time to go home, Paul thinks, and turns away.

5

PAUL OPENS HIS EYES TO FIND THE CAR PARKED in front of the Holiday gas station in Mirer, the last town before the lodge. Tim gets in the car and hands the *Mirer Times* to Christine. She reads the obituary notice in the paper. "Well, that's one thing Fran did right." She passes it back to Paul.

> Joyce Ann Bauer, age 68, owner of Spirit Lodge and Resort on Spirit Lake. Preceded in death by husband William. Survived by sons Francis and Paul; daughter Christine and son-in-law Timothy Bensen; and two grand-children, Richard and Steven. Visitation Friday 7 to 9 PM. Funeral service Saturday 10 AM at Johnson Funeral Home.

Paul stares at the notice for several minutes, trying to make sense of the conundrum that his mother's long life could so easily be buried beneath a few, short lines of print.

They take the only road heading east out of town. He knows this twenty-five-mile strip as if it were from a film he'd seen so often he could anticipate every scene. The blacktop unrolls across the contours of the landscape; around curves sharp enough for the tires to squeal and down long straightaways, where they make good time; through a forest of birch and white and Norwegian pine, with shafts of sunlight that reach from lofty peaks all the way to the bed of dead pine needles, broken branches, and curled strips of bark; past slopes and bluffs that look down onto low-lying marshlands with jack pine, swamp grass, and all kinds of scrub. A startling sparkle of sunlight on water suddenly appears at a bend and disappears. They cross the bridge over the Snake River and less than a mile later slow to nearly a stop as they turn left at the sign *Spirit Lodge/ Resort/Outfitters.* The dirt road twists around tree trunks and boulders, lurches over roots that ripple the ground, and dips through shallow gullies before leading, after a quarter of a mile, to a clearing, the north wall of the lodge rising before them to nearly the same height as the Norwegian and white pine that cast a dark shadow across it.

Tim, Christine, and Paul get out of the car, stretch their limbs, and walk around to the front of the lodge. Paul stops. His gaze follows the gravel road that leads from the parking area in front of the lodge down a steep slope, past the fish house on the right, to the boathouse and the main dock at the bottom of the hill. Spirit Lake lies perfectly still beneath the pale autumn sun. On the opposite shore pine and birch rise like a wall from the lake's edge and climb the hills and bluffs. Paul's gaze drifts back, past the small island covered with boulders and jack pine about a hundred yards from shore, to the path on the left that meanders off toward the string of seventeen log cabins on the west shore, the north shore with its two rocky fingers, and the east shore, where two docks serve as the only sign of cabins hidden just a few feet away.

Paul knows what everyone calls "the lake" is just a large inlet, one of many. Spirit Lake spans at least ten square miles, but it covers many of those miles through its

inlets, some of which are connected by long, narrow channels that resemble rivers. Canoeists setting out from the
lodge usually seek the channel at the southeast end of the
inlet and follow it for about a quarter of a mile to the open
lake. There they confront confusion: islands, appearing to
be peninsulas, conceal expanses of water, and peninsulas,
appearing to be islands, draw canoeists into deep inlets.
People wander about the lake, watching birch, pine, and
moss-scabbed boulders deploy before them on the water's
surface, while trying to navigate through the maze of water
and land formations. This maze, in turn, is one of many
entrances to a huge labyrinth of lakes, connected by rivers,
channels, and portages, that covers the hundreds of square
miles that make up the Boundary Waters in northern
Minnesota and Quetico National Park on the Canadian
side of the border. To inexperienced canoeists, the lakes
tend to look alike, but they never look like themselves on
the return voyage. Campers would comment upon their
return—relieved to be back—that their sometimes illusory
perceptions had caused them to spend hours if not days
getting lost and finding their way.

Paul's gaze wanders back to the bottom of the hill and
the boathouse. The big, old, brown corrugated aluminum
structure brings back memories of working alone in the
closed, cavernous, murky space where he would disappear
among backpacks; tents and tarps piled on the floor; and
canoe paddles, life jackets, and boat cushions hanging from
beams a few feet above his head. He takes a deep breath and
remembers the smell of canvas and lake water that permeated the boathouse. The constant hum of the two refrigera-
tors (full of tubs of leeches and boxes of night crawlers) and
the sound of waves rippling beneath the floorboards and
lapping against the piles would buoy his psyche like a lazy
current. While he found peace inside, the radio brought him
the energy of the outside world in the music of Bob Dylan,

the Beatles, and Crosby, Stills, and Nash. He remembers singing "Here Comes the Sun" and throwing open the two big doors at the north end of the building (as they are open now) to bring the sun inside. He loved working in the heat of the sun, getting the backpacks ready, setting them out on the main dock (just an extension of the platform on which the boathouse rests), spreading out wet camping gear, boat cushions, and life jackets to dry. He'd stop periodically to stretch and look out upon his little world—the spur of land, about half-way up the west side of the inlet, that protects the boathouse from winds and high waves; the narrow channel, just inside the spur, through which flows the Kawishiwi River (the only waterway out of the inlet aside from the channel at the southeast end); and between the channel and the boathouse, the calm waters where ducks would flock to nap during the day and sleep at night.

Seeing a huge backpack standing on the main dock, he wonders who's doing his old job. While two men in jeans and light jackets—probably campers—walk along the sandy shore toward the dock, a man in old faded jeans and a blue sweatshirt, with long wolf-gray hair combed back and a short gray beard, steps out of the boathouse and crosses the dock with a powerful, gliding gait, in spite of the weight of the second backpack he carries in one hand and drops next to the first. He arches his back and scans the clear sky. A black Labrador, trotting along the shore, freezes, eyes fixed on the man, then dashes along the beach, cutting in front of the two men walking toward the dock. The dog reaches the man on the dock, scampers back and forth in semi-circles around his legs, sniffing his pants. It follows its nose around the backpacks and along the planks to the far end of the dock where it finally stops, just beyond a bench, and looks out over the lake. The campers talk with the bearded man, then load the backpacks in a canoe and push off. The man watches them until they disappear down the channel through which the Kawishiwi River flows, then turns back to the boathouse. His eye must have caught sight of Paul, because for a minute he stops and seems to stare right at him. Paul whispers, "Stone." And the man, almost as if he has heard his name, appears to nod his head in recognition, then disappears through the open doors of the boathouse.

Paul lets the screen door slam shut behind him. Christine and Fran, off to his left, talk in hushed voices to one another. Christine appears to have nothing in common with her brother, a gangling man in a flannel shirt with the sleeves rolled up, thick black hair swirling across his left hand and arm and curling out of the neck of his shirt, and baggy jeans with threadbare knees. Resting his weight on his left leg and his left hand on his hip, he stands hunched over, looking down at the floor, like an animal beaten into submission or feigning indifference, as if trying to appear not to tower over his sister. The second and third fingers of his hand are gone, cut off in an accident that happened long before Paul was old enough to remember. The stumps where his fingers had been give the impression of a paw and a human hand fused into one. Fran raises his head to peer into Christine's face.

"Hi Fran," Paul calls.

Fran doesn't seem to hear him.

Wondering when Fran will acknowledge his presence, Paul stares at Fran's jutting black beard, shaggy hair, weathered skin, long nose, high cheekbones, and the generally angular features of his face, and sees again a resemblance to Abraham Lincoln, a likeness strengthened by his gaunt stature. It's so ironic, Paul muses, that a man capable of such cruelty and violence, and so utterly incapable of coherent speech, a true infant, should resemble Lincoln. Christine snaps, in a tone sharp as a bite, something about the catering; the muscles in Fran's cheek twitch, even when he bites back. In a moment when you can't tell the difference between *chien et loup*, Paul thinks, best to assume wolf and keep your distance.

He focuses on what is at hand, running his fingers across the back of a chair and a table top, feeling the warmth of the sunlight on the pine surface smooth as silk. The grain of the wood flows like honey beneath the varnish. The "new dining room," built before Paul was even born, has always been the only room on the first floor of the lodge that he has liked, because the sun entering the banks of windows set in the north, east, and south walls fills this space with warm pools of light throughout the day. At one time, when business was still good, the room, extending from the original east exterior wall of the lodge, provided an additional ten feet of dining space to accommodate all the customers. By the time Paul was growing up, this dining room was a peaceful place where a few tourists or campers might stop for sandwiches, coffee, or a beer, sit in the clear golden sunlight gazing at the lake, settle into a meditative torpor, and enjoy the silence, in which the slightest sound—the splash of a duck landing on the lake, footsteps on a dock, a red squirrel chattering in a tree— resonated as clearly and distinctly as musical notes.

Paul reaches the end of the log wall on his right and looks down the deep, narrow space of the barroom, where the sunlight from the windows behind him gradually fades to gloom dimly lit by the blue glow of a Hamm's beer lamp hanging on the wall behind the bar. The end of the barroom would be lost in total darkness had not someone left the back door open, through which a shaft of sunlight shines like a ray of hope, like a light at the end of the tunnel.

He overhears Christine ask Fran if he has thought about her suggestion for flowers, a question posed with the authority of a command.

Fran looks at Paul. His hazel eyes get a gleam in them that make Paul think of shamans and mad prophets.

Approaching with his arms extended, like a sleepwalker, Fran embraces him; Paul feels his brother's bearded cheek press against his forehead and smells the accumulated odors of sweat, dirt, pine, fish, and whatever else he might've picked up. Fran's body shudders, and from deep in his chest comes a guttural sound, followed by a moan, and then silence. The long arms and big hands feel heavy, like dead game. Finally Fran pulls back, his powerful hands slide down to grip Paul's arms, and his little hazel eyes, dilated wide open, stare at him as if seeking in his eyes the answer to a mystery. Deep grooves cut into Fran's skin like the weathered cracks in the moss-covered boulders that line the shores of the lakes; a few long white and silver hairs bristle and snake from his beard; and something yellow— probably a little egg yolk from breakfast or mustard from lunch—clings to his mustache. Fran's head, long face, crazed gaze, and gaunt, hirsute body evoke at once Lincoln, Rasputin, a lunatic, and an animal, adept and agile in the woods, awkward and clumsy in the world of men.

"You're looking your usual self, Fran."

"The Lord has provided for my needs," Fran mumbles.

"Is that Stone I saw down by the boat house?

"He's just helping with the outfitting. And the cabins."

"That's pretty nice of him."

Fran shakes his head. "Not many people come around here anymore."

"The old farts scare them off?"

Fran gives him a look of contempt. "They're all dead!" He looks at Christine. "How long you gonna be stayin'?" The tone of his voice suggests Christine's welcome is limited.

"We'll go back Sunday. Tim has to work Monday. Can we talk about what you've already taken care of?"

"Everything's done."

"Is all of the food ordered?"

"Everything's done."

"And my suggestion about the flowers?"

Fran turns around without bothering to answer her and walks down the tunnel leading to the light, turns right, and disappears into the kitchen. Christine, with Tim in tow, follows him.

Paul looks around the bar. This is where he learned much of what he knows about the past. His teachers were the "old farts," a motley mess of men in their forties, fifties, and sixties who took over the bar pretty much every day of the week, spring, summer, and fall. They'd wander in during the afternoon—dressed in their tropical short-sleeved shirts or graying or fading t-shirts (with images of fighting fish, big game, and bait-store logos stretched over swelling, sagging guts or hanging from skinny frames) and baggy blue jeans, sweatpants, and shirts, or plaid Bermuda shorts—and each would order a "beer and a bump" or a "boilermaker," get a good shine on, and a few hours later they'd be lit. They'd stagger out, often enough with six-packs under their arms, and head for home. The next afternoon they'd be at it again. From the time they walked in until they stumbled out, these raconteurs—oral historians, buffoons, and purveyors of the raunchiest jokes he'd ever heard—held court in the bar, always a bit pompous toward those who were younger or—God forbid! —from somewhere else.

Paul always kept a respectful distance and silence, busying himself with cleaning condiment containers, washing tables, sorting silverware, folding napkins—any little task that allowed him to hang around and listen in. The war stories (about "krauts" and "japs," the fire-bombing of Dresden and Tokyo, the Battle of Stalingrad and cannibalism, the concentration camps and what we knew or didn't know) and conspiracy theories interested him far less than did the stories about the lodge. Stories about a time when the mines were operating, the logging camps still open, Mirer had two or three times the population it had when he was a teenager, and the lodge had one of the few restaurants and bars in the area that attracted young people who came to eat huge platters of walleye and venison, drink beer, whiskey, and gin, and dance to the music of whatever bands "ol' man Bauer, ol' Francis, your grand-papa"—could entice into coming. They danced the polkas they'd grown up with as well as the jitterbugs and lindies they'd seen projected in the movie palaces. Paul would imagine women on the dance floor in the old dining room twirling and flying around like birds, some wild and exotic, others familiar and homely. The music and dancing and drinking went on until after midnight, and then drunken couples swayed and stumbled out the door and teetered toward their cars; the women opened their lips and their legs while the men, mad with booze and the taste of sex, plunged into them head first (the old guys would smirk and snicker at this idea). A couple of the old farts talked about walking through the parking lot and hearing the slap slap of belly to belly or belly to buttocks and screams and groans and peals of laughter. Some nights fists flew, knives flashed, and bottles gashed skulls, but ol' man Bauer and his "big strapping boys" most times prevented the violence from being fatal with their brawn and Big Bertha, the 12-gauge double-barrel shotgun kept behind the bar.

"Back then people knew how to have fun," one of the old farts would say. "And die young," another would chime in. They'd all laugh, and then compete with one another to describe the most gruesome accidents on the gravel road from the lodge to Mirer. Like the man who'd been found pinned alive to the seat by the steering wheel, babbling like a lunatic, his girlfriend's twisted body, the head almost entirely decapitated, pitched halfway out of the car on the hood. And the roadster with the rumble seat that catapulted the two men in the back a hundred yards if it threw them a foot. And a hundred other stories that got richer in gore and more grotesque in detail with each telling.

Sooner or later the old farts would talk about the whores. When the loggers—and years later, the miners—came on payday to spend their wages, they'd find all sorts of women hanging around: young and not-so-young, abused, abandoned, broke, bored, going nowhere, or ready to do anything to get the money to get out. The women would just happen to make the drive from town to spend a couple days in a cabin they'd rent. The right number of bills in ol' man Bauer's shirt pocket and he'd look the other way, while the men, having drunk their fill, stumbled arm and arm with a whore down to a bed where they'd contribute their seed to the slowly drying slime that saturated the sheets. "Hey, big ears, did you hear that?" the old farts would ask Paul, laughing, and he'd continue wiping the condiment bottles, jars, and shakers at the table where he was sitting and nod his head, so they wouldn't know he was feeling ashamed.

With all the nasty stuff that could be traced back to the lodge—the drinking and brawling, bashed-in skulls and knife slashes, whoring, girls with VD or scarred, sick, or dead from illegal abortions—it wasn't surprising that ol' Francis had his enemies. Probably the man who detested him most was Roger Swenson, the sheriff of Lake County for more years than anyone could remember. For years, word was Roger wanted to get Francis's liquor license revoked and shut him down. But the old man, he was a fox. He attended Mass and took communion every Sunday morning, placed an envelope that everyone knew was from him in the collection plate, and always lingered by the door after the service to talk with parishioners, as if he were the priest. Everyone knew he greased the hands of any city, county, or state employee who could make life difficult for him, but Roger could never get him for bribery. He never succeeded in shutting down Francis, and Francis never succeeded in getting Roger to stop trying. This feud lasted until Francis got frozen in a blizzard; a few years later, Roger's car went through the ice. People just couldn't figure out why someone who hadn't touched a drop in years (he'd been the town drunk at one time) would all of a sudden drink a pint of whiskey and then go driving out on thin ice in the fall. Nope, no one could figure that one out. The old farts would roll their eyes and laugh. They always knew.

When Paul was growing up, the person who was supposed to be keeping order in the bar was Fran. The old farts liked to prove they reigned in spite of Fran's presence. Paul recalls a summer afternoon when he was thirteen. A woman walked past the table where he was busy cleaning and filling salt and peppershakers. She sat down on a bar stool just two places to the right of Lyle, the leader of the old farts, and ordered a drink. She was blond, pretty, and way too well dressed for the lodge. The regulars couldn't take their eyes off her; nor could Fran, who spilled part of her drink when he served it to her, stuttered an apology, and repeated several times the drink was on the house— the first time he'd ever told anyone that.

Lyle and three of his buddies sitting to his right were trying to get her attention: "Hey, beautiful, how about some company?" Snicker snicker. She ignored them, so they escalated the assault. "Hey baby, how about some physical therapy? Free. The kind that makes you feel so good inside you'll just want more and more ... What's a matter, honey, you think you're too good to talk to us?" Finally Lyle slammed his palm down on the bar so hard it sounded like one two-by-four hitting another and spit his words into her face: "If you think your fucking pussy's so great, put it up here on the fucking bar so we can all have a look at it!" She immediately turned crimson, got up, and tried to leave, but Gordy, a fired or retired fireman from Mirer, shuffled and danced in half-circles around her as she left, leering up into her face while calling, "Here, pussy. Here, pussy." The screen door slammed shut. The regulars laughed until they had tears in their eyes.

Once they stopped shaking with laughter, they asked Fran if he didn't think Lyle was right to ask her to put her pussy on the bar if she thought it was so great. Fran tried to ignore them, but as he bent over the sink to wash some glasses, the muscles in his jaws twitched and red blotches mottled his skin, suddenly pale except for the carbuncular acne. They laughed again; he turned crimson. They stayed on him like black flies, telling him if he didn't like their manners maybe he should do something about it, maybe he should get big bad Bertha and blow them away, and they laughed some more, confident he wouldn't do anything.

Paul hadn't shared their confidence. He remembers an incident when Fran was about sixteen and two of his friends from school—Freddy Froelich and another kid—came out to the lodge one September weekend to go hunting. Fran allowed Paul, about nine at the time, to tag along. It was rare that anyone from town came out to the lodge to do something with Fran, known to everyone as a loner and a loser. They'd been walking through the woods for about an hour, shooting their .22 rifles at squirrels and pretty much anything else that moved, when they stopped to reload.

Freddy started making jokes about Queenie, a family nickname for Christine that had been leaked at school. Someone Freddy knew had claimed to have scored with Queenie, and this rumor, along with some dirty jokes about her, had begun to circulate. One of the jokes Freddy repeated was that Queenie was out to make every boy in the high school "King for a Day," and at the rate she was going, every boy would have his day. Freddy had looked at Fran and asked him if he'd ever had the pleasure of being King for a Day, and as Freddy and his friend laughed, Paul watched Fran's facial muscles near his jaw twitch.

Freddy glanced over at a box of ammunition that Fran

had set on a large rock and commented to his friend that Fran was obviously offering his ammunition to them and they should help themselves. That was the straw. Fran told them to use their own ammunition. When Freddy picked up the box of ammo and was about to offer some shells to his friend, Fran, who had already loaded his rifle, pointed it directly at Freddy's chest, turned off the safety, and, with his finger on the trigger, told him to put the ammo down. By this time Fran's face had turned white, his eyes looked deadly, and the facial muscles continued to twitch. Freddy set the box of ammo down on the rock and he and his friend backed away, then turned and ran toward the lodge. Fran turned the other way, pushed back the long lock of Brylcreamed hair that hung over his right temple like a broken wing, and, with tears in his eyes, waved Paul off and headed deeper into the woods.

So, Paul thinks, maybe Fran should've dealt with the old farts the same way he dealt with Freddy and his buddy, but he didn't. And that was good. Because in spite of their drunken sadism, they had stories to tell, and he had wanted to hear them. By the time he was old enough to remember anything, his paternal grandparents were in the church cemetery, his father was gone, the logging and mining industries had died, and Mirer had lost more than half its population. The gravel road from Mirer to the lodge had been covered over with blacktop, tourism had become the region's only industry, and the past—with all its energy—was dead. Every year on his way home from school, Paul would see a new sign posted on the road for yet another resort, and another, and another, until the lodge was just the last in a twenty-five mile directory of resorts.

Listening to the old men tell their stories had been like attending a séance and feeling the living presence of something long dead. As he grew from the little kid with the big ears to an adult standing behind the bar, home from college, helping out for the summer, he came to see the old regulars for what they were—alcoholics, with no lives outside their drunken bull sessions—and the past as something mean, petty, and provincial. That's the truth he saw on the way out of his labyrinth.

Paul walks along the bar, grazing the surface with his fingertips. The wood feels smooth as leather, as if fashioned from the hide of some huge animal. He remembers rubbing oil into the wood periodically to protect it from the spills and the beating it took. He glances up at the beer lamp, with a dancing brown bear in the foreground and behind it a luminescent blue lake with moonlight shining on its surface, and wonders if Hamm's beer still exists. He reaches the display cabinets, installed where about half the bar was ripped out after the collapse of the logging and mining industries, when a clientele of tourists replaced the hard-drinking loggers and miners. He continues walking, fingering swivel racks with displays of sunglasses and snacks, stopping to look at a rack of postcards: soft-focus sunsets on the lake in various shades of pink and tangerine; a white wolf standing in snow with its head turned toward the camera; a moose standing in an inlet amid water lilies; and a close-up of a loon in profile with a red eye and a band of moon diamonds on its black neck. Piles of green t-shirts and blue sweatshirts with Spirit Lodge/Mirer/Minnesota printed on them lay displayed on display shelves next to arrangements of lures, hooks, leaders, and sinkers.

The smell of cold, dead ashes stops him in the entry to the old dining room. His mouth and lungs feel full of grit, and the memory of living in this dark space penetrates him before his eyes can adjust to the gloom. Pale shafts of light enter the room from two windows that flank the stone fireplace directly in front of him. A moose head mounted above the mantle peers at him out of the dark with a glassy stare. The frayed couch on his left sections off a part of the old dining room into a kind of living room that includes a second couch, a coffee table, with a mess of newspapers, and a television. He watched the Lone Ranger, Charlie Chaplin, and Laurel and Hardy in this murky darkness on Saturday mornings during the off-season.

He walks past the fireplace toward the pool table in the center of the room on his right that seems to squat on its stout legs like a mammoth beast petrified by a mysterious force, never to move again. Circling the table, his eyes fixed on the varnished pine walls, he takes inventory of all that remains from the past: a circular saw at least six feet in diameter, salvaged from one of the lumber mills; next to it, a two-handed saw, at least seven feet long, used to cut the forests of virgin pine that the old farts claimed reached two hundred feet if they measured a foot; a pair of snowshoes pointing up in a V; a rampant black bear in the northeast corner gazing with its brown glass eyes through a thick layer of dust at some distant being that it was prepared to embrace; two pinball machines set against the east wall on either side of the open doorway leading to the new dining room; a bobcat mounted on a stand just below the ceiling, its mouth open in a snarl, as if ready to attack; display cabinets with glass shelves, similar to those in the barroom, set against the south wall; and above the cabinets, the head of a whitetail buck gazing stoically into the distance, as if its death were something it might overcome with patience. The cabinets display yellowed newspapers from Mirer with headlines announcing the stock market crash, a Fed raid on a still and brewery outside town, the bombing of Pearl Harbor, FDR's third presidential victory, Truman's defeat of Dewey, and the assassination of JFK. Arranged next to and among the newspapers like odd paper weights are two old flat irons, an assortment of Ojibwa necklaces and bracelets, a small handbell, some hand-forged iron spikes, and a variety of beaver and muskrat traps. Paul stops to look at

the Wurlitzer juke box and finds the same names he came
to know as a teenager: Glenn Miller, Hank Williams, Patsy
Kline, Elvis Presley, the Platters, Gene Vincent, Chuck
Berry, Sam Cook, Buddy Holly, the Everly Brothers, and
Roy Orbison.

He scans the room. Nothing has changed. A place full
of junk, full of dead things.

Weighed down by two days of traveling with little sleep,
he heads upstairs, the distant voices of Christine, Tim,
and Fran following him from the kitchen. He stops at the
top. The door on his right leads to his mother's room. He
turns left. He knows this space perfectly, even in the dark.
On the left, a storage room (shelves with piles of sheets,
blankets, towels, wash cloths, and table cloths) and the
bathroom (he remembers it clouded with steam, because
it felt so good to take hot baths when it was fifty degrees
below zero); on the right, his sister's room; and in front of
him, two doors, the one on the right leading to Fran's room,
the one on the left to his.

Standing in the doorway, blinking until his eyes adapt
to the sunlight flooding the three windows, he watches
everything fall into place. The bed pushed against one of
the windows and the desk against another so he could look
out at the lake during the day and up at the sky at night.
Books that he read in high school collecting dust on the
bookshelves near the north window. A chest of drawers
against the wall on his left. He enters the room, stops in
the middle, and turns in a circle, looking at all of the maps,
hand drawn with black lead pencil, colored pencils, and pen
and ink. Mounted on poster board, from the recent past as
well as other historical periods, maps of Europe, France,
the Russia of the czars, the United States, Asia, Viet Nam
and the countries that surround it, Central and South
America, Mexico, Brazil, Minnesota, the Boundary Waters
and Quetico, and the Rocky Mountains from Montana to

Alberta. He had developed the skill of drawing accurate maps freehand, and to any scale he chose, just by studying maps in books. Every time he could, he chose a map exercise for a homework assignment. He used to lie on his bed and stare at the maps, imagining the countries and cities, culling details for his fantasies from novels, histories, photographs, and illustrations.

He walks over toward the desk, sits down, runs his fingertips across the light varnished wood and gouged initials, and opens all the drawers except one, the bottom left, which is locked. Searching for the key, he finds nothing but some blunt lead pencils and a few sheets of Spirit Lodge and Resort letterhead (its logo, a canoe with two canoeists paddling in the midst of what appears to be mist beneath tall letters in a serif script), and makes a mental note to ask Fran about the key. He looks out the window at the landscape, so familiar, so much a part of himself he can see the lake and every rock, tree, and building in his sleep.

He sits down on the bed and looks at his old dreams of exploration tacked to the walls all around him. Somehow those dreams led to the person he has become. He has the uncanny sensation of being in the same room with the boy who drew the maps and wants to tell him he has already made the voyage, and the boy better ... better what? He doesn't know. But he feels affection for this boy with so many dreams. Bouncing lightly on the bed, he continues gazing at the maps, but they're too far away for him to see the details, too far away to draw him in: they're just maps.

He lies down and stares at the ceiling. The room feels so familiar, like an old pair of jeans and a loose fitting sweatshirt. He gathers the quilt, bunches it up in fistfuls, wraps himself in a cocoon, closes his eyes just long enough to feel himself drifting off, then rouses himself awake. He still has two or three more hours before he can seek sleep beneath the comforter.

6

PAUL ENTERS THE KITCHEN HEARING CHRISTINE exclaim, "I want to eat in the new dining room. There's sunlight, and we can actually look out the windows at the lake." Seeing Paul, she says, "He insists on eating in this awful kitchen," shakes her head, sighs in frustration, and rolls her eyes.

Paul quickly scans the kitchen. He knows it so well, he can see it, smell it, and feel it all in a few seconds: long, narrow, dark, with just one window over the sink; industry size stove, grill, refrigerator, freezer, and mixer from that time years ago when the family still had to produce up to a hundred meals per night; and fluorescent lights over the table and counters that (if turned on) would only enhance the gloom—a cold gloom, with an odor like the smell of old bacon grease or lard. The space feels like a back room, or a storage room, not a kitchen where a family would eat together—although this is where the family ate. In silence. He gets angry just thinking about it.

"I second Christine."

Fran says, "We ate in the dining room only on special

occasions, when Mother had guests."

Christine asks, "Well, what are we? Stray cats? It can't be that much trouble to carry four TV dinners from here to there! I'll do it myself."

Paul says to Fran, "Mother never had any guests. She was a recluse, for God's sake."

"We're not doing anything differently just because Mother's not here."

"Instead of fighting over this, why don't we just eat here?"

Christine looks at Tim. "There's no reason ..."

"There's no reason to fight. We can do what Fran wants. We're just here for a few days."

Christine says, barely loud enough for Tim to hear, and Paul to overhear, "You're soooo conciliatory. Such a peacemaker."

They're about to sit down at the table when Paul asks Fran if there's any wine.

He shakes his head. "Beer and pop."

"Okay. I'll have beer. It's behind the bar?"

"I'll get it."

"I can get it."

"Nope."

Fran walks off to get the beer.

Christine says, "Better be careful, Paul. You might rock his little canoe. I'm surprised he didn't tell you that we don't drink beer in the kitchen because Mother never did."

Christine stares at her TV dinner, then uses her fork to lift the edge of a thin slice of roast beef covered with thick, glutinous brown gravy, lets it fall back in place, picks out a wafer of the potatoes au gratin coated with a fluorescent orange cheese sauce, and nibbles at it. She notices Tim grinning at her. "What's so funny?"

"You remind me of this cat I used to have when I was a student. If I gave it food it didn't like, it would scratch the floor next to its bowl the same way it scratched in the litter box."

"You're being conciliatory again." A trace of anger lingers in her voice.

"Maybe." His fingers walk across the table, tentatively, until they touch her hand, and then cover it.

After a short while she withdraws her hand, leans back, and smiles at him, as if she were lobbing him a kiss.

He smiles, returning the volley, matching hers with love.

Paul watches the game. They're so lucky; he wishes he were with Claire. The game stops as soon as Fran returns.

"Oh," Paul says, "we have Hamm's beer. How about that. I was wondering if it still existed. It would've been so in character for us ... for the lodge to advertise a beer that no longer exists."

"Paul, better be careful about what you say," Christine says in a singsong, little-girl voice. "Things might get out of hand and Tim will have to do some more peacemaking."

Feeling Christine's eagerness to pick a fight with Fran, Paul ignores her and focuses on eating, as does Tim. Fran, bent over in silence, shovels in his beef au jus and potatoes au gratin. Christine continues picking at the roast beef with the coagulated gravy (even thicker now that it has cooled) and the fluorescent orange potatoes, then finally stops and lights a cigarette. Paul glances over at her. She has a way of tensing the muscles in her cheeks and puckering her lips when she draws on the cigarette that turns smoking into an intensely physical, aggressive act. She notices Tim, his fork held still in midair, staring at her. She quickly exhales: "What? Well, what?" He doesn't answer. She shakes her head. "I have to do something. I can't just sit here." She draws again on the cigarette, sets her hand next to her plate, and repeatedly taps the cigarette with her index finger, peppering the au gratin with ash. She glances at Paul, then looks away.

Tim finishes eating and looks at Fran. "This was pretty good, for a TV dinner. Is there anything for dessert?"

Fran, mopping up little puddles of gravy and cheese sauce with a piece of bread, ignores him.

"Is there dessert, Fran?" Christine throws the question at him like a punch.

Fran grumbles, "Might be some ice cream."

Christine glares at him. "Could you look?"

He stares at her for a second, as if wondering whether or not he should, then goes to the freezer, returns with a half-gallon tub of ice cream, and is about to set it on the table when Tim asks what kind it is. Fran peers at the side of the tub, answers, "Rocky Road," sets it down, gets a scooper and four bowls, and he and Tim serve themselves ice cream. While they eat, Christine returns again to the subject of the wake and funeral arrangements.

"Fran, you still haven't told me about the flowers. What did you order?"

She watches with an expression of irritation and disgust as he inserts the spoon in his mouth, purses his lips to put pressure on the ice cream, shapes it on the spoon, and then, having drawn out the spoon, studies the ice cream, the smooth chocolate surface broken here and there by a protruding nut or marshmallow. He reinserts the spoon in his mouth, sucks off the remaining ice cream, then spoons more ice cream and reindulges his retentive pleasures. Studying her face as she stares at Fran and waits for an answer, watching her expression evolve from disgust to repulsion, Paul is surprised to see a resemblance between the two of them that he never noticed before—an angular quality about the nose and the facial structure. The older they get, the more they look alike. He wonders if he's beginning to resemble them more as well.

Fran finally comments, between one spoonful of ice cream and the next, "It's too late to worry about the flowers,

Christine. Everything's done."

"You can't even tell me what you ordered?"

"I don't remember. And what difference does it make, anyhow? People aren't coming to see flowers. They're coming to see Mother."

Christine lights another cigarette, exhales, and stares at her brother, who continues eating his ice cream with the same oral-retentive pleasure.

"That minister you hired, how did you find him?"

"Fellow at the funeral parlor recommended him."

"And he never knew Mother?"

Fran slowly draws his spoon out of his mouth, examines the ice cream remaining on the spoon, then reinserts the spoon, swallows the ice cream, looks at Christine, and finally answers, "Nope."

Christine looks at him with snake eyes. She takes a long drag on her cigarette and exhales the smoke in Fran's direction. "Well, what 's he going to say about her?" The question drips venom.

Fran takes his time, replying only when he has completed his labor of love on another spoonful of ice cream. "I don't know what he'll say."

"Didn't you tell him something? Give him some ideas?"

Fran finally finishes, tosses his spoon into the bowl, and looks at her with a smirk. "I told him to say whatever he usually says. I told him he probably knows a lot better than me what to say."

"Well, I could have told him what to say. You should have called me."

"Mother didn't care about that kind of stuff, and you know it. She never thought twice about what people might say about her."

"Would it really have required that much of an effort on your part?" She flicks the ash off her cigarette onto the fluorescent orange, takes another drag, and exhales the stream of smoke at Fran. "You could have tried."

"It's not something she wanted."

Christine jabs her cigarette into the au gratin. "And you're the only one who knows what she wanted?"

He leaps to his feet and slams his right fist on the table in front of Christine so hard the bowls jump five inches. "You're goddamn right I am! I'm the one who stayed. All these years I stayed. And you, you ran off to college. Couldn't wait to get out of here. And then she's sick and you come runnin' back, wantin' to be Queenie all over again. Wantin' to boss everyone, like you'd never left." Fran jabs his finger toward her face. "She never forgot! You hear? Never forgot you were too busy all those years to care about anyone else. You goddamned ... you ungrateful bitch! You'll burn in hell!" Tim grabs Fran's hand from behind. Fran stops cold, his face blood red as if it were about to explode, not more than a few inches from hers. Supporting his weight on his mutilated left hand, he looks as if he's just beginning to come out of a state induced by a drug or hypnosis. He shakes his head and closes his eyes, panting.

With his hands on Fran's shoulders, Tim sits him down. "I think we've all had a long day. And we're all tired."

Christine is sobbing. Tim walks around the table, helps her to her feet, and holds her up as she leans on him and staggers toward the stairway. The sobbing continues as they climb the stairs.

Fran collapses in his chair, stares into space. The muscles in his cheeks, now pale, twitch spasmodically. He looks sick. Paul leans over him, touches his arm, and whispers his name. Fran doesn't respond. Paul whispers his name again. Finally Fran looks at him, then closes his dead eyes, letting go of anything outside. Paul squats next to him and puts his arms around him.

*
*   *

Paul lies stretched across his bed, the muscles in his arms twitching as his body tries to relax after the jolt it received from Fran's outburst. His back muscles tighten into knots; he rolls up to stretch them, then lies back down again and stares at the ceiling. Fran's rage—it was like a supernatural force that used his body and then discarded it. This rage could strike someone dead before Fran would even know what he'd done. Why is he like this? Unable to express himself, to find some kind of release before his anger becomes lethal. And what did Mother do to deserve his loyalty? Paul can't think of any answers; he's too tired to think; he just wants to sleep. He undresses, crawls under the comforter, and turns off the light, but adrenalin is pumping through his body like electricity. He's still galvanized by what he has seen, and questions keep popping up, like the eels in the old lady's pie. He gets up, throws his clothes back on, and tiptoes out of his room.

At the top of the stairs, he notices the door to his mother's room is ajar. He hesitates, then, curious, steps inside. He hasn't been in here since he was a boy. It's always been off-limits. He's about to leave when he sees a strange shape on the bed. He can't tell if it's a person or a heap of clothes or blankets. The floorboards creak in spite of his tiptoeing. Fran, fully dressed, lies in the fetal position on top of a white bedspread, a blanket covering him from his waist to his ankles. Paul imagines him completely spent by his outburst of rage. He pulls the blanket over Fran's shoulders and leaves.

Outside, the cold moon casts its silver light on the gray clouds gliding across the sky. His footsteps echo off the surface of the water underneath the planks as he walks to the end of the dock. He gazes at the black lake and the shadows on its surface. A point lies about a hundred feet out from shore. Just inside it—and only because he knows it's there—he detects the opening of the channel, which appears as absolute blackness with neither form nor shadow, a hole in the midst of rock. He remembers as a teenager canoeing at night, entering the darkness of the channel through which the Kawishiwi River flows out of Spirit Lake. He would let the current carry the canoe along the deepest part of the channel to avoid the huge rocks, boulders, and fallen trees in the water. At certain points along the channel, the current would carry the canoe within three or four feet of land, and though he had no fear of being on the lake at night, land was different. You never know who or what might be there. He shivers in the cold air. Still afraid of the dark!

"Welcome back, Paulie."

His entire body flinches and he looks to his right, half expecting to see a ghost. The open doors of the boathouse reveal nothing but blackness.

"Stone?"

"That's me." A man emerges from the cavernous opening into the moonlight.

"What are you doing?"

"Just putting some things away."

"In the dark?"

"I know my way around." He extends his hand to shake Paul's. "Been a long time, Paulie."

Paul feels amazed at the hardness of the big, bony hand that grips his. This isn't a man who needs to fear anything that might be about in the night. "Yes, it has. I wasn't expecting to see you this afternoon. It took me a minute to realize it was you." Stone finally releases his hand. "Even though you look the same."

Stone snorts. "Bullshit. You didn't recognize me this afternoon 'cause I look every goddamn one of my fifty-four years and then some. You've always tried to be nice, Paulie."

Paul starts. He hears claws scuttling across the dock. A dog, the Labrador, is jumping around the two men, sniffing their legs, wagging its tail.

"You still have a dog. Same one you had before?"

"Dogs don't live that long, Paulie."

"How long's it been?"

"About ten years."

"That's a long time."

"Yep."

"A dog can't live ten years?"

"Not if he's already lived about ten, and then you add ten more."

"Makes sense."

The dog plops down at Stone's feet, then quickly jumps up to run around the dock, sniffs along the edge near the water, trots back toward Stone, flops down again, and then once again jumps to its feet. Paul sits down on the bench; Stone joins him. The dog comes over and sniffs the air, whips their legs with its tail, and drops near the edge of the dock at Stone's feet.

"So you came back for your mother's funeral. I thought it was even odds you would."

"Just even odds?"

"Oh, maybe better than even." After a silence he adds, "You still livin' in gay Paree? With all the froufrous?"

"I'm still living in gay Paree with all the froufrous and the Frenchies."

Stone nods his head, as if he approves.

"Still writing for a living?"

"Yes."

"Never understood how you could do that. But I never read anything you wrote."

"Want to?"

"Nope."

The two men stare into the darkness for a while before

Paul comments, "Fran said you were helping out."

"Fran needed helping out. Real bad."

"Tell me about it."

"Oh, shit! Ever since your mother got real sick this spring, he just let the cabins go to hell. Plumbing got backed up, broken screens didn't get fixed, a roof leaked, and he didn't do a fucking thing about it. People were skipping out without paying. He didn't even have records of who'd paid and who hadn't. A real fucking mess."

Paul sees Fran lying in the fetal position on their mother's bed and wonders how could Fran take care of anything. Remembering Stone's presence, he says, "Well, I hope he's paying you something for your help."

"I've been living in the sticks too long for money to count."

"Hmm." This is so like Stone. Things fall apart, he shows up, puts them back together again, and goes his way, never expecting a thing. And he's not even a member of the family. Not really. A cousin, but Paul doesn't even know how close. He leans back and looks up to see a cloud pass like some nocturnal ghost ship in front of the moon and continue on its voyage, occasionally eclipsing some of the stars. He glances at Stone, who seems to be looking deep into the night, as if it held the answer to a riddle. His eyes having adjusted to the moonlit darkness, Paul can see the features of Stone's face and occasionally detect the nebulous expressions that drift across it.

Stone sighs, as if unshouldering a huge burden, leans back, stretches his legs, laces his fingers behind his neck, and looks up at the sky. "Yeah, that's quite a brother you got! Never know what the fuck he's gonna do. Like this summer. He just let people walk all over him." Stone falls silent for a while, then looks at Paul. "You remember those guys who used to hang out at the lodge all the time? Spend the whole day drinking and bullshitting."

"Lyle and Gordy and their pals."

Stone turns his gaze back toward the sky. "Yeah, that's 'em."

"I was just thinking about them this afternoon."

"Those guys didn't start hangin' around the lodge until after Grandpa and your dad were both gone. And Fran was old enough to tend bar. Well, wasn't old enough, but he did. Grandpa wouldn't have put up with those SOBs for one fucking minute. He would've kicked their fucking asses right out of there. Or shot 'em. You didn't mess around with him. He was the law, and everyone knew it. But Fran," Stone slowly shakes his head, "he let those blowhards run the place. When I came back to help out, there they were. One of 'em got so drunk he couldn't walk to the head. Pissed in his pants. Sitting right at the bar. I got ol' Bertha and nudged those stinking shit bags right out the door. They never paid any attention to Fran, but starin' into the barrel of a shotgun, they listened real well to me."

Paul chuckles. "That's kind of illegal, isn't it?"

"That was just my way of communicatin' with 'em. I told 'em they should think of me as being just as fucking mean as the old man. They didn't ask who. But, you know, it was still spring, no tourists around, I could've blown those mother fuckers to kingdom come and nobody would've missed 'em. And if anyone did find out, they'd probably say thanks."

"They ever come back?"

"Naw."

"Fran said they're all dead."

"He'd probably like to think that."

"You think he just didn't have the nerve to throw those guys out."

Stone shakes his head.

"Because I can think of times when people have said or done things that really touched a nerve, and he's gone ballistic. He's not afraid of anyone. He'd kill ..."

"Just my point. Guy's totally unpredictable. Those old farts don't know how lucky they were, 'cause if Fran had ever decided to pick up Bertha, he would've blown 'em away, blown 'em into chunks out in the woods." He laughs quietly. "Snack food for the wildlife." He shakes his head. "The trouble with Fran is, you never know what the hell he's gonna do."

"Yeah," Paul says, thinking about Fran's explosion earlier. He leans back, stretches his legs, arches his back, laces his fingers behind his head, and looks up at the moon and the stars. He remembers how that unpredictableness could get really mean. Like the time Fran twisted his fingers back to see how far he could bend them before Paul would start to cry. Fran threatened him with more of the same if he told anyone. He never did. There wasn't anyone to tell. But that was a long time ago. No sense in looking back.

He'd rather look at the stars that had increased from just a few to innumerable points of light that deepened the sky. He imagines falling through its fathomless, infinite depth. How can anyone comprehend infinity? He can't hold it in his mind; it holds him. He can only think of this infinite blackness in finite, historical terms. He remembers sailing into it, like some ancient voyager, guiding himself not by the stars but by the maps and the books that had become fantasies, and discovering in place of infinity a country, a city, a magical place, and then finding himself at the end of his dream still lying on a dock on the shore of Spirit Lake, looking up at the black fathomless sky.

Stone says, "The Milky Way flows even in the cold."

"You said Fran wasn't taking care of the lodge. So what was he doing?"

"Spending a lot of time with your mother. Other than that, I don't know. He never was much for talking."

Paul laughs. "That's an understatement!"

"Sure didn't mean it to be one."

Paul laughs again. "And how was she?"

"She was dying."

"That was a dumb question."

"Yeah, it was."

"I mean, what was she doing when she felt well enough to do something?"

"I don't know. Only time I saw her was when I went fishing in the Black Hole at night. She'd be sitting in the window."

"The Black Hole—you'd go back there at night?"

"Some real big walleye in there. They come up at night. Hungry."

"I didn't think anyone was crazy enough to do that."

"I guess I'm crazy."

Yes, Paul thinks, you've got to be crazy. He remembers the one time—a sunny summer afternoon—he paddled back into the Black Hole. He penetrated the tall grass that concealed the narrow channel, not more than three feet wide. He paddled for nearly a hundred feet in shallow water, stirring up muck that smelled of decomposing matter; penetrating reeds, cattails, and swamp grass that dragged across his face, arms, and shoulders; swatting the mosquitoes that the dragon flies, hovering and darting like helicopters, had yet to eat; frightening a three-foot garter snake slithering across the muck to hunt frogs; and finally entering an open pool, at least a hundred feet in diameter, pitch black from the depth, the muck bottom, and the iron, and ringed with more cattails and reeds and swamp grass. From there Stone could easily have seen the bedroom window. But to go into the Black Hole at night! That takes guts.

Stone asks, "How does it feel to be back in the lodge with your sister and brother?"

"I'm wondering how to survive the next few days with them at one another's throats."

"What are they up to?"

"They want to kill each other. Not really, but the way they're going at it, you would think they were both glued to some invisible object. They can get their hands on it, but they can't have it, they can't take it away from the other, and they can't let go."

"If the thing they're fighting over is Joyce, they won't have much to fight over after she's cremated."

The remark feels like a left hook out of nowhere. He leans forward so he can look at Stone's face. "Cremated? I haven't heard anything about that."

Stone turns toward Paul. "No one told you?"

"No. I just assumed she was going to be buried."

Stone looks out over the lake. "Just a few weeks before she died she told Fran she wanted to be cremated. And her ashes scattered on the Black Hole."

"The Black Hole? Why in the hell would she want her ashes spread there?"

Stone remains silent.

Paul's eyes follow his gaze fixed on the black water flowing into the channel, the gap between shadowy forms of rock ledges where the moonlight cannot penetrate. Paul finally says, "Well, she's dead, so what difference does it make?"

"None."

Paul feels the past, his past, will soon be gone, irretrievably gone, like his mother's dust slowly sifting through black water until it settles in the muck.

"I always feel real calm on nights like this. Just as calm as the lake." Stone falls silent for a while, and then continues. "Most people are afraid of the night. Afraid of shadows. I'm not. They kind of keep me company. I talk to the lake, the shadows ... like thinking out loud ... Tonight, you're like one of those shadows, Paulie. It's been good to talk to you."

"I think you've been spending too much time alone."

"Yeah, well, that's pretty easy to do around here." Stone leans forward and scratches, rubs, and pats his dog's back and neck. "Com'on, Jason, let's go."

"Jason? That's the name of the dog you had when I was a kid!"

"They've all been named Jason. Sort of gives me the feeling of having a friend won't never die."

"Your brand of marriage?"

"A dog won't drive you crazy the way a woman can."

"Speaking from experience?"

"Nah. I've just lived long enough to see a lot."

Stone remains seated, in spite of his decision to leave.

The moon glow on the black surface disappears and the night darkens. Paul looks up to see another ghost ship sail silently across the moon. A distant loon wails, filling the night with its piercing cry. Jason, resting at Stone's feet, starts, jumps up, and looks in the direction of the cry. Stone continues scratching the dog on its back and neck until it calms down.

Paul says, "That's got to be the most forlorn, baleful sound in the world."

"Yep. It's a crazy, lonely call. You can see why the Indians have so many stories about 'em. The white spots on their necks look like stars, and the red eyes look like the devil's. Strange birds. They mate once, and never again. They never forget. Never. They get separated, they call back and forth, sometimes from one lake to another." He shakes his head. "I've heard people say if they ever come back in this world, they'd like to come back as a loon. If your mother ever came back, she'd be a loon. I can imagine her out there at night calling to her mate."

Paul can't imagine his mother even having a mate, let alone calling to him. He doesn't want to talk about her. He doesn't want to tell Stone that love and his mother will always make, as the French say, two, and never one. It's been good to see Stone again. He'd like this encounter to end well.

"Hey!" Stone exclaims. "Sounds like this one's mate heard the call." A response echoes across the lake. Jason quivers with excitement. Stone scratches his back, pats him on the ribs a few times until he lies back down at his feet, and continues the scratching, appearing to take as much pleasure from it as Jason.

"He's calling again."

"He's back there, in that big bay. That's where you usually see 'em." The other loon responds. "Maybe they're sayin' hey, it's time, let's make whoopie."

Paul laughs. "I'm sure that's an accurate translation."

"I've seen 'em at night on the river. Strange birds. Keep strange hours. "

"So do you."

Stone glances at Paul, then looks back down at Jason. "Yeah, well, you live alone out here, nothin' to tie you down to the world of clocks and all that, you keep your own time."

"You still live in the same place?"

"Same ol' shack, same ol' lake, same ol' road from here to there. Same ol' everything."

"I remember a potbellied stove in the living room. And an old couch I used to sleep on."

"Everything was old then and just gotten older."

"A rack of antlers mounted on the wall."

"In the trophy room."

Paul laughs. "That's rich. Trophy room? It's the only room!"

"I got a bedroom too."

"Yeah, well, sort of. You also had an old gun. In the trophy room, of course."

"A 30 Ot 6. Came with the place. Belonged to the old fart who lived there before I did. I guess one night he didn't wake up to put another log on the fire. They found him in bed, frozen stiff as a board. That's what they say, anyhow. I also heard they found him on that couch you used to sleep on."

Paul chuckles and shakes his head. "How did you get me to believe that bullshit when I was a kid?"

Stone plays opossum. "Don't believe it? Fine by me. But the rifle was there when I moved in. Dirty, rusted. I cleaned it up. Still use it for deer hunting ... No, the shack hasn't changed much since you were a boy. Course, there's not much to change. Simple things don't change much."

"Simple things can be good."

A few minutes pass in silence.

"It's good you could come home for the funeral, Paulie. I think she'd be happy. She might've seemed kind of weird, like she didn't feel for anyone. But she felt a lot more than you think. I don't judge your mother, Paulie. I don't judge someone who had that much love in her."

"And how do you know?"

Stone's eyes fix on him, an expression of anger seeming to drift across his moonlit face; then he looks back down at Jason. "She put you and your sister through college, didn't she? Find me someone else around here who's done that for their kids."

"Maybe that was just a way for her to hang on to us, so we would keep on coming back and run the lodge for her in the summer."

"I'm not sayin' she didn't have her faults. Everyone does. Still, she loved you. An' she really loved your ol' man. "

"She never talked about him. Never."

"Doesn't mean she didn't think about him." Stone gives a short, quiet laugh. "Like I said, if she ever comes back from the dead, she'll be a loon."

7

PAUL WALKS INTO THE KITCHEN TO GET SOME OF the coffee he smelled as he came downstairs and finds Christine and Tim sitting across from one another at the table, busily talking in hushed voices. Cupping a mug in his hands, Tim blows on the coffee and inhales the steam as he looks up at Paul.

Christine glances back over her right shoulder at him and asks, "Did you hear him last night?"

Regretting having entered the room just then, Paul considers ignoring the question, then finally asks, "Who?"

"Fran." She bodyslams the name.

He walks around the table, gets a mug out of the cupboard behind Tim, and pours himself some coffee, wondering if he should perhaps take his coffee down to the dock and give Tim and Christine time to clear out so he won't have to listen to her complain about Fran. He leans against the counter and surveys the table, sipping his coffee. Plates covered with toast crumbs, purple smears of jam, bacon bits, and puddles of coagulated egg yolk have been pushed toward the center of the table along with salt and pepper shakers, a jar of jam, and scattered sections of the *Mirer Times*. He finally answers, barely able to conceal his irritation. "No. What was he doing?"

"He was howling."

Paul sits down at the head of the table. "What do you mean, howling?'"

"I mean howling. Like a wolf." She stares at him, eyes bloodshot, waiting for him to react.

"More of a wailing sound," Tim adds, holding the mug just below his chin as he speaks. "Like a baby crying. Or a cat in heat." He slurps some coffee.

"Howling, wailing, crying. What the hell are you talking about?"

Christine doesn't allow Tim a chance to reply. "We heard this wailing sound. At first it sounded like a baby crying, then we thought it might be a cat in heat, but then we were sure it was a wolf howling."

"I thought at one point it sounded like a wounded animal or something."

Christine scowls and shakes her head. "At first, maybe, but then you agreed it sounded like a wolf howling."

"Well, yeah, you're right."

Paul looks from Tim to Christine, seeking an explanation. "So ... what did you find out?"

Christine lights a cigarette, leans back in her chair, and before answering inhales slowly and deeply, so as to prolong the moment and the taste of what she and Tim have to offer; she exhales, then comments, a grin on her face, "Ask Tim."

Paul looks from Christine to Tim.

"The sound seemed to be coming from behind the lodge."

"A wolf wouldn't come that close to the lodge."

"Maybe not. But, at two in the morning, you're not thinking clearly. At any rate, I got up and turned on the hall light and was going to go downstairs, but ..."

"He was too scared!"

Tim throws his hands up. "You want to tell what happened, or should I?"

Christine shrugs her shoulders and takes a long drag on her cigarette.

Tim continues. "I went into Joyce's room, so I could see the back yard without going downstairs. There he was, on his knees, bent over, pounding his head with his fists, making this wailing sound, like he was crying."

Christine interjects, "Howling. He was howling like a wolf."

Paul says, "You know, when I woke up this morning I thought I'd heard a strange sound in my sleep. I thought I'd dreamt it."

"That was him!" Christine gloats, like a wrestler towering over her flattened opponent. Paul half expects her to jab her fists at the ceiling. "He's gone off the deep end. Don't you think it's time we bring a doctor in? Have him look at Fran?"

"For what? Grieving?"

"Howling and wailing and hitting himself on the head, that's a pretty extreme form of grieving, don't you think?"

Leaning back in his chair, Paul takes a long sip of coffee. "If all you're talking about is having a doctor give him a prescription, I'm for it—if Fran is."

"He might need to stay in a hospital for a while."

"Christine, what are you talking about? You can't have someone committed for grieving—even if they do it in a bizarre way."

Tim nods his head. "Chris, I think he might be right."

She glares at him, then looks at Paul. "My point is that he's not capable of looking after himself."

"So, we'll just ask Stone to keep an eye on him. He doesn't seem to mind."

"Stone," she grumbles, shaking her head. She stubs

her cigarette out in the egg yolk smeared on her plate and forces a smile. "Okay, that's fine with me. I'm all for it."

Paul takes another sip of his coffee, looks at Tim. "Where is he now?"

"He hasn't come down yet. He's probably pretty tired."

"Or suffering from one of his migraines."

She can't resist picking at him, Paul thinks. "He still gets those?"

"We'll see. It used to be every time Mother got depressed, he got a migraine."

Tim chuckles and mumbles, "Kind of like women who work together getting their periods at the same time."

Christine rolls her eyes, but otherwise ignores him. She lights another cigarette and immediately starts coughing, hacking, rattling loose phlegm in her chest. She grimaces and presses her hand clenched in a fist against her chest while grinding out the cigarette in the egg yolk next to the other butt. After several more seconds of coughing she takes a sip of coffee, a second sip, and then slowly leans back in her chair. Tears fill her bloodshot eyes. "Two more days, and then we're out of here, and I'm going to quit and never start again." She looks across the table at Tim and tries to smile through the pain. "What an ordeal! This can't end soon enough!" She sighs, then after a short while says she's going to go sit on the dock, picks up her cigarettes, lighter, and coffee mug, and walks out.

"She's right about that. This can't end soon enough." Tim stares vacantly at the place where she had been sitting and finishes his coffee. "I think I'll have another cup, and then get going on the dishes."

"Don't worry about that. I'll clean up."

"Were those two like this when you were kids?"

"At one another's throats?"

"Yeah."

"Sometimes I noticed a little tension, but nothing like

this. Usually they got along okay. But, you know, Christine is nearly six years older than I am, and Fran is about eight years older, so they didn't confide much in me, and I probably missed some things." That's a tough situation, Paul thinks, trying to back up your wife, even in her crazier moments, keep the peace, and avoid confrontation. "I guess this family must seem a little weird to you."

"All families are probably a little weird. You should meet mine! Oh," he feigns a worried look, "on second thought, it's probably better that you don't." He laughs.

Paul smiles. "We all have our neuroses."

A few hours later Paul returns to his room after a long walk and a late lunch. Still four hours to kill before the wake. He rummages through his tote bag, looking for something to read, and takes out *Arctic Dreams: Imagination and Desire in a Northern Landscape*, a book he bought at an American bookstore in Paris around Christmas the previous year. He opens the book to the bookmark he'd left when he stopped reading and discovers the wedding invitation and the picture that his mother sent him. Gazing at the invitation, he recalls her obituary. Her life went by so fast. Not yet married, and she's already dead.

He looks at the photograph of the three little girls carrying parasols and wearing white summer dresses. Gazing at the little girl in the center, smiling, so happy, sunshine and laughter, he tries to remember when he received the picture and the invitation, but can't.

He feels tired, a little depressed; he'd like to have all of this over. He lies across his bed and closes his eyes. And just as he feels sleep coming on, he remembers: it was snowing. And then it all comes back: one day shortly before Christmas, he received the invitation and the picture in lieu of a Christmas card. What could she have been thinking? And then it hits him: last December she probably knew that she had cancer and that by the same time the following year she'd be dead. How stupid of him! So obvious now. She sent the picture and the invitation because she was thinking about dying, and about who she'd been. The little girl, all sunshine and smiles, who has her whole life ahead of her, and the young bride marrying his father. The girl and the woman he'd never known.

Standing over her body at the wake, he gazes at her wispy white hair, closed eyes, sharp nose, and thin lips. Dead. The mortician tried to bring back an illusion of life with makeup. Paul feels a sudden impulse to touch her cheek, the soft smoothness of her skin. He extends his hand a few inches and immediately pulls it back.

It seems strange that so many people should come to see this body, since it's no longer hers. Someone else has bathed it, dressed it, filled the mouth with cotton, glazed the cheeks with cream and smoothed the face of wrinkles, combed the white hair, put the glasses on, and folded the hands over one another. This is a corpse. Were it not for the freckles that looked like a handful of light brown sugar granules sprinkled across her nose, he would have felt nothing. They catch him by surprise. They make him think of something childish and impish, like the grin of the little girl in the picture.

He takes a deep breath, inhaling the rich fragrance of death. Bouquets of roses, carnations, and lilies flank the casket.

The ambiance in the funeral parlor is at once sancti-monious and saccharine. Barely audible, quasi-religious organ music penetrates the room through various speakers, combining with the sound of hushed whispers to create a funerary muzak. Thick red carpet silences footsteps so that people seem to appear and disappear at his side in the softly lit room like ghosts. In comparison with these wandering, whispering spirits, Mother seems remarkably real and present. She is matter: white, smooth, cold. Dead.

An elderly couple appears in front of the casket and stands next to him. They gaze in silence at the corpse. He turns to his left and wanders off, picking his way among the small clusters of strangers.

He takes up a position at the opposite end of the room from the casket, looks around, and notices Fran standing at attention at the end of a row of flowers to the left of the coffin. His black suit, too short and too tight, fits like a monkey suit. The sleeves of his white shirt, while extending beyond the cuffs of his jacket, barely reach his wrists, and his hairy hands hang limp like those of a chimpanzee. The elderly couple that just minutes before came to stand before the coffin passes before the flowers and stops to talk with Fran. Meanwhile Christine, standing about twenty feet directly in front of the coffin, is talking with an elderly woman. As he watches his brother and sister, Paul senses that they have strategically positioned themselves in relationship to the coffin, as if they were vying for something. The elderly couple that has been talking with Fran gravitates toward Christine. Fran shifts his weight from one foot to the other, grasps his left, mutilated hand with his right hand, and stares impassively into space as if he were standing at a street corner, waiting for a bus. The elderly couple embrace Christine and talk to her, slowly shake their heads, rueful expressions on their faces, then smile, the sunshine through the clouds. Fran drifts off in the direction of the lounge reserved for the immediate family.

Paul is about to follow him when a man—short, slight of build, with a bit of a paunch—steps in front of him, extends his hand, and asks Paul if he remembers him. Paul studies his thin face: gold wire-rimmed glasses, slightly pockmarked cheeks, sandy colored hair fading to gray, and a bald pate. The man has to remind him: Phil Swenson, same class in high school, with friends in common, friends like Molly. Paul remembers that name. Molly, the beautiful girl with the long brown hair parted down the middle that draped over her shoulders like a shawl. The girl he always thought of when he'd hear Leonard Cohen sing, "Suzanne takes you down to her place near the river." Molly, with her "rags and feathers from Salvation Army counters," who'd been abused by her old man, and was so desperate for love, she gave all she had to the few she chose. Paul took so much and gave so little. And now he learns she was found dead a few months ago. Murdered. He asks the messenger all about Molly, and as Phil tells him everything he knows, Paul sees the skinny little kid with sandy brown hair and eyes that always seemed to be looking up at the world with a great longing to belong—finding his purpose now in keeping Molly's unhappy spirit alive.

Phil leaves, a woman steps forward, and Paul's heart balloons into his throat. She's much thinner now, she has lines around her eyes and lips and a few gray hairs, but when she smiles, her brown eyes warm into the lustrous deep pools he remembers. Her thin hand slides into his, and the feeling leaves him speechless.

"Paul."

He stares at her until his heart stops ballooning; his throat clear, he answers, "Hello, Rose."

"I didn't know if I'd recognize you."

"I didn't know you'd be here."

"I hope it's okay."

"Why wouldn't it be?"

"I don't know. I just wanted to tell you how sorry I am about your mother's death."

They talk briefly about his family, her family, her life in Mirer, his life in Paris, people they have known. Paul remembers the last time he spent the night with her—in a hotel, homecoming weekend, his freshman year—and the following day, when he talked about his new discovery, Dostoyevsky. To be a writer like him, that was his dream. He always had a dream. He was always going to move away to a big city, New York or Paris, and he was going to do something extraordinary: become a writer, a playwright, maybe an actor. He'd be someone. That night he ran his fingertips across the arch of her hip as he dreamed out loud. She asked how they would live in the meantime. That wasn't important. They'd find a way. And then a few weeks later, the letter arrived telling him she was seeing someone else. Someone, he learned after going home to see her, who might be able to give her the life and family she wanted. He'd lost her for a dream, he thought then, for some crazy, stupid dream. Now he listens to her talk about the days of her life that to him seem empty. He did become a writer; maybe not a Dostoyevsky, but he can make a living, and he can be happy. She talks about the difficulty of raising two teenage children, and wonders what life will be like when they have both left home and she and her husband will be alone. A lull in the conversation. A gap opens between them. Widens. She has nothing more to say, nor does he. They hug one another; she walks away.

A plump woman with white hair and thick glasses stands in front of him, a look of astonishment on her face. "When your sister pointed you out to me I thought I was seeing your father. I couldn't believe it! The resemblance is just amazing!"

Paul stares into lenses thick as shot glasses, at eyes that resemble large, milky, blue marbles.

She responds to the baffled look on his face. "I know you don't recognize me. There's no reason you should. I'm Ruth Langston. One of your mother's oldest friends."

He shakes her small, thin hand, feeling skin as soft and

smooth as parchment. "Happy to meet you, Ruth. I'm Paul, the youngest ..."

"Oh, I know who you are."

"No one's ever told me I look like my father."

"You didn't always. When you were a boy you looked more like your mother. I used to see you at threshing time when you'd stay with your grandma and grandpa. I grew up on a farm real close to theirs. I used to go home sometimes in the summers and help out with the cooking for the threshing crews."

He studies her face as she talks. Her sparse white hair is fluffed and curled, almost concealing the balding on the top of her head; blue veins spread across her temples like vines; her cheeks look soft and puffy, like rising bread dough; a thin, dark mustache gives her face a slightly masculine appearance that contrasts sharply with the thick, bright red lipstick that occasionally wanders from her lips and smudges the black hairs. He smiles as he imagines a woman with her eyesight trying to put on lipstick in the morning and warms to her immediately.

"So you were one of the women who cooked those meals. I'll never forget them." He still cannot place her in his memories of the farm, but he smiles as he recalls the meals she helped prepare. "Roast beef and chicken, sweet corn, homemade watermelon pickles, and bread and preserves, and rhubarb pies for dessert. What feasts! Do people still eat like that? Is it possible?"

Ruth beams with pride. "And," she nods, looking into his eyes, "those feasts gave me a wonderful excuse for writing to your mother. I'd tell her how happy and healthy you looked and how everything was going just fine. That's what she wanted to hear, and it was true. I didn't have to lie to make her happy."

Ruth's take on that enigma, Mother, startles him. "Did you know her when she was a girl?"

"Girl? She was a tomboy. She definitely did not like to wear skirts or dresses."

"Really? That's interesting, because last Christmas she sent me a picture of her when she was a little girl, wearing a white dress. But her hair looked like she'd had a Dutch cut, which made her look like a boy. Do you remember Dutch Boy Paints?"

"Uh huh."

"She looked just like the boy on the label."

"I can just see her: a little blond boy in a dress."

"There were two other girls, just a little taller, standing next to her. Both of them wearing white dresses. I wonder if one of them might have been you."

"I don't remember ever seeing that picture, but I suppose one of them could've been me."

"What was really strange was that she sent the picture with her wedding invitation."

"Her wedding invitation?"

"Yeah. And no explanation."

"Now that's strange, isn't it? Well, I'm sure she still loved him."

"Loved him?" He looks into Ruth's eyes, as if they might reveal an answer to this question that continues to reverberate inside him. He hadn't really thought much about his father, and what his mother and father might have meant to one another. "I don't even know how they met. That's a real mystery for me. He was up here in the boonies and she was down there nearly three hundred miles away."

She looks puzzled. "You don't know how your parents met?"

"My mother never talked about the past. At least, not to me."

"Well, this probably isn't the place or time …" Ruth looks around, her eyes coming to rest on the open casket several feet away, her view partially blocked by other mourners.

"We can go over there." Paul gestures toward a closed door in the back of the funeral parlor. Ruth has piqued his curiosity; this is a conversation he wants to pursue. "It's a room for family members. We can sit down and talk."

She hesitates, then agrees. They enter the room. She sets her shiny black purse down on a table covered by a white vinyl cloth with a pattern of roses, sits down, and looks around at the pine cupboards and gray Formica counters. Paul carries cups and saucers to the table, sits down across from her, and watches her pour a couple of sachets of sugar and some half-and-half in her cup and stir. She takes a sip of the syrupy coffee, leaving a bright red print of her lips on the edge of the cup, while she composes her thoughts.

"I was going to tell you how your parents met."

Paul nods his head.

"I'm still just amazed you don't know. But that's not my business. Well, Joyce had an aunt and uncle who lived in St. Paul or Minneapolis, I can't remember which, and every summer they'd go on a vacation and bring her along so she could watch the kids. Her folks almost never left the farm, so for her that was the only way to see the world. Now this one summer—let's see, it was the summer after her junior year in high school—Joyce went with her aunt and uncle and the kids to your grandparents' resort."

Paul smiles at the idea that someone who wants to "see the world" might come to the lodge.

"That's when she met Bill. I remember that time so well because Joyce ... she was so excited, she would've burst if she couldn't tell someone everything. So I got letters—lots of them." Ruth's eyes twinkle with mischief through the thick glasses.

That look makes him trust her. She seems happy, down to earth, nothing twisted. "What was she excited about?"

"Bill! She talked about how handsome and strong he was, and what a beautiful smile he had, and what beautiful eyes, oh … she just went on and on and on. Everything about him was perfect!" Ruth shakes her head and smiles. "She was seventeen and in love."

Paul remembers seventeen and in love, and the woman. "A potent mix."

"Oh, yes. He was her god. He really was. Anytime he looked at her or got close to her when he was waiting on tables or whatever, she'd have to tell me all about it."

"I can't imagine her like that."

"It's hard to see in an old woman the young girl she used to be." Ruth pauses a few seconds, seems to reflect about what she has said, and adds, "Above all if she's been deeply disappointed." Paul is about to ask her what she means, but she starts talking before he has a chance. "She told me when she came home she was going to marry him." She smiles, the twinkle lighting her eyes again. "She hadn't talked with him about it, but she knew."

"Determined!"

"Like most girls who didn't want to get stuck on a farm." Ruth appears to feel the weight of memory, and then seems to let go. "She kept everything secret from her aunt and uncle, and when they decided to go back to the resort the next summer, they brought her along. This time she didn't try to hide a thing. She and Bill watched the kids together during the day, and after everyone was asleep, she'd sneak out and meet him." Ruth grins. "She was so excited she couldn't keep anything to herself." Her eyes sparkle through her shot glasses. "I got all the details."

Paul laughs. "Did they make good reading?"

"You betcha! I probably enjoyed reading her letters every bit as much as she enjoyed writing them. Maybe more. I didn't have a boyfriend then." She reflects, searching for the thread of her thoughts. "Where was I? Oh, yes … well, to make a long story short, a few weeks after she got back she learned she was in the family way, and they got married that December."

"Shotgun wedding?"

"No one needed a shotgun back then. People knew the right thing to do."

"Did you go to the wedding?"

"I was the maid of honor. She was such a beautiful bride! A snow bride. It started snowing that morning—those huge flakes that fall so slow you can pick one out as it goes by and watch it all the way to the ground. Everything was white and beautiful. Like the world put on a white dress just for her. She was so lovely—all in white, and all that snow, it was like a dream." Ruth remains quiet, as if seeing the memory she described.

Don't stop, he thinks, talk my ear off. He gets up, careful not to scrape his chair on the floor, gets the coffee pot, and gestures to pour some coffee in her cup. She places her hand over the cup just as he is about to pour. He warms up his coffee, puts the pot back on the coffeemaker, and sits down across from her again.

"There's something I don't understand. Fran's birthday is in October. She probably would've given birth to this baby sometime in May."

"You really don't know anything about your mother, do you!"

"No."

"Well, just do some arithmetic. How much older than you is Fran?"

"Almost eight years."

"When were you born?"

"May 1950."

"So when would he've been born?"

"In, ahhh … 1942."

"The child I'm talking about was born in May of 1940."

"I don't get it."

"He was stillborn."

"A boy?"

"Yes. She was so certain it was going to be a boy, she'd already picked out his name—William Paul."

"William Paul! I can't ... Did she name me after him?"

"She's the only person could answer that." She pauses, looking pensive and sad, and then adds, "She mourned that baby for a long time. For years. Sometimes you need someone to help you carry the love you have for someone who's dead. It's just too much to bear alone."

"You're saying she did name me after him?"

"No. I'm just thinking out loud." She looks at him. "Guess I've lived alone too many years. Spend too much time talking to myself. "

"So do I. It's a common affliction." He looks down at the table, thinking of the dead brother about whom he has never known and whose name he bears, wondering if his mother thought of him as a substitute for the child she had lost. A resurrection of the dead. Maybe an unhappy reminder. He looks up, sees that Ruth has her shiny black purse in her left hand, and, not wanting her to leave, asks her if she would like some more coffee.

"No, I think it's time I get back to the motel. I'll just finish this cup."

"You haven't talked at all about my father. Did you know him?"

"Not really. I only met him twice—once when your mother got married, and again just after you were born."

"What was he like?"

She studies his face carefully. "Maybe I'll have some more coffee after all."

Paul fills her cup.

She sips coffee through pursed lips as she stares off into the distance, appearing to think about what she's going to say. "The first time I met him, it was at the wedding rehearsal. And what really struck me was that he looked so different from what I expected. I mean, he looked like what Joyce had described. He was tall, dark, and handsome, and all that,"—Ruth nods her head as she repeats the cliché—"but, well, she had always talked about how he was really open and affectionate; to me he seemed cool as a cucumber. Always holding something back."

She seems to have gotten stuck in her memories, so Paul prods her. "And the second time?"

She looks startled. "Oh, the second time. Yes. Well, after Joyce had you, she asked me to come and stay with her. Bill picked me up at the bus station in Mirer and drove me to the lodge. It was a beautiful day, bright and sunny. Still some patches of snow in the woods. He hardly said a word—even though he had a new baby, and so much to be happy for. When he opened the door to your mother's room, it was like a burst of sunlight. You know, that lodge is so dark, and suddenly there she was, just as bright as the day, nursing you. So happy, she just beamed. I sat down on the bed next to her, gave her a hug and a kiss, and there you were, a little red face, pretty blue eyes looking up at me, sucking away. I turned to congratulate Bill, but he was already gone. And that's the way the whole week went. He hardly talked, and always disappeared as soon as I looked the other way. He just needed a second to be gone."

"Why do you think he acted that way?"

"I have no idea. I never got to know him. A few years later he disappeared for good. And that was that."

"Died in a snow storm."

"Well, disappeared."

"What do you mean?"

"They never found him."

"But he's dead."

She looked puzzled. "Probably. That's what everyone assumed."

"But they never found his body?"

"No."

Paul feels as if he has just fallen flat on his back, looking at the world from a totally new perspective. Mother, Fran, and Christine rarely mentioned his father when he was growing up, and though he never visited a grave, he always assumed there was one. Now, for the first time, the possibility that his father might be alive looms before him.

The door suddenly swings open and Christine walks in. "Oh, here you are. I was wondering where you'd gone."

"I've been talking with Ruth. Have you met?"

"I was the one who pointed you out to her."

"Oh, that's right."

"Hi, Ruth. I really appreciate your coming. How do you know Mother?"

"She and I grew up together—as together as you can on a farm a half-mile away."

"Oh, did you visit her a few months ago?"

Ruth nodded.

"I'm sure it made her very happy."

"It was good for both of us. And now, I think the best thing for me is to go back to the motel and get some rest. I drove up this morning and ... I guess I'm a little old for trips this long."

"Will we see you tomorrow?"

"I'll be at the funeral."

Christine pours herself a cup of coffee as Paul opens the door for Ruth. "Paul." He stops to look at Christine. "I need to talk to you sometime."

"Sure. What's it about?"

"I'll tell you later."

He walks with Ruth to the entrance of the funeral home.

"You know, I think I might just drive back to St. Paul in the morning, rather than attend the funeral. I came to see her one last time, and I've done that."

He holds her parchment-smooth hand, looks into her

face warmed by the sunshine inside, and wishes her a safe trip. She opens the door to a burst of sunlight and disappears, taking the sunshine with her. He's sorry to see her leave. He could listen to her talk all day. And she told him something about his father. He might be alive. He'd be in his seventies. How, Paul wonders, if his father were alive—and that's a huge, almost impossible "if"—could he even talk to him? He can't imagine. The more he thinks about it, the more unimaginable his father becomes. Wishful thinking. He'll leave soon for Paris and forget everything. This part of his life will resemble a dream from which he's awakened. A dream quickly forgotten.

All the mourners have left. He stops in front of his mother's casket for a last goodbye. She seems at peace, dressed in a sky blue suit jacket with a cream blouse, her silence so incongruous with all the talk, all the reminiscing. Her body indifferent to the event that has been organized specifically around its presence. Indifferent to the memories, the thoughts, the feelings of those who were still struggling with life, and the gulf between life and death. He gazes at her hands folded over her abdomen—a mesh of gray vines in winter clinging to a bare wall. Her fingers look brittle, as if they might snap like sticks. He touches them. They're smooth as bleached wood, cold as porcelain. Her body has the absolute vulnerability of an object that cannot defend itself from whatever one might do to it. Touch it. Cut it. Throw it on an incinerator. He imagines it on a huge grill, torched from beneath by flames, thick gray fumes rising from its charred form. It won't burn cleanly. It'll smoke, stink, and produce a sweet putrid odor that will make a person want to puke.

He pulls his hand back from her fingers, and his gaze wanders to her face. Her mouth is open a fraction of an inch, enough so he can see her teeth. Her skin looks gray now; cheeks, gaunt. Her glasses, much too large, having been designed for a full, living face and not this skeletal head. This corpse has everything it needs to be human but life, and without that, it's just a thing, and no prayer, no funeral oration, no poem can bridge the gap between the live body and this thing. Nothing can. Except perhaps the freckles sprinkled across her nose and beneath her eyes. They recall that she was once very much alive, and for a second he feels himself stretched from life to death. Stretched like a rubber band, ready to snap. Sometime over the next couple days she will burn to ashes.

Bizarre, Paul thinks, that he and Christine should sit in the back seat while Tim sits alone in the front, like a chauffeur, following Fran's pickup truck. They pass the old State Theater; the bulbs on the marquee light up the night with the title *Dead Poets Society*. Paul read a review; the movie is supposed to deal with carpe diem. He thinks of the picture of his mother, little blond sunshine, and the corpse he has just left.

"What did you want to talk about?" And what, he wonders, is so important that you would insist I ride with you, and not, as I'd planned, with Fran?

"I just need to talk."

Paul glances at Tim and wonders why she doesn't talk with him. He notices that Tim just glanced at them in the rear view mirror.

"I was thinking this afternoon about Mother being cremated." She remains silent for a while; then continues. "I can't imagine her body being burnt to ashes ... and nothing left of her at all. It's so ... final."

Paul is about to comment that he has had similar feelings and then decides to remain silent. He sits back and looks out the window at white frame houses nestled beneath the limbs of old oaks and elms, a weeping willow in a front yard here and there.

"I went to her room this afternoon. I wanted to find something of hers to keep." Christine takes a deep breath and continues. "Everything was just as I remembered it. Same chair in front of the window. Same comforter on the bed. Same tables and lamps. That room looked and felt like her. It even smelled like her. Like her perfume and soap. I felt she might suddenly appear and ask me what I was doing there. Like I didn't have a right to be there. I came so seldom to see her when she was alive."

Paul remembers the night before, when he found Fran asleep on his mother's bed, also feeling as if he'd committed a transgression, just by entering the room.

"We try to hold on to things only after they're gone," she says.

Paul nods his head in agreement.

"I saw a picture on top of the chest of drawers. She must've seen it every day. That made me curious. I looked. It was a picture of all four of us—Mother, you, Fran, and me. We were all dressed up; it must've been a special occasion. I still had my permed curls, like some little doll. You had on shorts, and your hair was cut short. What did they used to call that?"

"Ah ... a butch."

"A butch," she repeats, nodding her head. "The picture was taken down by the lake. You could see the old Adirondack chairs. I wanted to take it, but it seemed wrong. I felt like a thief or something. Suddenly I noticed someone out of the corner of my eye. And there he was. Standing over me. Staring at me with that ... that insane look he has."

The brake lights of the pickup in front of them suddenly shine bright red in the night as it enters a curve ending the long straightaway and disappears. A few seconds later the tail lights reappear, but much further off ahead, and the truck careens along the twisting roller-coaster road.

"Look at the way he's driving. Tim, don't try to keep up with him."

"I'm not."

Paul feels the car slowing down.

"That man is a menace." She shakes her head. "I felt like I had to justify being in my mother's room—but why should I?" She looks at Paul. "Why should I? All I wanted was something that belonged to her. Something that would always remind me of her, after she's nothing but ashes."

"So, what did you do?"

"I took the picture and left."

Paul glares at her. "You got the picture, so what do you want from me?"

"He's sick."

"Look, Christine, I'm not getting involved in whatever is going on between the two of you." He turns away and looks out the window. "My flight for Paris leaves in three days. I'll never set foot in the lodge again." He shakes his head. "I'll never come back. Never."

He wanted to be able to get through all of this without any problems, without conflicts, without anyone getting angry or hurt, and now everything's a mess. Damn it!

"Well, I hope you and Ann find happiness together."

"Claire. Her name is Claire."

"I'm sorry. I hope you and Claire find—"

"I hope so too."

Stop trying, he thinks, just stop trying to patch things up. Please, don't say another word.

She says in a soft, seductive tone, "If we were to sell the lodge—"

He cuts her off. "Fran can't live anywhere else."

After a long silence she says, "I was surprised at the number of people who came tonight. Most of them looked

Mother's age. I didn't know she knew so many people. I wonder if they were friends."

"I wouldn't know. I only talked to three people."

"I noticed. You sure talked a long time to Mother's friend. What's her name?"

"Ruth."

"Oh, yeah. Ruth."

Paul ignores Christine and stares out the window. The night feels like a balm.

"What in the world did the two of you find to talk about for such a long time?"

He looks at her. "She said our father disappeared in a snow storm. I always understood he had died."

"He did. The body wasn't found, that's all. Everyone knows he's dead."

Paul notices Tim looking at them again in the rear view mirror.

"And why is everyone so sure?"

"Believe me, he's dead. You were so young when it happened. We all wanted to forget. We'd suffered enough."

Everyone wanted to forget? Hardly a reasonable explanation for everyone believing he was dead. He leans his head back and closes his eyes, expecting Christine to leave him alone. Instead she asks him, in a tone that expresses only mild interest in his response, as if she were just making conversation, if Ruth told him anything else about their father. He ignores her at first, then asks her why she wants to know.

"No reason. Just thought I'd ask."

"No," he murmurs. He doesn't open his eyes for a long while, but he feels both Christine and Tim are watching him. Maybe he's paranoid. About what? He opens his eyes. Her face is turned away toward the other window, and Tim seems to have his eyes fixed on the road.

A few minutes later the car comes to a stop next to

Fran's pickup, parked on the side of the lodge. As they walk by the truck, Christine touches the hood. "It's not even warm."

Paul says goodnight to everyone, goes straight to his room, and lies down across his bed in the dark. He feels troubled by the whole evening. About a half hour later he gets up and as he walks down the stairs he hears voices in the kitchen. He looks in and sees Christine and Tim sitting at the table. Tim stops talking when he sees Paul, and Christine turns around to look at him.

She asks, "Do you want to have some tea with us?"

He shakes his head. "No, I feel wide awake. I'm just going to get some fresh air."

Christine asks, "In this cold?"

Paul tugs at his jacket. "I'll be warm."

"Well, don't let the wildlife get you." Tim smiles.

Paul walks out into the cold and down to the dock, sits on the bench at its end, just where he and Stone sat the night before, looking out over the black water. If only he'd returned a few months ago, he would've been able to see Mother when she was still alive. He could've asked her about the picture and the wedding invitation. And about his father. What happened that night? Was there any chance he could be alive?

Dark mountainous clouds hover above the lake and threaten days of unremitting rain that could turn to snow. A canoe, its silver shape barely visible, emerges from the deep darkness of the channel a hundred feet from the dock. The paddling ceases and the canoe slowly drifts to a stop. Paul can make out the shape of the person who starts paddling again. The canoe glides silently toward the dock. When it's a few feet away a voice says, "Hey, Paulie, that you?"

"Stone?"

"Yeah. Can't see a fucking thing. What are you doing out here on a night like this?"

"I should ask you the same thing."

"Well, I've got a good answer: I went fishin'. What's yours?"

"Oh, I just wanted to get away from things and clear my head."

Stone guides the canoe through an arc so that it comes up parallel to the dock. Paul walks to the bow where he finds some rope and loops a length of it a couple times around one of the piles, while Stone pulls himself up on the dock, walks over to the bench, mumbling something that includes "holy fucking Christ," and sits down.

"Make room, old man," Paul says as he settles into the space that Stone gives him. It's too dark to see anything more than shades of darkness, so they just stare into the night.

"Where's your dog?"

"Oh, I don't take him fishin' with me. Too much trouble. So, what's foggin' up your head?"

"Kind of hard to explain." Paul thinks of the conversation with Ruth that had stirred up his past as if it were sediment. "Maybe it's the ghosts. Every time I turn around, there seems to be another one."

"If you weren't ready to see ghosts, you shouldn't've come home."

"I suppose."

"Who's been spookin' you?"

Paul shakes his head. "I can't even put a name on it."

"Ghost of a ghost, huh?"

Paul nods. "Yeah, ghost of a ghost in the fog. Just about that clear and tangible."

"Aw, shit! I bet it's just an old girlfriend, and you don't wanna tell me about her."

Paul laughs, shaking his head. "Sure." He adds, "I did actually run into an old girlfriend. Rosemary Gordon. You remember her?"

"Nope."

"Once the great love of my life. First time I've talked to her in twenty years." He pauses for a minute. "I wonder why in hell she decided to see me after all these years, and at my mother's wake on top of it all."

"She still live around here?"

"Yeah."

"Maybe she wonders what her life might've been if she'd gone a different direction. And you come from a long way off, from gay Paree. The road she didn't take."

"You're dreaming."

"Oh, you'd be surprised how many people live in the past. But I'm not telling you anything. You're the educated one."

Paul shakes his head. "Fuck you, Stone."

"Course, maybe you were doing a little bit of the same kind of dreaming."

"No regrets, believe me." He gazes at the mountainous clouds hovering above the lake like impending doom. "I did see someone who brought back good memories. Did you know a woman by the name of Ruth Langston?"

"Name doesn't mean a thing to me."

"She was a friend of Mother's. Grew up on a farm by Grandpa's."

Stone shakes his head again.

"She said she saw me a few times when I used to go to Grandpa's in the summer. She cooked for the threshing and baling crews."

"The what?"

"The threshing and baling crews."

"Don't know what you're talking about."

"All the farmers who lived near Grandpa's, when it came time to bale hay and thresh grain, they'd get together and work each other's farms. Ruth's family owned one of the farms."

"And you worked on those crews?"

"I drove tractor at threshing time. One or two guys would walk along either side of the trailer and pitch sheaves of grain into it. Then we'd drive over to the combine. It would blow away the chaff and straw, like a dust storm. We'd be dripping sweat, so the chaff would stick to us, and we'd end up covered with the stuff. It got everywhere. Even in the Kool-Aid. We'd keep it in a big jar, pass it around, take turns. The jar had a cover, but you'd have to keep your eye on the chaff and the bugs floating on the surface, so you'd hold the jar at just the right angle to get the Kool-Aid and not the rest."

Stone laughs. "No wonder you ran off to college."

"Actually, it was fun. Baling hay was even more fun. We'd stack the bales eight high, and then all the kids would ride back from the fields to the hay barn on the loaded wagons. The bales would shift and sway a little with each bump, and every once in a while you'd think, oops!, this is it, we're going down. But it never happened. It was like a ride at a carnival, everyone screaming and laughing. And lunch. Unbelievable. All the women from the different farms would get together and make these huge feasts, and we'd sit at long tables and pass food back and forth, and listen to the men tell their stories. Then I turned thirteen, and it ended. Mother decided she needed me at the lodge."

"That was probably about the time Christine left for the university."

"She did come back in the summers."

"Yeah, but your mother needed someone else involved. It's a lot of work getting ready for the season. And wasn't there a summer or two Christine didn't come home?"

"Might've been."

"Another thing, your mother never had a lot of confidence in Fran."

"So why did she put him in charge after I left for college?"

"Who else?"

"Why not you?"

"Naw. She wanted one of her kids to manage."

"Well, it's too bad she felt she needed my help, because there's nothing I loved more than living on that farm. And by the time I was thirteen I hated the lodge. The farm was paradise. Every day was sunshine, even when it rained."

"If it was such a great life, why didn't you become a farmer?"

Paul shrugged. "I moved on, that's all."

"Yeah, and maybe you knew your memories were nothing but quicksand."

"That farm was the best thing I remember. And Ruth brought it all back. I didn't want her to leave, it felt so good to listen to her talk."

"Gotta hang on to the good memories."

"She also talked about my father. No one's ever talked to me about him before." Paul stares into the darkness hovering over the lake as he recalls Ruth's memories of that mysterious man, uncommunicative, quick to disappear. "Did you know my father?"

"He was a hard man to get to know. Real hard."

"Why?"

"He didn't talk much. Course, he might've had pretty good reason not to, with all he'd been through. He lost his mom and dad, then Art went off to the war and left him with the resort."

"Who's Art?"

"Younger brother. Got killed in Normandy. And his sister died of cancer. All that happened before you came along. That's a lot to lose in the space of just a few years."

Paul feels a heavy sadness in Stone's voice fade into the blackness of the night.

"But you know," Stone says, "even if all that hadn't happened, even if times had been good, he would've been hard to get to know."

"Ruth said something that really surprised me. She said he disappeared. His body was never found." Paul glances at Stone, wishing he could see his face, then looks back at the lake. "I never thought about him much growing up. He was always ... just gone. Like he'd never been there. But there were times. Other kids talked about their dads having been in the war and all that, and I remember asking my mother about him. She said he'd died in a snowstorm. No details. And I didn't try to get any because ... well, I didn't feel I'd lost anything. Not then. What did I know?" Paul bows his head in his hands until the feelings that he has stirred have settled again. "So what do you know about all this?"

"Not much. He went into town one night. There was a big snowstorm. He never came back. End of story."

"It couldn't have been that simple. What did my mother do when he didn't come home?"

"She called the police the next day. They went looking for him. Called back that night. They'd found his car in the ditch, not more than a quarter of a mile from here, but he wasn't in it, or anywhere near it. They came back the next morning and looked until sunset. Never found a trace. Came back again the day after that, still nothin'. They even came back in the spring, hoping I guess that once the snow had melted they'd find his body—or what was left of it. But they never found a thing. So, he must've wandered off and died somehow. You can die pretty fast in the cold if you're drunk. And he'd probably had a few."

"He drank a lot?"

"Oh yeah. Every day. Above all at night, alone."

Paul glances again at the dark form of Stone's face. "You think my mother and father were happy together?"

"Yes and no."

"What do you mean?"

"Well ..." He takes a minute to formulate his thought. "Hard to describe. They were always kind of coming together and going apart." He adds, "But maybe that's normal. How would I know?"

"Do you think they were really in love with one another?"

"Yeah. Sometimes in kind of a strange way. They watched one another a lot. Like each one was tryin' to understand what the other one was doin', so he could figure out what to do. Like they were huntin' one another. Hard people to understand."

"Well it doesn't sound like they were very happy."

"Your father probably wasn't. I always had the feeling that he'd just gotten nailed to the wall with too many things too soon. The lodge, her, you kids. She wanted every ounce of him. The air he breathed, the body he lived in, even his soul, if there is such a thing." He looks at Paul. "Why do you want to know all this? They're dead. What difference does it make whether they were happy together, or loved one another, or whether your father drank?"

Paul feels Stone's eyes staring at him in the dark. He returns the stare, even though he can see nothing but a dark form that resembles a face. "No one knows where my father's body is. And in a couple days my mother's going to be incinerated, and she'll be nothing but ashes."

"So?"

"So I want to find out who these people were while there are at least a few traces of their lives left. They're disappearing. Time's not on my side."

After a minute of silence, Stone looks up at the sky, then stands up. "Well, it's not on my side either. I gotta get going or I'm gonna get soaked."

Paul stands up, watches Stone's dark form walk off to his right toward the bow of the canoe and squat to loosen the rope securing the canoe to the dock.

"Just one other thing. I didn't know there was a William Paul."

"There wasn't."

Paul walks over to the canoe and, bending over, takes hold of the edge with both hands to stabilize the canoe for Stone. "I didn't know she'd had a miscarriage."

Stone threw the rope in the bow and walks around Paul to the stern so he can board the canoe. "As I said, there wasn't a William Paul. He never lived." Paul watches the shadowy figure board the canoe.

"Did she name me after a dead baby?"

Stone takes his paddle and looks up at Paul. His words seem to come from the darkness itself. "Let go of the past, Paulie. There's nothing you can learn that will do you any good."

PAUL ENTERS THE KITCHEN FEELING HUNGOVER from the dream of snow that returned again that night and finds the others already sitting at the table. Tim looks up from a newspaper with a smile and nod. He has already showered (his hair washed and blown dry), shaved, and put on a white dress shirt and tie with diagonal bands of maroon, blue, and gold. Christine, in a white blouse with a black jacket, her face finished with airbrush smoothness, asks Paul if he slept as poorly as everyone else.

Walking past Fran's chair at the end of the table, Paul shakes his head and sighs, as if trying to expel the depression that still inhabits him. "I've been having the most awful dreams."

"You're not the only one," Christine mumbles as she looks down at the newspaper spread out before her.

Tim looks at her and then at Paul. "Have some coffee." He raises a white mug with a loon on it. "It'll brace you for the day."

"I intend to." Paul's feeling better already. It's good not to be alone. He pours his coffee and, after blowing on it and breathing the aroma, takes a sip, then another, and continues sipping while gazing out the window above the sink at the back yard, the old picnic table, and the long gradual slope ending in the reeds and cattails around the Black Hole. He refills his mug, turns around, and looks over the table. The usual breakfast clutter of plates with smears of butter and jam and toast crumbs; glasses with orange pulp clinging to the inside; coffee mugs; and sections of the newspaper laid open in front of Tim and Christine. He leans against the counter and stares at the back of Christine's head, for want of anything better to look at. No one talks for several minutes. He feels the depression, the futility of it all, grip him again as he watches Christine play with the curls on the right side of her head, twisting them around her fingers, releasing them and patting them in place, then twisting and patting them all over again. The back of a person's head is so extraordinarily vulnerable, he thinks, like a big egg that could easily be cracked open. He turns away from the thought and glances over at Fran, whose left hand is resting on the table, and wonders if Fran still feels pain where the two missing fingers used to be.

Tim looks up from the paper. "Pretty amazing. Thousands of East Germans at a rally yesterday chanted 'down with the Wall.' Can you imagine the Wall coming down? It's been there almost as long as we've been alive."

Paul remembers his editor's response to his article: "Speculative journalism." The Wall will come down; but what happens then?

"I wouldn't count on it disappearing too quickly," Christine says, without looking up from her newspaper.

"The evil empire. It has no more chance of surviving than Jericho."

Paul looks at Fran. He has that Rasputin look.

Tim responds, "It might be the evil empire, Fran, but I haven't read any reports of trumpets blaring. That's not what's bringing down the walls." He adds, with a laugh, trying perhaps to soften the tone of his remarks, "But maybe I haven't been reading the right reports."

Fran glares at Tim and slowly shakes his head as if confronted by a pathetic fool.

Christine says, "Tim, you probably haven't been reading the news from the spirit world, so how could you possibly know about the evil empire and Jericho?"

Tim spreads his hands before him, as if trying to calm a mounting storm. "Chris, please, let's not get anything started."

But it is too late. Looking at Fran, nodding her head slowly, she speaks in a hushed voice while carefully articulating each syllable. "You're a really sick person, Fran. Really sick. The people in the white coats should come and take you away. Lock you up and throw away the key."

"You're the one who's sick!"

Christine repeats in a singsong voice, "They're going to come and take you away, come and take you away."

Oh, God, she's as crazy as he is. Paul watches, amazed.

"Chris! Chris!"

She ignores Tim and continues chanting, "Come and take you away, oh yes, come and take you away, you nut!"

Fran leans back in his chair and fixes Christine as if she were a voodoo doll at which his eyes were shooting pins, while she chants, "Come and take you away from your mother!"

"Chris! For Christ's sake, stop!"

She remains silent for a second, and then adds, "You really need help, Fran. Serious help."

Silence.

Tim exhales some of his tension in a long sigh. "Oh, God." Shakes his head. "You know, it would be great if the two of you could knock down your own wall." He looks from one to the other. "But that's obviously too much to hope for.

If you did, you'd probably end up throwing the bricks and mortar at one another, so maybe it's best you keep it up." He folds the newspaper, lays it on the table, stands up, puts on his jacket. "Well, I'm dressed and ready to go, so I think I'll walk down to the dock and enjoy some peace." He leaves. A minute later the front screen door slams shut.

Fran's eyes remain fixed on Christine; she seems to be staring at Tim's chair. Paul feels the tension, and knows they feel it too. After a long silence he asks, "What's for breakfast?" The question does nothing to reduce the voltage.

Fran, his eyes still fixed on Christine, doesn't bother to look at him. "Same thing as yesterday."

Paul finds two grease-filled pans on the stove, washes and rinses them, clanging them against the sides of the sink, hoping the noise will make them leave. With the bacon starting to sizzle, he sets about making another pot of coffee and some toast. He'll hold off on the eggs until the bacon is mostly cooked; maybe by then they'll have left.

"You know, Fran, I was thinking, since the minister doesn't know Mother, maybe we could do something to personalize the funeral."

Oh shit, Paul thinks, leave it alone. He looks over his shoulder at the two of them. This is really going to set him off.

Fran's eyes seem to penetrate her. "Like what?"

"Maybe we could talk about our memories of her."

Paul leans against the counter and stares again at the back of her head, while the bacon sizzles and the coffee drips. "What memories would you like to talk about?"

She turns around to look at him. "Well, I don't know. But the only person who's saying anything is someone who never knew her." Turning back to look at Fran. "He's just going to read something and fill in the blanks with her name."

Seeing Fran is not going to respond, Paul does. "Well, that's kind of what death is, isn't it? It's like a form. Someone dies every day. Pretty much the same thing could be said about each person. You change the names and the dates. Christine, we've been over this already. I think Fran did the best he could. Let's just leave it alone."

"I can't. There's no church. No priest. She's not being buried."

Paul responds. "But she didn't want what you want. She wasn't really Catholic. She probably wasn't anything."

Fran glares at him. "Yes she was!"

"Yeah? What was she?"

"She was ... she is, part of the spiritual."

Paul continues staring at Fran, ignoring the toast that has popped up in the toaster. "Part of the spiritual! Can you be a little more specific, Fran?"

"You know what I'm talking about. When you're alone in the woods, or out on the lake ... you can feel there are people out there."

Paul responds, as if questioning a child. "People? What kind of people, Fran?"

"People who've been dead for a long time."

"Like, spirits?"

"The Indians used to call this the land of the spirits."

Christine blurts out, "Oh, Lord! Who cares what the Indians called this land? I think she should have a real funeral and a burial. It's just like her not to think about us. Not to think about whether or not we want to come back and visit her. And if she was buried—"

"Visit her? You had plenty of chances to visit her when she was alive, but no, you—"

"Fran, don't you try to tell me—"

Paul interrupts her. "Let it be, goddamn it! Christine, get this through your head; it was her fucking decision to make, not ours!"

"The people who count after someone has died are the ones who go on living. I can't accept the fact that a day from now there'll be nothing left of her."

"Ashes, Christine. There'll be ashes."

"Yeah, that we're supposed to scatter on the Black Hole. That's not a place I'd ever want to return to."

Fran looks directly into Christine's eyes. "That's a place she never wanted to leave."

A long silence.

She responds, resignation in her voice. "You're right. It makes sense." The storm that seemed to rage inside has suddenly subsided.

How is that possible, Paul wonders, as he looks into Fran's face that seems transformed: its craggy, rough surface looks weathered by a lifetime of suffering, and the hazel eyes, no longer gleaming with that Rasputin righteousness, project sorrow and commiseration instead of rage. This face has communicated something to her, but what? When Fran said, "'That's a place she never wanted to leave,'" Christine understood something that he didn't, that he couldn't, and that she and Fran knew he couldn't. Just like when they were kids. Something binds them together, and excludes him. It's obvious, and yet not so obvious he can point to it, can say, see, I know what you're doing. It's a game they play, they know they play it, and one of the rules is that you never talk about it, you never acknowledge it even exists.

Fran continues staring at Christine. "Her spirit will rise with the other spirits over the water at night like mist, and in the morning sun they'll seem to disappear. But they'll be there, and she'll be happy."

"Did she tell you that, Fran?"

He looks at Paul. "She didn't need to. There were some things we didn't need words for. You only need words ... when you can't understand one another."

Paul nods. "Certainly in this family."

"When are you going to perform this ... ceremony ...

of spreading the ashes? I ask, because we'd planned on returning home tomorrow. I hadn't thought about the need to do this."

"I don't know. I'll do it when I feel she wants me to do it."

"Okay. I certainly don't need to be here." Christine remains silent for a long time, then adds, "We'll leave tomorrow, right after breakfast."

Just as she gets up from the table, Fran looks at her and says, in a conciliatory tone, "The minister asked me lots of questions about Mother. He has some good things to say." Christine nods, hesitates, then walks out of the kitchen toward the front of the lodge. The screen door again slams shut. Fran gets up, walks around the other side of the table and out the back door.

Paul goes back over the conversation, wondering what really happened between Fran and Christine.

Paul stands next to Fran in the back of the room in the funeral home, with its thick dark red carpet and muted sound and light, and stares at the coffin and the flowers that have been moved to the far end of the room. A tall, big-boned, middle-aged man in a black suit, a huge head of brown hair, and glasses with thick black rims stands at the lectern. He appears to be reading something. He raises his head from time to time to scan the rows of folding chairs and the ten to fifteen elderly people—people with white hair or balding heads, broad hips or sparrow limbs, thick paunches and triple chins or scrawny necks and loose-hanging clothes, stooped and leaning on canes or one another—shuffling in and sitting down. Tim and Christine arrive, join Paul and Fran, and they all walk up the central aisle. Fran introduces the others to Reverend

John Schultz. They chat for a few minutes. Paul looks for Ruth, but doesn't find her.

Christine leads the way to the second row. The minister clears his throat loudly enough for everyone to hear and begins to speak, looking frequently down at his sermon.

"We are gathered here today because of our bond to Joyce ... Bauer. Her death is cause for all of us to mourn, to join with her family at this hour of need, and to offer them our support and comfort. Their loss is our loss. We know the bell that tolls for her will some day toll for each and every one of us.

"Joyce was a wife, a mother, and a sister. Hers was a heavy cross to bear. Her husband died when her three children were still young. She raised them alone, while operating a ... a business here in town. She taught them the importance of faith, charity, and love. And she provided for their education by sending all three of them to the university. She did this without complaining, because she knew that to give was to receive and to love was to be loved.

"Joan was also a friend. She lived in this community for many years and formed many bonds. She left a deep impression on all of us. She was seventy-one when she died. Most of those seventy-one years she spent here, among us."

Paul leans forward and glances at Christine. Her face reveals no reaction to the minister's mistakes. He settles back in his seat and listens to the rest of the sermon. It's so predictable. As the minister proceeds through the major points in his argument that it is only by dying that we can live, he continues to substitute the name of Joan for Joyce and make other mistakes as well. Christine was right to assume the minister might make mistakes, but did it really matter? The sermon would have been the same. Fran seemed equally right to be unconcerned.

*
*   *

Paul listens to the tires hum on the blacktop as he looks out the window of Fran's pickup at the beautiful autumn day. The sun captures the red in the scaly bark of the Norwegian pines and sets it aglow. It feels good to escape the minister's rhetoric, with its tortured logic, twists and turns to make us feel that the road to death is really a road to life, and to ride instead down a real road with his silent brother beside him. He thinks of Mother in her coffin, freckles sprinkled like granules of brown sugar across her nose, and wonders if the little blond girl in the picture had freckles too. She must've. Freckles go with the sunshine and love in that smile, that grin. Full of the dickens, as his grandmother might say. He rolls down the window, puts his arm out, feels the cold wind rip at his shirt sleeve and blow through the cab, replacing the warm, stale air with the same wind that gusts through the tree tops. It feels good to be with someone who won't make any effort to talk.

Paul is surprised to see Stone, whom he can't recall ever seeing in the lodge before, standing behind the bar and looking down at a newspaper. A couple of men in t-shirts and jeans sit at the end of the bar, drinking beer. They might've just returned from a camping trip. Stone looks up, strokes a long lock of oily gray hair out of his eye, nods to him, and goes back to reading the newspaper. He wears his usual clothes—jeans and a sweatshirt. As if nothing special had happened.

The pool table in the old dining room has been covered with sheets of plywood and tablecloths to convert it into a buffet table. The funeral lunch includes platters of roast beef, ham, turkey, cheese, breads, pastries, and bowls of potato salad, cold slaw, pickles, beets, and olives, all sealed with plastic wrapping. Paul positions himself next to the rampant bear that always looks as if it's about to embrace someone it sees in the distance and waits. He looks up at the bobcat mounted on its stand and suspended from the ceiling. While the cat snarls, ready to attack, the whitetail buck still gazes into the distance, stoic as ever. Christine and Tim arrive, then a half-dozen people who were at the funeral. Paul doesn't know any of them. They fill their plates and make their way to the tables in the new dining room. Even the two fishermen go through the serving line, then return to the bar to eat. There's almost enough people to make this feel like a normal funeral lunch. But again, Mother seems somehow irrelevant to everything that's being done to honor her.

Christine moves next to him.

He continues watching people serve themselves and head for the outer dining room and the sunlight. "The lunch looks like it's going to turn out okay. Why don't you eat something?"

She shakes her head.

"That sermon," he says, "I'm sure the minister knows it by heart. I could've given it for him."

Her hand grasps his and grips it so tight it almost hurts. "It's over."

Paul hesitates outside the door. He planned on going to his room and resting after lunch, but the image of the little blond girl kept returning, and looking at the door to his mother's room as he reached the top of the stairs, he remembers Christine's story about finding the family picture. He wonders if he should go in. The room is taboo. Has always been, as far back as he can remember. But she's dead now. A corpse. Vulnerable. He remembers looking at her body at the funeral parlor and thinking it had been washed, dressed, and prepared for public view by others, and would soon be incinerated by others. Her room now is like a corpse, completely vulnerable, and totally indifferent. It has no private parts, no modesty. He can look and touch and smell all he wants. Only the feeling of transgression holds him back. But he's not doing anything wrong. Nothing will happen. He opens the door, hesitates again; no screams, no flames of hell, no adult looking down at him; he slips in and closes the door.

The afternoon sunlight flows into the room through the white lace curtains covering three windows, the two across from him and the third window to his left. The filtered light forms a warm pool on the maple floor and on the comforter's white field with faded roses covering the mahogany bed on his right. Night tables matching the bed stand on each side of it, a matching chest of drawers had been placed to his right, against the east wall, and on the other side of the bed, a dresser with a large mirror held by two lyrelike arms, faces the west wall. An armchair—one of those high-backed armchairs that he remembers curling up inside like an animal hibernating in its den—and a round table next to it face the window on the west side farthest from where he stands. The third window, facing south, presents a picture of birch and pine in the foreground and just beyond them, water that reflects the blue sky. Between that window and the east wall, a cabinet with two doors, each with myriad small panes of glass set in wooden frames, appears to be filled with books.

The bed, with its tall headboard, seems to dominate the room like a massive throne. He imagines her sitting up high, her back resting on a pile of pillows, reigning over the room and all that's in it, perusing her books, perhaps talking to herself. She spent so much time alone, he can't imagine her not being a little neurotic, keeping herself company with her own monologues and soliloquies.

He sits down on the bed and picks up a picture on the night table. A wedding picture, a six-by-eight sepia-tinted studio photo, in a tarnished gold frame. The bride and groom in the center, the best man and the bridesmaid on either side, and a young boy, about five, standing in front of and between the two men on the left. The bride wears a long white silk gown with a high collar that opens like a petal around her neck, so that her head seems to blossom out of the gown, and her smile seems the expression of burgeoning happiness. Her hair, parted in the middle and arranged in tight waves along the side of her head, reminds him of movie stars from the 1930s. From the small white headdress in the form of a starburst on the back of her head descends a lace veil that disappears behind her back, then reappears draped diagonally across her legs and splayed across the floor, where it covers her feet. Both she and the bridesmaid wear long sheath gowns that remind him of Gothic statues of fluted figures. And they both carry huge bouquets of flowers. The men wear dark suits, white shirts and ties, and a flower in each lapel. All four of them look very young. From what Ruth Langston told him, his mother would have been about eighteen or nineteen when she married, and his father could not have been much older than that.

Paul doesn't recognize the best man or the bridesmaid, but there's something about the boy—dressed completely in white (from his shirt, open at the collar, to his jacket and shorts to his socks and shoes) and standing at attention with a sprig of green fernlike leaves and a long stemmed rose in his hands—that intrigues him. The longer he looks, the more he sees a slight resemblance between the boy and the men—above all the long face and nose, the deep-set eyes, the small lips and the broad forehead—that makes him think they might be related by blood. The best man might be an uncle, the boy might well be Stone. He makes a mental note to be sure to ask Stone how exactly they're related, what in their relationship has brought him so close to his family, from the wedding right up until today. Stone turns up in the most unexpected ways—on the dock, the day Paul arrived; out of the darkness of the night on the lake, a shadow coming out of the shadows; in the lodge, behind the bar, where Paul had never seen him before; and now in this picture, with these people who are probably all dead. He seems to have wandering rights through past and present, day and night, life and death.

Paul puts the picture on the table and picks up a book (dark blue, cloth bound, with frayed gray corners) and opens it to the title page. *Rebecca*, by Daphne du Maurier. Someone wrote "1952" in pencil near the top right corner of the title page. He flips through a few pages, browses, flips through a few more, and browses. The pages feel soft, worn by time and perhaps the fingers that turned them repeatedly. The corners of some of the pages have been turned down to mark a place and then turned back up again. Was she fascinated by this story? Did she identify with the main character? Why would she read this book before she died? But maybe he assumes too much. Maybe someone placed it on the table after she'd been taken to the hospital.

He sets the book down, looks around, walks past the chest of drawers to the cabinet, and opens the doors with the little panes of glass. Books—paperback, hardcover, mostly old and worn. His eyes scan the spines, picking out titles: *A Mind to Murder*; *Death of an Expert Witness*; *The Secret Adversary*; *Murder on the Orient Express*; *Death on the Nile*; *Murder with Mirrors*; *Sleeping Murder*, and another dozen by Agatha Christie; *The Big Sleep*; *Farewell, My Lovely*; *The Long Goodbye*; *Where Are the Children?*; *The Cradle Will Fall*; *A Cry in the Night*; *Edith's Diary*; *This Sweet Sickness*, and half a shelf of paperbacks by Georges Simenon. Why all the mysteries? He takes *Edith's Diary* off the shelf, skims through a few pages, then stops, and stares at one of the pages without reading. The only conclusion he can draw is the obvious: she liked to read mysteries.

And while reading mysteries, she became a mystery for the rest of them. A sphinx, speaking in riddles—like the picture and the wedding invitation she sent him. Probably the most personal message he'd received from her in fifteen years. But no less ambiguous than the rest of her behavior: her abrupt announcements when he was a boy that he'd be going to his grandparents' farm; her equally abrupt manifestations of affection that always seemed excessive, as if she felt some extraordinary urgency to show him love; the way she slowly disappeared from their lives without any explanation, while Christine took over and ran everything, telling Fran and him what to do; her increasing coolness toward him as he grew older and became more independent, and yet her desire that he return. Why did she want him to return? Why did she send him the wedding invitation and the picture? Was that another attempt to manipulate, to draw him back? Well, he's back, maybe not in the palm of her hand, but spinning like a yo-yo just beneath her palm, almost in her grasp. That's absurd. She's dead. She has no control over him; the thread of her life has been measured and cut; the string of the yo-yo cut with it; it's all over with. He looks at the description of *Edith's Diary* on the jacket: "A chilling, harrowing, heartbreaking novel about separation and loneliness, mirrored in the eyes of a woman at midlife whose familiar world collapses into a chaos she is powerless to avoid." Cheerful stuff.

He closes the book, puts it back on the shelf, wanders over to the armchair in front of the window, opens the lace curtains, and sits down. The chair, which seems to enclose him and hold him, faces south. This is what she saw every time she sat here: the Black Hole and the surrounding marsh, thick with yellow reeds and cat tails; the inlet, the water lilies, and the large flat rock on which loons sometimes nest in late spring; and the river that broadens into a lakelike expanse, where sunlight shimmers like millions of rippling lures, before flowing through a narrow channel further south and disappearing. She might've sat here watching the wood ducks and mallards land, like fighter planes returning from a sortie, or the loons plunge and resurface as they hunted for food, or deer come down to drink at dusk. At night she might've heard the loons calling to one another in the darkness, like forlorn lovers, or gazed at the moonlight and stars sparkling and shimmering on the surface of the black pool like an entire galaxy rising from the water. And she would've been ignorant of what her own children were doing, or thinking, or feeling.

He gets up from the chair and walks over to the dresser between the two windows, idly inspects perfume and eau de toilette bottles, a plastic brush and comb, and a round rose-colored satin box of facial powder. The drawers contain brassieres, panties, socks, stockings, hankies, scarves, t-shirts, nightdresses. His fingers caress a flannel nightgown, soft and warm. He sees his reflection in the mirror and turns away.

He opens the closet door and breathes the dry, musty smell of old age, the smell of clothes that have been cleaned and hung and stored with moth balls and aired and cleaned and hung again, clothes that were never replaced because the person wearing them wasn't active enough to wear them out. Light cotton dresses and shirts with flower prints and blouses and skirts of white, black, or cream rayon or silk and cotton blends suspended from hangers seem to have ghostly lives of their own. He touches a dress, feels a skeletal frame as thin and light as china, and lets go, leaving the dress where it is and where it will remain, out of respect for her.

The closet on the other side of the bed reveals clothes from another era. Clothes that a young woman would have worn. Décolleté dresses; a black velvet sheath dress that must have just reached her knees; square-dancing dresses; dresses of exotic colors evoking limes, oranges, and lemons, or Gauguin's Tahiti and beautiful brown women bearing mangos, papayas, and passion fruit. Round hatboxes on a shelf above the hangers with black velvet hats and lace veils. And the faint odor of mothballs that have preserved the clothes and embalmed her youth. She's far more present in the dresses, blouses, shirts, coats, and hats in the closets than in that corpse in the casket. The corpse was just three-dimensional; it existed only in space. The closets accumulated the years of her life. They are a fourth dimension, time, without which the other three seem meaningless. Time, the unknown territory.

He looks through the chest of drawers, each drawer full of winter things—scarves, mittens, sweaters, wool socks, long underwear, wool pants. The bottom drawer contains a large shoe or boot box, and next to it two black photo albums. The albums prove to be empty. He opens the box and discovers a mess of pictures: all sizes, black and white, sepia monochromes, hand colored, a few in color, some looking as if they might be sixty years old or more, others more recent, none of them taken within the last few years. He sits down on the bed and starts taking them out. Almost every picture had sustained some kind of damage—creases where a picture had been folded or crumpled, or a white jagged line, like a scar, where a picture had been torn and the pieces taped together on the back. Others are simply missing corners. And one picture after another has slivers of black paper adhering to the bottom edges. Someone must've ripped these pictures out of an album. He wonders why anyone would've done that. The pictures are so old; most of the people are probably dead.

Certainly this man is dead. Paul looks at a five-by-seven photograph of a young man in a dark pinstripe suit coat, white shirt with a full starched collar, and a broad dark tie. A medium close-up, in sepia with a shallow depth of field creating a blur of light and shadow behind him. Round face, full lips; strong nose; hair parted on the left, combed straight across his head and cropped as if someone had placed a shallow bowl over his head and shaved around it down to the scalp. In his mind's eye Paul sees an old man with a thick shock of white hair laying on his head like wheat blown flat by the wind. Yes, this is Grandpa, still young in the photograph, his youth mummified in this chemical impression, wondering perhaps what lies ahead on a road that had already ended in a funeral and a cemetery near the outskirts of town. What had this man—who was not yet his grandfather—hoped to find? And what did he find? Dead, his whole life still lies ahead of him. Paul feels for Grandpa. He wants to warn him, to let him know his life is already over—but what would Grandpa have done if he'd been able to see his life as still to be lived and already finished?—and finds he can't imagine thinking that contradiction anymore than he can imagine finding a way out of one of Escher's drawings of divergent and convergent planes.

He flips through pictures of people he doesn't know, then stops to look at some photos of children—blond children with dark tans who clearly spent their summers outdoors in the sun and the water. Snapshots that caught them on the wing and pinned them still. Like this boy and girl, about six and four, running across a lawn toward the photographer, the boy smiling and leading the girl by the hand. A short, light-colored dress, white socks and shoes; dark pants and a white shirt. Paul recognizes the log cabins in the background beyond the trunks of Norwegian pine. The children must be Fran and Christine. On a Sunday. After or before church. Then a picture of the two of them in their bathing suits, tanned like Pacific Islanders, Fran crouching with a play shovel, digging a round canal in the sand and clay of the lake shore, Christine kneeling on the sand inside the moat, a pail next to a sand turret that she appears to be patting—the way she might pat her hair today. Both of them completely absorbed by their construction. Behind them, the dock, and in the background, a corner of the boathouse.

This must be me in the next picture, Paul thinks: about three or four years old, in bed, sitting up and leaning toward the camera, a big grin on his face, his eyes squinted shut, round cheeks, hair cut in a buzz, skin deeply tanned. He looks at the picture for a long time, then shuffles through the stack again, encountering one picture after another of Fran, Christine, and himself. Pictures of children who were loved, and whose every move, every expression, was worth recording. He stares at the pictures for a long time, mesmerized. Like his mother's dresses, they add another dimension to Fran and Christine and to himself: time—forgotten time, and time he had never known. A time when they were all happy. What happened to change all that?

He moves on, finds some pictures—posed pictures—of his mother with her children, and stops to look at one. He easily recognizes Fran and Christine now. Shoulder to shoulder, standing on the white bench that used to be in front of the dining room, looking directly at the camera and holding hands. Mother's wearing a knee-length, light-colored coat, dark high heels with ankle straps, and a narrow-brimmed hat with flowers on the front and a veil pulled back over the top. Her lips parted, as if she were about to say something while looking directly into the camera. She's wearing lipstick and looks sexy, like a movie star in one of those films right after World War II, when people wanted to celebrate, drink highballs, and dance jitterbugs and lindies. But who is this teenager, behind and to the left of Fran? Thirteen or fourteen years old, a long face, broad forehead, light brown or sandy hair. He stands just a little shorter than Mother, on the opposite side of the picture, slightly behind and to the right of Christine. Is this the boy who was also in the wedding picture? Could it be Stone? Who else?

Another picture of Mother, this time with a little boy standing on a picnic table and dressed in dark shorts, a light t-shirt, and white baby shoes. A plump little boy with stout legs, round face, tanned skin, and blond hair, who might well have been himself. His mother standing next to the table, in profile, looks at him, not at the camera, smiling, happy, and proud. A woman still young, in a summer dress, with a barrette in her long hair, saddle shoes, and bobby socks. The table he remembers had once been in the backyard. The photographer must have been kneeling about ten feet away when he took the picture, or perhaps he was standing on the slope, because the low angle makes the child—him, he's sure now—look like a little prince, a little Mussolini, with a puffed out chest, who rules over this woman. She looks up into his eyes, as if he'd once been the object of her desire. He smiles. What an extraordinary sight!

She's been the object of someone's desire too, he thinks, as he looks at a picture of her, alone, in a dress with a pleated light skirt and a black décolleté top, her dark hair permed and piled in curls, looking directly at the camera, her face still young, open, and innocent. A small pendant hung on a black ribbon around her neck rests on her white skin, the whiteness highlighted by the rectilinear décolletage, and a small corsage is pinned to her right breast. A floral curtain hangs in loose folds, framing Venetian blinds that conceal the window behind her. Flowers wherever he looks: fragments of large, dark leaves and blossoms that look like irises and carnations on the folds of the curtains; a stem with small leaves and a delicate rose splayed across the bulbous white base of the lamp; and the corsage on her chest. She's Flora—beautiful, radiant, receptive. And young. She couldn't have been much over twenty. He puts down the picture, then picks it up again, turns sideways on the bed so that he can see the windows with their drawn white lace curtains. The round table, a little behind her, resembles the table in front of the second window, the one further from the bed. He looks back and forth from the table in the picture to the one in the room. They're definitely the same. So this room, the one he has always thought of as the den of a recluse, now contains the ghost of this beautiful woman who was his mother. He smiles at the thought.

He slowly looks through another stack of pictures and stops at a close-up, three-quarter frontal shot of his mother sitting on a lawn, facing toward her left, pensive. The picture taken from her right side shows her entire face. She looks as if she were twenty, perhaps even younger. Dark brown hair in waves cut at the neck. Dressed in a white skirt, a matching white jacket with a ruffled collar around her neck and a row of five dark buttons down her right sleeve, and a white blouse with a pattern of heavy dark lines in the form of diamonds. Lawn and trees in the background. Obviously a park. The photo, a direct imprint of her body, is so clear it looks as if it were taken just hours before. There she is, poised at the beginning of a new life. Just on the brink, ready to leap. Did she want to go ahead? Turn back? Was she eager? Anxious? Her face is ambiguous. He can't see her eyes directly, and yet, because she's looking away, she reveals a pensiveness that she probably would have concealed had she been looking directly at the camera. She's so young, so beautiful, she had every reason to imagine that life would be worth living. He stares at the photo for several minutes. He has that Escher feeling again: she's already dead, and yet she still has her whole life ahead of her. That feeling is accompanied by another, far more intense: desperation. He wants to warn her: whatever you want to do, you have to do it all very fast; you have very little time; you're going to be dead soon; you're already dead. He continues staring at the photograph, feeling the desperate futility of being alive.

Other photographs suggest her life wasn't all rose tint and soft focus. A picture of her standing outside the door leading to the kitchen and wearing a nightgown with a floral pattern. This time she's not soft, receptive, delicate, with her petals open and waiting for penetration. No Flora this time, she looks directly at the camera with expressionless eyes that challenge the right of the person taking the picture to pose her like a still life.

In another picture of her in profile she stands in front of one of the kitchen counters, wearing a halter and shorts. The numeral "45" is written in ink on the border at the top of the picture. Paul does some quick calculations. Forty-five—a year after Christine was born. His mother was born in ... 1921. She was only twenty-four when this picture was taken. She looks down toward the counter, which is covered with condiments, packages, bowls, and other kitchen things, her face impassive. The fingers of both hands poised on the counter top as if she might begin tapping her nails until she can stop posing. Something in this picture of a young woman with dark waves and curls and a halter that emphasizes the contours of her breasts and reveals her bare arms and abdomen evokes the pinups he remembers from gas stations when he was a boy. The longer he looks at the picture, the more he thinks he can read in the relationship between her and the person who took it—perhaps his father—a power struggle pitting the subject behind the camera against the object in front of it.

He lays the picture on the bed next to him and finds a photograph of a man sitting in an Adirondack chair. A medium long shot in half profile. He's smiling, quite content with himself; he might be twenty-seven or twenty-eight. Paul sees the resemblance to the man in the wedding picture; it's his father.

He sets the photo aside and confronts another medium long shot of his father standing in front of a dark car from the 1940s, wearing a light double-breasted suit, white shirt, and tie. The hood, directly behind him, tapers to a point like the front end of a submarine. Enormous fenders, each with a blind glass eye in the center, flank the tapered hood and reflect the branches above the car and outside the picture frame. Trees in the background—might be a park. A sunny day. Large shadows on the car and grass. He looks a little older in this picture. A hint of a smile, not much more. Dark hair lies across his right temple. His head cocked just a little to the side. A handsome man. Well built under the suit. Proud of his car. A man who by this time in his life feels he has accomplished something—owning a car, and maybe something, or someone, else. The longer Paul looks at the picture, the younger his father becomes, until finally he can see in him someone not much older than a teenager, dressed up as an adult and proudly standing in front of a car that might well have been his first. He looks both proud and insecure, as if he were afraid he might not measure up to the image he wants to project. To whom? To Mother? Paul wonders whether she took this picture of the boy smiling through the man.

He continues flipping through the pictures until he comes to one of the entire family. The only one he has seen. A black-and-white photo, also torn from top to bottom and taped together. His father (Paul recognizes him easily now) on the left side of the group, in a dark overcoat that he wears unbuttoned over a dark suit, white shirt, and tie. A fedora pulled down over his forehead. His gloved hands hold Christine's upper arms. She stands in front of him, the top of her head reaching to the level of his chest. Dressed in a knee-length coat, lighter in color than the one her father wears, and a hat with a small brim over her forehead and flaps pulled down over her ears. Then Fran, standing stiff, already tall and gaunt, a head shorter than his father, a dark parka with the hood down, hair hanging down over his forehead, his hands enclosed in the deerskin mittens with wool liners they called choppers when he was a boy. The jagged tear, barely visible, passes between Fran, to the left, and a young man on the right, who must be Stone. About the same height as Father. Wearing a dark jacket and jeans. No hat. His brown hair combed back off his forehead. Head tilted, a cocky look. Then Mother, in a knee-length dark coat, her left hand in a dark leather glove grasping her coat and holding it tightly against her chest, her right arm hanging to her side. And, Paul thinks, this must be him, the little boy, three or four years old, standing just in front of and between Stone and his mother, on the wooden cover over the old concrete well next to the cement walk leading to the side entrance to his grandparents' house. Bundled up and hidden in a dark jacket, probably wool, a scarf wrapped around his neck, and a hat with earflaps tied beneath his chin. Behind them a tree barren of leaves, and beyond the tree, a field rising gently in the distance, black dirt powdered with snow on the crest. Patches of snow on the lawn too, around the old covered well. Late fall or early winter, or perhaps early spring. Paul has no memory of the trip. Nor of the family. The picture, though, proves that it once existed. He wonders how much longer it survived. It might have been that winter his father disappeared. He looks again at all the faces. No one smiles. The absence of emotion makes the picture resemble an official document that one might find in a government archive.

He continues sorting through photographs until one stops him cold. The resemblance, amazing. A permanent imprint of a man who, at the moment the picture was taken, could have been his double. The same high cheekbones, large forehead, wave of dark hair like a wing across his right temple, receding hairline on the left side, and the eyes that look vaguely Indian. His father, with whom he never identified, is the mirror image of himself. Suddenly the ten-year-old blows off the adult like an erupting volcano blowing off the top of a mountain and Paul feels all of the boy's loss. He never had a father when he was growing up, never could identify with an adult male, never knew what it was like to follow in a man's footsteps. Not a man who was really there, with whom he could talk and of whom he could ask questions, and listen to what he had to say. Tears fill his eyes as he gazes at this father he never knew. He wants that father just as strongly now as he did thirty years ago, and that desire spews forth streams of contradictory wishes: wishing his father hadn't died; angry that he had; wondering if he was alive, because after all, his body was never found; then hoping he was; and then, because he never returned, hoping he was dead. He deserves to be dead. All the streams flow together.

Paul closes his eyes and takes a few deep breaths, until he feels a measure of calm return. As he wipes away the tears, he wonders what it would've been like to identify with a real father who was there, present, in front of him—someone he could watch, hear, touch. Someone who had to struggle and to learn to cope with those things Paul never discussed with older men. Things like sex, love, marriage, children, success. And purpose. Why do we live, love, hurt one another, or try to make one another whole? Why do we go on doing all that? Could this man have shown him some logical way to go, a clear direction? Would his life have had more meaning? Instead of all this doubt, the feeling that he was never going the right way, that he'd better change direction, go somewhere else, be someone else, prove something to someone—he didn't know exactly what or to whom—would he've been sure of himself and confident in the significance of what he was doing? And could this certitude and knowledge have enabled him to forget those things that still caused him pain? Perhaps. He felt a rush of retroactive hope. If this man had been there all through his childhood and youth, perhaps... and then it sinks in. A life has been lost—his. Something of himself—something still in the future, but now, just like the people in all these pictures, already in the past—died with this man.

Paul stares at the pictures while thinking of what a normal life would be. The kind of life his friends in Paris lead. They argued with their fathers when they were young—that's what young people do—but as they matured, married, and had kids, they returned to their fathers and grew closer. Arguments and reconciliations were a normal part of life, of growth. But he never had that.

He fights the urge toward self-pity by focusing on the picture, studying its detail, trying to understand it, as if it inscribed somehow his destiny. His father is sitting in front of a window, wearing a dark turtleneck. Trunks of Norwegian or white pine in the background. Snow that buries the world in white silence. Eerie silence, in which time seems to stand still, and the mind, freed from its structured view of the world, can wander across the surface of life like a spider across water and take a long look at what it sees and sees through. And what, Paul wonders, does his father see and see through? He isn't looking at the camera, nor at the person shooting the picture. He seems to be looking a long way off, as if what's in front of him doesn't mean anything. The gaze of a dreamer, but a dreamer who knows nothing will come of the dream. A strange look, at once pensive and cynical. Or, Paul wonders, is he reading this into the picture? Perhaps this image is out of character, and might not reflect who his father really is. Or was. The longer Paul studies the picture, the less it yields. This picture is an imprint of Father's body; it brings him so close, and now he's disappeared again. Frustrated, Paul turns it over, as if there might be miraculously a third dimension, but all he finds is a date—December 1953. The month his father disappeared. Maybe for good.

Paul sets the picture on the bed beside him, puts the others back into the box, then sorts through those he previously placed there until he finds the three-quarter frontal close-up of his mother, so pensive, sitting on a lawn and facing away from the camera, toward her left. He studies it again, wondering what she could have been thinking about. She seems so acutely alive in this picture, he decides to keep it. He also keeps the picture of his father in the turtleneck sweater, sitting in front of the window. And then he rummages through the remaining photographs until he finds the picture of the entire family, all five—or six—of them, taken at his grandparents' farm, and the picture of himself, the plump little prince standing on the picnic table, and his mother, next to him, looking up at him. He places the box back in the chest of drawers, sits down in the chair in front of the window, where his mother used to sit, and stares at the Black Hole.

All the photographs prove there had once been a time of happiness and love in his past. But a big piece of that past is missing. He's never more than three or four years old in these pictures, Christine's never more than about ten, or Fran about twelve, so there have to be more pictures somewhere. Maybe in the attic, or perhaps Fran has them. But would he take them out of their mother's room? That depends on what she would've wanted. But how important were they to her, if she threw them in an old shoebox? If she treasured them and wanted to be sure not to lose or damage them, wouldn't she have put them in the albums he found in the drawer? Wouldn't she have wanted to escape in albums the way she escaped in books? But perhaps she wasn't escaping. The fact was he didn't have any idea what she used to do in her room. Perhaps she just watched the ducks land on the river and listened to the loons.

The floor creaks behind him. He almost turns to see who it is, but checks his impulse and continues looking out the window. Finally he hears Fran's voice—thin, cold, and sharp as a razor.

"What the hell are you doing here?" Paul can't answer, because the question and the tone in which it is asked evoke an image he has long forgotten: Fran walking toward him, his hands and the knife he's holding red with blood, his face bulbous with rage, a lunatic look in his eyes, jabbing him with the question, "What the hell are you doing here?"

Paul looks at the four photographs in his hand, pretending to be unshaken by Fran's voice, almost like one tom cat lying still and feigning indifference to another tom circling it in slow motion to position itself for an attack. "Nothing to get excited about, Fran."

"I'm not excited." Fran slowly walks around Paul's left side.

"I was just looking at some pictures I found in one of Mother's drawers. Very interesting. I'd never seen them before, but then … it's not like we looked at family albums much when we were kids." He feels Fran's eyes bore a hole right through him. "Did you know about them? They were in a shoebox."

Paul raises his head to see Fran standing almost directly in front of the window, his hazel eyes fixed on him, a cougar ready to pounce.

"That beard, you've got to do something about it. Look! You've got gray hairs sticking straight out like cat's whiskers … and a few that look like snakes. My God!" Paul laughs. "Some of those whiskers have got to be five inches long. Fran, you've got to get that goddamn thing trimmed." Leaning forward and peering more closely at the beard. "Yeah, just as I thought. You've got some of your lunch in there. Or is it breakfast? Can't tell if it's mayonnaise or yogurt. What else have you got in there, Fran? A few bird eggs?"

"You found some pictures."

"I sure did. In a shoebox. I found it in the chest of drawers. Interesting pictures. I'd never seen any of them. Have you?"

"Just because she's gone don't give you the right to come in here and snoop through her things."

"You know, Fran, you've been telling me for years to stay out. Ever since I was a kid, that's what I've heard. Well, you really don't have any fucking right to tell me that. No right at all."

Fran stoops from his towering height, places his hands on the arms of the chair, and with his face just a few inches away hisses, "She didn't want you here before she died, so—"

"Don't try to intimidate me. We're too old for that kind of shit." Paul laughs. "One of us might have a heart attack."

Fran backs off a couple steps, crosses his arms, and looks down on Paul like a torturer surveying his victim.

Paul takes a deep breath. "You know, Fran, when you asked me what the hell I was doing here, it reminded me of something that happened about thirty years ago. You had gone into the woods with Stone to hunt deer. I wanted to go too, but you told me I was too young, said if I tried to follow you, you'd shoot my ass. You remember?"

"You followed us."

"Yeah, I sure did. Just as any kid would've. I followed your tracks in the snow until I heard a shot, and then a second. When I caught up, you were crouched over a deer laying on its side. You'd pushed one of the legs up on your shoulder so you could get in between the legs and dress it. You were jabbing it with a knife, and it jerked each time. Stone told you to be careful or you'd cut through its intestines and get shit all over the place. You went berserk. You started shouting, 'You do it, goddamn you. And I'll tell you everything you do wrong.' You saw he wasn't looking at you. That's when you turned and saw me. You came at me with that knife, covered with blood, and you were shouting, 'What the hell are you doing here?' I thought you were going to slit my throat. If Stone hadn't grabbed your shoulder, you might've."

Fran slowly shakes his head no while Paul continues talking.

"I was going to run home, even though Stone had you by the shoulder, but he told me to stay. He took the knife and told you to go wash the blood off your hands with some snow. Then he went about dressing the deer. Worked like a surgeon. Very efficient. Focused. Never said a word. I stood as close to him as I could." Paul stood up and faced Fran. "You know what I learned, Fran?"

Fran shrugs his shoulders. "All I ever tried to do was protect you. That's what we were always supposed to do, Christine and me. Protect the little darling."

"I learned, Fran, that you were a bully. Learned that you used your rage to intimidate me. Learned you couldn't stand up to anyone who could keep his cool. And I learned if I could keep my cool, I could hold my ground. So, Fran, when you come in here and ask me what the hell I'm doing here, which really means get the hell out of here, I'm going to ignore you. I'm not leaving."

"You're leaving tomorrow morning. That's a done deal."

"Yeah, I'm riding back with Christine and Tim tomorrow, but today I'll go where I want to. And right now I want to go back into the past. And I want you to help me."

Fran has been staring at Paul's right hand. "What are those pictures?"

Paul holds up the pictures. "What are they? Just some pictures I found in that box." Paul grins and slowly shakes his head. "One of them is a picture of our family. How about that? Us, a family! Papa Bear, Mama Bear, and the three little baby bears. And Stone. I'm keeping it as proof we were once a family. And all five people could stand close enough together to have their picture taken at the same time. What do you think of that?"

"Don't think nothing of it."

"Well, I do. And I've got questions. And you're the person who can answer them. Here's one of the really big questions: who was this woman I've called Mother for nearly forty years? Who was she?" Paul searches Fran's eyes, as if he might find an answer there. "In one of these pictures she's a young woman with her whole life ahead of her. She's lived her life. Today, tomorrow, she's being cremated. I know almost nothing about her."

"If you'd known her, she'd be with you right now."

"The way she is with you?"

"Yeah."

"Even now?"

"I can feel her presence."

"You know, Fran, I can understand you not wanting to share anything with me. You probably think I'm a real shit for—"

"You're unworthy."

"Why?"

"You've got the gall to ask me why?"

"I want to hear it from you."

"You know why. You couldn't wait to get out of here. Go to college. Then you go away to Paris. And now, after not showing any interest in Mother all those years, now you want to know everything about her."

"There are reasons, Fran. You know that. Most of my memories have to do with leaving. Leaving Mother alone—she's not feeling well, she's busy, she's this, she's that. Leaving for Grandma and Grandpa's. Leaving, just to come back on cue. So I left to make a new life. Can you blame me?"

"None of that makes any difference one way or another. You're leaving tomorrow. For good."

"Fran, what are you afraid of?"

Frustrated with getting nothing out of Fran, Paul returns to his room, paces back and forth, sits down at the desk and stares out the window, but too tense to sit still, leaves the lodge and sets out on a walk. He follows the gravel road that snakes around huge pines and boulders garbed in a mottled lace of light and dark green moss, descends a long slope, passes within a hundred feet of the marsh and the Black Hole, ascends a hill and continues on, winding its way toward the blacktop road to Mirer.

He walks along the edge of the road, so caught up with his own thoughts he's oblivious to everything else. That conversation with Ruth changed everything. Why didn't someone tell me my father's body had never been found, that it's possible he didn't die that night? Why's Fran so possessive and secretive about Mother? Does he think I'll somehow steal her away from him? And those pictures— what happened to the happiness this family used to have? How did we end up the way we did? And what do we do now? Fran can't live here by himself. And he can't live anywhere else. What would I do about that? He's dangerous. Unpredictable. Calm one minute, ready to kill someone the next. Thank god I'm leaving tomorrow. Thank god I've got Claire, a career, a life.

Paul shakes his head and smiles. The day after tomorrow Claire will be meeting him at the airport. He imagines everything from her smile when they first make eye contact at the airport to the dinner and the wine and her questions—because she's so curious about this family she's never met—and her lips smiling above the stemmed glass full of dark red wine, and the kiss she'll blow to him, and feeling her skin next to his that night as they make love. And sleeping together. After three years he still loves falling asleep with her at night and waking up with her in the morning.

He hears something in the woods and freezes. The sun is fading and the trees along the highway are merging into two tenebrous walls. He feels a chill along his spine and turns back. By the time he reaches the gravel road it's almost dark. As he passes a boulder at the crest of a small hill, just before the gravel road dips and passes the marsh next to the Black Hole, he notices the lights in his mother's room glowing, the two windows like eyes in the dark. He stands there for a while, waiting to see someone in the room, but no one appears. The lights go off and the house becomes a dark form in the darkness. He picks his way along the road in the night without stars or moon, relying on his memory of the twists and turns to reassure himself he'll reach the lodge.

That night he sees the windows of his mother's room in a dream. Two large yellow eyes glow in the darkness. The lodge seems somehow alive, with all of its attention focused on something outside. He awakes, a shiver penetrates his body, the yellow eyes glowing in his mind. He picks up *Arctic Dreams* again and lies in bed reading, occasionally looking at the alarm clock—1:50; 2:25; 3:10.

He's so tired his vision blurs, but still he can't sleep. He lays the open book face down on his chest, closes his eyes, and sees the deer, its rear legs like pool sticks pointing lugubriously up at the sky and jerking while Fran, crouched over the animal's crotch, jabs and pokes as if doing something perverse to the dead animal. And all the while Stone sits on a fallen tree, still and calm, smoking his cigarette, watching Fran make a mess of things, until he sees Paul. He takes a drag off his cigarette, exhales, smiles and slowly nods his head, and continues looking at him until Fran, with blood all over the knife and his hands and an insane look in his eyes, starts toward Paul, screaming, "What the hell are you doing here?"

After Stone grabs Fran by the shoulder and stops his charge, he sets about dressing the deer, totally focused on the task at hand, unfazed by Fran's tirade of profanities. He makes an incision around the anus and the genital area, staying away from the gouge Fran made near the anus; slides his fingers into the incision just above the genital area and lifts the skin and membrane, separating them from the organs; and inserting the knife between his fingers, makes an incision from the genital area to the diaphragm. He ties a thick cross stick three or four feet long to the antlers, makes a knot around the center of the stick, and throws the rope over a tree limb. It's a big, eight-point buck, too big for one man to handle, so Stone has Fran, who has cooled off, pull on the rope and bring the animal's head up, while he stands the buck up on its hind legs. When Fran pulls, the rope knocks some snow down on the buck's face. White dust covers its big brown eyes, still as marbles. It doesn't blink. The deer fully strung up, its lungs, entrails, and genitals spill out onto the ground. Plop! A huge pile of steaming offal. Blood drips from the deer and oozes from the pile, staining the snow dark red.

Stone pushes it all aside with his boot and faces the animal, as if the two of them were involved in some intimate act that should remain private. He holds open the flap of skin that encloses the abdomen, first one side of the incision and then the other, and with his knife he carefully scrapes away dangling pieces of fat and membrane speckled with thick red clots of blood. When he finishes, he and Fran lower the deer and Paul follows them, carrying the rifles, as they drag it back to the boathouse where they'll hang it from a rafter and butcher it.

As Paul finally drifts off to sleep again, he sees Stone facing the animal hanging from the tree limb, open the flaps of skin as if they were part of a robe, step inside the naked cavity, and merge with the animal that the two are almost one. A voice says, "The hunter passionately loves what he kills—that's why he kills it."

The next morning he walks down the gravel road, turns around, and walks back toward the lodge, then turns around again and walks back down the road. He stops next to a boulder, runs his fingers across the lace of moss, and looks out over the marsh, with its cattails and yellow reeds that border the Black Hole. A wedge of geese flies high overhead, honking. They've already started their migration. The loons will follow soon, probably after the first snow.

He makes his decision and walks back to the lodge.

Claire's voice from the other end of the line feels like sunshine on his soul.

"C'est toi."

"Oui, c'est moi."

He listens to her tell him how happy she is he'll be home in just another day. And then he tells her the bad news.

"Claire, I'm not coming back." She doesn't respond; he continues. "At least, not for a while."

"Why?"

"Well, one reason is that my brother, Fran ... he's not in a ... he can't really be left alone here at the lodge. He's not in a state where he can take care of himself."

After a brief silence she asks, "Can't someone else take

care of him?"

"I don't think anyone else would want to. But there are other reasons too. Some things have happened. I've, ah ... I've learned that my father didn't die; he disappeared and ..."

"But he's dead, isn't he?"

"That's what everyone seems to assume. But that's just one of the reasons. I've been learning things about my mother and father, and actually, Christine and Fran too. I think my past might be different from what I thought it was. Very different. I need to find out who these people were, and why Christine and Fran and I ended up the way we did."

He waits for her to respond; she doesn't.

"There's nothing I want more than to be with you, but I feel I need to do this. My mother's being cremated."

"Does that upset you?"

"I have this huge fear that my entire past is going to just disappear, like ashes, before I can understand it."

There's a long silence.

"How long do you think it'll be before you come home?"

"I don't know. I'll come as soon as I can."

Another long silence.

Finally he asks, "Are you there?"

"I'm just in shock. I was so excited about seeing you, and now you're not coming."

"I know." He can hear her sniffle; she's crying. "I need to know that you're okay with me doing this."

"Would it make any difference if I weren't?"

He hesitates, then says, "Yes."

After a long silence she says, "Take the time you need. Just promise me you'll come as soon as you can." She adds, through her tears, "And I want letters and phone calls."

"Every day. I promise."

He enters the kitchen. Fran, Christine, and Tim are still drinking coffee over their breakfast plates. Christine looks up and smiles.

"I bet Claire is happy you're on your way back."

"I've decided to stay on for a while. That okay with you, Fran?"

All three of them look stunned. Finally Christine asks, "Why?"

"I don't know. I just feel I need to do this." He looks at Fran and adds, "No need to worry about money. I have enough to cover our expenses."

"But what about Claire? She's going to be so disappointed. I'm sure she's counting the days. I would, if my husband were—"

"I just talked with her. She wants me to do this."

"Do what?" Christine's voice has an aggressive tone. "You talk as if you had, I don't know, some kind of mission to accomplish."

"No."

Fran finally speaks. "There's nothing here for you."

"Fran, I'm definitely staying."

Paul looks around the room: Fran slowly shakes his head, the muscles in his jaws twitching; Christine lights a cigarette and exhales like a raspy bellows; and Tim leans back to watch the scene.

A half hour later Christine, her eyes hidden behind her dark glasses, gives Paul and Fran a small wave as the car pulls out of the lot. Paul waves back and then turns around to face Fran, whose eyes challenge his right to be there. Instead of accepting the challenge, Paul suggests it's time they clean up the kitchen and look into what needs to be done around the lodge. As Paul rinses off the plates and stacks the dishes, coffee mugs, and juice glasses in the dishwasher, he thinks of the long winter ahead and of the silence that will force him to live in the echo chamber of his mind. He looks out the window over the sink and feels grateful for this opening onto the outside world. Fran wipes off the table and counters, scattering crumbs on the floor. Paul wonders if he can survive whatever Fran might have in store for him.

The next day, Fran drives into town. That evening, just before sunset, as Paul stands behind the lodge looking toward the Black Hole, he notices Fran in a canoe, tipping an urn from which a thin gray stream of ashes flows onto the surface of the water. Fran empties the urn, holds it on his lap for a few minutes, then slowly submerges it in the water and releases it. He sits in the canoe without moving for fifteen minutes, a half hour, an hour, while the sun sets and all the colors fade to darkness.

PART III
Winter 1989–1990

9

"IF YOU LOOK AT THE FACE OF GOD IT WILL BLIND you," Fran bellows, as he enters the kitchen from the second floor landing and sets a pair of sun goggles down on the table. "Better take these with you."

Paul turns around to see what Fran put on the table and turns back to the cold venison he's slicing at the kitchen counter. "Who's talking about looking at the face of God? I'm just going skiing."

"Snow," Fran says loudly, as if he were blowing a trumpet to announce the Lord. "Snow reveals the face of God."

When he's in one of his manic states, Paul reflects, he sounds like an archangel proclaiming the revelations to John. All because I'm going skiing for the day. "Snow reflects the sun, Fran. "

"Yes, it does."

"It doesn't reveal the face of God."

"Yes, it does."

"Okay, Fran, I'm not going to argue with you. Thanks for the goggles. I've got some sunglasses, but I'll take these along just in case. Don't want to be blinded."

"Blindness isn't necessarily a bad thing," Fran muses, staring out the kitchen window at the back yard while Paul, standing next to him, spreads mayonnaise and mustard on two slices of bread. "Sometimes people see better with their eyes closed."

"That's what the surrealists used to say."

"Who were they?"

"A bunch of artsy-fartsy guys in Paris about sixty years ago."

"There ya be. Yeah, sometimes I have to close my eyes to see."

"I believe you, Fran."

"People get to thinking the world's just what it looks like, nothing else. Their eyes are open, but they're sealed shut."

Paul nods while he layers the venison on the bread, then slices the sandwich in half and wraps it in a couple of paper towels. He's been nodding in agreement a lot over the last several weeks.

Fran continues uttering his pronouncements to his audience of one. "You have to see with your eyes closed to remove the seals from your eyes and really see."

"Can I get in here for a second?"

Fran steps out of the way so Paul can move in front of the sink to rinse an apple and a tomato under the faucet.

"Fran, I'm sure you have a far greater appreciation of the world than the likes of me. I guess for you the world is an open book."

"A scroll."

"A scroll?"

"A scroll. That's what the Bible says. To open the scroll you must lift the seals to see what's revealed. To see the world as it was and is and will be."

"Ah! The Bible. At first I didn't pick up on what you were saying." Paul wipes the apple and tomato dry, puts them in a brown paper bag on top of the sandwich, and then puts the lunch in a backpack. "If you think everything is somehow God's will, what if something bizarre happens and you can't figure out what his will is? Doesn't that make you feel a little paranoid?" Paul looks back at Fran leaning against the kitchen table to see how he will react.

"It's all there. All the devils and the murderers and the fornicators and the Jezebels and the death and poverty that's visited on their children—it's all there. The fulfillment of the Word."

Paul laughs. "Fornicators and Jezebels, eh? Well, Fran, I guess you part company with the surrealists on the issue of sex." He glances back at Fran's green eyes staring at him and adds, "I don't mean to make light of what you're saying."

"We're all the children of fornicators and Jezebels."

"You're absolutely right, Fran. And the world would be an empty place without those fornicators and Jezebels."

Paul pours coffee into a thermos, puts the thermos in the backpack, and takes a sip from his mug. An emerald fly buzzes feebly up the window, revived for a few seconds by the pale sunlight, then falls back onto the windowsill. He nudges it with his fingertip. It buzzes, rises a few inches, and falls back onto his finger. He holds his finger up in front of the window and studies its body, while murmuring, "'The small gilded fly does lecher in my sight.'" He becomes aware of Fran staring at the fly on his finger and looks him in the eye. "He, or she, needs a partner."

Fran flicks the fly off Paul's finger and says, "It's nearly dead." Fran turns on the faucet and washes the fly down the drain.

"It's dead now," Paul says. He turns around, leans against the counter, and takes another sip of coffee. "It's ironic that you talk about fornicators and Jezebels, since you're the person who first taught me something about women and sex." He glances at Fran to see if he will react; Fran simply stares at him. "Do you know what I'm talking about?"

Fran shakes his head no.

"You remember a deck of cards you used to keep in your desk drawer?"

Fran still shows no reaction.

"They had pictures of women from the waist up, all with huge breasts. Trophy size. You don't remember that?"

Fran shakes his head.

"Or the magazines I found on the top shelf in your closet? I still remember the issue of *Playboy* with the prostitutes of Paris—soft focus, delectable nudes with pixie cuts and big brown eyes. I used to sneak it into my closet and, you know ... use it for inspiration." Paul smiles. "You must've been doing the same thing, right?"

Fran's jaw muscles twitch; he raises his mug and sips some coffee, concealing most of the lower half of his face.

"All the magazines disappeared one day, so ..."

"Don't forget the goggles. That sun will burn your eyes."

Paul nods. "Thanks. It's good to know you're concerned." Paul's eyes try to fix them both on a moment of truth, but Fran looks into the cup from which he sips. Paul watches him for a few seconds, but Fran continues avoiding eye contact. Paul pulls a map out of the backpack, walks over to the kitchen table, and, standing next to Fran, sets his mug down, spreads out the map, and studies the chain of lakes and the portages he'll follow.

Fran peers over his shoulder. "You can't remember your way without a map?"

"I'm not a visionary, Fran, just a poor mortal. For me, a wood covered with snow looks totally different from the same wood in the summer." Paul studies the map, then asks, "What are you going to do while I'm gone?"

"I've gotta get a cabin ready. Some people are coming up

from the cities."

"Why didn't you tell me? I would've helped you."

"Naw. I don't need no help."

"No, really. I could stay and help you, and then you could come with me."

The phone rings once, twice.

"That's probably her."

"Oh," Paul arches his eyebrows, "you're telepathic, as well as a seer?"

"I'm gonna get started on that cabin."

"You don't have to leave."

Fran grabs his old wool jacket off the back of a kitchen chair and throws it on as he heads for the back door; Paul hurries to the barroom where the phone is ringing.

"*Allô*? Paul?"

"*Bonjour. Ça va?*"

"I'm so glad you're there. I felt awful about calling you in the middle of the night just because of that dream."

"It was the middle of the night for you, not me."

"I know. But still … I feel silly for having called you. It's just that it was one of the most terrifying dreams I've ever had. The feeling that Fran was lurking somewhere in the shadows and he was going to do something horrible to you. And there was nothing I could do. I felt so helpless."

"As I said last night, he's not going to hurt me."

"But when I think of what you've told me about his temper, and the way he rants about spirits and everything, and the migraines that send him to bed for a whole day, I can't help but feel he's mentally unstable. There's something eating away at him. I wish you'd come home."

"Actually, you know, he hasn't been violent in any way since … I don't know … since he threatened Christine when she was here for the funeral."

"I don't care. There's something wrong with him."

"There's probably a lot wrong with him. When I think of

what he went through growing up here ... But that doesn't mean he'd hurt me." Paul pauses, reflects, and continues talking. "I was a little worried in the beginning. You know, when someone hardly talks to you, you start wondering. I got kind of paranoid. But he's come to trust me. The biggest problem I have with him now is the way he mothers me."

"I find that hard to believe."

"You should've seen him just a few minutes ago. I was getting ready to go skiing, and he gave me a pair of snow goggles to wear, so the sun wouldn't burn my eyes. A good pair of sunglasses would do the job, but he absolutely insisted on the goggles. He reminded me at least twice not to forget them."

"That's reassuring."

"How's your book coming?"

"It's going well. Even though I spend a lot of time thinking about a guy in the United States. Wondering when he's coming home. Trying to understand why he's not here."

Paul doesn't know what to say.

"You're going skiing today? What does that have to do with what you're trying to accomplish there?"

"I told you. I didn't feel right about leaving Fran alone."

"What about leaving me alone? It's been almost two months now."

"I also told you, I need to find out ... what happened to my father—he might still be alive—and what happened to my family. And no one's going to just tell me."

"And how does spending the day skiing help?"

Paul exhales his growing frustration. "Look, I'll come home just as soon as I can." He listens for an answer, and not getting one asks, "How are your parents?"

"They're fine. They asked about you, of course. I told them you're doing well."

"Good."

"I almost couldn't visit them last weekend. The car wouldn't start." Claire pauses, then continues. "Luckily one of our neighbors helped me out."

"Oh, who?"

"Philippe. I don't know his last name. He lives two floors up from us."

"So, what was wrong with the car?"

"I flooded it. That's what Philippe said. I should've known. You could smell gas. He said we should let it set for a while, so we went to a café. When we returned, he started it without any trouble."

"Well, that was certainly kind of him."

"I thought so."

"Sounds like he's got the right touch—for starting the car."

"He's a very nice man."

"Are you planning on seeing him again?"

After a pause she answers, "It's nothing like that, Paul."

"Nothing like what, Claire?"

"Like what you're thinking."

"And what am I thinking?"

"Aren't you going to ask me about our other neighbor? You're always so curious about him."

"Our other neighbor?"

"The insomniac, as you call him."

"Oh, him. Okay, what's happening with the insomniac?"

"Well, he looks fully recovered. And he's gone back to performing all his little rituals—you know, standing in his window on weekend mornings, listening to Edith Piaf, flicking his cigarette ashes on the people below. The only difference is that now there's just one woman in the apartment. Guess who?"

Paul reflects a minute, then says, "The one who tried to kill him?"

"None other. She's always there. I can recognize her voice now. She's a real song bird."

"Interesting he should stick it out with a woman who tried to kill him."

"Interesting she would stay with a man she tried to kill."

"Of course none of this may be true but ..."

"It's given everyone something to talk about."

"Well, you'll have to keep me updated—on the insomniac and Philippe."

"There won't be anything to tell you as far as Philippe is concerned. All I want, Paul, is for you to come home."

Paul nods his head.

"I love you, Paul."

"I love you, too. I'll call you tomorrow."

He waits until he hears the line go dead and then hangs up. He stares down at the telephone, in a small island of light surrounded by a world of darkness, wondering about this Philippe. He can't expect a woman like her, alone in Paris, never to be approached by another man. But there's nothing he can do. He just won't think about it.

A few minutes later he clamps on his skis and pushes off from land onto the frozen lake. He veers right after the point and heads for the southeast corner of the inlet and the channel that leads to the main body of Spirit Lake. Settling into an easy loping stride, he feels the pleasure of moving almost magically as he glides across the thick crust of snow burnished by the wind. In some places the snow is only three or four inches deep, in others up to seven or eight. The sun flashes on the snow in incendiary sparks. He stops to put on Fran's goggles, then continues. A few minutes later he reaches the channel. Bluffs about ten feet high and huge boulders with patches of snow form its walls for about five hundred yards. Jack pine and scraggly birch grow from crevices in the rocks, sometimes at bizarre angles. He passes the narrow island in the middle of the channel and, upon reaching the main part of the lake, now a desert of snow with occasional wisps blowing across the surface, veers left and heads for an open space between two islands. He goes between, rounds the end of a point, and heads for the mainland, where he knows there's a portage trail. He finds it easily enough and follows it up a slope as it skirts a river of rocks and boulders, their sharp angles softened by thick snow, and delves into a forest of red pine. Then he glides downhill toward the open expanse of a frozen lake, too small to have its own name, crosses it in less than ten minutes, and skis directly onto another portage trail.

After a while, breathing heavily and feeling the cold air nipping at his hot, sweaty face, he stops near a fallen tree to eat lunch. He takes off his goggles and puts them in his pocket. The sun isn't as bright in the woods as it is on the open lake and there's no longer danger of a sudden gust of wind blowing snow crystals, sharp as sand, into his eyes. He brushes snow off the trunk, sets his backpack down, and maneuvers with his ski poles until he has positioned himself so he can sit down. He unfastens his skis, lifts his feet out of the clamps, and rests them on the skis where they will be out of the snow and remain dry. He pours himself some coffee and warms his hands with the cup before raising it to his lips and allowing the steam to warm his nostrils and cheeks. He stops eating his lunch from time to time to look around. He hears a toc-toc-toc, but he can't find the woodpecker. In the silence of the winter forest the slightest sound carries hundreds of yards. He finishes eating, stands up, fastens his skis, puts on his nearly empty backpack, and, keeping his legs spread, pisses a yellow hole in the snow, which steams as he finishes.

After skiing for a short while, he comes across a deer path that intersects with his and he stops. Scattered droppings just a few feet off to the right, but no deer. He looks up in response to a crow flying overhead, warning the other animals of his presence. The cawing continues to echo through the woods long after the crow is out of sight.

Treetops sway back and forth, as sensitive to the slightest breeze as antennae to stimuli. He decides to follow the deer path and sets off, resting from time to time as he labors through the deeper snow. An occasional gust of wind suddenly roars through the pine peaks like a conflagration, without ever penetrating the deep stillness at the bottom of the forest, and then abruptly dies. The sharp, crisp light of winter, with its low angle to the surface of the earth, makes every tree seem more distinct and somehow more real than the trees he saw during the fall. He gazes at the warm, red tone of the scaly gray pine trunks, the green needles, the sharp black shadows cast across the brilliant whiteness. The wind returns, and the upper trunks creak like the mammoth masts of a ship at sea. He looks up again. The virgin pine forests that the Sioux, the Ojibwa, the voyageurs, and the immigrants found were supposed to have been two hundred feet tall. And these? He couldn't even guess. But they're tall enough to inspire awe, and he continues gazing upward until blue dots prick his eyes and he feels he might lose his balance.

He labors yet a while on the path, then stops again and looks at the deep snow that lies ahead as far as he can see. The path is taking him too far inland. If he continues on it, he's likely to find more deep snow instead of the hard crust over which he can glide across the lakes, and he might lose his way. The fear of freezing to death haunts him. He turns around, follows his ski tracks back to the portage path. He eventually arrives at an inlet. He enters a narrow channel that leads him to a lake. He stops to look at his map, and once reassured of his location, turns north out of the channel and skis across the middle of the lake. As he scans the shorelines he sees three wolves trotting near the western shore a little further north. A fourth suddenly leaps from the deep snow of the woods onto the smooth plane of the lake and joins the pack. They sniff the ground and the air, loping along the ice near the shore, looking no doubt for an isolated deer or moose. Downwind, he escapes detection. They continue trotting back and forth, sniffing, stopping, and looking around, and then trotting some more until something draws them charging back into the forest.

Still heading north, gliding silently across the hard snow, he rounds a point where the lake narrows and he comes face to face with a doe, not more than forty feet away, his approach concealed by some boulders. She couldn't see him, smell him, or hear him until he confronts her. Startled, she freezes and stares at him. He too remains perfectly still. In the summer, her tawny coat would have blended in with her surroundings; but now, isolated against the whiteness of the snow, she stands out as if she were on stage. Her beautiful black eyes remain fixed on him as she waits for him to move. He and the doe continue staring at one another for several minutes, as if they vaguely recognize one another. Finally she turns and runs halfway up the slope of a hill, swift and graceful in spite of the deep snow, and then stops to look back at him, her white tail raised like a salute. She stops one more time at the crest of the hill and then disappears. Long after the doe has left, he continues staring at the hill, listening to the wind in the trees and the silence of an infinite universe in which he feels no more significant than any other animal. He looks up at the pines, towering above him, swaying back and forth in the wind, until he starts feeling dizzy, and glances down at the snow before him. He feels impelled to go on, to keep moving deeper into this wilderness, to merge with the universe.

He remembers feeling this way when he was a boy. He would hear the wind in the trees and the silence in this landscape muffled with snow and he would want to set out and just keep on going. He recalls stories of explorers who set off alone in the arctic and were found years later still frozen solid, their bodies perfectly preserved in ice. And of the man who discovered, peering at him through a wall of ice, the corpse of his father who had disappeared years before when he was the same age as the son who discovered him. Was it a novel? A film? An old story he'd heard? He didn't know, but as he imagines the son discovering his father entombed in ice, a father who looked so much like him they could've been twins, he sees his own father, who looks the way he did in the picture with the snow in the background, staring out at him through a thin wall of ice, his eyes holding him, refusing to let him go. It's like looking at himself dead in a mirror.

The shadows from the trees lengthen, and his own lies before him like a thing he might step into. He has at most three hours of sunlight; he'll retrace his tracks rather than continuing north and then circling back. He turns around and sets forth, his foreshortened shadow preceding him on his left, and as he follows his shadow, he thinks about the world of snow to which he has returned and about which he began to dream in Paris.

Perhaps everyone has a landscape in their mind that feels like home. His is a landscape of snow—snow, silence, a certain light—where objects, animals, and even his own shadow are endowed with a surreal presence. A snowscape is a stage of tremendous depth, where a wolf, a deer, or a fox might suddenly seem to appear, an apparition, when it had been there all along, eluding our vision because we're not accustomed to seeing at that depth. His mind can wander into that depth and follow phantoms across the stage without leaving the real world of snow, ice, trees, and sun. A part of himself that he cannot find anywhere else inhabits that stage. These are all familiar thoughts. He might forget them, but they return as easily as old habits.

His shadow has gotten longer and the light paler. The sun will set soon and the temperature, which has already dropped several degrees, will plummet. Luckily there's almost no wind. He quickens his pace across the open, frozen lake, his skis gliding across the burnished crust of the snow. The sun sets about the same time that he sees the entrance to the channel about two hundred yards away. It's dark, but the snow captures what little light remains. Slowly the channel comes into view until before him lies the broad, white highway lined with boulders and bluffs, partially concealed by snow, and small naked birch and tenacious jack pines. He enters the channel, the road home, where he recognizes every rock, every tree. The island appears to rise in the middle of the channel, about a hundred yards ahead, like a submerged ship of granite. He passes the island and the dark forms of jack pine, round boulders, and flat slabs of gray rock partially covered by snow, and after another few hundred feet, following the channel as it narrows and curves north, he finally reaches the large, elliptical inlet—"the lake," as people always called it when he was growing up—which was as much a part of his home as the lodge itself.

He skis another hundred feet and stops to rest. The inlet extends like a white field, the snow glowing in the light of the full moon. The white field ends in darkness on the east shore where trees grow densely right down to the shoreline, but ahead of him, at the northern and northwestern end of the inlet, he can almost see individual pines standing out against the snow. What a great day, he thinks, as he gazes at the moonlit snowscape. The wilderness makes you feel small and insignificant, yet part of something so vast your mind can't comprehend it. It feels like the threshold to infinity. You can almost see it. It's a contradiction, but one that makes sense when you're looking at this. Fran this morning was talking about snow reflecting the face of God. What is God but a human face we project in the place of infinity and eternity? Maybe Fran isn't totally nuts. Sunlight, moonlight on snow, it's so unspeakably beautiful, why not reach for something like the "face of God" to describe it? He pulls back. As long as you realize it's just language.

A sudden gust of wind from the north stings his face and chills him to the bone. Thinking now of the fire Fran would certainly have built in the fireplace, he sets off again with an extra kick in his stride, and after another hundred yards he can see beyond the point on the west side of the inlet the bright yard light above the fish house halfway up the hill—a beacon welcoming him home. At the top of the hill the lodge windows glow with a warm, yellow light. Fran is waiting for him.

He's walking with a woman in a birch forest. It's winter. He looks at her. Claire. They're walking along a path through the deep snow. He stops to look up at the birch trees, the white limbs against the blue sky. It's unnaturally quiet. A squirrel runs somewhere across birch bark. The toc-toc-toc of a woodpecker echoes through the forest. He can tell which direction the sound is coming from, but cannot see the bird. It might be a mile away. He has never experienced this silence before. He looks up again. His eyes fill with burning blue spots. He looks down and covers his eyes to protect them. When he opens them, he's alone. As far as he can see, there's just the whiteness of snow and birch. A deer appears out of nowhere and stares at him, large eyes black as night. Then the deer is gone, and there's just the white-ness and the silence. Such a tremendous sense of loneliness and emptiness invades him that he wants to scream.

He awakes to find himself sitting in his bed, feeling he's lost her forever.

10

CLAIRE ARCHES HER BACK AS SHE PULLS LOOSE strands of hair together and twists them into a bun. She reminds Paul of a painting—or rather, a theme, a topos, as he would've said when he was a student: woman doing her toilet. She's here, in his room, like a Christmas present, bringing together by her very presence two worlds that for him have always been separate. He stretches his arm across the tussled bedclothes and touches the nape of her neck; she shivers. He drags his fingertips across the curves of her back, into the slope of her spine (the stem of a molded leaf of flesh), all the way down to the crevice between her cheeks. Amazing that her body never ceases to excite him, as if it were always new, always virgin, always ready to be explored again, even as he feels, while touching her, burrowing into all the familiar little crooks and crevices, smelling and tasting the salt and perfume of her skin, that he's come home. His fingers glide upward toward her neck, across the top of her left ear where he discovers again the tiny piece of cartilage that forms a point; she snares his hand, pulls it around to her chest, and cradles it between her breasts. He nibbles at her ear and whispers, "*Petit elfe de mon coeur.*" His lips graze her breasts, kiss the little mushroom on the top of her thigh, just beneath the pubic hair soft as silk against his cheek, and his tongue glides between the wet labia into the pungent warmth, succulent as the flesh of a peach.

After they finish making love again—the fourth time since they arrived at the lodge the day before—he lies, totally spent, eyes closed, stroking her hair as she lies on his right, her head resting on his chest. It's magic, making love to her in this room where he dreamed his escape. Her presence in the lodge illuminates the cavernous old building and gives it a warmth he never felt here before.

When he found the message she'd left on the recorder the day after he'd gone skiing, he played it back repeatedly until he knew it by heart. "I decided I can't live anymore with just phone calls and letters. I need to see you and touch you. I need all three dimensions." Now she's here, body and voice, for a whole week.

"Mmm. It feels so good," she murmurs.

"Uh-huh."

"That's so considerate of Fran ... letting us have time alone ... last night and this morning."

Paul smiles. "I don't think he's being considerate. He's probably afraid of meeting you."

"Why would he be afraid?"

"Who knows? He was nervous about meeting me my first day back, and I'm his brother."

"I hope he gets used to me."

"Uh-huh."

He opens his eyes. She's still here. Magically here. Like a vision. Sitting on the edge of the bed, looking around the room.

"It's like being in our study at home, with all these maps." She stands up, her arms across her breasts, protecting them from the cold. She picks his shirt up off the floor near the end of the bed where he threw it the night before, pulls it on, draws one side of it close to her face, and breathes deeply. "Mmm. I can smell you. It's like being wrapped up inside you."

He likes seeing her in his shirt, knowing she wants to be wrapped in him even as she moves independently of him, and knowing too that at any minute she could drop the shirt to the floor. She looks like an elegant pinup. A few strands of hair hang in wispy curls along her graceful neck. She could've been a dancer with those long, sculpted legs. She becomes aware of him staring at her and, knowing what he's thinking because they've had this conversation before, does a little pirouette, flashing a smile.

"You look at me; I'll look at your maps." She walks around the room. "How old were you when you drew these?"

"The earliest ones probably go back to fifth or sixth grade. The most recent I did in high school."

"What got you so interested in maps?"

"I don't know."

"After I got back from driving you to the airport, when you left for the funeral, I was standing in our study, looking at all the maps, and I remembered a comment you made to me once: learning a new language is like becoming a new person. Do you remember that?"

"Vaguely."

"Hmm. Vaguely. Well, do you think it's true?"

"Maybe."

"What do you mean, maybe?"

"Okay. I think in a way you might develop a different ... persona."

"A different persona," she repeats. "Hmm." After gazing at the maps a while longer, she says, "I realized when I was looking at the maps, thinking about your comment about learning languages, that I knew almost nothing about you prior to your arrival in Paris. Nearly fifteen years ago. And I wondered, what is he like in English, at home?"

"So, what am I like?"

"I thought you'd help me with that."

"You'll just have to observe."

"In the spirit of getting to know the pre-Paris Paul better, I'm going to indulge one of my obsessions and see what you have on your bookshelves."

"Indulge away."

She begins scanning authors' names and book titles. "I wonder, did you always use books to store your pictures?" She looks at him. "You know, you're the only person I've ever known who does that."

He nods his head.

She looks at a picture she has found in Dostoyevsky's *Crime and Punishment*. "You used to have a mustache."

"I wanted to be Russian."

"Why?"

"I loved Dostoyevsky and the characters he created." He assumes a deep, dramatic tone to amuse her. "Complex, brooding, intense, impulsive. And so theatrical. A world of anarchists, revolutionaries, students, aristocrats, artists, beggars, and gamblers. And the holy whores. Can't forget the holy whores!" He assumes again his natural voice. "Dostoyevsky's world seemed so much more interesting than mine, when I was eighteen."

Claire smiles. She continues scanning names and titles, occasionally taking books off the shelf and flipping pages, until she finds a picture in Fitzgerald, *The Great Gatsby*. "Very pretty. Who is she?"

"Rose."

"That's all? Just Rose?"

"She was my Dolly."

"Ah. Sounds tragic."

"First loves always are."

She shrugs. "Not always." She gazes at the picture. "So, what happened?"

"She didn't want to marry someone who wanted to be Dostoyevsky."

"I wonder why."

She opens one of the books next to Fitzgerald and stops at an illustration, looking confused. "I didn't know Forester wrote sea stories."

"C. S. Forester, not E. M. Author of the Hornblower series. I read them all when I was in grade school."

"Never heard of him. But, sea lit isn't my field."

"I loved his novels. I was always impatient to see how everything turned out at the end, but when I got there I was so sad to see the book end. I wanted it to continue forever."

She nods her head. "I remember that feeling." She flips through a few more pages and puts the book back.

She scans the names and titles more quickly now, until she comes to Proust. She takes the first volume of *A la recherche du temps perdu* off the shelf and discovers more pictures. Paul remembers each image clearly: himself as a toddler, standing on a picnic table next to his mother; his father, in the black turtleneck, all alone, snow in the background; his mother, a young woman, sitting on the grass in a park, gazing wistfully into the distance; and the family, at his grandparents' farm.

"Who are these pictures of?"

"I found them in my mother's room. I talked to you about them."

"When Fran nearly attacked you?"

"That's right."

"Your mother was very beautiful." She looks at the next picture. "And your father ... " She shakes her head. "You do resemble him. A lot. And this one; it's priceless. Such a little prince. You should frame these." She studies the pictures, then looks up at him. "So, why did you put them in Proust?"

He shrugs. "Search for a lost past."

"Is *that* what you're doing?"

"Trying to. Haven't had much success." He blushes.

"No, you haven't." She studies his face for a long time.

He knows what she's thinking. How much longer is this going to continue? When are you coming home? Are you coming home? These questions have come up in letters and phone calls, and during the two hours it took them to drive from Duluth to the lodge he could feel them on the tip of her tongue.

"I could send you some madeleines. Drink some tea, maybe you'll have an epiphany."

"You're speaking in rhyme today."

She's not amused. She takes more books off the shelf, picking at random. Thomas Wolfe, *You Can't Go Home Again*. She holds up a picture of Paul: clean shaven, dressed in a suit, a lawn in the background. Taken on the University of Minnesota campus, after his graduation. "You lost your mustache."

"I'd given up on becoming Dostoyevsky."

"So, why in this book?"

"The sequel to *Look Homeward, Angel*. And a reminder."

She nods her head. "So, why are you still here?"

Obviously it was just too much to hope she'd leave this alone. But why shouldn't she want some answers, after several weeks of phone calls and letters adding up to an "I don't know when I'll be coming home." She was patient in the beginning, but it's gone on too long. It pisses him off he can't give her a clear answer. And he's not stupid. He knows only too well that a woman like her—as he watches her, he feels something deep inside himself, attached to his stomach, heart, lungs, and throat, attach to her, stretch to the point of snapping like a taut violin string—a woman like her is attractive to a lot of men. This Philippe, so interested in getting her motor to turn over, he's probably got his eye on her all the time. Waiting for his next chance to help. Maybe with the shopping. Carrying the bags as they make the rounds to the shops and vendors. *"Monsieur-Dame, vous désirez?"* What does he look like, this Monsieur Philippe? He tries to recall all the men from their apartment building, but no likely image comes to mind. Maybe he should ask. No, she'd get angry, accuse him of being jealous.

She walks along the end of the bed to the desk on his left. "Your friends have been asking about you. Mom and Dad too."

He nods his head.

"I don't have any answers." She stops in front of his desk, runs her fingers across the surface, focuses on something, then picks up an envelope—the one in which she mailed her last letter. She starts to read the letter, looks as if she's about to say something, then gazes instead out the window, like a Vermeer.

He approaches her, places his hands on her waist, nuzzles his cheek against her hair, and whispers in her ear, "What are you thinking about?" She remains silent. He looks out the window. Snow, ubiquitous snow, blown across the ice, accumulating in great depths in the forests and on the slopes, clinging to branches and window frames.

"I can understand that you love this place. The snow is so beautiful. It's … otherworldly."

He wraps his arms around her waist; she pushes back just enough to give her diaphragm room to expand.

"I never think about snow, but for you, it's part of your vocabulary. I don't mean the word, I mean the reality, and everything you associate with it. You dream with snow. That dream you had several times this fall, with the boy running on the snow. And the dream you had the other day, in which you and I are walking through a white forest deep with snow. Your imagination speaks to you through snow, and through the landscapes you see here. Why would you ever want to leave?"

"I do want to leave. I just have to ..."

She's already shaking her head. "You're not being honest. Not with me, not with yourself."

He feels the sutures tightening and tugging on his heart as she seems to pull away. He's about to ask her what she means, but ... his last few letters surprised even him with their long descriptions and reflections about his life at the lodge.

She continues looking out the window. "I can't help but wonder what it would be like to live here."

"You can't live here."

"People can live anywhere."

"You'd have to give up your family, your friends, your career, everything."

After a long silence, she says, "You're right. And it would be suicide to give up everything and move for someone. Even more so for someone who doesn't know who he is."

"I'm coming home."

"Maybe you are home."

He shakes his head. "No," he murmurs. He just wants everything to be okay. He brushes her hair with his lips, kisses the point on her ear, and whispers, "*Petit elfe de mon coeur.*" Her body doesn't give.

"I love you, Paul. I want you to work everything out. And be happy. But my name's not Penelope. The odyssey can't go on forever."

"I decided, if Paul wasn't going to come to me for Christmas, I'd come to him."

Claire's French pronunciation draws smiles from Christine and Tim. They arrived two days after Christmas, eager to meet her.

"A Christmas present for all of us," Christine answers, smiling.

"And what a great way to spend an evening," Tim says, putting his arm around Christine's shoulder. He looks at Paul and Claire. "A warm fire, good company, and some great cognac. Thank you, Claire." Tim holds up his snifter, in tribute to her.

Paul smiles. Tim is so transparent, so openly happy.

"Don't thank me. It's Paul's gift"—Claire turns toward him and smiles a benediction—"that he's chosen to share with us."

"Well, I wasn't going to take the bottle to my room and drink it alone."

"That's thoughtful of you, old man." Tim affects an accent that sounds vaguely British.

Christine smiles at Claire. "And thanks for the perfume. It's heavenly."

"And the scotch," Tim adds, "my favorite kind. How did you know?"

"It's quite amazing," Christine says, before Claire has a chance to respond, "to see what Fran and Paul have done with this room." Looking at Claire, she continues, "They got rid of a mammoth monstrosity of a pool table, and the pinball machines that used to be in the corner over there. They moved the couches and the chair that used to be in a corner over there"—she turns her head and nods over her shoulder in the direction of the doorway to the kitchen, beneath the stairway—"and arranged them around the fireplace. Now this feels like a place where people might actually *want* to be."

Tim nods his head in agreement. "Absolutely. A lodge should be organized around a stone fireplace." Tim's gaze fixes on the huge stone fireplace, where flames dance like dervishes from the coal-encrusted logs. "Huge beams, varnished logs, pine and birch everywhere you look, all that's important, but the center has to be the fireplace, where people can talk and feel warm. You want to think of the snow and the wind whipping across that frozen lake, and then look at the glass of cognac in your hand"—Tim holds up his glass, nearly empty—"and say to yourself, I'm so happy to be in here and not out there." He laughs. "That's what it's all about." He swirls the cognac in the snifter, inhales the fumes, drinks the glass dry, exhales with a huge *ah* and a big smile. "This is the best I've had in years!" His eyes plead for a refill.

"Help yourself to more." Paul nods in the direction of the bottle on the coffee table.

Christine looks at Paul. "It's wonderful to see you and Fran living together. Like brothers." She laughs, as if she finds the idea so bizarre it's funny, shakes her head, and adds, "Who would've ever thought?"

Claire looks around the room. "Where is Fran?"

Paul says, "He went downstairs to fix the plumbing. Although I didn't notice any problems."

"Maybe he broke something so he could spend the evening fixing it." Tim smiles at his own joke.

Christine looks at Claire and says, "Fran isn't really big on communicating."

"I've noticed. I've rarely seen him for more than a few minutes since I've been here."

"That's Fran for you," Christine replies. "Paul brought him to our house for Thanksgiving." She looks at Paul. "I'm sure you practically had to drag him."

Paul nods his head.

"That's the furthest Fran's been from the lodge in at

least thirty years. They arrived Wednesday night and left Friday morning, and we rarely heard a peep out of him. Of course, Rick and Steve, my two boys, were home for Thanksgiving break, so that might've been enough of a crowd to scare him off."

"He seems painfully shy," Claire interjects.

"With strangers," Tim adds. "Chris and I've been married for nearly twenty-five years and I'm ... no longer a stranger."

"He can be almost talkative," Christine says. "In fact, we talk about once a week on the phone. He tells me everything that goes on. Now that Mother's gone, he has to report to somebody."

Paul says, "I didn't know he was talking to you that often."

"Oh, yes. A couple weeks ago he mentioned you were rummaging through the attic looking for something."

"Reporting on me, huh?"

"No, no. Nothing like that. He was just surprised, that's all." Christine stays focused on Paul. "So, what were you looking for?"

Paul feels all three of them staring at him. "Nothing in particular. Just seeing if there's anything I might want to bring back to Paris with me."

"I think Fran's probably confused because he doesn't know why you're still here. You didn't stay just to rearrange the furniture. So, what's keeping you?" Christine adds, when her eyes meet Claire's, "Above all, when you have a beautiful, talented woman like Claire waiting for you in Paris."

"Nothing's keeping me here. When I'm ready to go back, I will. I do have every bit as much right to live here as you or Fran." He can hear the tension and the anger in his voice.

"Of course you do. And you should stay as long as you like. We're concerned about you, that's all."

Paul looks at Christine, trying to read her intent in her face, and not seeing a trace of dissimulation, responds, "The only thing I found of any interest was a garment bag with a wedding dress and a man's suit. The amazing thing isn't what I found, but what I didn't find. Mother saved so little. It makes me wonder if she was more interested in forgetting than remembering."

Christine remains silent, a placid smile fixed like a mask on her face.

"I found a whole slew of pictures in her room," Paul continues, "all of them very old. The most recent dated from the early to mid-fifties. Nothing after that."

"Really?" Christine's face remains inscrutable.

"Was she trying to forget something?"

"I wouldn't know."

"Fran doesn't seem to know anything either."

"Where is Fran? I wish he would join us." Claire looks around again, as if he might be lurking somewhere in the shadows beyond the light of the fire. "I hope I didn't scare him off." She laughs nervously.

She frequently looks around, as if suspecting Fran's watching her. Paul recalls her dream, in which she felt Fran was lurking somewhere in the shadows, ready to harm him. It's not surprising she's anxious, with the comments he's made about his brother—the confrontation in his mother's bedroom, Fran's first experience with dressing a deer, the incident when Fran turned a gun on one of his friends, the outburst of rage against Christine at breakfast, and of course the howling, at night, like a wolf. She probably has images of Lon Chaney in fur.

He hasn't talked to her enough about the Fran he has gotten to know. Or the way being back here has changed him, so that what Fran sees no longer strikes him as so bizarre. He remembers the night he returned from his ski trip, found Fran alone in front of the fireplace, and told him about his "strange experience."

"I was skiing around a point on Otter Lake. I came around a big boulder, and all of a sudden there was this deer—a doe. I was downwind of her so she didn't smell me or hear me. When she saw me, she froze. She must've been just as surprised as I was. We stared at one another. And I had this eerie feeling as we looked into one another's eyes— which is a pretty strange thing to do with an animal—I had this weird feeling that somehow we were part of one another. Or both part of something that was a lot bigger than either one of us. It was bizarre."

"I feel that all the time," Fran answered. "Every animal has a spirit."

"Come on, Fran, I've seen you kill deer. And you seem to enjoy doing it."

"I kill just for the meat. And after I give thanks to God, I do what the Indians used to do: I say a prayer to appease the animal's spirit. I ask everything I kill to forgive me. You felt you and the deer were connected. Well, you are. You're connected in the same spirit."

"The great spirit?"

"Yeah. It's not complicated. You don't need all your education to understand what's right in front of your eyes."

"I'm not sure that's what was right in front of my eyes. My feeling was that we were just two living things that were part of a larger thing, which is the universe. And in that larger thing, we were essentially the same. I felt like a little speck in the universe. And someday I'll be gone. There are thousands of people who die every day, and what difference does it make? Where did we ever get the idea we're the most important thing in the world?"

Fran chuckled. "Another year up here, you'll see. You'll see what I'm talking about. You just need to learn how to see."

Paul laughed. "I doubt it, Fran." He reflected for a few

seconds. "But who knows, maybe you're right. Maybe in a year I'll be talking about the spirit world too."

Fran was partly right. What they saw wasn't all that different. A connected universe, of which they're just a part. And perhaps Fran has found some peace and happiness in that realization, that he sees confirmed every day. And maybe he's not totally crazy after all.

"Fran's just fine, whatever he's doing," Paul says. He leans over toward Claire and whispers, "He's harmless. No werewolf. No Lon Chaney in fur."

Claire looks at him, puzzled.

"Paul's right, Claire, there's no reason to worry about Fran. He likes to be alone—that's just the way he is. And you never know, he might have one of his migraines. He used to get them all the time when we were growing up."

"Oh, that's sad."

"Although I often thought the migraines were an excuse to go to his room so he wouldn't have to deal with people anymore."

Paul smiles and nods his head in agreement.

"But, we're here," Christine says with a friendly smile, "and we're so happy to get to know you. It's too bad we couldn't have left earlier, so we could have all come together, but, with our boys home for Christmas, and one of them brought a house guest—"

Tim interjects, "Rick brought his girlfriend home to meet the parents."

"I didn't want to put you to any trouble. And of course, I couldn't wait to see Paul." Claire smiles at Paul and places her right hand on his knee. She looks back at Christine. "And I got a chance to see some of the country. Although it was nerve raking to drive on those icy roads. "

Paul smiles, knowing she means to say nerve-racking. He's always been amused by her few pronunciation problems with English, as when she pronounces "sheet" as "shit," says *shit* for *sheet*, or puts the accent on the second syllable in "capitalist," making the word sound as if it derived from "capitulate." He finds these errors as endearing as her elf-ear.

"Driving those icy roads for a hundred and fifty miles is a lot less challenging than dog sledding—the other means of transportation around here this time of year."

Claire looks into his eyes to see if he's serious, then shakes her head and laughs.

"It's amazing to see this side of Paul," Christine says. "He was always so serious, I just came to believe that's the way he was. I never knew this Paul existed."

"Well, he can be pretty serious too." Claire looks at Paul. "Can't you?" She pokes her fingers into his ribs to get a response.

Paul squirms and tries to act amused by the attention.

Christine says, "You get along so well. You must have a lot in common."

"We do share a lot," says Claire. "Books, films, art exhibits, travel, politics."

"And politics," Paul laughs.

"And politics. We have great conversations. And we both write—although very different kinds of things. Paul writes his articles, and I have a book on women writers I'm trying to finish." She looks at Paul and whispers, knowing he'll understand, "If I can ever finish that section on Hélène Cixous!"

"I never could write," Christine says.

Tim chimes in, with a big grin. "If I had a choice between writing a book and dying, I'd choose dying."

Claire laughs. "Sometimes dying looks pretty good." She puts her right hand on Paul's knee and gives it a gentle squeeze. "Paul is one of those rare people who writes with ease. And meets all his deadlines. Don't you?"

"Usually."

"Although he did have some problems finishing articles this fall. He was so upset about his mother's illness." She shakes her head.

"Really? I didn't know."

Paul hears the sarcasm dripping from Christine's words.

"It got to the point," Claire continues, "where he couldn't finish anything. And then one editor refused to publish something he did finish—a piece on the Berlin Wall coming down—because he claimed it was speculative journalism." Claire raises two fingers on each hand to designate quotation marks for the editor's phrase. "Paul went into a rage." She looks at him. "You did kind of go over the top, didn't you?"

"I had some arguments with him at three in the morning—which I always won."

Tim says, "The good thing about those arguments is you always win them. The bad thing is they always happen at three in the morning."

"But," Claire says, beaming, "Paul was right." She looks at him. "History vindicated you, didn't it, my prophet." She winks at him and laughs.

"That it did. But a prophecy of a month and a half doesn't exactly make me a prophet." He's surprised to find he feels uneasy with Claire talking about his problems in front of Christine. As if, by knowing about his problems, Christine could do him harm.

Christine says, "Fran told me you've been publishing articles in the *Mirer Times*, right?"

"Yeah, just to have some fun."

Claire's smile fades, her ebullience deflates. He can almost hear the questions going through her mind. Is he coming back, or is he going to develop a life here?

"Well, I'm so happy you can finish what you start. That must make you feel good." He's about to say something, but she quickly adds, "I imagine you're sleeping well too." She looks at Christine and Tim. "That's the other thing. Paul couldn't sleep last fall. He was having nightmares. It was such an awful time." She looks at Paul. "For both of us."

Christine says, "I had no idea."

Claire nods her head, still looking at Paul. "But, you seem so much happier now. You're finishing articles for the ... the *Mirer Times*?"

Paul nods.

"You don't seem to be having nightmares anymore."

"Oh yes, I told you about that dream ..."

"Okay, one nightmare. But otherwise, you seem to have found sleep. You like to say, the innocent sleep well. You must feel you have regained your innocence." She glares at him, then smiles. "Hmm. Is that kind of like a woman regaining her virginity?" She laughs.

Paul sees pain and anger in her eyes, and wants to calm and reassure her.

Claire continues. "But then, how would anyone know what Paul really feels, he keeps so much to himself."

"A family trait," he responds, just to somehow get himself back in the conversation so he can guide it in another direction. But he immediately regrets his comment. "Well, I'm not keeping anything to myself now."

They continue looking at one another until he sees a glimmer of trust return.

He becomes aware of Christine, who has been watching them closely, and looks in her direction. She appears stunned by what has happened. Finally she finds her tongue, and says to Claire, "It's so good to see the two of you so ... so happy." She seems to be trying to think of something to say. "And it's good to see Paul and Fran happy too. The difference in their relationship—it's just amazing."

"Yeah," Tim adds, glancing away for a minute from the fire that has mesmerized him, "a real odd couple."

Christine smiles, looking relieved now that she's received help from Tim. "You are a kind of odd couple, aren't you?"

Paul is about to ignore this glib talk of happiness and the odd couple, when he decides to say something that has been on his mind for a while. He looks at Christine and says, "You know, one thing about Fran really amazes me."

Tim asks, "Just one thing?" And again laughs at his own joke. No one else laughs, so he shrugs off the failure and sips his cognac.

Paul continues to fix his gaze on Christine. "The one who stayed is—between the three of us siblings—the one who received the least support from Mother. She treated him more like a servant than a son. He was the oldest, and yet she didn't let him manage the lodge and the resort until you and I were gone. Think of how humiliating that must've been."

Christine nods in agreement. She knows. He can see it in her eyes. She has thought about all of this before. Perhaps many times. But still, he's going to say this, because he needs to—the injustice of it infuriates him.

"I don't recall him ever being encouraged to think he might have a brain in his head, that maybe he was smart enough to go to college, manage the lodge, or do anything. And she let him care for her only because there was no one else. Except Stone."

"No," Christine murmurs. "She would've never accepted Stone."

"Who's Stone?" Claire looks back and forth from Paul to Christine.

Christine shakes her head.

Paul mumbles, "A cousin." He looks down at the floor, thinking about Fran. Someone doesn't end up the way Fran did without having suffered a lot of pain. He remembers that day in the woods, watching Fran try to dress a deer for the first time, overcome with rage because he couldn't do it, and screaming at Stone that he should dress it, and Fran would tell him everything he did wrong. And then the humiliation of watching Stone do it to perfection. Shame has been a huge part of Fran's life. It has shaped—or misshaped—him.

Paul looks at Claire. "Stone was at times a mentor to Fran and me when we were kids. He taught us some tough lessons. But he's the kind of guy who always shows up just when you need him. He fixes things for the family."

Paul looks at Tim and Christine. "If an odd couple is two people who are exact opposites fitting perfectly together, then Fran and I are an odd couple. He's an extraordinary hunter. He has already stocked the freezer with enough duck, goose, and venison to last the winter. And no one's better at dressing game in a forest than Fran. It would take me years to learn how to do what he does without even having to think about it. He hunts; I write. And what I've enjoyed writing about these last few weeks is the wilderness—from which he takes game, and I take words."

The others look at him in silence. He adds, just in case anyone didn't get the message, "I feel for Fran. He got screwed."

Tim, who seems to have been waiting for the tension level to drop, asks, "These articles, what are they about?"

"What it's like for someone to return and re-discover the wilderness. To have again that experience of standing at night at the threshold of an infinite universe, teeming with billions of stars, and feel you could step right into it. And fall forever. It's been fun writing about my ... my home."

Christine eyes him. "Your home?"

Paul feels hot from the blush.

Christine continues, "But you are going back to Paris, aren't you?"

"I'm going back. Don't worry."

"I'm not worried. I just think, with your education and

everything you've done ... and your amazing luck in having found someone like Claire ... " She embraces Claire with her big-sister smile, approving of her younger brother's wise choice in a mate. She turns her attention back toward Paul. "You need to go back to Paris. That's where your life is."

"I plan on going back."

Christine nods her head, smiling. She looks at the chunks of ember encrusted logs covered over with gray ash, then at Tim, who has leaned back on the couch and, covering a yawn, looks at her with sleepy eyes. Christine places her hand on his knee, which she rubs as if it needed to be awakened, and says, "Well, my tired man, shall we call it a night?"

He returns her smile and says, "You betcha."

Paul lies in bed, Claire's head on his chest. It feels good to stroke her hair, to feel close, to know she loves laying her head on his chest and feel his fingers—his magic touch, as she has often said. Too much has happened for either one of them to sleep.

Finally Claire says, "You are returning."

"Yes."

"When."

"Soon. I promise." He continues stroking her hair. "Well, now that you've met my family, what do you think of them?"

Claire is quiet for a long time before responding. "Christine's definitely a big sister. She could be everyone's big sister."

Paul chuckles. "Yeah, that's for sure."

"When I walked into the living room—or the old dining room, whatever you want to call it—she and Tim were kissing. It looked as if they'd been fooling around. How can you not like two people who still feel passion for one another after so many years?" She raises her head so she can see his face. "It gives reason for hope." She lays her head back on his chest. "Tim is very sweet. I think he would do anything to make Christine happy."

"Uh-huh. What else?"

"Well, I didn't sense any of the animosity between Christine and Fran that you talked about in August. But maybe he wasn't around enough to irritate her."

"Yeah. That's something I don't understand. They were constantly at each other's throats. Christine was even trying to get me to agree to having him committed. Then all of a sudden everything changed." Paul strokes the little elf point on her ear, while recalling that day. "They'd been arguing about Mother wanting her body cremated and the ashes spread on the Black Hole, and Fran said something … it didn't really make sense to me. Something about Mother never wanting to be far from there, and then Christine became very quiet. From then on they were so nice to one another. A 180-degree turn. Weird."

"That is strange."

"When I was growing up, I sometimes felt the two of them shared a secret language." He laughs. "It used to make me feel kind of paranoid."

"Well, I can't imagine Christine wanting anything but what's best for you."

"And what about Fran? You haven't said much about him."

Claire doesn't answer. Paul lifts his head to see if she's fallen asleep, but she's still awake.

"How did he lose those two fingers?"

"I asked him once. He just shook his head." Paul adds, "Fran's the master of silence. When he doesn't want to talk, he doesn't talk."

"He makes me uneasy."

"Why?"

"I don't know. I guess because he always disappears, but at the same time I feel he's lurking somewhere, watching us. Like in that dream I told you about. I know how you feel about him, Paul, but you have to admit, he is a little strange."

Paul laughs.

"You probably think I'm paranoid."

"Fran's harmless. He's just shy." He continues stroking her hair and her elf ear. "All he needs is to mother someone. Just one person will do. Otherwise, he's much happier alone, on the lake or in the woods."

"A romantic loner, hmm? Maybe he should write poetry."

Paul chuckles. "I don't know that he can write." It's easy to turn into a loner here. He remembers a day, years ago, fishing alone on the lake. It had started to rain. He sat for at least a half hour huddled under a poncho, in a peaceful, meditative state. He noticed someone else also hunched over in a canoe, shrouded by a poncho. On his way home, he paddled close enough to the other canoe to talk. A man with a long narrow face and dark, emotionless eyes peered at him from beneath the hood. He had started coming here with his parents when he was still a boy. His father had died the previous year. He liked coming back, spending time alone on the lake. "The sound of rain on a lake is solace for the soul," he said. The words stuck in Paul's mind like a mantra. He whispers, "'The sound of rain on a lake is solace for the soul.'"

"Where did that come from?"

"A guy I met on the lake. A long time ago."

"If you love this place so much, why would you ever want to leave?"

"Maybe I'm trying to assimilate it, so I never have to return."

Claire draws close to him. Later they make love again and fall asleep in one another's arms.

*
* *

Paul leans against the wall near the desk and watches Claire snatch underwear, a pullover, and a sweater out of the chest of drawers, and dresses and slacks out of the closet, and toss them at the open suitcase on his bed.

"I thought after a week together I'd have a better idea of what's going on. You keep saying you're coming back, and yet you continue to develop a life here with Fran. You're obviously intent on staying."

"I'm not."

"Then get a plane ticket and come back with me."

"What were you and Christine talking about?"

Claire bends over to pick up a pair of shoes and tosses them onto the bed.

"Christine has nothing to do with this."

"Well, what did she talk to you about?"

"She thinks exactly what I think—that you're staying here permanently."

"Well, I'm not."

"Then get a plane ticket."

Paul doesn't respond.

She opens a drawer, finds some wool socks, tosses them onto the bed, opens another drawer and slams it shut, and another, and another, takes a look in the closet, slams the door, all the while complaining. "It's true you haven't lied to me. You just haven't told me the truth. You haven't explained anything. What exactly are you trying to find out? What happened to your father? Who were your parents? You act as if Christine and Fran are hiding something from you. What is it? Tell me!"

"I don't know. That's what I want to find out."

"Well, why don't you just ask them?"

"Because they get evasive. They act as if they don't know anything. But I know they do."

"And maybe they don't. Maybe this is all in your head, Paul."

"That's what they'd like me to think."

"Or maybe," she slams the suitcase shut, then looks him in the eye, "maybe you're afraid to find out. Maybe you don't want to know what happened." She waits; he says nothing. "Is that it, Paul? Is that why you haven't done anything all this time?"

"I don't know," he shouts. Then, in a more reflective tone, repeats, "I don't know."

She stares at him, as if she might find the answer on his face. She crosses over to the window and looks out at the snow and ice. "You remember the swan that got frozen in the ice?"

He nods his head.

"Don't wait too long, Paul."

"That's pretty tough."

"I love you. I want you to come back. But I won't wait forever."

He feels the sutures tugging at his heart as he shuts the car door, wondering if he and Claire will ever be together again. She looks away.

Christine, before getting in, hugs him and whispers, "She's perfect for you. Don't let her get away."

Claire looks up at him through the window. A look that seems to ask, what are you going to do? And then she's gone.

He turns around and finds Fran standing a few feet away, his breath forming clouds in the cold air. "Where the hell have you been all this time?"

"Here."

"You could've made an effort with Claire."

Fran doesn't respond. Paul wants to launch into a tirade against him, but catches himself. No use beating up on Fran for being who he is. No use beating up on himself, either. He just needs to move ahead, somehow.

11

"YOU SPEND MORE TIME SITTING IN THE DARK THAN anyone I've ever known," Paul says, collapsing on the couch facing the fireplace, perpendicular to the one Fran is sitting on.

"What do I need lights for? I'm not too likely to get lost here anytime soon."

The fire roars, crackling and popping hot coals against the wire mesh screen, igniting air pockets in the logs that suddenly hiss and blaze like miniature flame throwers. The bright red-yellow glow illuminates Fran's profile. He has a child's love for big fires.

"Why did you turn the television off?"

Fran turns his face toward the fire. "It's a rerun. I'm going to bed."

"Already? It can't be later than 9:30."

"There's a plate of venison and potatoes on the counter you can warm up."

"How was your day?"

"Okay. How was yours?"

"I had dinner with a friend in town."

"Didn't know you had any."

"Rose. Someone I knew when I was growing up. She was my girlfriend in high school." Paul stares mesmerized at the fire for a while. "Did you know a Molly Morgan?"

Fran shakes his head.

"I knew her in high school. She was found dead last May. Murdered."

"I didn't do it."

Paul laughs. "I know you didn't do it. I'm just wondering what you've heard."

Fran shakes his head. Stares at the fire.

The logs collapse in the fireplace, a stream of sparks shoots up the chimney, and Fran's face glows red. He gets up, throws three more logs on the fire, and remains standing, looking down at the blue and yellow flames crackling crazily around the white birch bark.

Well, Paul thinks, he apparently doesn't want to go to bed, doesn't want to be with anyone, and doesn't want to be alone.

"I thought you were going to bed."

Fran shrugs. After a while, the logs singed black, the flame recedes into a constant flicker that slowly grows into an intense steady flame. Fran turns back toward the couch, sits down, and stares at the fire as if in a trance, half of his face in darkness.

Finally he speaks. "Oh, I forgot to tell you. Stone stopped by. He left some walleye fillets." He falls silent, then adds, deadpan, "I asked him if he'd like some of ours."

Paul laughs and shakes his head. "Walleye fillets—the currency of the realm."

Fran, still staring at the fire, seems oblivious to the humor. "He said you should come by sometime. Said he'd expected you by now."

"Does he have a phone?"

"When he pays the bill."

"Has he paid it?"

"Give him a call. You'll find out soon enough."

"I should do that. Maybe tomorrow. Anything else happen?"

"Christine called."

"Again? I leave and everyone calls or stops by. What about Claire?"

Fran shakes his head no.

"What did Christine want?"

"Just wanted to know how we're doing."

"Did she want to know if I'd made reservations for Paris?"

He shakes his head.

Paul watches him as he stares at the fire and wonders what put him in this mood—other than just winter. He's moved to the dark side of the moon tonight. He could stay there for days. "Fran." Paul leans toward him, wishing he'd respond. "Fran?" He knows he's listening, even if he won't look. "What did she talk to you about?"

"Who?"

"Christine."

"She wanted to know how I was doing without Mother."

"And what—"

" I told her Mother's here and everything's just fine."

"Fran, she died two months ago. You took care of the ashes yourself."

"She's here in spirit."

"Okay," Paul nods his head, "she's here in spirit." He continues watching Fran stare into the fire. "It's been a long time since we've talked about her." He pauses, then continues, "And I don't know when we've ever really talked about our father." Another pause. "You know, Fran, when I was a kid and someone at school would ask me about my family, I'd make up some of the wildest stories. I used to tell kids my mother sent me off to Grandma and Grandpa's because she had some rare disease that baffled the whole medical establishment, and sometimes she was so sick she couldn't keep me at home. And as for our father, well, I made up a glorious life for him. He'd been an air force pilot, had shot down as many German planes as Chuck Yeager, and finally he got killed in a dog fight. But I wasn't a very good liar. I didn't think of all the details. So when Bobby Rickett asked how my dad managed to have me if he'd been killed in World War II, I had to think up a new story fast. I switched the Korean War for the Second World War. He knew I was lying. He got me. After that, when anyone would ask me about my dad, I'd just say he died when I was too young to know him. I'd hide in my ignorance. But now, before I go any further with my life, I want to find out who my father was, and my mother."

Fran remains silent.

"I really want to know."

Fran leans back in the couch, rests his head on the cushion, gazes at the ceiling, and sighs. "It's too late. They're both dead."

"You've said many times they're both alive—in spirit."

"If you're already close to them, yeah, they're still alive."

"Well then, help me get close to them. Tell me about them."

Fran remains silent, his head, silhouetted by the red glow of the fire, still turned toward the ceiling. "It's a little late for getting close."

"I think Mother wanted me to get close."

"Bullshit."

"No, Fran, this isn't bullshit. I told you about the weird thing she did a little over a year ago. She sent me her wedding invitation and a picture of herself as a little girl. A very happy little girl. Something I could never have imagined before looking at that picture. No note, no explanation. Why, Fran, why do you think she did that?"

After a long silence Fran answers, "She knew she was gonna die."

"I'm sure she did. But why send me the invitation and the picture?"

Fran continues staring at the ceiling. "I don't know. People do strange things when they know they're gonna die."

"I think she wanted me to learn about her past ... find out who she was. And no one can help me do that more than you."

"I'll wait 'til she gives me a sign."

Paul arches his eyebrows and nods his head. "I think she already has." Fran doesn't respond, so Paul continues talking, hoping something he says might draw him out. "She must've been pretty happy in that marriage. The wedding invitation was fifty years old. And it was still important to her."

Fran leans forward, rests his elbows on his knees, and stares at the floor. "Probably was. But I don't remember much about Mom and him as a couple. I was only eleven when he died."

"Eleven! You must remember something."

He shakes his head no.

"Well, did he love her? Was he affectionate? Did he beat her?"

"No!"

Paul leans forward and tries to make eye contact with Fran. "What did he do to her, Fran?"

"He was a good man. A good father. We respected him. And loved him." Fran's voice sounds mechanical, as if he were reciting a script. He glances at Paul, with a look that seems almost accusatory. "You loved him too, even though you might not remember."

"I'm sure I did, Fran." Paul sighs, looks down at the floor and shakes his head, then looks up again at Fran. "Tell me about his death."

Fran has turned his gaze back toward the dying fire,

the visible side of his face fading into the shadow.

Paul is about to repeat his request when Fran, without turning away from the fire, finally replies. "There was a snow storm. He didn't come home. No one ever saw him again. That's all there is."

"Where was he going?"

Fran leans his head back on the couch, closes his eyes, and mumbles, "Into town."

"What was he doing?"

"I don't know."

"Hmm. Why didn't someone call the police?"

"Sometimes he came home late."

"Why?"

"I don't know."

"Did he hang out in bars?"

"I don't know what he did."

"You were eleven, and you didn't know what he did?"

"That's right."

"Were there nights when he didn't come home?"

"Nope."

"Did he—"

"Just that night he didn't. The next day Mom called the police to tell 'em he'd gone into town and hadn't come back. They came out and talked to her. Looked around. Never found any sign of him."

"Why didn't she call them the night before?"

"I don't know. She probably fell asleep."

"So she called in the morning when she woke up."

"I guess so." Fran raises his head from the cushion and looks at Paul. "You're trying to learn about something that happened over thirty-five years ago. I've forgotten a lot ... and there's no reason for me to make an effort to remember. I'm at peace with the past."

"Really? Not many people can honestly say that. I sure can't."

"You're not going to learn anything here that will make any difference in your life."

"I guess that's for me to decide."

"I guess it is."

Fran looks back at the fire.

"Was there some kind of an investigation?"

Fran looks at him. "Investigation? Into what?"

"Father's disappearance."

"I told you, the sheriff's people poked around a few days and then gave up. Never found a clue."

"Why did they look around here?"

"I don't know. Probably because this is where he lived."

"Wouldn't they look for him wherever he was seen last, or where they found his car? I assume he drove to town."

"They found his car. In a ditch."

"Where?"

"On the road to Mirer. Maybe a half mile from the turnoff. "

"The turnoff to the lodge?"

Fran nods his head.

"But they never found a trace of him? That's hard to believe."

Fran shakes his head. "It's not hard to believe a man could disappear in a whiteout. Not hard at all." Fran leans his head back on the cushion and closes his eyes. "There was so much snow the sheriff couldn't get here until a plow had gone through. By then it was afternoon. The snow had finally stopped. The sheriff and his men came back in the spring, after the snow had melted. Looked around. Never found a thing. Whatever was left of him probably was eaten by dogs or wolves … vultures … whatever. Any bones left probably got scattered. That's what the sheriff said." He falls silent, then adds, "A whole lot of scavengers up here. Come spring, they're pretty hungry."

"What did you—"

Ignoring Paul, Fran continues speaking, almost as if he were in a trance. "Mom really hurt. We all hurt. Even you. You kept on asking, 'Where Papa go? Where Papa go?' We'd tell you, 'Papa's gonna come back.' And you just kept on asking, 'Where Papa go?' Until you drove us crazy." Fran leans his head back on the cushion and closes his eyes.

Stunned into silence by this description of him asking repeatedly for his father, Paul stares at the fist-size coals glowing in the fireplace. He is about to get up and put more logs on the fire when Fran begins talking again in a low, monotone voice.

"Mom couldn't do much of anything the first few months. Walked around the lodge in her old blue housecoat, crying and whimpering." He seems to reflect for a few seconds, then adds, "She had Stone run the lodge for her."

"Stone?"

"Yeah. Stone. And Queenie took orders from him. How about that!" Fran smirks.

"I'm amazed!"

"For about a year. Then Mom took over. She helped him buy that old shack and the land it's on."

"Is that what he wanted?"

"I guess."

"I remember, years ago, when I learned he was a cousin, I was amazed. For a long time I thought he was just a hired hand."

"That was his own doing."

"How so?"

"Don't know. He might've stroked her fur the wrong way."

In the morning Paul heads into town, goes straight to the library and the periodicals room, and asks the librarian where he might find issues of the *Mirer Times* for December of 1953. She leads him to the rolls of microfilm. Scrolling through each issue on a viewer, he finds articles about Christmas, ice fishing, Ike and Mamie in the White House during the holidays, Communist spies, and the U-2 incident, but nothing about William Bauer. As he approaches the end of the month he begins to wonder if he's going to find anything, when he comes to the issue for Friday, December 29. There it is, in the bottom right corner of the front page: "Lodge Owner Missing."

> William (Bill) F. Bauer, owner of the Spirit Lake Lodge and Resort located 25 miles east of Mirer, was reported missing Wednesday when he did not return from a trip into Mirer the night before.
>
> According to his wife, Joyce Bauer, Bill left home Tuesday, between 7:00 and 8:00 PM, saying only that he was going into town. She did not hear from him again and called police Wednesday shortly after 9:00 AM to report him missing.
>
> The police, who were unable to drive out to the lodge immediately because of the blizzard that had blanketed the area in nearly two feet of snow, followed a snowplow as it cleared a path along the Old Lindgren Road. Bauer's car, a 1951 Packard, was discovered in the ditch, buried beneath snow, just 200 yards before the turnoff to the lodge.
>
> The car was empty. There were no signs of injury or footprints in the snow. According to Sheriff Roger Swenson, whose office is heading up the investigation, any footprints that Bauer might have left would have quickly

been covered by falling and drifting snow in the blizzard.

Police searched the area surrounding the car yesterday, but failed to find any sign of Bauer. They plan to continue the search today.

A picture of the Packard, still buried in the snow, is positioned to the left of the article. The car seems familiar. It teases Paul with a memory, just beyond his mind's grasp, like a word on the tip of the tongue that refuses to be recalled. He concentrates on the memory, but gets nothing, and lets go.

He scrolls through the rest of the paper so quickly it's just a blur, and then slowly scrolls back and forth a few times until he finds page one of the Saturday, December 30 issue. A picture of his father, eyes fixed on the camera, a wave of black hair partially covering his right temple and receding hairline, is in the bottom right quarter of the page. He's wearing a black turtleneck just like the one in the picture Paul found in Mother's room. He gazes at his father for a long time, transfixed by the absent stare. Finally he succeeds in lowering his eyes to read the caption beneath the photo: "Bill Bauer, 34, disappeared in the blizzard Tuesday night." The article, laid out around the picture, bears the title, "Bauer Still Missing."

The Mirer Sheriff's Office reported no progress yesterday in the search for Bill Bauer, the longtime resident and owner of the Spirit Lake Lodge and Resort who disappeared during the blizzard Tuesday night.

Bauer was reported to have been seen around 8:30 PM in The Haven, a Mirer bar. He left the bar a few minutes later with a woman. Police discovered his car the next morning in the ditch along the Old Lindgren Road, not far from the turnoff to the lodge. The search for Bauer focused on the area around the car.

Sheriff Roger Swenson said, "I'm amazed Bauer would try something as crazy as driving in a blizzard, above all knowing what happened to his folks."

As many longtime Mirer residents know, Bauer's parents, Francis and Nora Bauer, died in the Armistice Day blizzard of 1940 on the same road, about five miles from the place where Bauer's car was found. The driver of a snowplow found the Bauers frozen to death in their car, which had gone off the road and into the ditch.

Police have scheduled a broader search of the area around Bauer's car for today.

Holy shit, he thinks, what are the chances of that happening—his father getting caught in a blizzard on the same road where his parents died? Rereading the article, amazed at the coincidence, Paul stops at the name Swenson. Swenson. It tugs at his memory. Where had he heard it? It could've been anywhere, a common name like that. He starts to scroll forward when he remembers—Roger Swenson, the sheriff whose car sank through thin ice on a lake just a few miles from the lodge. The old farts always talked about Swenson's death as if it had happened soon after his grandfather's, suggesting there had been a connection between the two, but Swenson must've died much later ... at least—Paul calculates—thirteen years later. He tries to remember if any of the stories directly linked Swenson's death to his grandfather's, but he can't remember.

He finally lets go of the name and scrolls forward to the next issue, where he finds another article about his father's disappearance: "Bauer Search Continues."

> The Sheriff's Office continued its investigation yesterday into the disappearance of Bill Bauer, the owner of the Spirit Lake Lodge and Resort, whose car was found buried in snow in a ditch along the Old Lindgren Road Wednesday afternoon.
>
> Police released the name of the last person in Mirer known to have seen Bauer— Miss Valery Night, a teacher at Mirer High School. Bauer and Night met at The Haven at 8:30 PM. They left about fifteen minutes later for Night's house, located on Pine Street. A neighbor confirmed seeing Bauer and Night arrive there around 9:00. According to Night, Bauer left at 11:00 to drive home. His departure could not be confirmed by witnesses.

Paul recalls taking Molly to The Haven once for a beer. They were kids. Underage, but they knew they'd get served. She was wearing a flower print skirt, sandals, a shawl over a loose low-cut blouse, and daisies in her hair. As he sat next to her in a booth, the juke box played Leonard Cohen singing, "Suzanne takes you down to her place by the river," and he kissed her, feeling her loose breasts, soft and swaying as she moved close to him, brushing against his ribs. Molly, who lived in a place by the river with her alcoholic father, became his Suzanne. The thought that his father went to the same bar to meet a woman, to drink with her and go home with her and perhaps to make love with her, made him seem human and real. What was she like, and what did she mean to him?

> Yesterday Sheriff Swenson and several depu-
> ties searched the Spirit Lake Lodge, home to
> the Bauers, and all the cabins in the resort
> that the Bauers operate. Police are reported
> to have again interviewed Joyce Bauer, Bill
> Bauer's wife, as well as their three oldest
> children—Robert (19), an adopted nephew;
> Francis (11); and Christine (nine).

Paul stares at the last sentence, wondering who Robert, the adopted nephew, might be. He doesn't have a clue. Then he realizes: Stone. He never thought of him as anything but a distant cousin, a hired hand, and here he's mentioned as one of Mother's children—as if he were a brother. She never referred to him as her adopted son, or her nephew. Never by any name but Stone. Never. How could she ignore him like that? Or ignore telling him, her son, that Stone was his adopted brother?

He finishes reading the article, which concludes by saying the search has yielded no clues to his father's disappearance, and gets the roll of microfilm for January 1954. The front page headline on the issue for Tuesday, January 2, immediately grabs his attention: "Investigation Takes Dramatic Turn."

> The investigation into the disappearance
> of Bill Bauer a week ago took a dramatic
> turn yesterday afternoon when Sheriff Roger
> Swenson said he could not rule out "foul play."
> Swenson made the statement in response
> to a question from a *Mirer Times* journalist
> who had asked if Bauer's disappearance was
> still being treated as a missing persons case.
> Swenson refused to elaborate.
>
> In other news related to the case, police

brought in two people for questioning: Joyce Bauer, the wife of Bill Bauer, and Valery Night, a Mirer High School teacher believed to be the last person to see Bauer the day he disappeared. Reliable sources have indicated that Bauer had been having an affair with Night for approximately a year when he disappeared.

Meanwhile police searching the area where Bauer's car had been found discovered no clues that might help solve the case.

Paul reads the article several times, as if re-reading it would enable him to understand what connection there could possibly be between his father, mother, Valery Night, and "foul play."

Baffled, he scrolls forward, looking for the paper for Wednesday, January 3. He knows there'll be an article. The title stops him dead: "Bauer Attempts Suicide."

An ambulance rushed Joyce Bauer to Lake County Hospital shortly before midnight Tuesday after a failed suicide attempt. Bauer's husband disappeared during the snow storm that passed through this area last Tuesday and Wednesday.

Mrs. Bauer's son Robert called the hospital when he found her lying sick on the floor of her bedroom. He told police he had seen her take a bottle of whiskey earlier in the evening from the bar in the lodge and carry it to her room. This surprised him, he said, because she rarely drank alcohol.

About an hour later he heard vomiting in her room. He found her lying unconscious on the floor. He then called the hospital.

The hospital reported that Mrs. Bauer was in serious but stable condition and was expected to live, after taking tranquilizers with whiskey.

The sounds of whispering voices, turning pages, and the slamming of book covers on counter tops and tables seem to come from a long way off, far removed from the incomprehensible fact of his mother's attempted suicide. He can't comprehend this, nor deny it. It just doesn't fit. Not in the puzzle he put together. And put away. Now everything's messed up. Nothing fits.

Again he looks at the headline: it screams, "Bauer Attempts Suicide." He stares at it for a few more seconds, then slowly scrolls forward to Thursday's paper: "Bauer Search Called Off." The first two paragraphs summarize the unsuccessful search for his missing father, report Sheriff Swenson's commitment to conduct another search in the spring, when the snow's gone, and repeat his response to a journalist who asked if he still suspected "foul play"—he does not. It's the last few paragraphs that catch Paul's attention.

> While the search for Bauer has come to a temporary halt, the effects of his disappearance continue to be felt. Joyce Bauer, who attempted suicide, remains hospitalized, and Valery Night, the teacher with whom Bill Bauer had a relationship, has come under criticism from the community.
>
> The principal of Mirer High School, Michael Kapucinski, has received several letters from parents demanding the dismissal

of Night, who has been employed at the school as an English teacher for over six years. Kapucinski confirmed having received the letters, but refused to comment on their content.

However, some of the parents who wrote letters have told the *Times* they feel Night should be fired for having an affair with Bauer, a husband and father of three children. The parents said they would circulate a petition to have Night removed if she does not leave immediately.

Kapucinski told the *Times* that Night had not done anything unlawful and would remain on the school's staff. He added, "She is an outstanding teacher, admired by colleagues and students alike."

She must've felt horribly alone in that god-awful town, where everyone knew everyone's business, and the newspaper wasn't much more than a gossip rag. *A* for adultery. Accused, judged, and condemned. Leading a father of four astray. He wonders what she was like, what she looked like (he finds no picture of her), what attracted his father to her. What he wanted and why. What was missing in his parents' marriage. Maybe nothing. Maybe she was available. Maybe he could, so he did, and that was that. And maybe if he hadn't had the affair, he wouldn't have gone into town, wouldn't have died or gotten lost in a whiteout, and would've been a father to his son. Paul looks again for a picture of her, but finds none.

Nothing in the paper Friday, but Saturday's paper carries a headline that confirms Paul's sentiments toward both the town and the newspaper: "Night Resigns."

Valery Night, the last person to see Bill Bauer the day he disappeared in the blizzard a week ago, has resigned her position at Mirer High School.

Michael Kapucinski, the school's principal, confirmed reports Tuesday that several parents had sent letters to the school demanding Night's resignation. Yesterday afternoon he announced in a staff meeting that Night had resigned her position.

A member of the school staff, who asked to remain anonymous, commented that Kapucinski received a petition Wednesday afternoon signed by nearly 100 parents demanding that Night be fired. He spoke with Night about the petition Thursday morning. Yesterday morning she tendered her letter of resignation.

Kapucinski deplored the move. He said, "This is a brutal expulsion of a fine person and teacher from our school." However, some students and parents have claimed that Night had her classes read pornographic books, such as *Lady Chatterley's Lover* by the English novelist D. H. Lawrence.

The *Times* has also learned the Sheriff's office is concerned with Night's safety. A reliable source reported that Night has received several death threats over the phone and in writing. Sheriff Roger Swenson refused to either confirm or deny the existence of these threats, but Night's neighbors have reported seeing police cars in the area.

Meanwhile life for the Bauer family goes on. Francis and Christine, ages 11 and nine, attended Emerson School Friday. They stayed out of school Wednesday and Thursday following the failed suicide attempt by their mother Tuesday night. The school nurse, Mrs. Runyon, said, "The little dears are trying to keep their chins up, but you can see they're just traumatized by what has happened."

Robert Bauer, the 19-year-old adopted son and nephew of Mr. and Mrs. Bauer, has been caring for their three children. Members of the community who would like to help this family in need should contact the Church of the Holy Spirit in Mirer.

He rereads the paragraphs about Fran and Christine. All of this must've been traumatic for them, but it probably brought them closer together. For a while. He must've felt something too if he kept on asking, Where Papa go? But he remembers nothing. He hits a wall. If only he could reach the little boy on the other side.

His eyes move up the column to the paragraphs about Valery Night, who brought D. H. Lawrence to this little town. And had an affair with one of its married men. Did she come from somewhere else? An outsider? She had to have been, because an English teacher from Mirer just would not have had her students read *Lady Chatterley's Lover*. Was she an experienced teacher, in her thirties or forties, on some kind of mission, ready to do battle with the small minds of small towns? Or was she young? First teaching job. Probably not aware of the risks she was taking. Not used to thinking the people she saw every day considered her life their business. Paul looks around the room. The librarian at the circulation desk, a woman in her thirties with straw blond hair and black rimmed glasses who helped him find the microfilm rolls; clusters of high school kids sitting at different reading tables, talking, giggling, laughing behind their cupped hands, their radar on the alert for adults ready to reprimand; an old man sitting in a reading chair over in the corner looking at a newspaper. Just ordinary people. Why wouldn't anyone trust them? Again Paul looks for a picture, wanting to know who Night was, to better understand who his father was. Nothing.

He scrolls forward, not really expecting to find anything, but discovers yet another article about the Bauers in Monday's paper.

BAUER GOES HOME

Joyce Bauer, who attempted suicide last Tuesday evening and has been hospitalized since then, was released from the hospital yesterday morning. She is the wife of Bill Bauer, the owner of the Spirit Lake Lodge and Resort who disappeared during a snow storm that hit this area almost two weeks ago.

A search conducted by the Sheriff's Office uncovered no clues about his disappearance. Sheriff Roger Swenson called off the search last Wednesday.

The *Times* has learned that Valery Night, the last person to see Bauer before he disappeared, has also vanished. While the Sheriff's Office confirmed reports that shots had been fired through a window in the front of her house around 11:30 PM Friday, it refused to comment on her whereabouts.

Bauer's disappearance drew public attention to Night and her behavior. She had been having an affair with him for nearly two years when he disappeared, and according to neighbors she increasingly flaunted the illicit relationship.

Parents of Night's students at Mirer High School, where she worked as an English teacher, complained that she had students read and discuss pornographic books. She resigned her position at the school Friday.

In related news the Church of the Holy Spirit announced that the Bauer family has requested the church no longer accept donations on its behalf.

Paul leans back and stares off into space, thinking about the mother he knew, or thought he knew, and the mother who attempted suicide. He tries to imagine her so passionately in love with her husband that his loss could compel her to her own destruction, but cannot. His thoughts turn to the other woman, Valery Night. He wishes he could have known her, and known what she knew about his father. But she too was gone.

Paul scrolls through the remaining issues of January, March, and April, finding nothing. The Sunday, May 1 issue carries a small article headlined, "Final Search for Resort Owner." The follow-up article published the next day bears the title, "Bauer Search Over."

A team of police officers and volunteers searched for clues to the disappearance of Bill Bauer from 8:00 AM until dark yesterday, but found nothing. They fanned out in all directions from the spot where Bauer's car was found in a ditch along the Old Lindgren Road last December.

Talking to reporters at Spirit Lake lodge and Resort, the home of the Bauer family,

Sheriff Roger Swenson, who headed up the search, described this as one of the most baffling cases he had ever worked on, adding that the search was over and wouldn't be resumed unless someone found a new lead.

When asked if he still suspected foul play in Bauer's disappearance, Swenson said, "When someone disappears there are all kinds of questions that remain unanswered. People want answers, but we can't find any. Or can't find enough. That's real frustrating."

Asked if Bauer could still be alive, Swenson commented it was possible, but not likely.

Expressing sympathy for Joyce Bauer and her four children, he remarked that the family had experienced more than its share of tragedy. The Sheriff talked about Bill Bauer's parents who died in a snowstorm on the same road on Armistice Day 1940; about his older sister, Helen, who died of cancer less than two years later, leaving her son, Robert, in the care of Bill and Joyce; and about his brother, Art, who died in the Normandy invasion. The Sheriff, who had known all these people, said, "That's a hell of a lot of dying for one family to cope with."

Mrs. Bauer refused questions from the press, saying only, "We will continue praying Bill is still alive somewhere, but we'll have to go on without him for now."

They're all dead. His mother and father, his father's parents, his father's brother and sister. Fran knew all those people. It's time for him to talk.

Paul's about to leave the library when he remembers the picture of the Packard buried in the snow. Something about that picture. He gets the microfilm for December 1953, and returns to the viewer. There's not much to look at. Drifts of snow cover all of the car but the windows, roof, and part of the hood. He studies the grainy image, and is just about to rewind the role when he notices two silver wings sticking up through the snow. The hood ornament of the '51 Packard. Now he remembers. A silver Pegasus, or a bird of prey, wings raised close to one another, as if it were about to take off and soar. In the peripheral vision of his mind's eye, he glimpses the silver flashing in the sun, directly in front of him, as if it were a gun sight, and feels the steering wheel in his hands, the thick tuft of the upholstery in which his feet sink, and the strength of his father's hands. He tries to look directly at his father's face, but the silver flashing in the sun has already disappeared, and with it the feeling of the hands and the upholstery that nearly resurrected the dead. The picture that opened like a window has closed on a part of himself that brought with it a piece of his father. He stares at the grainy image for a while, wishing the past would come back. Finally he rewinds the microfilm.

He doesn't notice anything as he drives back to the lodge. A feeling like hot metal has flowed over him and cooled, containing him in its mold, holding him fast. His heart feels like lead, pulling him deep down inside. About a half mile before the turnoff to the lodge he slows to a crawl and scans the snow-filled ditch. A last glint of the dying sun on the snow, and he thinks he sees the wings. Then it's gone. Nothing but snow. There should at least be a marker. Here is where my father disappeared. Forever.

The car glides silently along the plowed driveway between walls of snow three feet high, the packed snow the plow left behind absorbing the sound of the tires. He moves in a dreamlike state: enters the lodge, slams the door shut, stomps his boots on the rug out of habit. The sound gives him a feeling of authority. He walks through the bar, the living room, the kitchen, looking for Fran, his boots striking the wood floors, breaking the somnolent silence. Then up the stairs and across the hall to Fran's room, his heavy footsteps punctuating every move.

He pounds on the door. No answer. He flings it open and finds Fran lying on his bed, his back propped up by a couple of pillows, asleep, mouth agape, a book lying on the bed under his right hand. Paul walks over to the side of the bed and looks down at Fran's head and the bald spot near the back that makes him look like a tonsured monk; he wants to give this melon a judo chop and split it wide open. Fran makes a snorting sound as he breathes. Paul slips the red, hardbound library book with frayed edges out from underneath his fingers and reads the title in the crepuscular light: *Flintlock and Paddle.* He opens to the title page and finds beneath the title the description, "A novel about eighteenth-century voyageurs in northern Minnesota." He leafs through the book, then tosses it on the bed. A boy's adventure book. How pathetic! Still reading this stuff. Well, he's had more adventures this afternoon at the library than anyone could want. He touches his brother's shoulder, then grasps it firmly in his fist, tugging and pulling at this person who has always given him so little.

"Fran, wake up. Goddamn it, wake up!" Fran tries to roll away. "Wake up, you fucking son of a bitch!" Paul yanks the shoulder back and forth, and finally Fran's eyes open, a startled look on his face. "What's the matter?" He tries to sit sideways so he can get out of bed, but Paul pushes him back and then straightens up, stands above him, and looks down, dominating him with his eyes and his anger while Fran looks up at him.

"I've been to the library. Read a lot of newspaper articles

today. All dated 1953 and '54. Those years mean anything to you?"

Fran looks disoriented and confused. He scans the room, as if his surroundings might somehow explain what's happening.

"Do you remember anything of any significance about that time? I mean, something that might even be of significance to me as well as to you?" Fran doesn't talk. "You insolent son of a bitch. Why didn't you tell me our father might've been murdered? Huh? And some woman by the name of Valery Night was fucking him? And Mother tried to commit suicide? And Stone's my brother, our brother! Why didn't you tell me about all that? Don't look at me with that fucking granite face. I want some answers. Now!"

Fran directs his gaze toward the wall in front of him, across the room, and folds his arms across his chest. "You didn't need to know."

"I didn't need to know? What the fuck are you talking about, I didn't need to know?"

"What you didn't know couldn't hurt you."

"Couldn't hurt me? It's hurt me all my life, you asshole! That's part of my life you kept secret from me." Paul stares at the head below him with the bald spot and feels again an almost uncontrollable urge to pound this melon with his fist. "Tell me what you know, Fran." The threatening tone of his voice must have seemed deadly, because Fran starts to talk.

"I don't know much more than what I told you yesterday."

"Was he murdered?"

"No."

"How do you know?"

"I just don't think he was."

"How else could he have disappeared?"

"Oh, there's a thousand ways a man can get lost in a blizzard. You can wander around for hours thinking you're going in a straight line and drop a hundred feet from where you started out. And if you'd had too much to drink, well ..."

"He drank a lot?"

Fran nods his head.

Paul slowly walks to the end of the bed and toward the wall at which Fran is looking and then turns to face him. Fran continues staring straight ahead without looking at anything, as if he were blind. The pale light entering the room from Paul's left hardly reaches the top of the bed, and Fran's face with its ashen skin is slowly merging with the shadow of the far wall.

"Why did the sheriff suspect foul play?"

"He didn't."

"Yes, he did!"

"That's not what I remember."

"What do you know about Valery Night?"

"Who?"

"You know who I mean. Valery Night, the woman our father was with the night he disappeared. The woman he was having an affair with."

"Oh, her."

"Yeah, her. How long had Mother known about her?"

"I have no idea."

"Did she know about her before he disappeared?"

"I couldn't tell you."

Paul pauses in front of the window that looks out on long black shadows and the snow-covered lake, then turns around and moves closer to the bed so he can see Fran's face in the twilight. "Did they fight a lot?"

"Who?"

"You know who."

"Not that I know of."

"You were living in the same house. How could you know so little?"

"I was only eleven. What do you expect?"

"I expect you had the same curiosity all kids have about their parents and you tried to understand them, that's what I expect."

"Guess I'm just not like other people."

"What about Stone? Why didn't someone tell me he was our brother?"

"Mom didn't want you to know."

"Why not?"

"I don't know. All I know is a few months after Dad disappeared, Stone moved out of the lodge. The next day she told us he was never to set foot in the lodge again. He could work down by the docks and help with the cabins, but that was it. And you didn't need to know he was our brother."

"Why do you think she did that to him?"

"I don't know."

"Thanks, Fran, you've helped a lot."

Paul tries to control his rage. He'd still like to smash his skull. Why did he conceal so much? Is he telling the truth now? He notices Fran has turned his gaze up toward him. His eyes seem to see him perfectly and fix him with that maniac glare.

"I can't tell you what I don't know. No one can. Get on with your life. There's nothing for you here. You don't belong here. You never did."

"Maybe not." Paul starts to pace slowly at the end of the bed. Fran follows him with his eyes.

"Leave."

Paul continues pacing. "And maybe what I should do is stop by Stone's place and talk with him. The other brother who doesn't belong here." Paul stops pacing, looks down at Fran, and says, "You can go back to sleep. Sorry I disturbed your rest."

Paul goes downstairs and calls Stone. No answer. He walks around behind the bar, pours himself a shot of the scotch he keeps there, and tosses half of it down. It burns; he flinches. He empties the shot. It has a warm, rich taste. He feels his muscles distend and his nerves relax. He pours himself another shot, leans back against the counter, and drinks, looking toward the windows. It can't be later than six, but it's almost dark outside. He takes the bottle into the living room and sits down on the couch Fran sat on the night before. He tries to recall the conversation with Fran, but there's too much emotion and his brain can't stay on track. Maybe it's the whiskey. He takes another sip. It mainlines to his brain. He feels a little woozy; he hasn't eaten since breakfast. He could get up and fix something to eat, but that takes too much effort. He pours himself another shot.

Later he's awakened by a phone ringing. It rings again and again. He wonders why a phone is ringing in his room. His eyes seek among the dark forms that surround him his desk and chest of drawers. He starts to panic; he's not in his room. The phone rings again. Someone is shuffling in stocking feet down stairs on the other side of a wall. His head hurting, he tries not to breathe, lies perfectly still as a black form in the darkness, not bothering to turn on any lights, walks around dark forms—the arm chair and the couch in front of the fireplace. The phone rings again. Fran's dark form, surrounded by a pale blue aura from the luminescent beer sign, passes through the entry to the barroom.

As Paul tries to understand why he's lying on the couch and what time it could possibly be, he hears whispering on the other side of the wall and wonders if he isn't dreaming. He lies still, afraid to move and draw attention to himself, while trying to decipher the words murmured in a hushed, anxious, or angry voice: "No (or was it "know"?) ... old newspapers ... way too young! ... Stone ... no (know?) ... no (know?) ... dead ... too long ... no idea ... Swenson ... Stone... no (know?) ... Mother ... gone ... Mother ... new (knew?) ... suicide ... Why? ... no (know?) ... secret ... nothing ... yeah ... good-bye." Paul hears the click of the receiver placed back on the phone. Then nothing.

He tries to breathe as quietly as possible, while questions clamor in his brain: Who was Fran talking to? Who would call at this time of night or morning? What time was it? Eleven? Three? Why was Fran whispering? Finally Paul hears the creaking of floorboards as Fran passes through the entry, shuffles past the couch and chair, climbs the stairs, and walks to his room.

Paul listens to the blood throb in his head until he's sure Fran's in bed, then, shoes in hand, tiptoes upstairs to his room. He feels so relieved when he finally shuts the door. He turns on the reading light next to his bed and checks his watch: 12:20. Who would call Fran at this time? It wasn't Stone, because Fran and the person at the other end of the line seemed to be talking about Stone. It was someone who knew Stone and who was concerned about what someone knew. He wonders if Fran and the other person were talking about him.

12

"I'VE LEARNED WE'RE BROTHERS." PAUL STUDIES Stone's face, looking for a response. He hears Jason's claws on the bare wood floor of Stone's shack as the dog walks around the table and curls up in front of the potbellied stove. A green log hisses in the fire.

Stone continues looking straight at Paul, still smiling. He leans back in his chair, runs his fingers through a long lock of oily wolf-gray hair drooping over his right eye, then leans forward, his elbows resting on the table. "Actually, we're cousins, not brothers."

"No, we're brothers. We're cousins too, but we're also brothers."

"Who told you?" Stone snorts. "Shit. I don't know why I ask, 'cause the only person who could've told you is Fran."

"Wrong. Fran didn't tell me. One thing Fran does really well is keep a secret. No, I read it in the papers."

"The papers?"

"Yeah. The *Mirer Times*. It's public knowledge. I didn't know it, but everyone else did—at least, thirty-five years ago they did."

Stone shrugs, still smiling. "So, my aunt and uncle adopted me. Is there something wrong with that?"

"No, but I find it strange neither you nor anyone else ever told me."

Stone slowly shakes his head. "Maybe it just slipped our minds."

"My mother threw you out. Then she told Fran and Christine never to tell me you were my adopted brother."

"You didn't get that out of the papers."

"No, that's one thing Fran did tell me. After I'd found out you're my brother. So, why'd she throw you out? And why the secret?"

"That's a long story."

"I've got time."

"It'd take a lot longer than you think."

"Test me."

Stone nods his head. "Okay. Your mother and I ... Well, she did a lot for me." Stone leans back in his chair and gazes up toward the ceiling. "She took care of me at a time when I felt so goddamn alone. So ..." He slowly shakes his head, takes a deep breath, and continues. "When my mother died ... Until then I'd been just as happy as a tadpole in a pond." Stone smiles. "I was her sunshine. Her precious this and that. She used to call me her little diamond, her little jewel, because she got me instead of a ring from the asshole who fathered me. She made the sun shine on my little pond. When she died, the sun died too. And I was a scared little kid lost in the night."

Paul sees all the sadness of Stone's loss on his face, and all he can say is, "I'm sorry."

Stone looks at him and smiles. "It happened a long time ago." He leans forward and adds, "But if it hadn't been for Joyce ..." He shakes his head.

"What about her?"

"That was a hard time. Grandpa and Grandma were

already gone." He falls silent, remembering that time, and then continues. "You really missed out, Paulie. They were great people. Big-hearted people. Everything about 'em was big. He was just huge—tall, big shoulders, big hands. A real pioneer. He used to tell about coming here at a time when there was nothing, not a goddamn thing, and how he got that land down by the lake for a prayer and built the first cabin himself. Had to get it done before winter so he and Grandma could live in it." Stone pauses, remembering. "He had a big voice. It just boomed through the lodge, rattling the windows like it was the voice of God ..."

"Rattling the windows? Come on!"

Stone chuckles. "No, I'm serious. Should've heard him. I can still remember him at the dinner table, reciting a string of Our Fathers, Hail Marys, and Glory Be's like they were all one long prayer, and his voice would just rattle the whole lodge, and we'd sit there—my mom and me, Grandma, Art, Bill, Joyce—all of us, with our heads bowed, and we'd join in, but the only voice you ever heard was his. You could feel the muscle in his voice. He was ..." Stone shakes his head. "He was as tough as old shoe leather. And she was just as soft as soft could be. And warm as the oven she baked in. She had these huge"—he holds his hands cupped in front of his chest—"like loaves of bread dough rising on her chest. She'd pick me up, and hug me, and smother my face in those loaves, soft like they'd been rubbed with flour, and they'd smell so good I'd wanna take a bite."

Paul laughs. He tries to remember. Was there a picture of her with those loaves, with her big-hearted pioneer, in that box of photos he found in Mother's room?

Stone chuckles. "She would've whacked my fuckin' head off if I'd tried, but I was tempted." His smile fades. "There was a time ... there was a time when we were a happy family."

Paul nods his head. Takes a sip of coffee. It's cold. He

pushes his cup to the side. "I always seem to arrive after the good times are over. Terrible case of bad timing."

"Bad timing? Hmm. How about getting caught in a whiteout five miles from home. Now that's bad timing."

"Or getting caught on the same road in a whiteout thirteen years later."

Stone nods his head. "I guess dying always comes at a bad time. Wasn't a good time for my mom to die, with an eight-year-old kid. Or for Art, his whole life ahead of him. The war put a lot of people in the wrong place at the wrong time."

"Art?"

"Uncle Art."

"Oh, yeah. Killed in Normandy."

Stone nods. "My mother's other brother. A real nut. Kind of guy who'd do anything to make a kid laugh. Walk into a door and fall on his ass, just to see how you'd react. Had to go get himself killed." Stone shakes his head. "Then it was just Bill, Joyce, and me."

"So you must've gotten to know them really well."

Stone picks up his cup, sees it's empty. "Shit! Want some more coffee?"

Paul shakes his head no.

"I'm making some fresh."

"Okay."

Stone shuffles in his stocking feet over to the stove and back and forth between the stove and adjacent sink as he rinses out and fills the pot and sets it on the stove to boil. He stares out the window above the sink. After a few minutes he says, "You know, the shack's so close to the river, you could've just skied down here." He laughs and adds, "Shit, in the winter, with all the ice and snow, that river's the best road around."

Paul wonders why he didn't ski from the lodge to the shack. And in the next breath he smells the same odor he smelled the second he opened the door to the shack: the smell of food cooked and eaten, of bacon grease and fried potatoes, of game and fish, of oil, vinegar, and butter that impregnates the walls and permeates the air. Unforgettable, this warm, fetid odor that makes him think of entrails and bowels, of a man living alone in the smell of his own body, with little to look forward to other than preparing the next meal or going to bed at night. The second he opened the door, that odor hit him in the gut and evoked his entire memory of the shack whole and intact.

Water steams out of the coffee pot and hisses on the burner. Stone lifts the pot off the fire, lowers the flame, and puts the pot back on to percolate.

Paul finally says, "I guess I just got too busy."

Stone snorts a laugh of contempt. He turns around to face Paul and leans against the sink. "I'll probably end up like the old guy who lived here all alone before me. One day the mailman came in and found him frozen stiff. I ever tell you about that?"

"A million times."

Stone snorts another laugh. "Yeah, I bet I did." He reflects, then continues. "You know, that ol' guy teaches me humility. Anytime I start hopin' for really big things, I think, I'm already sleeping in a dead man's bed, and before long someone's gonna find me frozen, haul me out like a big ol' log, throw me in the rear end of a pickup, and that's that. Kindling for the devil. You sleep in a dead man's bed, gives you a different look on life."

"Yeah. I'm sure we can learn a lot from the dead."

"You wanna hear about the ol' boy's 30 Ot 6?"

"I've already heard—"

"You wanna see it?" Stone arches his eyebrows and feigns excitement. "I can get it for you. Got it right here in the closet." He nods his head in the direction of the bedroom door on Paul's right.

"No, that's okay. I'm not interested in looking at guns. I came here to talk about something else."

Stone turns off the burner, carries the pot over to the table, pours the coffee, sets the pot on the table, on the newspaper he was reading when Paul interrupted his breakfast, and sits down. He nods at the newspaper, opened to the comic strips on one page and an ad for women's lingerie on the other. "There's my entertainment for the day."

Paul forces a smile.

After a while Stone says, "You're not going to let go of this thing, are you?"

"No. I'm not."

"You oughta."

"It's natural to want to understand the people who made you."

"Shit, I never knew my father, and from what I learned about him, I'm not any the worse for it."

"Sure about that?"

Stone snaps, "Yeah, I'm sure. The guy was an asshole. No reason to miss an asshole, right?" His face breaks into a grin. "Plenty of 'em left. Got one of my own. And you only need one."

Paul stares at him.

"Okay, you won't let go. So here it is, the little I can tell you about your ol' man. And I mean little, because it was impossible to get to know him. He had a great disappearing act. Not the kind my ol' man had—you know, running off with another woman. Bill disappeared all the time ... somewhere in his head."

Stone falls silent. He stares off into space, his jaw set, and taps the rim of his mug with his fingernail. Finally he begins talking again.

"I remember going out fishing for walleye at night. I'd get done filleting, and I'd be walking from the fish house to the lodge ... and all of a sudden through the screen, I'd see a red glow in the dark. He'd sit in there by himself, at the table near the end of the bar. I'd go in, let the screen door shut real slow, walk by him on my way to the kitchen. Sometimes he'd ask me what I'd caught. Other times he wouldn't say a fucking word. Just kept on smokin', sittin' in the dark, like I wasn't there." Stone shakes his head. "I didn't wanna say anything 'cause ... I don't know. It was like I was supposed to pretend I didn't exist. Or he didn't exist."

"Why do you think—"

"He'd just fucking ignore you—ignore you so much you felt like you weren't real." Stone falls silent again.

Paul watches him stare off into space, a sullen look on his face. "Tell me more."

"Tell you more? You like to make people suffer?" Stone returns Paul's stare. "You're kind of an asshole yourself, aren't you?"

"I just want the truth."

"The truth? The truth is, your father was an asshole."

"Go on."

"Just like my father was an asshole. He might've loved Joyce at one time, but by the time I was in high school, he was humpin' all the girls who worked at the lodge. Young girls, college kids, high school kids. Some of 'em were still babysitting. Shit, a couple of 'em might still've been playing with dolls. They'd be there for a while, a month or two, everything just fine, then all of a sudden they'd be gone."

"How do you know he was having sex with them?"

Stone laughs. "Let's see, maybe it was the way he'd put his hand on a girl's ass, and she'd just let him do it. Or come up behind her and put his hands on her tits. That's kind of a dead giveaway, don't you think?" Stone stops to sip some coffee, peering over the rim of his mug at Paul.

"He liked playing with fire."

Stone nods his head and smiles. "Yeah. One summer he got a girl pregnant. Had to pay for the abortion. I remember him saying to me one night, when he was sitting in the dark, and I was just tiptoeing by—he said, 'Women are nothing but fly paper. Land for a second and you're stuck, stuck 'til you die.'" Stone sips his coffee again. "She knew about it, you know."

"Who knew about what?"

"Joyce. She knew about the abortion. The sad thing is, she never stopped loving him. Never. Not even later, when ..." Stone falls silent.

"When? When what?"

Stone picks up the knife off his egg-smeared plate and traces the outline of a model's figure in an illustration for lingerie, leaving streaks of grease and egg yolk on the newspaper.

"When he had the affair with Valery Night?"

Stone looks at him, startled. "You're pretty good at finding things out."

"One of the things I do to make a living." Paul studies Stone's face, refusing to let go. "She knew about that too?"

Stone tosses the knife on the newspaper and nods. "Everyone did. The two of 'em would meet in town at the bars. Or he'd go to her place. Neighbors would see 'em. People talked."

"What did my mother do about it?"

"Nothin'."

"Nothing?"

"Sometimes I think he did it just to hurt her. Every so often, on a weekday night, Valery would go out to the lodge, when there weren't a lot of people. Kind of late. Joyce would be upstairs with you, and Fran, and Christine. I'd be the only one downstairs. She'd have a drink at the bar with him and leave. Then he'd close, and a few minutes later he'd be gone. I knew sooner or later Joyce would come down and find her. And she did. The first time she didn't know who Valery was and didn't catch on to what was happening, but the second time she did, and with all the screaming and crying it sounded like a slaughter house. The kids came running downstairs, scared out of their minds. Joyce was hitting Valery and trying to pull her hair out, at least until Bill grabbed her hands. Then she attacked him, and Valery got away."

"Jesus. I have no memory of this at all."

"You were only about three, so why would you?" Stone finishes his coffee and looks past Paul at Jason still lying down in front of the wood stove. Jason raises his head off his paws and gazes at Stone, thumping his tail against the floor.

"What the fuck do you want, dog?"

Jason jumps up as if on cue, runs around Paul's chair, and nuzzles Stone's thigh. Stone pushes his chair back, and Jason leaps up, puts his front paws on Stone's lap, and lays his head on his paws. Stone slowly and rhythmically scratches his neck.

Paul says, "I get the feeling, reading the newspaper articles, that Valery was run out of town."

"Getting your windows shot out and your tires slashed might make you feel like getting out of town. Above all if the sheriff lets you know he can't protect you."

"I wonder if I could find her."

A boyish grin spreads across Stone's face as he leans back and digs his fingers into the dog's fur. After massaging Jason's skin, Stone puts his arms around the dog's neck, pulls him up, hugs him, then pushes him away. "You whore." Jason jumps back toward his lap, Stone pushes him away again, and the two repeat this game several times before Stone allows Jason to rest his paws and head on his lap again. "Always come back for more, don't you?"

Paul smiles as he watches Stone play with Jason. He would have liked to have had a dog when he was a boy, but his mother wouldn't allow it, so he played with the Jason that Stone had at the time. There were other things he did without that were a whole lot more important than a dog.

"I was thinking the other day about when I was a boy. I used to have these daydreams about … about the parents I would have liked to've had. Teachers, doctors, parents of friends. I'd match them in happy couples; they all loved me. They never talked or moved, they just smiled, like wax figures in a diorama depicting some family scene."

Stone stops stroking Jason's fur and stares at him. "Jesus! You're even nuttier than your brother, and that's sayin' something."

"I've never told anyone that before."

"If I was you, I'd never tell anyone again."

"I need help."

"You need the kind of help I can't give."

"No, I need exactly the kind of help you can give. I've spent my whole life finding ways to ignore and forget the parents I had. Now I need help finding them. Finding the real people."

"I don't understand all this, Paulie. You're just too smart for me."

"Don't play dumb."

"There's a reason people call me Stone."

"Which is?"

"A stone always sinks to the bottom."

"Who gave you that name?"

"Pretty much the whole third grade."

"That was a shitty thing to do."

"Yeah, I thought so too. At least until Joyce taught me to like the name."

"Come again?"

"You remember those cigar boxes she saved for special things?"

"No. Wait. Yeah, I do."

"Well, one day she gave me one of those boxes and told

me to open it. I found … here, let me show you."

Stone pushes Jason away, walks around Paul's chair, past the wood stove, and disappears in the bedroom; he returns with a cigar box, sits down, and opens it.

"I found a white stone with pink colored rings." Stone takes the rock out of the box for Paul to see. "She said, 'A stone can be beautiful to look at,' and she smiled this beautiful smile. I picked up a flat grayish black stone, polished real smooth by waves." Stone takes the rock out of the box. "She said, 'A stone can feel good.' The rock felt almost as good as her smile. I picked up a lump of crystal"—he shows Paul the rock—"and she said, 'A stone like that can shine if you put it in the light.' She kissed me on the forehead, and I felt like … like she was shining her light on me."

"So, if my mother cared so much about you, why did she throw you out and tell Fran and Christine never to tell me you were my brother?"

Stone gets up from the table and scoops up the plate and mugs. "That, Paulie, is a very long story. It'll have to wait until another time."

Paul's eyes follow him as he carries the dishes to the sink. "You're cheating me!"

Stone spins around and confronts him. "You're cheating me. You ask all the questions, and you tell me nothing, nothing but bullshit, about what you're doing here. Why didn't you go back to gay Paree," he sneers, "where you belong? 'Cause you sure as fuck don't belong here."

"I need your help."

"I got other things to do than sit around and talk all day."

"Like what?"

Stone pushes his boots away from the wall with his toe, slips his feet into the boots, and bends to one knee. "Gotta go into town."

"Really? Busy schedule? Things to do, people to see?

What bullshit!"

Stone shuffles and bends the other knee so he can tie the other boot.

"Come on, Stone, let's sit down and finish talking."

"I have finished talking."

Paul watches him for a few seconds, shakes his head, mumbles, "Shit!," angry he'll not find out what happened between his mother and Stone. He puts on his boots, grabs his jacket, and follows Stone out the door.

Almost blinded by the sun's reflection on the snow, Paul stops, covers his eyes, and blinks until the blue dots disappear. Stone, who has also stopped, gazes at the limbs of the red pines with their green needles; the brilliant snow carpet strewn across rocks, downed trees, and flattened grass; and the path that leads past a chopping block, with honey-colored wood chips strewn about, a stack of logs, and an old shed, down to the Kawishiwi.

"I've lived most of my life next to that river."

Paul follows Stone's gaze in the direction of the river, wondering why he's stopping to look at it now.

Stone continues talking, as if to no one in particular. "People tend to think of this wilderness as huge, but if you've grown up around here, it's not really so big. You go down the river; it circles back. You go from one lake to another and somehow end up where you began. In the winter, the shack closes in on you, till it smells just like you. It could be you. The snow melts, the ice breaks up. You look up and see the sky, you look around at the shore, the rocks, the trees, and then you look in the water and see everything all over again. Like it's closing in on you. It's so damn still, so quiet, you can hear your own thoughts just as clear as if someone was saying 'em out loud. You're so alone, you may as well be dead. You get to a place where you're okay with never coming back, never knowing people again."

Paul, baffled, looks at Stone and then again at the river.

Stone continues. "That used to scare the shit out of me, when I'd get that feeling. Now, I'm there. Ready."

"Ready for what?"

Stone looks Paul up and down, and shakes his head. "You better get your ass out of here. Get out while the gettin's good."

"What do you mean?"

"Paulie, don't mess with this shit. It's more than you ever dreamed."

The phone is ringing when Paul walks through the front door of the lodge. He rushes to the counter to answer before the ringing stops. A woman's voice—a voice whose edge has been softened by time—asks for him. She introduces herself as Ruth, his mother's friend whom he met at the wake. Yes, he remembers her very well. Her own health has suffered lately. He's sorry to hear that. She came across a letter Joyce had written last October and thought he should have it. Now that she knows he's still at the lodge she'll send it to him right away. Why? The letter will make it clear. She hopes he's well, wishes him good luck, says goodbye, and hangs up. Paul, wondering what the letter could possibly be about, holds the receiver until it starts to beep, then hangs up as well.

A few days pass.

Fran is always gone somewhere or on his way out by the time Paul gets up in the morning, and he never tells Paul where he's going. Things have been that way since Paul confronted him in his bedroom. So Paul takes his breakfasts alone. He stands in front of the window, drinking his coffee, staring at the world outside. A couple of sparrows peck at the bread crumbs he leaves on the tree stump in front of the window; a squirrel, upside down, pauses halfway down a tree trunk as it descends to search for food; and much further off, down by the marsh surrounding the Black Hole, deer forage for the tall grass that lies beneath the snow, stopping frequently to raise their heads and smell for danger. After breakfast he sits at his desk, staring at the frozen lake that lies beneath him like a white mirror, trying to think of a way to go forward. He can sit like that for hours, trying to find a way, and ending up mesmerized by the light on the mirror, his mind blank.

If his brother returns while he's downstairs in the kitchen or the bar or the dining room, Fran steps deftly around him with an economy of movement that minimizes the time they spend together. At lunch Fran might open a can of tuna fish, boil water for ramen soup, eat, and leave without uttering anything more than monosyllabic responses to Paul's greetings, comments, and questions. Dinners, when they happen to eat at the same time, are equally silent, brief, and tense. Paul thinks of returning to Paris, but that's just what Fran wants, so he stays.

Four days after Ruth's call, Paul receives an envelope with a French stamp and Claire's handwriting. The envelope is covered with a mess of lines and arrows, a handwritten "Not Here!," a "RETURN TO SENDER" stamped on and then crossed out with a ballpoint pen. His correct address is printed above this mess. The envelope had gone though quite a labyrinth to reach him. Inside he finds a card with a picture on it, a reproduction of Botticelli's *Virgin and Child with the Young St. John the Baptist*, from the Louvre. The Virgin looks down at the child who, while looking up at her, appears to reach for her face with his eyes and her neck with his right hand. Paul opens the card and reads Claire's note. She misses him and wishes she could be with him for Christmas. He looks at the envelope; she mailed the card before she decided to drop everything and fly to Minnesota for Christmas. He returns to her note.

> *It's the strangest thing: I find myself lingering over every Madonna and Child I see, whether at a museum, in a book, or on a card. I wonder why?* (Paul smiles, imagining her smiling as she writes this.) *Yesterday, when I should've been working on my book, I found myself instead thinking about you and wanting you (this is not uncommon!), and wanting a baby with you. I remembered how moved you were by this painting when we saw it together at the Louvre, and I knew we had a card with a reproduction somewhere, but I couldn't find it. Then last night I dreamed you and I were in bed together, and between us lay a beautiful baby boy, who looked just like Botticelli's infant. I woke up and immediately found the card in a desk drawer where I'd put it one day to try to put my desire for you out of my mind so I could work. And now it's going to be harder than ever for me to wait until you come back. I have more time now that classes are over. I miss you so much. Please come back soon.*
>
> *Love,*
> *Claire*

Paul remembers when she visited at Christmas she asked him if he'd received her card yet; when he said no, she refused to tell him what was in it, teasing him with the different sexual proposals she might've made. As he rereads her note, he tries to remember when they might've seen the painting together at the Louvre. Finally it comes to him. Last winter sometime. A day they'd taken off—their own holiday. They would pretend they were tourists and wander through the Louvre. He remembers how Claire, gazing at the painting, leaned back against him; she trusted him completely to hold her up. And while he was holding her and looking at the painting, he remembered the picture and wedding invitation he'd received a few days earlier from his mother, and thinking he'd never want to make a family, not even with Claire. Now that thought seems so rigid, so unforgiving.

He's about to put the card away, when he notices the adolescent Saint John the Baptist. He looks like an intruder, in the corner of the painting, staring at the spectators as if they'd caught him in the act of spying on the Virgin and the infant Jesus. He doesn't belong. The figure wasn't even painted by Botticelli. He disturbs this perfect couple.

The next day a six-by-eight-inch manila envelope arrives. He opens it and finds a letter folded and attached to a white envelope with a paper clip. He unfolds the letter, written with a blue ballpoint pen on three small sheets of ruled stationery. He recognizes his mother's handwriting, with its loops and flourishes, an occasional hitch here and there where her hand must have had trouble controlling the pen, and lines that were lighter or darker, thinner or wider, depending on the pressure exerted by that hand.

> *October 20, 1989*
> *Dear Ruth,*
>
> *I've been laying here all day just remembering.*
> *So many memories. They're all aglow now,*
> *and they're lighting up more memories, like so*
> *many rooms in a big house where I can wander*
> *about as much as I like. I'm not getting out*

of bed anymore, so the only walking I do is in my head. The doctor's got me taking so many pills right now I feel like I've always just had a drink and it's given me a little bit of a buzz. Maybe that's why Bill liked his whiskey so much. Did I tell you the doctor said if he were in my condition he'd get a case of scotch and go to his cabin and drink 'til the end? Well, I'm already in a place just as good as a cabin, and these pills sure are a lot better than whiskey. I have bad memories of that stuff.

I've dreamed a couple three times about walking around in that big house. There's so much sunshine and stillness in all the rooms. It's real strange. I never see anyone there. Just rooms that look like different rooms I've known. But I remember lots of things when I go into a room. The hall is very long. There must be at least ten rooms that open onto the hall. And at the very end, instead of a wall, all I see is sunshine and the lake. And every time I enter the hall, I start walking toward the sunshine and the lake. I never get there though before I wake up. Maybe I have to die to get there.

Listen to me chatter away like an old ninny and forget to tell you why I'm writing. I'm sending a letter for Paul. Please give it to him sometime after I'm gone. But wait a few months. And give it to him only if he stays on here instead of going back to France. I hurt him so much when he was growing up, I don't want to open any old wounds unless it's for a reason. I can't explain why you should do what I want, just please do it.

*Goodbye, Ruthie. You've been more than a
friend to me, more than a sister. I'll have you
with me in my heart to the very end.*

With every bit of my love,
Joyce

Paul tore open the white envelope and found a short
letter, not even two pages long, on the same stationery as
the first, and dated October 18, 1989.

Dear Paul,

*You must have been puzzled by the wedding
invitation and picture I sent you at Christmas.
I didn't know when you were coming home
again, if ever. I know you don't like returning
home. You'd just as soon forget us all. I can't
blame you. I sent you those things because we
can't talk to one another. That's my fault. But
I want you to know that once there was a lot
of love in this family. Something happened to
it. I can't explain what. It's too hard. It would
take more time than I have left. I know you
got hurt. And I know you still hurt. Your pain
hurts me. I want to talk to you, I want to tell
you my story, so you'll understand and maybe
you'll hurt less. The cigar lady has the key to
the story. By the time you remember her, you'll
be ready to read my story. And your father's.*

*I want you to know, Paul, that I love you
and I have always loved you, even though
it might not have seemed that way. There's
nothing I want more than to be able to tell you*

*to your face that I love you, and to hear you
tell me that you love me too, but that's more
than I have a right to expect.*

Goodbye,
Mother

He stares at the letter for several minutes, seeing only
the words, "I love you and I have always loved you." Tears
soothe his burning eyes and cheeks. Why couldn't she have
just told him that when she was alive? He rereads the first
sentence. "You must have been puzzled by the invitation
and picture I sent you at Christmas." Puzzled? No, dumb-
founded—at receiving something so bizarre. As bizarre as
this letter. And the way it was delivered.

He rereads the letter from his mother to Ruth. "I'm
sending a letter for Paul. Please give it to him sometime
after I'm gone. But wait a few months. And give it to him
only if he stays on here instead of going back to France."
She toyed with him. As if he were a character in a book
and she was the author. She knew the picture and invitation she sent in lieu of a Christmas card would raise questions he couldn't ignore or forget. She knew Ruth would do
what she wanted her to do—talk to him at the wake and
tell him enough to pique his curiosity about his past. And
then this letter that Ruth was to give him only if he stayed
at the lodge instead of returning to France. A master of
manipulation. You've played me like a yo-yo. You might
be dead, but you knew which strings to pluck to make us
dance, which threads to weave to plot our destiny—even
after you're gone. Your sense of timing is impeccable. The
cigar lady has the key, and by the time I remember her,
I'll be ready to read the story. And who in the hell is the
cigar lady?

He's ready to pack it all up and leave. But that would make too many people happy. He walks around behind the bar and pours himself a double shot of scotch. A while later, after staring at the two letters spread out on the bar, he pours himself a second glass, then carries the bottle, the glass, and the letters upstairs to his room. He sits down at his desk and stares at the frozen lake. And stares. Concealed beneath the snow, frozen in the ice years ago, are dreams, desires that never took wing, never flew. Never tried. Or waited, until it was too late, and the wings could not tear themselves away from the encroaching ice. He can see the effort to fly in the gray striations layered upon one another in the transparent ice. Voices, that barely separate themselves from the silence, from the absolute whiteness of snow, whisper to him of flights not made, journeys never taken, words never said. Then a little girl with long blond curls appears, as if out of a trap door in a stage, and walks upon the ice, carrying a parasol. The sun's burning red fingers splayed across the snow. She has an impish grin on her face, and as she twirls her parasol, she says, in a singsong, teasing voice, "The cigar lady has the key."

13

PAUL LIES IN BED, STARING AT THE CEILING. ALL
night he has labored to find the cigar lady. Then, click. He
rolls over onto his stomach and, still half asleep, reaches
under the bed, lifts a loose floor board, and pulls out an
old cigar box, the word "Corona," surrounded by a pattern
of gold leaves, on the cover. On the inside of the cover, a
cameo portrait of Queen Isabelle of Spain, in semi-profile,
her black hair in curls that fall to her neck, blue across
her eyelids, dark eyes, pale skin, and bright red lips. He
smiles: he has found the "cigar lady." And a mess of objects
inside. String that feels as fine as flax. Popsicle sticks. A
dried black feather. A small white stone polished smooth by
waves. A red devil lure, its hooks a dull silver spotted with
rust. The entire jaw of a walleye or a northern pike with
all of its teeth. A tangle of black fishing line. A tarnished
silver pocket watch, the glass face cracked. Pennies. Three
of them. And a key.

Lying on his belly, staring down at the key, he tries to
think of what it might open, and finally gives up and sets

it aside. He fingers the other objects, all of them vaguely familiar, as if their surface and texture contained inscriptions from another era. He places them in the box, rolls over on his back, and closes his eyes. His thoughts lead him to his threshold of remembered time, when there were open cigar boxes displayed on a shelf behind the bar and men would sit long afternoons smoking their cigars while they drank and told stories. Gray clouds of smoke would hover a few feet above the floor. If Paul got too close to the smoke, it burned his nostrils. He'd look up at leather faces, pockmarked faces, ruddy faces, beards and stubble, grinning and gaping mouths with black gaps where there had once been teeth, and stagger backward into his mother's legs that he would touch to reassure himself of her presence, and the men—the old farts, not so old then—would laugh like thunder. And then in no time he'd be running around like a windup toy, flying with his wings extended, orbiting around his mother, touching her legs again when he came near. A man—unclear, his father, perhaps—stood behind the bar, looking down on all of this.

Paul used the cigar box for his treasures, hiding it under his bed, beneath the loose plank, for several years. And then he forgot about it, until he read her letter. "The cigar lady has the key to the story. By the time you remember her, you'll be ready to read my story. And your father's." The key started to turn in his memory. He's ready. He fingers the key, trying to ... and then he remembers.

He inserts the key in the bottom left drawer of the desk. It turns easily in the lock. He discovers two bundles of letters, each about three or four inches thick and wrapped with a rubber band. Dry as parchment, the letters feel as if they might tear with each fold he opens. He immediately recognizes his mother's handwriting in the first letter.

September 5, 1938
Dear Bill,

*Today is Labor Day, and in just two days I
start school. I really dont want to go back,
but I guess there's not much I can do about
it. Thats the trouble with being seventeen. You
always have to do what someone else wants.*

*Right now I would like to be canoeing with
you. We sure didn't have much time! You took
almost two weeks to ask me to go for a ride. I
guess you thought I might say no. And I kept
on wondering when were you going to talk to
me! Finally you did. Boy, you sure know how
to canoe well. And you know all the best places
to go too. Maybe next summer my aunt and
uncle will want to go back and take me along
again. I sure hope so! I had so much fun this
summer.*

*Well, your going back to the U in just a
couple weeks. I bet there are alot of gals who
will be happy about that. I can just hear them
talking about what a good looker you are.
Dont forget to study! And maybe you can even
write a letter to me. I bet you write real good
letters. I'll be expecting one.*

Yours truly,
Joyce

. . .

Saturday, September 17
Dear Joyce.

I didn't think I'd get a letter from you. Im sorry
I didn't answer sooner. It arrived after I left for
the U, so Mom had to send it to me. Like I told
you this summer, I've got a football scholarship.
I guess I forgot to tell you football players have
to come three weeks before school starts. I
play defense, and all day we've been hitting
and tackling, and roasting in the hot sun, its
enough to make you sick. Im not sure Im good
enough to be on this team. Mom and Dad say
I must be, because why else would the U give
me a football scholarship? Another week until
classes start. Im hoping some of the guys Ive
met will be in class with me too. Ive heard the
U is real big. Mom and Dad say everything will
work out and not to worry. Im sure there right.

By now you've started school. From what
you told me this summer, you cant wait to get
out on your own. Wow! Your very brave.

Well its already supper time, and then
another team meeting. Thanks again for the
letter.

Yours truly,
Bill

P.S. If you want to write, my address at the
U is Pioneer Hall, University of Minnesota,
Minneapolis, Minnesota.

Paul looks for Joyce's response to this letter; finding
none, he continues reading.

November 26, 1938
Dear Joyce,

Im sorry I haven't written sooner. Ive been so busy with classes and football. I felt like I was drowning under the work, running a race and never getting caught up. But now, with football over, its getting easier. We had a winning season, and I got to play alot, so football turned out good. I had exams in all my classes. I didnt do great, but good enough to keep my football scholarship for next year. I have a lot to learn, but Im liking it here. Now that football's over, Im having a swell time.

Its been fun listening to some of the professors lecture. They're really good at it. No one at Mirer ever even talked about lecturing. They just talked. We have been reading a lot of poems in English. Mostly love poems. Id already memorized one in high school that we read, and that kind of helped. It's called "Let us not to the marriage of true minds admit impediments." That's not really the title, but a lot of these poems don't have titles so people just call them by their first lines. It seems as if these poets just spent their lives writing poems to women. Must be swell to have so much time, don't you think? I guess they didn't have to worry about making money. You kind of wonder why they didn't just talk to them. But I guess if they did they wouldn't need to write the poems.

I also have Math and Chemistry and French. They're real hard. I promised myself I wouldn't even think about them over the vacation. I sure am glad I don't have to take any more math or science after this year. And French, why study a language if you know you're probably never going to leave the good old US of A? May as well study Latin.

My other courses are History and Philosophy. They both deal with Greece. We have been studying the wars between Athens and Sparta in history and weve been reading Plato in philosophy. Plato wrote long conversations called dialogues, with one person named Socrates in all of them. Socrates always seems to find a way to win the arguments he gets into. He's a clever guy. A lot more clever than anyone else. Its fun to see how he does it.

We were told that some time next year were supposed to decide what we want to major in. I think Id like to major in English or Philosophy, but I can't decide which. I like reading. Everyone in my family reads a lot. And Im not good at science or math. So the choice isnt too hard. But I dont know why Im here. Its fun, but I dont know how I can use what Im learning. I guess I'll just have to wait and see. I have a year to decide.

Gee, I just realized how much Im talking about myself. Ive been going on and on. You must think Im interested only in myself. I sure hope everything is going well for you. I bet your looking forward to graduation at the end of this year. I sure was happy to leave high school. I dont understand people who dont want to. Maybe you can come to the resort again this coming summer. That would be

*swell. We could do a lot more canoeing and
explore some real interesting places I know. We
should be able to go much further than we did
last summer. Well, let me know if your gonna
come back next summer.*

Yours truly,
Bill

• • •

Friday, December 2
Dear Bill,

*What a wonderful surprise awaited me when
I walked in the door today! A letter from you.
Mother put it on the dining room table all
by itself where she knew I would see it right
away. I couldn't stop myself from running to it
like it was a long lost friend. There could be
no denying it—it was my name and address
in your handwriting! Id almost given up on
getting a letter from you ever again, and here
it was, finally. I knew there must've been a
very good reason for you not writing so long,
and now that I know how hard it is for you
to stay caught up at college with everything
you have to do I feel embarrassed about even
wondering why you weren't writing. And Im
embarrassed about telling you all this. I hope
you don't think less of me. Please don't think
I'm a fool. Or worse. I almost feel sick.*

*There. I laid down on my bed for a while
and feel much better now. Are you going
home for Christmas? I bet the lodge is really*

beautiful at Christmas time. All those big pine trees standing so tall in the snow. And the lake must be all frozen over. I have a picture of you in my head skating on the lake. Its like a Christmas card. I love Christmas. Everyone is always so happy. The house is warm as toast with all the baking and it smells so good.

We had a heavy snowfall last night and this morning our farm looked like a winter wonderland. Even the old shed where we keep the tractor looks beautiful with a thick heavy blanket of snow hanging from the eves and nearly touching the white drifts. Beyond the shed is an open space that was a field of alfalfa last summer, but now it's all white. I've never seen the ocean, but when I look out at a field like this, I have the feeling that I'm looking at the ocean, a very special ocean. One that is always still and calm. It makes me feel peaceful and calm inside.

Oh, I almost forgot to tell you. I asked my mother if she'd heard anything from my aunt and uncle about them going back to the resort this coming summer and she said no. But I think they might want to because my uncle caught a lot of fish, and that's all he wants to do. If I go with them on vacation we can be together for fourteen days. I can hardly believe it! Fourteen days! Just think of how much time that is! I cant let myself think about it anymore. It might bring bad luck. No, I wont think about it. But as soon as I start thinking of you I imagine us together again. I start scheming and thinking up things I can do to be with you. Then I get so excited I almost feel sick and I

have to stop because it hurts not to be with you.
I had better stop. Im sure Mom can use
some help in the kitchen. Please write to me.

Sincerest wishes,
Joyce

• • •

Monday, December 19
Hi Kiddo,

Thanks for the Christmas card and the letter.
The picture of the couple skating together on
a frozen lake in the moonlight is beautiful. I
haven't gone skating in years. Me and my
brother Art did go skiing yesterday. The lakes
are covered with snow, and we glided across
them like we were blown by the wind. Its easy
skiing, until you try to go into the woods. Then
the snow gets deep and it can be alot of work
getting anywhere. It felt good to get outside
after sitting at a desk for such a long time.
We saw some deer and a fox. They kept their
distance and watched every move we made.
Tomorrow I have to start working on a paper
for English. Boy, it looks like Im never going to
get a real vacation.
And about vacations, I sure hope you can
come here next summer too. I'll take you down
river like we talked about last summer. Not
many people go that far down the river because
there are some rapids in a couple of places that
are pretty risky and most people don't want to
try them. I portage around them, but there's

*not much of a path so people don't portage
either. Once we get past the rapids we won't
see anyone anymore. We'll be totally free. We'll
have to start early, because we'll need a whole
day, and we'll want to get home before dark.
I'm not afraid to canoe at night, but I'm sure
your aunt and uncle would be real angry if you
got home after dark.*

*I get excited every time I think about you
being here for two weeks. And this summer
we wont waste any of those fourteen days just
to meet one another. You'll have to think up
excuses to get away from your aunt and uncle.
I'll help. I'm sure we'll come up with a lot of
nifty ideas.*

*Love,
Bill*

• • •

*Tuesday, December 20
Dear Bill,*

*Guess what! You wont believe this. We got a
Christmas card from my aunt and uncle in
St. Paul, and in her note my aunt said they're
planning on going back to your resort next
summer and I can come along to help take
care of the kids if I want to. If I want to! Can
you imagine? I started laughing and crying at
the same time and mother looked at me like
Id just gone loony. Its really going to happen!
Were really going to be together for two whole
weeks! Now I can let myself think about it. I*

dont have to worry anymore about whether I'll
get to see you again. I wish you were here now
so we could be happy together.

I feel like such a fool. Im talking like this
and I havent received a letter from you in a
month. For all I know you might not even care
if I come. Please write to me right away. I wont
write again until I hear from you.

Yours truly—and impatiently,
Joyce,

• • •

Thursday, December 29
Dear Bill,

I just received your letter today and now I feel
like such a fool for doubting you would write.
It must have been held up by the Christmas
mail. You signed your letter with love. I love
you too. This is so embarrassing, but I can't
think of anything else to write. Im such a
ninny. Im sitting here in my bedroom with
your letter in front of me and all I can think
about is the way you closed it. I cant quite
believe this is really happening. Im not even
sure what's happening. We're writing to one
another, and this summer were going to be
together again. When I think of the girl I was
only six months ago, I just can't believe that
her and me are the same person. My whole life
is different. I might not even recognize myself
in a mirror. Im going to go look at myself in
the mirror just to see if I look different too.

*There, I looked, and I can see my love for you
glowing in my eyes. I wonder if my mother and
my sister can see it. What am I talking about?
I cant write anything that makes sense right
now. I don't even know if I should mail this
letter.*

*I love you,
Joyce*

*P.S. If I do mail this, please dont think badly
of me.
P.P.S. Do you have a picture you could send
me? I want so much to look at you and talk to
you. If I had a picture I could at least look at
you and pretend Im hearing your words as I
read them and speaking to you as I write.*

• • •

*February 14, 1939
Dear Bill,*

*It's such a long time since you last wrote!
Almost two months! I've written letters to you
and thrown them away, because I dont want
to be a pest. But why dont you write? I cant
help but wonder if something's wrong. Im sure
there are a lot of pretty gals on campus. Why
should you even think about me, stuck out here
on a farm in the middle of winter. Not very
romantic! Certainly not like being on the U's
campus with a lot of other swell young people
who are probably good lookers and some of
them have a lot of money I'm sure. But maybe*

*you're real busy with your studies and I'm just
being silly and any day a letter will arrive that
got lost in the mail or something. It sure hurts
though when I come home from school and
look through the mail on the dining room table
and there's nothing from you. Please write, Bill,
even if you are real busy, just write and tell me
everything's okay and I've got nothing to worry
about. Im so afraid you're going to meet some
girl. I shouldn't even tell you that. Please don't
laugh at me. I'm so upset I can't think straight.*

*Today is Valentine's Day. Some of the
kids at school were exchanging cards. They
probably dont do that at the U. I'm sure it's too
childish. But if they do, I bet you got a whole
bunch. I felt kind of sad when my friends got
cards, and I cant even see you or talk with you.
I'd call you at your dormitory, but I dont know
the number, and besides I'm afraid everyone
out here would listen in. My mother listens in
on our neighbors' conversations and they all
listen to ours too.*

*Please write soon. I'll be thinking of you, with
all my love,
Joyce*

Paul finds the last page of a letter, torn into pieces and
taped back together. He looks for the preceding page or
pages, and not finding anything, continues reading.

*I've been rambling on because I didn't want
to tell you something that I know I should.
I started seeing a gal on campus last fall.
Actually I met her in history last spring, but*

*we didn't start going out until this fall. We just
go to movies together and sometimes a play
in Scott Hall. It's nothing really serious, but I
don't want to give you the impression I'm not
seeing other women. I don't want to feel that
for some reason I'm supposed to be "true" to
you. And I don't think you should feel that way
either. I'm looking forward to seeing you this
summer. I sure hope everything works out with
your aunt and uncle.*

*Very best wishes,
Bill*

• • •

*Monday, March 6
Dear Bill,*

*I received your letter yesterday. It made me
sick. I vomited. I thought your feelings for me
were like mine for you. Obviously, there not.
I feel like such a fool! I didnt realize I was
putting pressure on you to feel you had to be
"true" to me. I guess because I dont even think
about being true to you. I just dont think about
anyone but you. But obviously we dont share
these feelings and I certainly wouldnt want
you to feel tied to me. You're free to go out with
whoever you choose. And I will too. Now that
things are clear, I will feel free to date those
~~boys~~ men who have been asking me out.*

*I suppose we can still be friends. Im going
to be in Minneapolis to visit a friend around
the beginning of April. If you want maybe we*

*can get together for lunch at the restaurant you
mentioned. (I think it was the Varsity Cafe.)
My friend and I will be busy but Im sure I
could find a couple of hours when we could get
together. Just for old time's sake. You know, I
cant even remember what you look like. You'll
have to send me a picture so I'll recognize you.*

*Best wishes,
Joyce*

• • •

*March 16, 1939
Dear Joyce,*

*That would be swell if we could get together for
lunch. I'm afraid I don't have any pictures that
I can send you, but I'm sure we will recognize
one another. There is a telephone at the front
desk, where you can call and leave a message.
The number is UM-1934. Call me before you
come to town and we can plan a date.*

*Yours truly,
Bill*

• • •

*April 1, 1939
Bill,*

*I cant think of a better time to be writing to
you than April Fool's Day, because I've been
such a fool. If nothing else, I thought you*

*wanted to be friends with me. Every time I
called the dormitory, they said you were out.
Now I understand what a fool I've been to
think I meant something to you. How heartless
of you to allow me to reveal my feelings in
letter after letter to you without telling me that
you don't share those feelings! How cruel! Did
you enjoy that? Did it make you feel superior
to me? Well, you'll have to find someone else
to boost your ego, because I won't be writing to
you anymore and I wont be going to the resort
with my aunt and uncle this summer.*

*Happily free of you,
Joyce*

• • •

*April 21, 1939
Dear Joyce,*

*I don't blame you for being angry at me. I
don't know what I can say to convince you that
I didn't want to hurt you and that I wasn't
looking to make you show feelings I didn't
share. Dolly and I were just friends last fall,
but then it got serious. I didn't realize when
I was writing to you that this was going to
happen. But then when I came back from
Christmas vacation we started going out to
movies and plays together and all of a sudden
everything started to change. I wish I could
tell you how much I love Dolly without hurting
you. I'd so like to be able to confide in you, but
I've felt I had to hide what I was doing—like I*

*did for spring break. The only reason I wanted
to stay here for the vacation and not go home
was so I could spend time with Dolly.*

*And now we're talking about getting
married. We don't know when, we haven't
had enough time to plan yet. All of this has
happened so fast. I'm really sorry if I hurt you.
I sure didn't mean to. I hope you won't hate me.
There's nothing I want more than to continue
being friends with you.*

Your contrite friend,
Bill

· · ·

May 1, 1939
Dear Bill,

*What makes you think I could ever hate you?
Im very happy for you. When I think of all
the suffering that people go through, like the
Orf family that just saw the bank auction off
their farm and everything they owned but the
clothes on their backs, well, its wonderful to
know that someone's happy. There's nothing I
would like more than to have you confide in
me. It would be just swell to hear about all the
great times you and Dolly are having together.
You cant imagine what it would mean to me!*

Your trustworthy friend,
Joyce

· · ·

June 11, 1939
Dear Joyce,

I feel like such a fool! Just two months ago
Dolly and I were talking about getting married.
Then two weeks ago she told me she was
going to France with her mother and sister.
And then she told me the only reason she was
going with them was so she could meet up
with her "beau." I didn't even know what she
was talking about at first. She had this funny
way of saying "beau," with her nose in the air
and her head kind of tilted to the side and her
lips puckered as if she was thinking of giving
someone a kiss.

Well finally I remembered "beau" means
handsome in French and a "beau" is a
handsome man, and the handsome man she
had in mind is someone she's been in love with
for a long time. I asked her why she led me
along all this time, she said she didn't—two
months ago she felt like marrying me but
today she doesn't feel that way anymore. She
seemed surprised I would even ask, as if you
have these kinds of feelings and then change
your mind to suit the season. She didn't seem
at all sad or sorry or anything. At first I was
so angry, because she was so happy she just
talked on and on about her "beau" and how
she couldn't wait to see him when he got
home from Princeton and how he lived in the
biggest and most beautiful house on Summit
Avenue and how they had planned on getting
married all along until they argued at the end
of last summer and how he didn't bother to

*see her when he came home from Princeton
for Christmas but then they saw one another
again just before he went back at the end of
Easter vacation and they started writing to
one another again and decided a couple weeks
ago they would get married as soon as they
both finished college. So all the while she was
going out with me and telling me how much
she loved me and wanted to marry me, she
was writing to him and telling him she wanted
to marry him. Only she must have meant what
she said to him.*

*She seemed to want to talk forever about
herself and her beau and didn't seem to care
a bit that what she was saying might hurt
me. She just wanted someone to listen to how
happy she was. I was so hot. She mentioned
Princeton every time she could, and suddenly
I realized that what college you go to means a
lot to some people. Just like living on Summit
Avenue in the biggest house just a few blocks
from the Cathedral means a lot. And I suppose
having maids and a servant who answers the
door and serves the meals and all that kind of
stuff that Dolly has and I'm sure her beau has
too means a lot. I felt kind of poor and shabby
sitting there on her front porch, holding the
lemonade her servant had given me, listening
to her talk about how swell her beau was. I felt
like I didn't really exist.*

*Their black Packard pulled up in the drive
and her mother got out of the back seat and
walked to the front porch. She said hello to us,
as if nothing had happened, and went into the
house, and I thought, I bet her parents never*

felt anything had happened or would happen between Dolly and me. They knew their daughter, she wasn't going to marry someone who didn't come from their class. I had just created a slight aberration in her orbit around the money and things that attracted her, but she would stay true to that orbit.

I walked all the way home. About two hours it must've taken me. I didn't want to talk to anyone. The walk did me a lot of good. It gave me time to think about who I am and how little I had in common with her.

I haven't had any problems studying for final exams. I like it here, and I want to come back. But I'm also looking forward to going home and seeing Mom and Dad and Art. And you too, if you're still coming. I hope you haven't changed your mind.

Yours truly,
Bill

• • •

Monday, June 19
My Dearest Bill,

Im so sorry for what you had to go through with that Dolly. What can be worse than having to listen to someone you love talk all the time about someone else? You were lucky you didn't really love her, or you would still be feeling the pain.

I'm happy we will be able to see one another this summer. I really want to go on

that canoe trip you promised. I cant wait!
Maybe we could even go on more than one. Its
so beautiful at your resort! I can never forget
waking up in the morning and walking out on
the dock in the fog and watching the mist rise
above the water and drift across the lake and
the sun glowing pink and getting brighter and
redder until the mist is gone. By then the kids
are up and it's time to make breakfast and
break up their squabbles and wipe up the spilt
milk. Taking care of them makes me wonder
if I would ever want to have any of my own. If
I was to have any, I dont think I would want
more than two. A boy and a girl. What do you
think? That's so silly, I cant believe I wrote it!

Im feeling very happy right now. This is
a time of the year that I really love. Schools
out. The crops are planted. Nothing's ready to
harvest yet. Theres just the routine things that
have to be done. Get up at 5:00 to make coffee,
milk the cows, make breakfast, help Ma keep up
the house and do the laundry, make lunch and
dinner, and then milk the cows again at night.

There's a lot of time during the day, above
all after lunch, when I'm pretty much free to
do what I want. I like to hide in the hayloft
and read. By June most of the hay that we
baled the summer before is gone, so there's a lot
of room between the bales that are still there
and the ceiling that rises so high above. If Im
standing I get dizzy looking up at the ceiling
its so high and the bales wobble and I feel like
Im going to fall. So I usually find a little nook
between some bales where there's enough light
to read, because there's a lot of light that comes

*in through the chinks between the boards,
and I curl up in my little nest and spend a
good part of the afternoon there, reading and
dreaming. In the evening I'll walk to the top
of the ridge surrounding the barnyard to see if
there aren't any cows still coming and the sun
will be sitting there on the horizon like a huge
ball and suddenly a flock of birds will come
flying above the ridge and they'll swoop in one
direction and then in another as if they were
just one big bird made up of hundreds of birds
all chirping at the same time so they almost
make you deaf and then they'll fly off and go
roost in the trees over by the hay field.*

*I guess there's not a whole lot to do here
other than work unless you like to read and
daydream a lot. Sometimes I feel as if I'm just
waiting, waiting for my chance to live, and
then I'll stop daydreaming and reading and
start living.*

*Well, I sure wrote a lot. Im such a
chatterbox. I could talk forever if I thought it
would bring you close to me. I get sick to my
stomach with longing when I think of our two
weeks together, so far away, when we'll be able
to look at one another and talk to one another
and touch one another.*

*Yours truly,
Joyce*

• • •

Thursday, July 6
Hey Kiddo!

This might be a slow time of the year for you,
but boy are things ever hectic for us. Art—he's
my brother. You probably remember him from
last summer. He's the tall thin guy with lots
of brown hair always hanging in his eyes.
Art and me (oops, I) are working constantly
cleaning cabins and fixing things the guests
break and outfitting campers and people
going fishing and hauling all the fish heads
and guts out of the fish house and waiting on
tables and just running errands for Mom and
Dad. By the time night gets here I'm really
bushed. I can hardly lift my legs up high
enough to get them on the bed when it's time to
hit the hay.

Some days it's not so bad and I've still
got enough energy after the sun sets to do
something, and so maybe I'll go down the river
through the channel and fish at the opening
there, or along the bank just off the weeds
where it gets deep in a hurry, and I'll catch a
few walleye, but I really go out just to get away
and be alone so I can think. There are few
places better suited to thinking than a canoe
on a lake or on a slow flowing river at night.
I can hear my thoughts more clearly there
than anywhere else. And what I'm thinking
more and more is that I don't want to spend
the rest of my life here. You talk about how
beautiful and mysterious the lake looks in the
morning when there's all that fog with sun
shining through and how the mist clears and

*the lake looks new, like it was just created,
and still pure with God's touch. Or when we'd
be canoeing, and you'd rhapsodize over the
reflection of the sky and the shore in the lake,
where you could see the colors of the clouds
and each detail of every rock and tree. I've seen
those things so often, they've lost their magic.
Sometimes, when I'm in a canoe paddling,
and I'm seeing the same thing over and over
again, I have the feeling I'm only paddling in
my mind, like I've become my own wilderness.
I get to a place where I'm all alone, and I don't
know how to get out.*

*The U looks like it might be a way out. I
can't wait to go back. It's really different from
what I'm used to here. At first the difference
was kind of hard for me and I got really
homesick. But once I got familiar with things,
I felt better. Having a roommate like George
Gardner sure helped a lot. We roomed together
all last year and we're going to room together
this year too. We're a lot alike. He reads a lot
too, so we stayed up at night talking about
books, and sometimes our friend Tom would
stop by and join in the conversation. We talked
about writers like Plato and Voltaire and F.
Scott Fitzgerald. I read his book Tender is the
Night and learned that the title comes from
a poem by John Keats about a nightingale.
Tom read it too. He said it taught him a lot
about the kind of women to avoid because
they always destroy men. He always seems to
be trying to learn about life from the books he
reads. That was kind of new to me. He's very
smart. I like him a lot, but he's not going to*

be back next year because he graduated. He's
going to Harvard University so he can get a
Ph.D. and be a professor and teach philosophy.
I'm sure he'll be a real good professor. I'll
miss him, but luckily I'll have George as my
roommate again. He's been real swell.

I started trying to write some stories this
year and George and Tom encouraged me to
publish one of them in the Ivory Tower. That's
the school's literary magazine. I left the story
in an envelope with the editor's name on it at
the Ivory Tower office and I no more than got
out of the building when I decided to go back
and get it, but when I reached the office the
girl I'd left it with was gone and the fellow
who was there couldn't find it. There wasn't
anything to be done so I left, and there it was
in the next issue, staring right back at me. It
was fun reading my words and listening to
them in my mind. I tried to imagine what it
would be like for someone else to read it, so I
pretended it wasn't mine, closed the magazine,
and opened it up, like I was waiting in a
doctor's office, but I just couldn't read it as if it
was someone else's. I kept on hearing my own
words in my mind before I could read them on
the page.

You can see I've had a lot of fun at the U,
but I don't know what I can do with the things
I'm learning. When I try to imagine the future,
I can't see a thing. All I can imagine doing is
going back home, even though I know now I
don't want to do that. But I don't know what
else I can do. I think when I go back to the
U in the fall I'm going to talk to some of my

*teachers and see if they can help me. I really
feel lost.*

*I just looked over this letter. It's nearly six
pages long! I'm embarrassed about talking so
much about myself. I think about you all the
time.*

*It's late so I'd better get to bed. Good night
and pleasant dreams. You'll be here in just a
month, can you believe it? I'll dream of holding
you in my arms, my sweet Joyce,*

Bill

• • •

*Sunday, July 23
Dear Joyce,*

*I can't believe how quickly the summer is
flying by. It's almost August and you'll be
here in less than two weeks. We've been so
busy this summer that I've hardly had time
to think, let alone write letters. Unfortunately
for Art and me, fishing's been good. We haul
a barrel of fish heads and guts to our dump
every day and feed the crows and gulls and
vultures that await us. The barrel stinks so
bad, when we dump it we almost drop our own
stomachs in with the fish guts. It's amazing
how quickly the whole smelly mess disappears.
The birds swoop in even while we're dumping
it and they've got it pretty well cleaned up by
the next day. When we get done hauling fish
guts, we still have a lot of other chores to do,
like outfitting people who want to go camping,*

doing repairs, fetching things for the kitchen,
waiting on tables, cleaning up the dining
room, and serving beer and booze. People start
arriving here at five or six on Saturday and
eat supper and dance polkas and get good and
drunk. Some of them can get real mean. An
empty beer bottle can do a lot of damage to
a head, and a broken one can do even more
damage to a face.

I haven't seen anything like that for a while,
but this morning I saw what these people can
do to themselves after they leave. Art and I
were on our way into town to go to mass and
about five miles down the road we came across
a car that had gone off the road and hit a
tree head on. The driver was dead. Blood
had flowed out of his nose and mouth onto
the steering wheel and his chest. A fly that
was buzzing around landed on his upper lip
and started feeding on the thick brown blood
under his nostrils. Another walked across his
eyeball. I kept waiting for him to blink, but
he didn't. I looked in the back seat and saw a
man and a woman out cold, lying in a heap
on the seat and on the floor, with their legs
and arms all tangled up. The car reeked of
booze. We walked around the front. The whole
windshield on the passenger side was blown
out. A woman went through the windshield
and flew into a tree. It was so gruesome, I
don't even want to tell you what she looked like.

Luckily someone stopped, drove back to the
lodge, and called the police. My dad talked to
us about having to deal with awful stuff in life,
and still having to carry on. And sometimes

having to carry on helped get through pain.
He's right. We changed into our work clothes,
loaded the barrel from the fish house onto the
back of the truck, and went to the dump. I
hardly even noticed the stink or the sight of the
fish heads and guts when we dumped them.
That was this morning. It may as well have
been a year ago.

I didn't plan on writing all of this. When I
started this letter I was just going to reply to
yours. I was going to tell you how busy we've
been and that's why I didn't answer your letter
right away. But as soon as I started writing,
everything that happened this morning just
took hold of me. You can probably see why I
don't plan on spending my life here, above all
now that I've seen something different at the U.

Yours truly,
Bill

• • •

Sunday, August 20
Oh Joy,

How fitting your name should include that
word, which expresses how I feel every time I
think of you. I've never been as happy as these
last two weeks with you and there's nothing I
wouldn't give for just two more weeks like that.

But boy, did I catch hell after your aunt
and uncle left yesterday. Oof! My mother
bawled me out, and when she got done my dad
started in, and that was even worse. He was

*so hot I thought he was going to take a swing
at me. I'm glad he didn't. I'm afraid of what
I might have done. At any rate, when I saw
the lights on in your aunt and uncle's cabin
the night before last, I had to go in with you. I
knew they were going to light into you and I
didn't want you to have to face the music all
alone. Maybe I made things worse. They sure
seemed to think I had a lot of nerve, and every
time I tried to say anything it just made them
angrier. You might have been able to make up
a story they would have believed, but I don't
think so. And besides, I don't like hiding, and
we don't have anything to feel ashamed about.
I sure hope you're okay now. I imagine they
told your parents all about it.*

*Once my mom and dad blew up it was all
over. There's just too much work to get done on
Saturdays to lose time and energy bickering. I
got going as soon as I could on my chores and
for once I was happy to do them. Hauling out
the dirty linen, putting clean sheets on the beds,
mopping floors, fixing anything that might
be broken, checking canoes for dents and
holes, making sure no one walked off with any
paddles, stacking equipment in the boathouse,
and then helping in the kitchen and waiting
on tables. I'm sick of doing all that, but I had
a smile on my face all day long because I was
thinking of you.*

*I woke up this morning thinking of you too.
I stayed in bed for over an hour remembering
the things we did the last two weeks. The
canoe trips during the day, and being all
alone with you. That first trip down the river,*

*when we decided to let the current carry us
right through the rapids, and then after the
really dangerous rapids where we portaged
and where the river opens up like a big lake
and we canoed around those huge boulders
that look like monstrous dice a giant might
have thrown. Sitting on one of those square
boulders in the sun, surrounded by water,
talking and watching the wood ducks that you
thought were so beautiful and then lying in
the sun, touching your warm skin, and cooling
off in the river that was so deep between the
boulders and holding onto one another.*

*And that night in the boathouse lying
on the floor and trying to be quiet so no one
could hear us. You got so embarrassed because
of that sliver in your bottom, and even more
embarrassed when I had to light a lantern so
we could get it out. I still think if we hadn't it
would have really festered, and how would you
have explained that to your aunt? And then
the bleeding. I feel like such a dummy for not
having understood right away. What a place
to make love the first time! The next day when
we hauled gear out of the boathouse I looked
at the spots and wondered if Art or Dad would
notice them, but no one said a word. Of course
the spots were so small no one would ever see
them except me. All I could think about was
the night before.*

*That's the way it was every day, thinking of
the night before. Looking for you as I paddled
over to your dock, seeing you step out of the
shadows of the trees, and then paddling back
to the boathouse, tying the canoe to the end of*

the dock so we wouldn't scrape the bottom on the sand, then sneaking into the boathouse, our little hideaway. I woke up every morning in a dream that I knew was real, and knowing we would make it come alive again that night.

But this morning when I woke up, still in that dream, I knew that's all I'd have. And now I just want to find a way to make it come alive again every day. Maybe once I get to the U you can find an excuse to visit your aunt and uncle in St. Paul again. I miss you so!

Your devoted lover,
Bill

• • •

Saturday
My Dear Sweet Bill,

I read and reread your letter until I knew it almost by heart. It was so beautiful! I feel as if Ive been living a dream and your letter let me know that the dream isn't going to end.

I'm glad your parents weren't too hard on you. My mom talked to me after my aunt and uncle brought me home last Sunday. They talked with my parents for about an hour while I was in my room unpacking. My mom wanted to be sure that I hadn't done anything with you that would put me in the family way. Of course I said no. And with just those few times, I'm sure I can't be.

I told her I love you, and why I love you. I told her how kind and handsome and smart

you are, and that you're a student at the U.
She was real impressed with that. No one from
around here has ever gone to college. And I
told her how courageous you are, because you
came to the cabin that night and told my aunt
and uncle that we had wandered too far off
and that it was your fault that I was so late
in getting back. I wonder how many other
men would have done what you did? And I
told her about our beautiful day and about
our trip down the rapids, and the portages,
and the lake with the beautiful sandy beach,
and the little stream that flowed through the
woods into the lake, and how we spent the
day sunning ourselves like turtles and talking
and picnicking and swimming. I loved telling
her about our day because that made it fresh
for me again. I didn't tell her that we were as
naked as angels when we went swimming or
what we did when we were lying on the beach.
But I blushed, and my face felt so hot I must
have looked like a beet. And then I did the
silliest thing. I started crying, I dont know
why. And she took me in her arms and said
she understood and patted my back as if I was
a little baby. I was real tired then and she left
me alone. I went to sleep and dreamed of you,
and of laying next to you on the blanket we
had spread out on the sand, and your hand
under the small of my back and your lips on
my mouth and then I felt you sliding into me.

I think perhaps I should be ashamed of
writing this to you, but then I wonder, why
should I? Im in love with you and your in love
with me, so why shouldn't we tell one another

about what were thinking and feeling. For
two beautiful weeks we revealed our hearts
to one another and I'm not going to give that
up. Those nights in the boathouse were all so
beautiful. That first night we were so clumsy,
but every night after that we knew how to be
with one another. And every day when Id see
you working Id think about how that night
we would be together again and I'd think of
all the things I wanted to tell you, but most of
all I wanted you to hold me and I wanted to
feel you inside of me. Once we spread all those
blankets out on the floor it was really like our
own little love nest, just as warm and comfy
as a bedroom could ever be—even more so,
because no one knew we were there. We didn't
need to talk. Sometimes just lying on the floor
with your hand in mine and listening to the
waves under the floor was all we needed to be
happy. And other times, I wanted every inch of
you pressed against me.

Now that were not together, all I want to
do is talk, because I cant stop thinking about
you, but if I dont stop writing I'll never get this
letter mailed, and if you dont get letters from
me someday you'll stop writing. I'll end this
letter only because I'm greedy. I want as much
of you as I can get.

I love you with all my heart, Bill. Your own
Joyce

P.S. Please destroy this letter. I hate to think
what anyone in your family might think of me
if they read it. Only we can understand how

we feel about one another and how we can
write to one another the way we do.

• • •

Saturday, September 2
My dearest Joyce,

I received your letter today and like you read
it and reread it until I knew it almost by heart.
I can't stop thinking of you either. I got so
spoiled seeing you every day and being with
you almost every night in the boathouse. Now
when I go in there I think of you lying with
me and I just want to make love with you. It
drives me crazy. I go outside and look at the
lake and think of the day we spent making
love on that beach. Everything we've done
seems right, and anyone who would try to stop
us is wrong. You say in your letter that I'm
courageous because I went in with you that
night to try to explain things to your aunt and
uncle, but like I said I just felt that we hadn't
done anything wrong and I didn't want you to
face the music all alone. I might have made
things worse for you, because the more I talked
the angrier they got. They didn't want to hear
anything about how we feel about one another.
Joyce, I can see you as if you were here.
I had so much time to look at you, I can
remember everything, right down to the scar
on your ankle and the little mole on your
tummy. I can smell your hair and feel your
skin. I'm going crazy. I think of you all day,
and sometimes I catch myself talking to you,

and I reread your letters until I know them by heart. I can recite practically every letter you've written to me. But I still want more. Please write soon.

It's late. I need to be off to bed. I'll dream of you. Good night and sweet dreams. Mine will be of you.

Your adoring lover,
Bill

. . .

Tuesday, September 5
Dear Joyce,

We've been talking about just one thing at home the last few days—what's happening in Europe. From what the papers say those planes that are bombing towns and cities are killing mostly women and children! Every time I read an article in the Mirer Times there's something about houses or hospitals being bombed and innocents killed. The papers make it sound as if the Poles are putting up a good fight, and I'm sure they are, but you have to wonder what lancers on horseback can do against men in tanks. I think this business about Germans being persecuted in Poland was just an excuse for the Fuhrer to invade that country. If he gets his way there, where will he send his nazi killers next?

Art thinks we should get in the war on the side of Poland, England, and France. This morning at breakfast, when we were talking about the ocean liner that was torpedoed by a German sub, Art said that should be reason enough right there. Dad said it was a ship that got us into the Great War, and he sure as hell hoped another ship wouldn't get us into this one. He seems really worried. He spent a year in France in the War, and he doesn't want to see us go to war again. He says President Roosevelt is doing the right thing. I don't know. Art said if the U.S. went to war he'd join the Army. Dad said he'd be a damn fool to do that. I think Dad's right. When you get to know Art, you'll see. He's real hot headed. Dad once called him a fool in waiting.

I wanted to get Dad talking a little bit about the Great War, but I couldn't. He doesn't like to talk about that war, or the one that's getting started now. I think one reason is that his parents are German. They had a farm near a town somewhere in Wisconsin where everyone spoke German, and they were all Catholics. Mom and Dad still speak German to each other sometimes, but never to us kids. Except my dad calls us little scheisters and stuff like that. I asked him if we still have family in Germany; he said maybe, but we wouldn't know one another anymore. I know we do, because my mother sends Christmas cards to some cousins over there. Dad acts as if the old country doesn't mean anything to him, but I know it does.

I'm packing and getting ready to leave tomorrow for the U. I should've left Sunday, but I had too many chores to get done. I really miss you and I keep on thinking about how

we can see one another again once I'm at the
U. Do you think you could find a way to come
to Minneapolis? Or maybe you could stay with
your aunt and uncle in St. Paul again.

In the meantime, Joy, my Joy, I will dream
of you,

Bill

P.S. Don't worry about anyone seeing your
letter. I put it in a safe place.

• • •

Wednesday
My Dearest Sweetheart,

*I read your letter four times, and then read it
again, because reading it made me feel as if
you were next to me, talking to me, and that's
what I want more than anything else. I need
to hear your voice and your thoughts, and I
need to tell you everything that's welling up in
me and feel your arms around me and I need
you, I need you to tell me you'll never go to this
cursed war if our country gets into it. Maybe
that's selfish and childish of me, but every
time I hear talk of war I just want to be with
you and know that you'll never leave. I know
how horrible the war in Poland is for all those
innocent people, but I could never let you go.
And I'm so afraid your father might be right,
this country might get into the war because of
a ship that was sunk, just as he said we got
into the Great War.*

But I'm convinced everything will turn out for the best, the way it did for the people on the ship the Germans sunk. I remember reading about those two sisters from Minneapolis the papers said drowned when the ship sank and thinking what an awful way to die, drowning in that dark cold water. And when I read the next day they were saved along with most of the other passengers I just felt so happy I almost started to cry. I know that God is looking out for us. He will keep you safe. He will protect us. I know He will.

I dont know what's the matter with me lately, maybe its just that I want to be with you so much. I feel constantly on edge and ready to cry at the drop of a hat. I looked at myself in the mirror today. I wanted to see myself with your eyes, so I can understand why you love me. Whatever part of me you love I'll love. Whatever part of me you don't love I'll not love. And those parts you dont love I'll find a way of getting rid of them until Im everything you love. Then none of those gals at the U will have a chance of getting you to fall in love with them because I'll be everything you love and you'll not have any love left for any of them.

Oh Bill Bill Bill you see how crazy I am! I love saying your name because it makes me feel your here and I'm talking to you and then I start thinking about those two beautiful weeks and all the times I said your name and I can feel my lips against your cheek whispering Bill, Bill I love you, I love you Bill. I can smell the canvas in the boathouse where we spent our beautiful nights, and I can feel

*the warm sand beneath me and all the ways
you kissed me that day we spent in the sun
on our own little lake where you made me feel
more alive than I'd ever felt before. I can feel
your lips on mine and your body on mine and
I feel as if my body is just a memory of yours.
I touch myself and I remember you. Isn't that
strange? I feel as if half of me is gone and I'm
not real without you. Sometimes I want to be
with you so bad I almost get sick and have to
lie down.*

*Other times I just want to get far away
from everyone so I can be alone with my
thoughts of you. I walk down the path that
leads to the old wood bridge and through the
forest on the other side to my favorite place,
where the woods slope down toward a bend
in the creek. I sit there in clear sunlight that
shines on the little slope and sparkles on the
tiny rapids where the creek flows across some
rocks and listen to the birds chirp, and feel the
sun warm my body right to the bone. It's so
calm I can hear a squirrel's claws scratching
bark as it runs around the trunk of a tree. I lie
back on the leaves that crumble beneath me
in the dust of last year's fall and let the sun
warm me until my body is so relaxed I feel
like a warm lake lying asleep beneath the hot
summer sun.*

*That's when I feel you are somehow
inside of me, like sunlight in a lake warming
its water. Your my sunshine and you shine
through and through me. Your in my fingers,
my lips, even my eyes beneath their closed lids.*

*It feels so good and I feel so happy! I stay there
until the sun starts to set. It gets cold quickly
in the woods at this time of year, so I hurry
home carrying all your sunshine inside. I feel
like a little stove with a fire in my chest that
warms me from the inside out. That fire is you,
my love. My dear sweet Bill. I go to sleep at
night with you all aglow inside me and dream
of you all night long.*

*My adorable lover, Im going to stop now. Its
already dark, and the only thing I want to do is
go to bed and dream of you. I love you love you
love you. I could repeat those words forever, and
if I stop repeating them it makes no difference,
because I keep right on thinking them.*

*Maybe I can find an excuse to go stay with
my aunt and uncle. If they'll have me again!
I'll find a way, because I can no longer be
apart from you.*

*I must go to bed, so I'll wish you a sleep
full of beautiful dreams and hope you wake up
thinking of,*

Your Loving Joyce

*P.S. Please write to me first chance you get.
Your letters feed my soul just as surely as food
nourishes the body. I love you, Bill, I love you
so much I feel I'm going to burst with all the
love inside me.*

• • •

Sunday, September 24
Dear Joyce,

*I'm sorry for not having written for such a long
time. I didn't get your letter, your beautiful
letter, which I've read so many times I know
it almost by heart—I didn't get it until last
Tuesday, and I've been so tired after football
practice that I haven't had the energy to do
anything, not even write.*

    *Everyone here is talking about one thing—
the war in Poland. We're all reading the
papers and listening to the radio. One of the
guys bought a map of Europe and put it up on
the bulletin board in the lounge. He put colored
pins in showing the parts of Poland still
controlled by the Polish Army and the parts
the nazis now control. There's a lot of red, the
color he uses for the Germans, and not much
blue. From what we read and hear, the few
cities the Poles still control have been bombed
and burned to nothing but rubble.*

    *There's a guy here by the name of Andrei
whose family is from Warsaw. His father's in
the grain markets and travels a lot between
Minneapolis, Chicago, and New York, but his
mother, younger sister, and his aunts, uncles,
and cousins, they're all still in Warsaw. He
told me his father hasn't been able to get any
news about them. They were all planning on
moving to Minneapolis next summer, but the
Germans, with their panzer divisions and dive
bombers, moved so fast, the whole family got
trapped in Warsaw.*

    All the fellows in the dorm seem angry

*and disgusted with the Germans killing all
these innocent people, blowing them to bits,
burying them beneath buildings, burning
them alive. But there's not a lot of agreement
about what we should be doing. Some of the
boys think we should declare war on Germany,
some think we should do whatever we can to
help the Poles, Brits, Canadians, and French,
short of sending our own men, and others
think we should remain absolutely neutral
and let the Europeans stop the Fuhrer. I think
the British and the French can take care of
him. They don't need our help. Hitler seems
to have caught the Europeans offguard, but
once they get organized they'll crush Germany.
I feel sick about just sitting on the sideline
watching what's happening. A couple of the
boys have been talking about going to Canada
and volunteering to fight in the Canadian
army, but talk's cheap. We'll see what they do.
I wonder what Art is thinking right now. I
haven't talked with him since I left for the U,
but even before I left he was saying we should
enter the war on the side of Poland, England,
and France.*

*This war makes me realize how lucky we
are. It's so far away! The nazis would have to
cross an entire ocean to get to us. We're free
to think only about what we want. And right
now I want you. Joyce, we have to find a way
for you to come here. I can't stand not seeing
you. You talk in your letter about trying to
see yourself with my eyes to see what I love
and don't love, but I love every part of you.
Love loves completely—even the mole on your*

tummy and the scar on your ankle. If you can see yourself with my eyes, then you must see yourself as perfect. So there's no need to worry about any of the gals on campus. It's as if they don't exist. The only thing I want now is to be with you. We have to find a way. Homecoming is always a big deal here. Maybe you could tell your parents that I've invited you for homecoming and you want to stay with your aunt and uncle in St. Paul. Or maybe we could find a way for me to come and visit you. Then we could walk through the woods together and go to your favorite place and lie in the sun. And I could kiss the little mole on your tummy. And so much more! Talk to your parents please and see if you can come here or if I can visit you there. I can't be satisfied with letters. They just frustrate me. I want to be able to hold you—touch you and hold you and put my arms around you and kiss you and be totally united with you. I love reading your letters, but they're not enough! They just tease me. I need you. And if I can't have you I'll go crazy. It's so hard without you. I have to concentrate as much as I can on what I'm doing each day or I'll go nuts. It's good that I've had football practice, because that keeps me busy so I don't have time to miss you, and at night after I've hung around with some of my friends I'm so tired I fall asleep and then I dream of you. Tomorrow classes start so that will help keep my mind occupied. I'm taking courses in Shakespeare, European history, French, Philosophy, and Rhetoric.

I'm going to try to write some more stories
for the U's literary magazine again this year.
It was such a strange feeling seeing my story
in print last spring, and ever since then I've
dreamed of seeing another one of my stories in
print. It's a real thrill. I can't do much during
the football season, but as soon as it ends I'd
like to get something done. I worked on a story
this summer. It's not done yet, but it might be
close. Sometimes I think I'd like to be a writer,
but then I wonder how I would earn a living. I
don't know that I can write well enough or fast
enough to really make a living at it. And then
I start wondering what I'm doing here. I know
if it hadn't been for football I would have never
been able to go to the U. Now that football has
gotten me here, I'm losing interest in it, but I
don't know where to go. Oh well, I'm sure the
answer will become clear and I just have to
have faith in myself. But I sure wish things
were clearer.

I will write to you much sooner next time,
I promise. And don't forget to talk with your
parents about coming here or me going there
(so I can kiss the little mole on your tummy!).

Love,
Bill

Paul does not find Joyce's response to this letter. He
continues reading.

Saturday, October 7
Dear Bill,

As soon as the mail came and I saw there
wasn't a letter from you I had to call. It took
so long for them to find you, I wondered where
you could be, and when I finally heard your
voice you seemed a million miles away, in
another world. I felt I didn't belong. I think
about you so much you're really part of me, but
when I heard your voice it was like a stranger
talking to me. I had this horrible feeling that
someday everything could end, and I wouldn't
mean anything to you. That's why I had to
hang up. I'm sorry. I guess I shouldn't have
called. Please write to me.

Love,
Joyce

• • •

Monday, October 9
My dear sweet Bill,

I'm so happy you called yesterday. You should
have seen the look on Mom's face when she
said it was for me. Almost no one ever calls
here for me, except sometimes Ruth, and Mom
was so surprised. Oh, it's for you, it's a man!
A man calling for me? It must be Bill! And it
was. Talking to you really settled me down.
I've been so excited lately, ready to cry or laugh
at the drop of a pin. I probably shouldn't tell
you this. You'll think I'm a real silly ninny. I'm

*just so happy you're coming and I'll be able to
see you at last. I'm so happy I feel like singing.*

*I love you, love of my life,
Joyce*

. . .

*Tuesday, October 17
My Dearest Bill,*

*You guessed right when you said you felt there
was something wrong. I couldn't bring myself to
talk about it, because I so wanted everything to
be perfect while you were here, but sometimes
I let my worrying get the best of me and I just
couldn't be happy, even though nothing makes
me happier than being with you.*

*I've told you many times I wished you were
inside of me. Well, you are inside of me. You
see, I have missed two periods, my breasts are
swollen and tender, and although I'm feeling
better now, for a while I was sick almost every
morning. I don't think Dad suspects I'm in
the family way, but I know Mom does. I can
tell from the way she looks at me and the
questions she asks—do I feel well this morning,
am I tired, and that sort of thing. And Arlene,
my dear sister, who is so envious of me because
of you, well, Arlene is watching me like a
hawk, and I'm sure she suspects something
too. Bill, I'm afraid. I can try to conceal my
condition for a while, but one day it will no
longer be possible. What shall we do? I feel so
confused and unsure right now. I'm so afraid*

*of how you will feel about me now that I'm in
this condition. Bill, I love you, I love you so
much it hurts. Please tell me what we should
do. Please love me and stay by me. Please. I
love you.*

Joyce

• • •

October 17, 1939
Dear Joyce,

*I was hoping to write to you yesterday, but
since I didn't do any studying over the weekend
I had to get caught up on Monday. I really
like your family. I was worried at first about
how your mom and dad might respond to me
after what happened last summer with your
aunt and uncle, but they were just as nice to
me as could be. Boy, did I breathe a sigh of
relief! They're so easy to talk to. Your dad's a
real character. Like that business about not
allowing hunters on his land because hunting
doesn't seem like much of a sport and hunters
just scare the animals away. I bet there aren't
many farmers who think like that. Thank your
mom again for the great dinner. That was sure
the biggest roast chicken I've ever seen and the
best I've ever eaten. I couldn't get over all the
food she made. Does she cook like that all the
time? I sure hope she didn't do all that just
because of me. She's really swell.*

*I bet Charles is a really great brother too.
He doesn't talk much, but I'm sure he has a*

*heart of gold, just as you said. It's too bad he
had to spend so much time working in the
barn, but I guess Sunday's as good a day as
any to do chores. As for Arlene, I see what you
mean. She sure likes to play the big sister.*

*All in all, I thought everything went
just grand. I really like your family, and I
feel they kind of like me too. I can't wait for
Thanksgiving. It seems such a long way off. I
hate time. I'm always waiting for it to pass,
waiting to see you. I love you even more now
after having spent just one more day with
you. All the way back on the train yesterday
I thought about you and what we might
have done if we had been alone. Last night I
dreamed about going for a walk with you in
the woods that we looked at from on top of
the hill Sunday morning, but then somehow
we were swimming in our birthday suits in
the lake last summer. We were just sort of
suspended in this warm water, and you kept
on laughing about doing this with Ruth, but
never before with a man. Soon enough there
was nothing more about Ruth and we were
making love under water. Somehow we didn't
need to breathe, but I had this horrible fear
that we had to hurry up so your parents
wouldn't catch us. You see why I have to throw
myself into football practice and my studies. I'd
go crazy otherwise! Being in a dorm with a lot
of guys who want to talk all the time keeps me
occupied too.*

*By the way, I learned something today
that made me feel so sad. Do you remember
me talking about Andrei, the guy from Poland*

whose entire family was trapped in Warsaw? He has a cousin who managed to get out just before the city fell to the nazis and escape somehow to Hungary. He got word to Andrei's father about the family. Apparently the building in which they lived took a direct hit from a bomb and was completely destroyed. There were no survivors. I guess the cousin's family was wiped out too. Andrei left a few hours ago to be with his dad, who's in New York. His dad is trying to get the cousin out of Europe and into the U.S. Hungary seems safe for now, but it looks as if this war could spread.

That Hitler really has a lot of nerve! The U-boat sinking that British battleship the other day made everyone realize the Nazis aren't going to back down from anyone. But Hitler's going to have his hands full with the British and the French, and once the Canadians get over there too he's really going to be in for it. It's hard to sit on the sidelines and just watch, but I think we have to let the Brits and the French take care of him. They'll give him what for. One of my friends wants to join the Canadian Air Force, but I told him by the time he got over to Europe the war might be over.

Well, I'd better finish this letter and get to bed. I miss you, Joyce, and I want to be with you. I'll be counting the days until Thanksgiving. I sure wish your aunt and uncle would let you stay with them for a few days. I don't know how I'm going to make it until Thanksgiving. I love you more than anything in the world.

Love,
Bill

P.S. You seemed kind of quiet from time to
time over the weekend. Is everything okay? I
sure hope you will tell me if it's not.

• • •

Sunday, October 22
Oh Joy Joy Joy!

What a surprise! I hadn't thought about you
getting pregnant. We should plan on getting
married as soon as possible. People can be
so cruel, and I don't want them to be able to
attack you because you're "in the family way"
and not married. But maybe I'm assuming too
much. We've spent so little time together. Do
you want to marry me? I wish you were here so
I could see your eyes when I talk to you. Please
let me know right away what you want to do.
You know what I want.

With all my love,
Bill

• • •

Saturday
My Dearest Bill,

I can't stop thinking of you, and you ask me
if I want to marry you! Yes of course I want
to marry you! I think I would die if you didn't

*ask me to. I can't tell you how much your letter
means to me. I was so afraid that you might
not want me because of my condition. And
then I would have to decide what to do with
the baby.*

*I'm going to tell Mom and Dad I'm in the
family way and we're getting married. Won't
they be surprised! Actually I don't think Mom
will be surprised, but I know Dad will. I hope
you don't mind if I tell them. I want to do it
now before Dad begins to wonder about the
change, this wonderful change that's taking
place in my body. Sometimes I think I can
feel something down there, but I know it's too
soon. You really are a part of me. That's what
love is, isn't it, two people becoming a part of
one another. That's what I want more than
anything else.*

*I love you with all my heart—
Your own Joyce*

• • •

*Monday, October 30
My Darling Bill,*

*I saw my chance Sunday, when Mom and
Dad were alone in the living room reading
the paper, to tell them we want to get married.
Dad seemed completely surprised. When I
told them I'm in the family way, he started to
get this look he gets when he's upset—stares
straight ahead with his jaw set like an anvil
and his eyes burning like hot metal. But when*

*Mom saw what he was doing she said, you
know, Peter, Robert was born less than nine
months after we were married. Dad didn't
say anything, but the look on his face softened,
and I knew he wouldn't do anything to stand
between us.*

*No one said anything more until after
dinner tonight. While Dad was finishing his
coffee, he announced to everyone you and me
are getting married. He said it like it wasn't
any different from saying there's a snow storm
predicted for tomorrow and maybe we better
keep the cows in the barn. Charles just stared
at his plate and then looked up at me and
stared at his plate again, nodding his head
up and down as if he was agreeing with what
Dad was saying. But Arlene, you should of
seen her, she had this smirk on her face, and
she looked at my bosom and then at my face
with this look that said I knew all along, you
can't hide anything from me. I saw such envy
in the way she looked. Oh, I wish Ruth was
my sister! That's mean, isn't it? I feel sorry for
Arlene. She's been out of high school for two
years, and no one has shown any interest in
marrying her. She has nowhere to go. How
awful!*

*Dad asked me if you had talked with
your parents about us getting married, and
I said I didn't know. Have you? I wonder if
they even remember who I am. I hope they
aren't angry. I so wish I could be with you
right now and see your face and hear your
voice and talk to you and know that your
going to reassure me everything's going to*

*work out and that your family is going to
accept me as your wife. What if they dont?
The thought makes me want to just shrivel
up and die.*

*I so wish I could call you and talk to
you, but all the women around here listen
in on the phone calls and know everything
that's going on. But every time I walk by
the telephone I think of calling you so I can
hear your voice. Your picture stands before
my eyes constantly as I write, tempting me
to give up my sanity and believe you can
see and hear me. Even now as I look at it
while I write I try to imagine it coming to
life, but it won't. See how much I miss you?
Oh please write soon, before I go completely
crazy with love.*

Your adoring Joyce

• • •

*Sunday, November 5
My dear wife-to-be,*

*I wrote to my parents shortly after I got your
letter telling me you were "in the family way."
They called the dorm today. We had a long
talk in the office with the doors closed. They
aren't opposed to us getting married, but
they had a lot of questions. They wonder
where we're going to live, what we're going
to live on, and what my plans are for school.
Joyce, I must admit, I didn't have any
answers. It's not that I hadn't thought of*

these questions before, it's just that I didn't want to contemplate the answers. The only solution I can think of is living at the lodge and helping my parents run the resort. I don't know where I could get a job right away that would pay enough for us to rent a place to live and take care of the baby. There's plenty of room at the lodge. Both of my sisters moved out when they got married, so there's just Mom, Dad and Art. We could get married perhaps right before Christmas, after the fall term at the U.

There is one other question my parents asked. Is she Catholic? We haven't talked much about religion. I know my parents want me to marry a Catholic. How do you feel about religion, and how do your parents feel? Would you be willing to convert to Catholicism?

Please let me know what you think about getting married in December and living at the lodge. I wish I could call you, but obviously I can't if all your neighbors will be listening in. So please write soon.

Your devoted partner in life,
Bill

• • •

Sunday, November 12
My darling Bill,

I will marry you today, tomorrow, on Christmas day, whenever you want. And I will

*be happy to live with your parents and Art,
and I will work hard to help your family run
the resort. I will even find a way to work with
the baby so maybe you can continue going to
college. But when I brought up the subject of
religion the day before yesterday, Dad seemed
pretty angry. We didn't talk about it much,
but that night I could hear Mom and Dad
talking about it in their room. I couldn't hear
everything they said, just enough to know
they weren't very happy. Well, this morning at
breakfast Dad told me I should do what I felt
was right. If your parents want me to convert
so that we can be married in the Catholic
Church, then I will. If they want us to be
married in Mirer, then that's what I want. Bill,
I would convert to paganism if that's what
I'd have to do to marry you. But please don't
tell your parents that! I love you love you love
you. I'm so happy we're going to be married. I
know there's nothing could stop us. We love one
another too much to let anything get in the way.
Please write soon and tell me what I must do.*

*Your Adoring Wife (to-be),
Joyce*

• • •

*Tuesday, December 5
Dear Bill,*

*You have been gone for a little more than a day
and already I miss you as if you'd been gone
for years. I'm so happy, but at the same time*

I'm frightened. I've never experienced anything like this before. In less than two weeks Im going to leave my home and my family forever and start a new life with you. Im frightened because I realize I can no longer live without you. And yet I cant wait until were married and I can curl up inside your arms and let you hold me against your chest like a little animal. I dream during the day and at night of lying next to you and feeling my body merge with yours. Right now I dont want anything else than to be part of you. I mean really a part of you, a part of your stomach and a part of your chest. And I want our baby to be a part of both of us. I can't wait until we can both feel this baby inside me. I dreamed the other night about Ruth's Russian dolls. There are three dolls, all alike, except each one is a different size. I put the smallest one inside the middle-sized one, and that one inside the largest one. Then I'd take them apart and do it again. It felt so good to do this, because I knew you were the largest doll and our baby was the littlest one. And now I feel like such a silly ninny for telling you this. Whenever I start talking this way I'm always afraid your going to think I'm a little loony and have second thoughts about marrying me. But I know you love me enough to forgive me for being silly sometimes.

As long as I'm talking about silly things, I should tell you I've been spending hours practicing writing my new name. I've written Mrs. Bill Bauer, Mrs. William Bauer, Mrs. W. Bauer, Mrs. Bauer, Joyce Bauer, and Joyce Marie Bauer. I like them all. I'm going to use

*every one of them. I've practiced all sorts of
fancy loops and curlicues. I'm sending the paper
on which I practiced so you can see for yourself.
Please let me know what you think. If we're
going to be married until death do us part, you
should at least like the way I sign our name.*

*It's already the 5th, and there's so much
to do before the wedding. Mom is making the
wedding dress. She got some beautiful white
satin and lace for my dress and Arlene's. I'm
afraid standing next to the bride is the closest
Arlene will ever come to getting married. I
would of preferred having Ruth as my maid of
honor, but when I suggested that to Mom she
gave me a look that said don't even think it.
She's stubborn about some things, and with the
wedding in Mirer and her not having much
to say about that, I don't argue with her. I've
never seen her so happy. While Mom's been
busy making our dresses, I've been sorting
through my things and deciding what I'm
going to bring with me. At first I wanted to
bring everything I've ever owned, but then I
decided to just bring some family pictures
and my clothes. It's a new life I'm beginning,
and I don't want to bring too much of the past
with me. I have been talking with some of our
friends, but only Ruth is going to come with us
to Mirer for the wedding. Dad was concerned
about leaving the farm for three days, but one
of our neighbors offered to help Charles with
the chores so Dad can go too. I wish Charles
and Robert could come too, but, well, they cant.*

*I still cant believe that in less then two
weeks we're going to be married. I love you Bill,*

I love you more than you can ever imagine.
Please take good care of me. I'm all yours.

All my love,
Joyce

. . .

December 8, 1939
Dear Joyce,

I was so happy to talk with you and hear
your voice! Yes, letters are too slow, but the
wonderful thing about letters is that you can
read them over and over again. Right now I
wish I had the letter you mailed on Wednesday.
You did the right thing, by the way, mailing
it to the lodge. I take my last final exam this
afternoon, and then I'm going to start packing
right away so I can leave on Sunday. Going is
even sweeter knowing that there's a letter from
you waiting for me. And you will be arriving
just five days after I get home. I can't wait
to see you and hold you. In just a little over
a week we will be husband and wife. Then
we can actually kiss in public, if we feel like
it, and go to bed together without hiding, as
if it were wrong. I want to see how you have
changed since I saw you at Thanksgiving. I
want to nibble at your breasts, kiss the little
mole on your tummy, and dissolve inside of you
like a sugar cube in your mouth. You can see
why it's so hard for me to focus on my exams!
My mother said everything will be ready
for the wedding. From what you said your

*dress sounds beautiful. I'm trying to imagine
you wearing a "veil of snow," as you described
the lace your mother used. You will be my
snow bride, beautiful and pure as the snow. I
can't tell you how lucky I feel!*

*That's what my friends have been telling
me too. I'm lucky. As I said when I talked to
you last night, I feel kind of sad about leaving
school and not knowing if I will ever be able to
come back. Part of the reason is that I've really
come to like school, in particular English. And I
think if I were to stay on I would want to major
in English. I'd love to be a writer and compose
novels. I don't know if I'm good enough to ever
be able to earn a living at it, but it's something
I'd sure love to do. I just finished reading a
novel called The Grapes of Wrath by a writer
named Steinbeck. I've never seen the kind of
suffering and exploitation that we know exists
in the world depicted so clearly. I realized as
I read that book that the writer must assume
responsibility for showing the world as it is,
and not as we might like to think it is. If I could
write something half as good as this book, I'd
consider myself a success. Someday I'm going to
find a way to become a writer. But for now, it's
go back home, help Mom and Dad take care of
the resort, and bide my time. I know my turn
will come.*

*George, my roommate, has organized a
going-away party for me on Saturday night. I
am really sad about leaving all of my friends.
We have grown so close over the last year and
a half, we're like one big family. We spend
hours meeting in the lounge, in one another's*

*rooms, or at a restaurant called The Varsity,
and we talk about everything—the depression,
the economy, FDR and the New Deal, the war,
our courses and profs, what we want to be
when we get out, and even our sweethearts. My
friends know all about you! I think I've done
more talking during the last fifteen months
than during all the preceding years of my
life. But I've done a lot of listening too. One
thing I've learned is everyone, even the most
shy, timid person, has something to say worth
listening to. And perhaps one of the reasons I
liked Steinbeck's book so much is it seemed to
include somehow a little of almost every story
I've heard, only in a much more dramatic
way. But there have been so many stories
about people doing the most desperate things
to try to hold body and soul together. What an
education this has been! Now, with the war
in Europe, I think we're in for something very
different. Sooner or later we're going to end up
fighting in this war. I just know it.*

*I can't believe I've written almost four
pages, and I have an exam in just a little over
an hour! I'm going to mail this right after the
exam with the hope it reaches you before you
leave for Mirer. Remember I love you, will
always love you, and marrying you is a dream
come true.*

*Love,
Bill*

• • •

May 11, 1940
My Dear Bill,

I have tried writing to you, but every time I think of our little William Paul I start to cry and get tears all over the letter. I need to talk to you, and yet words won't come. I love you. I need you.

Your Loving Wife,
Joyce

• • •

May 15, 1940
My Dearest Bill,

I so miss having you near and being able to talk to you. I want to tell you that for the first time since the death of our little William Paul, I felt the sun penetrate my body and bring warmth into this heart that has been like a room cold with death and the dark forms of a dead baby and grieving parents.

Ruth, who has been such a dear to me, visiting with me every day, succeeded in getting me out of the house today. Do you remember, my Sweetheart, when you were here at Thanksgiving and we walked to the top of the ridge next to the barn and looked out at the valley and the marsh below and I showed you that cow path along the west side of the marsh? That's where we went. Red-winged blackbirds flew from one cattail to another, and on the other side of the path where Papa

*had planted wheat some yellow finches
perched on the barbed wire singing their
hearts out. We came to the old wood bridge
that crosses the creek and stopped to watch
the water sparkling in the sun as if there was
electricity running through it. A big mud turtle
sunning itself on a rock gave us the idea to
do the same. We sat down on the edge of the
bridge and let the sun warm our backs and
watched the stream with all that silver energy
flashing. For the first time since the death
of William Paul I realized how lucky I am to
be your wife and to receive your love. That
thought charged me with a kind of energy I
haven't felt since that horrible day.*

    *Ruth and I continued our walk toward the
woods. The crows began cawing to warn the
forest creatures we were coming. We walked on
last fall's leaves, all brown and rust. We had to
climb over a fallen tree, and I stopped to look
up at the sun shining through the tree tops. It
shined like a pathway to heaven, and I thought
of walking up that pathway and taking back
my little William Paul. I felt my heart break
again. Ruth put her arm around me and we
walked some more until we came to my favorite
place, the place where I wanted to take you
when you were here at Thanksgiving. There's
a soft grassy slope where the creek bends and
flows quickly over some rocks. We laid down on
the slope. I closed my eyes and listened to the
creek spilling over the rocks, the birds chirping,
a squirrel running from one branch to another.
The sun warmed my eyelids. The thought of
you warmed my heart. We lay there for about*

*an hour and then I wanted to come home, look
at your picture, and write to you. You're my
sunshine. Your love gives me life. I want to
come home soon. I want to place my hand in
yours and walk with you to the end of our days.*

*Your Loving Wife,
Joyce*

• • •

*May 17, 1940
My Dear Sweet Bill,*

*I must tell you about the adventure Ruth
and I had yesterday. We drove all the way to
St. Paul and back again in one day! Ruthie
is learning how to drive her father's car. He
actually allowed her to drive all that way by
herself! Well, of course I was there too, but you
can imagine how much help I would have been
if anything had gone wrong. I'm afraid we
were real naughty, driving with the windows
open and the radio playing music that just
made me want to dance.*

*When we were in St. Paul we went to see a
movie called Rebecca. It was about a woman
who gets married and moves into a big house
by the ocean. Her husband and the maid and
everyone else expect her to behave just like
the man's first wife, Rebecca. And the woman
starts to feel Rebecca is everywhere in the house,
until finally Rebecca seems to live through
her. Ruth apologized after we left the theater
because she didn't think it was the right kind*

*of movie for me to see, after everything I've been
through. But I told her the movie gave me hope.
You see, I believe our William Paul will come
back to us somehow. He isn't really dead, he's
just gone, but he'll return. Do you believe people
can come back from the dead? I do. I really do.
Our love will bring him back.*

*Your Longing Wife,
Joyce*

• • •

Tears fall on the page, and ink that dried fifty years
before begins to bleed. Paul rolls over on his back, closes
his eyes, and lets the tears stream down his cheeks. It feels
good to cry, to let out all this emotion he'd brought into
himself. Exhausted, like a medium at the end of a séance
coming out of a trance, he lies dead still. Joyce and Bill
have lived in him. Everything. The dreams, the yearning,
the lovemaking, the belief that all their dreams would
come true and love would last forever. He felt like a father
wanting to protect his two children—so naive, so vulnerable, they don't know, they can't know, the betrayals and
the loss they'll experience. An immense sadness wells up
in him, and yet he returns to all that he shares with them
in his life—spending afternoons in the hay loft reading
novels and fantasizing magnificent flights into other
worlds, making love on the floor of the boathouse, wanting
a partner in life, someone in whom he could place all his
trust and who would say to him, "My hand in yours ... to
the end of our days," and the desire to escape from this
place, this cold gray place, where dead dreams accumulate,
a glacier, with layers of ice.

He breathes a heavy sigh, rolls over on his side, gathers

up the letters, carries them over to the desk and puts them back. No need to lock the drawer now. The secret's out. He's about to put the key back in the cigar box, when he stops to look at the queen—the "cigar lady." Mother gave Stone a similar box with his treasure—the three rocks. He smiles at the pun—Stone has his rocks in a lady's box—but the joke seems tacky. It cheapens Mother. He closes the box with the key in it and puts it back beneath the floor plank.

He lies in bed, staring at the ceiling. He sees men at the bar, drinking and smoking cigars, the smoke accumulating in a haze. The child touches his mother's thigh as if to reassure himself of her presence. Her legs, covered with black lace, rise high above him like graceful white columns covered with black shadow. From her great height she bends down, takes him in her arms; he feels himself raised into the cloud of acrid smoke, his head pressed against her breast. She turns him around and holds him with his back toward her so he can see the elderly men who gaze at her while rolling their cigars on their lips, slipping them in and out of their mouths like trombone slides, then lighting them. Such a funny sight. He looks at them as if he were about to bless them; but of course he doesn't, he's just a child. His father looks on, smiling, happy as a king, while the haze thickens and becomes a cloud that slowly consumes him. The old farts puff on their cigars and grin. He turns away from the leering elders, nestles his face in the hollow of her neck, places his hand on her breast, and looks over her shoulder at a teenage boy gazing at her with adoration.

14

PAUL FLIES DOWN THE ROAD TOWARD MIRER WITH-
out noticing his speed, he's so preoccupied by the dream
of snow. He had it again last night, the dream of the boy
running on a plane of snow, pursuing the tornadoes of white
dust ... or fleeing, the thick crust collapsing beneath his
feet. He's going to find out what all this means—the feeling
of panic, of danger; the relief when he reaches the summit
of the hill and stands on solid ground; the giddiness as he
plunges into the valley below and falls such a long way; the
power of his flight as he glides across the broad bosom of
snow, a deep, thick comforter of snow buoying him on its
surface, bearing him as if he were weightless. Everything—
the plane of snow, the hilltop, the valley below—everything
comes from his grandparents' farm.

From Mirer he turns southeast, driving past pine
forests, stands of leafless birch, frozen lakes, marsh-
land, fields buried in snow, Iron Range towns with a gas
station and a food mart, isolated white frame houses with
satellite dishes to receive the world and aluminum-sided
trailers parked along side. He follows a labyrinthine route

through Duluth to Superior and heads south again through Wisconsin, through a region of small hills and valleys, past isolated shacks and old rusting hulks of cars abandoned in snow covered fields and woods. Gradually the land levels off; stands of cottonwood and oak replace forests of pine and birch; and farms, driveways lined with trees standing guard, two-story white houses, and fields covered with snow dominate the landscape.

He feels a rush as he approaches the sign with the town's name, New Bremen, and the population: 8,396. He slows while crossing the old iron bridge to look at the frozen river covered with snow and swept by the streamers of willows. He opens his window and smells again the aroma of feed dust as he drives past the grain elevators where he used to go with his grandfather in the pickup truck loaded with corn or grain. Driving on instinct, he turns right at one stoplight, left at another, and soon finds himself barreling down the blacktop highway he and his grandfather used to take to town, remembering the old man driving thirty in a fifty-five-mile-per-hour speed zone while looking at every field of wheat, oats, or corn to see how his neighbors' crops were doing.

He turns off the highway onto a dirt road that looks familiar and accelerates, hoping to find a landmark that would tell him he's on the right track. He crosses a bridge over a creek, hits the brakes, nearly skids off the road, then backs up. This is it, the creek where he used to go swimming with the other farm kids. Bare asses, unless there were girls. Then they'd wear underpants. After swimming they'd come out of the water and inspect one another, rubbing the leeches with sand until they rolled up and fell off. He gets out of the car, walks around the front to the side of the bridge, and stares at the deep snow, knowing that beneath it is the creek and the swimming hole where the course of the stream broadens and slackens in a large pool before narrowing into a tight channel and coursing forward beneath oak and cottonwood. He drives on. A little further and the fields on his left start looking familiar. He remembers baling hay and threshing grain. He takes a left at the next intersection.

He slows to a stop at the top of the hill and gazes at the farm far below, amazed that something so deeply buried in the past can still exist. Suddenly it returns intact and complete—the images, sounds, smells, even the touch of things from the days and the weeks and the months spent on the farm: the pungent odor of fermenting yeast that permeated his grandmother's kitchen; the grid over the floor heater in the living room that would get so hot it burned stockinged feet; the creaking of steps and floorboards upstairs; the squeaking of old bedsprings and the hushed voices of his grandparents at night across the hall; the musty mattress that closed around him like a catcher's glove around a ball. And the cow barn: the extraordinary whiteness of stone walls and concrete floor covered with lime; white painted beams, posts, and planks that stood out with skeletal clarity among the shadows of animal pens and stalls; massive Holsteins, with their bloated bellies and swollen udders, lying on the straw with their necks in stanchions, ruminating, waiting for evening when they would be relieved of their milk, warming the barn with their body heat; the extraordinary silence of these animals whose breathing gave life and warmth to wood, stone, and straw; the silver fern and floral pattern of clear ice on the sparkling frost of the window panes and the sun that gleamed on the banks and drifts of snow outside.

He lets the car coast down the hill, then turns into the long driveway lined with oak, gazing at the drifts of snow across the field on the right and the yard on the left, and at the old white house that he approached from this driveway so many times when he was a boy. The two-story house, facing east, can be entered through a small covered porch with a white balustrade not much more than knee-high and two white posts that support the roof. He slows to nearly a stop as he stares at the porch. Something is different. He never paid much attention to the porch because this entrance wasn't generally used. People usually drove around to the back—the north side of the house—and entered through the washroom and coat room. The front entrance was used only for special occasions, when people would spill out onto the porch and the lawn.

He remembers uncles in white shirts with their sleeves rolled up on their forearms; aunts in black or royal blue silky dresses with white dots, or white dresses with floral patterns; young girls in white Sunday dresses and sapling boys dressed just like their fathers in white shirts and tugging at their collars. The men, drinking beer out of bottles while they waited for lunch, talked about work, hunting, fishing, and farm equipment; whispered dirty jokes, laughing raucously at the punch line; and told hushed stories, accompanied by sly looks, about their escapades in Europe during or after the war and their encounters with women, some enamored of American heroes who had saved or conquered their countries, others desperate for money. Their wives, bustling in and out of the house, checking on kids squirming in the sun and their Sunday clothes and wishing they could run down to the barn and climb up into the hay loft or ride two each bareback on the work horses, talked about kids, kitchens, pregnancies, recipes, diets, and cool nights at the movies when it was just too hot to do anything else. Later they would all quiet down as they sat on the porch or beneath the boughs of the surrounding trees that filtered the sun, eating from plates they balanced on their legs. At least one of the little urchins would spill gravy or preserves all over a white shirt or a dress and there'd be a flurry of activity. Paul can almost hear a mother's gentle scolding.

And then he sees it—the picture of his mother, the little blond girl with a Dutch cut who captured the sun in her smile and who radiated in that smile a wealth of love given and received. He remembers seeing in the background of the picture the stairs leading up to the porch, one of the columns holding up the roof, and part of the balustrade. So the picture was taken here. Suddenly the house, which he has always identified with his childhood, is part of her childhood as well. It's not only his memory, it's hers too, and perhaps one of her most treasured. He thinks of her getting ready to die, thinking of him, and mailing that picture— mailing her memory to his. He can imagine her so clearly, the little blond girl standing on the porch and smiling into the sun, just as he can remember himself taking advantage of his small size to slip into the circle of men as they stood in front of the porch and told their stories.

He slowly accelerates. As the driveway curves around to the back of the house, where everyone used to park, he wonders if his grandparents will step out of the back door and walk toward the end of the sidewalk to greet him. But no one comes out. He pulls alongside a new Ford parked next to the walk, goes up to the house, and knocks at the door. A man in his mid-thirties opens. When Paul explains that he frequently stayed there as a boy with his grandparents and asks if he can take a look around, a smile spreads across the man's face.

"I knew your grandpa. Adolph."

"He preferred to be called A.J."

"That he did. I remember now. I baled hay and threshed grain on his farm here when I was a kid." He gazes at the field off to his left, as if he could see himself working.

"I did too."

The man looks back at Paul. "Oh yeah? I wonder if we didn't work together. What's your name?"

"Paul. Paul Bauer." He extends his hand.

The man shakes his hand. "Pat Michels. My dad's George Michels. Owns a farm about a mile west of here."

The name seems familiar.

Pat studies Paul's face. "I don't remember you."

"Well, that was a long time ago. I'll turn forty in a few months, so ..."

"Oh, that explains it. I'm thirty-four. So if you came here when you were a boy ..."

Paul nods his head.

They recall shared memories of the men on the threshing and baling crews and how, when they'd stop work on AJ's fields to break for lunch, they'd gather underneath those old cottonwoods—Paul looks behind and sees the trees still standing there, on the other side of the driveway—where they'd parked their tractors, and they'd stand around in their bib overalls and sweat-soaked shirts and t-shirts, drink their Leinenkugel's, and tell stories about some of the local characters—like the one about the drunk who years before had a horse step on his lip. And the one Grandpa loved to tell, about his half-brother showing him photos in a family album and coming to a picture of a woman facing the camera and the rear end of a horse standing next to her, and saying "The one on the right is Aunt Cora." He never cracked a smile. Great deadpan humor. They all had it. And the ones who were listening, they'd nod their heads, might even laugh, but not too loud, look at one another and smile. Great storytellers.

"And," Paul adds, "the happiest people I've ever known."

"Those days are gone for good. A corporation in the cities has been buying up all the farms around here. They had to take this one too. The house and a couple acres, that's all they'd sell me."

Pat invites him to come on in and see the changes he and the wife have made. The old washroom where the men would take turns washing themselves in two basins placed in a wash stand, plunging their hands in the soapy water to wash the sweat and chaff off their arms, bending over to splash water on their faces, then dry themselves with towels that were soon soaked, is now an office. A computer screen, with numbers in rows and columns, faces them.

Paul stands in the kitchen, with its tiled floor, formica counter tops, and microwave, and breathes deeply, trying to find the smell of fermenting yeast, rising dough, and bread baking in the oven that always permeated the air. In the dining room there used to be a buffet with framed photographs of his mother, aunt, and two uncles, and a long table with a shallow bowl of plastic fruit (red apples, yellow bananas, and purple grapes). Up and down the table a crew of ten or twelve men and boys would pass platters of roast beef and chicken, bowls of mashed potatoes and gravy, plates with heaps of corn on the cob, layers of sliced tomatoes from the garden, and homemade pickles, bread, pies, and cakes. Now there's a small round table with four chairs. The hardwood floors, which Paul remembers being a dark, scuffed brown, have been sanded and refinished with a clear stain that gleams in the sunlight. A half-bath has been installed off the kitchen and a full bath on the floor just above it, so, Pat grins, no more chamber pots, or having to stumble outside to pee in the middle of the night; and he and the wife don't have to fill up a tub in the basement with hot water to take a bath anymore; and in the living room they never burn their feet on the grill of that goddamn floor heater because they got central air.

Paul notices something strange with each step as he walks with Pat through the house; they stop, he takes another step, and realizes what it is: the floors—they don't creak. As a boy he could track anyone in the house by the creaking floor boards. At night in bed he could hear his grandparents come up the stairs and go into their room, the bed springs squeaking as they got into bed, and his own springs squeaking too as he nestled into the mattress. The whole house, with all of its sighing, squeaking, and cracking, seemed to surround him and pull him into its warm bosom, just as his grandmother would draw him in between her ample breasts, where he would disappear in a huge hug. He remembers her not so much walking around the house as waddling, swaying from side to side with each step, an effort that made her gasp and sigh as she walked, marching like a steam fired machine across the floor that creaked with every step. That house is gone. This one has nothing in common with his grandmother or with him.

Paul stands at the end of the concrete sidewalk looking down the gravel road toward the barn, a tall, weathered, gray structure, once red, built into the side of a hill. He can see his grandfather, alone, walking up the road toward the house, his head bowed, his shock of white hair wild and unruly, a King Lear in bib overalls muttering to himself. He'd always been stooped, always had white hair, and was always muttering, perhaps whispering to the ghosts of his past, or cursing his fate, or just rambling incoherently. He'd raise his head to look up at the sky and out at the fields, gauging the likelihood of good or bad weather and of the crops making it to harvest. Hoping for good luck. He may as well have been playing Russian roulette—with nature instead of a gun. Every year he'd spin the wheel and hope it wouldn't stop on a loaded chamber—a couple of months without rain, or a couple of months with too much rain, or a hail storm that could flatten entire fields. But after everything the old man had been through—the death of his impoverished mother when he was just a boy; his father's rejection; his years wandering from one town to another, drinking in nearly every bar and saloon in Minnesota and the Dakotas; the death of his first wife during the flu epidemic at the end of World War I; and the death of one of his sons in World War II—losing a field of wheat or corn must have seemed trivial.

Paul starts down the road of frozen mud and gravel. He enters the machine shed, a hangarlike structure of corrugated steel with fiberglass skylights, and is startled by the sudden flutter of wings as sparrows swoop down from their nests in the cross joints of the metal beams and fly just over his head and out the open door. Tractors, wagons, hay cutters, rakes with long spindles, and a threshing machine used to fill the cavernous building. "Hello," he shouts, and listens to the faint echo. He leaves. The old machine shed, much smaller than the building that replaced it, not much bigger than a garage, was already old when he was a boy. The roof has rotted and caved in and the walls, the red paint weathered to a rusty gray, look as if they might follow. He takes a deep breath: the smell of oil and grease that penetrated the work bench and the dirt floor over the decades that men spent repairing farm machinery is gone.

He walks a little further, then stops to look at a huge old cottonwood tree behind a grain shed and some chicken coops, all caving in. Is this the same tree he climbed so high he could see the surrounding fields in every direction for at least a mile? Big patches of color—green fields of corn, yellow fields of wheat, rust fields of oats, and off in the distance toward the north a green forest. He looked down at the machine shed and the chicken coops so far below it was like looking through the wrong end of a telescope and saw Grandpa leave a chicken coop and walk down the road toward the house, carrying two pails full of eggs. He shouted to him; Grandpa stopped and looked around, but didn't see him. He shouted again. Grandpa looked up, but still didn't see him. He shouted a third time, and finally Grandpa looked way up, saw him, and dropped the pails he was carrying. One of them tipped over and the eggs rolled out. Grandpa started yelling to get down, and all the while he was yelling he was stepping on the eggs. By the time he got down Grandpa was so angry he grabbed him by the collar, hauled him into the house, and called the lodge. He told his mother he was sending this kid home and not to send him back until he learned to keep his goddamn feet on the ground. Paul was back in a few weeks, even though he hadn't learned to keep his feet on the ground.

Paul reaches the horse barn, a sturdy structure of stone walls and wood planks, built into the same hill as the cow barn. He tries to push the heavy wooden door far enough on the track from which it hangs to wedge his body in the entry, but the door won't move. All he can see in the darkness is the vague forms of wooden stalls and pens.

He follows the dirt road leading out of the barnyard and reaches the crest of the hill. From here he used to watch the sun sit on the horizon in the summer like a huge red ball, while birds (hundreds of them, perhaps thousands) would flock and fly together as if they were a wave, flowing in one direction, and then another, or an organism with invisible ligatures, a dancer using the huge red ball on the horizon as a backdrop. Wheeling in a swarm, all of them chirping so loud they'd almost make you deaf, they'd suddenly fly off and disperse among the trees that lined the end of the field just across the way and continue their cacophonous chorus until the sun set.

He turns around and walks east along the crest of the hill to the hayloft above the cow barn. He rocks the door back and forth on its track until he can push it open enough to step inside. He has always remembered the loft at least a third full of bales of hay. Now it's empty. A huge space lit only by the sunlight filtering through the cracks between the vertical planks of the walls. The ceiling seems so high that looking up almost makes him dizzy. Great timbers, probably twelve by twelves, rise gracefully like the masts of an old seafaring ship. This is one of the most beautiful places he has ever known. There's something magical and ethereal about it. The tall ceiling, the wooden beams, the shafts of sunlight piercing the west wall and lighting the space from floor to ceiling—all of this reminds him of the interior of a Gothic cathedral, except that here everything seems soft, warm, and homely. He squats and runs his fingertips across the wooden planks polished smooth as skin and soft as silk by all the bales that have been thrown on them. He stands up again and looks around. The chute— four vertical poles with cross poles nailed to them every few feet—rises at least twenty feet above the floor. Here and there baling twine hangs from the cross poles in long tresses like a woman's hair, once blond, now faded to gray. He remembers breaking open bales of hay over the chute, shaking the bales to break them up so they'd fall to the floor of the cow barn, and tossing the baling twine over the poles.

He used to come here with his cousins to play hide- and-seek and wrestle—in spite of his grandparents' warn- ings not to do so, after one of his cousins fell down the steps from the hayloft to the cow barn floor and broke his arm. When he outgrew that kind of play, he and an older cousin would bring their BB guns up here and, pretending they were sharpshooters, wait for sparrows to perch on a beam. The birds would fall with hardly a flutter to the cats waiting below, and after a few minutes their bones would crack like dry sticks as they were eaten.

Then one summer, finally a teenager, he came here with his cousin Sarah. They climbed the bales of hay stacked at least ten high and nestled in a corner where the air was so still and so hot they were immediately covered with sweat. That corner became their haven. One day she removed her blouse and allowed him to touch her newly formed breasts; another day she lay down on her belly, had him rub her back, pulling her pants down below her hips so he could touch her buttocks; another day she did the same thing, and when he was fondling her buttocks, she rolled over onto her back; and the next time she had him lie on top of her. He smelled sweat, alfalfa, and when he came, the pungent odor of sperm and pussy juice. It all seemed so easy and to end so quickly that he wondered, is that all? How could something that had seemed so complex be so simple? With Sarah, it was as natural as breathing.

As that summer wore on he immersed himself in novels, became the characters he read about, and wanted more than anything else, even more than making love with Sarah, to explore all the cities he'd first seen through their eyes. He feels so close to this boy, so primed and ready to voyage to New York and the cities of Europe, so certain he can realize his dreams, his whole life ahead of him; and then he feels the boy's vulnerability. He'd like to talk to the kid, to warn him. He feels a kind of fondness for him. But he lets go; that boy can only live in the past.

Mother would also come here, stretch out on the bales, read her letters by the sunlight entering the cracks, and roll up in the shadows of her dreams. He knows, like a pain in his stomach, her teenage hunger, her craving for a life beyond the farm that must've seemed impossible to satiate—until she met a man at a resort and fell in love. All of the bits and pieces of her that he found in the pictures and letters suddenly fuse, galvanized into something vital that pulses through him like blood, and he feels the exorbitance of her dreams and her fantasies catapulting her beyond the cycle of days and months and years that otherwise lay before her. He looks up at the ceiling so far above and at the massive timbers that rise to meet it, and he imagines her lying on the hay, a letter fallen from her hand, gazing upward, the ceiling to her dreams so high. No idea of the gap between what she fantasized and what she would encounter.

And yet, he thinks, remembering the wedding invitation,

she never let go. No matter how great the gap, how much the stretch, she never let go of the man she loved. Paul feels he has found her just as she really was, the girl who came here to dream. The girl lived in the old woman, and the old woman still loved the man she dreamed of when she was a girl. And Paul knows that she loved him too. Knows it because she has guided him to this moment. She loves him from beyond the grave.

Dizzy from standing and looking up, Paul sits down so he won't fall, lies back, stares up at the ceiling and at the mastlike timbers, and feels the whole loft might set sail and carry him off. He lies there for a long time, exhausted, in a daze, until a current of cold air from the open door blows down his neck. He shivers, pulls himself up, and steps outside.

He gazes at the valley below, the snow covered pond and the winding creek, and the hill in the distance. This is the place where it all started—the dream of the boy walking across snow drifts to the ridge, looking out over this valley, and flying, as if he were a bird. And the horrible feeling when Paul awakes of having lost something. This dream must mean something—why else would it have returned to him so frequently?—but what?

He heads west, walking until he passes the end of the barn, then stops and looks around. From that point he can see everything: on one side of the ridge, the long slope of snow leading down to the valley and the marsh below; on the other side, the deep drifts of snow that have filled the far side of the barnyard and form a bridge to the ridge at the top of the hill. None of this makes him feel the emotions he feels each time he dreams of the boy walking on the snow drift and standing on the ridge looking out at the valley below. There's no connection. He was so sure when he set out to come here he'd find one.

This is not the place he dreamed about. He doesn't

understand how this could be, yet he doesn't doubt his conclusion, which seems at once obvious and inexplicable.

It's late afternoon by the time he drives past the white porch on the east side of the house where his mother posed as a child, and early evening when he reaches St. Paul. He checks in at a Ramada Inn and calls Ruth Langston to tell her he received the packet of letters she'd sent and he'd like to stop by and visit with her for a while.

The next morning around nine thirty he pulls up in front of a small stucco bungalow in the Merriam Park neighborhood, an old part of the city, and walks up to the door. Ruth answers. She stands in the open door, dressed in a faded pink sweatshirt and matching pants, telling him, "Come in, come on in." She's been up and about for at least an hour, she tells Paul, just working with her plants, so no, his visit is definitely not a bother. She invites him to sit down on the couch and asks him if he'd like a cup of coffee, she's just brewed a pot. While she's in the kitchen, he looks around the small living room at the brick fireplace and oak mantelpiece, a television on a small table in the corner, an old black recliner, and a plump arm chair with an ottoman. All the furniture looks worn, but well cared for and inviting. The dark brown surface of the coffee table in front of him glistens from constant cleaning and oiling. He sits on the edge of the couch, his forearms resting on his knees, staring at an old scrapbook with black strings tied in a limp bow at the top right side, wondering if it was a good idea to come.

She reappears, hands him a mug with steaming black coffee, and sits down on the couch next to him. "Well, how are you getting on at the lodge?"

"Okay. A little bit of cabin fever. I'm ready to beat the walls down. That's probably one of the reasons I'm here—couldn't stand my own walls anymore."

"Mine weigh on me too, but probably not as much." She looks at him. "You said you wanted to talk about your mother."

"Yeah. My mother and my father."

"Like I told you before, I don't know much of anything about him, and most of what I know your mother told me." She looks him squarely in the eye. "I was always on her side."

He nods. "I know." He peers into the shot-glass lenses of her glasses and her milky blue marbles.

"What can I tell you?" she muses, turning away, staring at nothing in particular. "They sure didn't know one another when they got married. All totaled, they only spent a few days together during those two summers before they got married. Otherwise, it was just letters ... lots of letters. You don't need a college education to know that people are a lot different from the way they show themselves in letters."

"You talk as if their marriage was somehow doomed from the start."

She looks at him. "It was. Other people knew it ... and maybe Joyce and Bill knew it too. But I don't think anyone said anything to them. I sure didn't. You can't tell your best friend the man she's going to marry isn't right for her. She has to figure that out for herself."

"That must've been hard for you, to think they weren't right for one another and not say anything."

"It's hard to explain. It's kind of like a sound that you can hear only when it's completely quiet. Like hearing your heart beat." She remains silent for a while as if indeed listening to her heart. "I remember when my husband Eddy left for the war ..."

"I didn't know you were married."

"Twice ... and twice a widow." She pauses, then continues. "When Eddy left we were living in an apartment down by Como Avenue, just a few blocks from the railroad tracks. The first night he was gone I heard the sound of diesel engines starting up and pushing railroad cars, and making a kind of chugging, whining sound that would suddenly end with a crash, the sound railroad cars make when they're being coupled. It would be completely quiet, and then it would start all over again. That would go on all night. I never heard that sound before the day Eddy left, but I heard it that night and every night after."

She looks at Paul and smiles, her eyes twinkling at the bottom of the shot glasses. "I don't want you to think I sat around worrying about your mother. We're all selfish in the end, and you can think about someone else's problems for just so long."

He smiles and nods his head.

She turns her face away from him. "I was nineteen, still living on the farm with my mom and dad, and too worried about myself to worry about Joyce. There wasn't much to look forward to but marrying a farm boy and spending the rest of my life the way my mother had. I didn't want that. So I went to stay with a gal I knew who'd moved to St. Paul, and I got a job. The first one didn't work out, but after a while I got a job as a nanny for a doctor and his wife over on Summit. There was a bakery on Grand that used to deliver bread and rolls to the house Tuesdays and Saturdays. Usually it was a young boy who came to the house, but one Saturday this young man came. Dressed all in white and handsome as an angel. I let him in the kitchen while I went to get the money, and then we talked. And a few months later we were married. Everything went real fast." She falls silent.

Paul finally asks, "Did you, ah ... did you have any children?"

She starts. "No. We weren't together for a very long time. He left for the war about two years after we got married. Never came home again. He died at a place called Anzio. In Italy."

"I'm sorry to hear ..."

She nods her head slowly. "There were a lot of gals like me. A lot of young widows." She sighs, looks at him, and smiles. "See, you let me get started, I might just talk you to death. Here, I wanted to look at this with you."

She picks up the black scrapbook, unties the long frayed laces, and opens it. There were pictures: two teenage girls, Ruth and his mother, facing the camera, posing for it with the shyness and exuberance of their adolescence; Eddy, with wavy black hair, dressed in white work pants and a white t-shirt; and Eddy in an army uniform standing next to Ruth, both of them facing the camera, his right arm around her back; and several pictures of his mother, some of her alone with each of her infants, and a few group pictures of her and her family. Newspaper articles, mostly clippings from the *St. Paul Pioneer Press*: the snow storm on Armistice Day 1940, and a picture of the roof of a black car buried in snow; battles in the African campaign, in which Eddy had participated; and a clipping about Anzio, and yet another about those from Minnesota who had died there. And various memorabilia: his parents' wedding announcement; the wedding announcement for Ruth and Eddy; a Purple Heart and other medals and citations. And mixed in with the pictures, newspaper clippings, and mementos were letters, most of them from Eddy.

As she turns the pages she talks about her life and the people in it—her parents, brothers, Eddy, Lloyd, her second husband who died a few years earlier, Joyce, Bill, and the children. All these people seem inseparable parts of her life that she holds close to her, like threads woven together in a shawl. Talking about the chances his mother took in marrying Bill leads her to speak of the foolish things young women do for love and how quickly. Why, after a courtship of just a few months, she married Eddy, her one true love, the angel in white who loved to have a few drinks in a bar with his brother and his girlfriend down on the East side and then get into a good fight. The big blue marbles beneath the shot-glass lenses sparkle as she recalls throwing herself into these fights and hitting some guy or his gal over the head with her purse to help bail out her Eddy, and all the other happy-go-lucky times before the War when she was young and unhurt. The newspaper clipping about the Armistice Day snow storm reminds her of the death of Bill's parents in that storm and all of the misfortune that plagued him and Joyce—the deaths of his sister, of his brother during the war, of William Paul. She can't help but remember the day an army officer came to her apartment and told her Eddy was dead. And while Joyce had to raise three children on her own—not to mention her adoptive son, because hadn't Bill and Joyce adopted his nephew?—at least she didn't have to live with an empty house at night and listen to those engines and all the straining and screeching as those railroad cars banged into one another. And children, they allow you to live your life over again, to remember the wonderful friendships, the crazy times, as well as the heartaches.

"You know, I love to cook and bake for the church, and for my friends and neighbors. And I love my garden. I start it inside when it's cold, and as soon as it warms up I move everything outside. I have a busy life ... a good life. But I'll tell you a secret—one of the things I love to do most is live in the past. And for me there were two really happy times in my life: when your mother and I were growing up, and when Eddy and I were together. Oh, I was happy with Lloyd too, but there was something just real special about those times when you're young. With all the time Joyce spent alone, I hope she was able to have the kind of happy thoughts I had."

"I think she spent most of her time reading those mysteries."

She shrugs. "She might've. But she might've been reading the way we used to read in our little old schoolhouse—with the school book standing up and hiding the books we were really reading. Behind her mysteries, your mother might've been reading her life book."

"Well, we'll probably never know, will we?"

"One thing I know. Joyce felt real guilty about ... well, she felt she hadn't been much of a mother to you. Sending you away all the time to stay with your grandparents."

He nods his head.

"Why do I bring that up? You know all about it. Or at least, you know as much as I do. I'm happy you came by today, because there are some letters from your mother I think you might want to look at." She turns to the inside back cover of the scrapbook and some letters. "There were things Joyce wanted you to know, but she couldn't bring herself to tell you. I don't know why. I always felt I understood Joyce, at least until Bill died. After that, she changed. She didn't write or call quite so often."

"Thanks. I had no idea there were more."

"You can sit here and read them. Joyce wrote a lot of letters to me over the years. I didn't keep most of them. I can't tell you why I saved these. There was probably a different reason for each one. Well, I've got things to do."

"Thanks. That's really sweet of you."

"I'll be here."

She leaves in the direction of the kitchen; he picks up the letters and starts reading. The paper has yellowed, the ink has faded, but the handwriting is his mother's. He experiences a rush as he realizes again that her own hand wrote these letters.

February 13, 1940
Dear Ruthie,

Sorry for not writing sooner. Been very busy sewing, knitting, cleaning, cooking, and just helping out any way I can. I so want my new family to accept me and I want Bill to be proud. He laughs when I tell him that, but I know they're judging me, and I want to make a good impression.

My new life is not just work. Bill and I find time to have fun too. We drive into town almost every week if the road is clear and go to the movies. Go to the drugstore where Bill's sister works and have sodas with his friends. Sit around the fireplace at night and talk and read. Sometimes this little one gives me a good kick to let me know he's here too. We've picked out names. William Paul if it's a boy, Anna Marie if it's a girl. I think it's going to be a boy. A little Bill. Then I'll have two sweethearts. But I'll be just as happy if it's a girl.

Well I must tell you about my new family. Francis kind of frightened me at first. A huge man with a voice that just seems to boom through the whole house. He reminded me of a big bear, and I kept my distance, but he's turned out to be very kind and protective of me. Always asks how I feel and if that little one's ready to kick its way out yet. I heard him tell Bill I shouldn't be doing any work because of my condition. I'm glad he's so kind because he rules the roost and what he says is law.

I was a little worried about Nora. You know what they say about mothers and their sons' wives. But she seems to like me and is so nice! Treats me as if I was her own daughter. Both of hers have married and left home. One lives somewhere out West. No one even breathes a word about her. The other one, Helen, is the one who works at the drugstore in town. She has an apartment just above the store. Her son, Robert, is just as cute as a bug. She calls him by some French word I can't remember, but it means jewel. The two of them come out pretty much every Sunday for dinner when the road's clear—which isn't often this time of year. Poor thing is raising her boy all by herself. Bill told me Helen got divorced a few years back, and moved from St. Paul to Mirer. Sad that a woman has to raise a child all alone and try to earn a living too. Don't know how she does it!

Then there's Art. He's the same age I am. What a hothead, and just as wild as they come! One day he's ready to go off to war in Europe and next thing you know he wants to pack up and move to California. Got itchy feet and is rarin' to go somewhere. But where? Any gal marries him is going to have her hands full! The way he stares at me sometimes, I think he needs one real soon.

You see, I'm doing everything I can to fit in and feel part of the family. But this new life sometimes seems so strange and hard. The world outside is cold and frozen. Bill says the ice on the lake is probably three feet thick. One day he and I were walking on the ice where the wind had blown a lot of the snow clear, and suddenly I heard this really loud ping sound that was both very close and far away. Bill said it was the ice cracking. He said it contracts and expands because of the sun. Another day when I was outside by myself I heard wolves howling. It sounded like something from hell. I never felt so afraid. There I go, probably scaring you away.

Ruth, I sure hope you will come and visit us sometime. Maybe when the baby's born you could come for a few days. That's the fourth week of May. Please write.

Your bosom friend and soul sister,
Joyce

• • •

March 29, 1940
Dear Ruth,

Thanks so much for the letter. I miss you too, and so wish you could be here. But now might not be the best time because I'm so irritable!

Sitting in our bedroom in front of the window looking out at the lake I see this thick blanket of snow and wonder will winter ever end? Haven't seen a sign of spring yet. Feel I've been wrapped in a warm thick blanket for months, and now want to get outside and walk around without heavy

*layers of clothes and feel the warm sun and
see the lake sparkling in the sunlight and
leaves on the birch trees and hear birds
singing and smell the pine trees.*

    *And most of all, I want this baby born!
He's got cabin fever just as bad as I do
and he wants to come out! Ruth, I feel as
big as a house. Can hardly move. My back
aches almost all the time and I can't find
a position at night that will allow me to
sleep. The baby's turned, my belly looks just
like a watermelon, and my breasts feel like
they're going to explode. Bill said the other
day they're like champagne bottles ready
to pop! I've enjoyed being pregnant until
now. Bill constantly cares for me and he's
just as loving as can be. But I can't stand
one more day of being pregnant! This baby
has to come soon! I want to see him. I try to
imagine sometimes what he will look like,
but I can't. I dream about him, but I never
really see him clearly. All I know is, the way
he's been kicking and pushing, it's a boy. I've
already named him William Paul. Oh, he's
kicking right now. I must stop. Please write!*

*Ready to burst,
Joyce*

· · ·

May 4, 1940
My Dear Ruth,

*It's with a heavy heart that I write. My little
William Paul is dead. He arrived, quite
unexpected, a month early. Born with his
umbilical cord twisted around his neck. That's
what Bill said. No one would let me see him.
But I screamed until finally everyone stepped
aside, and there he was, his little body covered
with blood, his skin a horrible bluish gray. I
didn't believe he was dead until I saw him.
How could I believe that this little boy who was
nearly kicking his way out of my womb would
die before he even left? Why did this happen?
What reason was there for God to take the life
of this dear little infant before it could even
breathe his first breath? Everyone has tried to
comfort me, but I will not be comforted. I can
only think of this baby so alive, turning and
kicking inside of me, and then lying dead in
a blood soaked blanket. This baby's death is
unpardonable. He did nothing to deserve it.
Nothing. It's wrong. Wrong. And if God took
his life, then God was wrong to do so.*

*Ruth, I am picking up my pen again after
starting this letter yesterday. Such strange
thoughts I am having, criticizing God for
taking my baby. But they are my thoughts, why
should I hide them? What do I have to fear
now? Being damned to hell? I have no fear of
hell. I have no fear of God. If he were human,
I would kill him. What am I thinking? I don't
want to go on living. Why ...*

The ink has run, blurring a few words.

*Ruth, each time I begin writing I have to stop
after just a few lines or I'll get this letter all
wet with tears, the way I did earlier today.
I can't stop thinking about my dear little
William Paul, and wondering if he could not
have been saved. He was born here, at the
lodge, because with all the snow and the thaw
the road to town was too dangerous. A doctor
came to the house, but he didn't arrive until
after William Paul was born dead. I can't help
but wonder if we'd been living somewhere else,
if we'd been able to go to a hospital, or if we
could've had a doctor here when we realized
something was wrong, could we have saved
William Paul? I tell myself, could've, would've,
it doesn't make any difference.*

*Bill is taking the death of our little angel
real hard. I feel so sorry for him. He has tried
to comfort me, when he can't even comfort
himself. He needs me, but at the same time he
needs to be alone. He goes off sometimes by
himself in the woods and comes back hours
later, wet and covered with mud. I think we
all need some time alone to cry out in our
own silence against the injustice of this baby's
death.*

*Ruth, I can't talk about this anymore. I just
want to tell you that I'm going home to stay
with Mom and Dad for three weeks. Nora was
the one who suggested it, and I'm eternally
grateful to her. I think it will do me a world
of good to be away for a while and to be able
to spend some time with Mom and Dad and*

*of course with you. I am leaving in a week, on
May 11.*

Yours truly,
Joyce

. . .

December 4, 1940
Dear Ruth,

*This family seems to be cursed. We lost
William Paul in April. And now we've lost
Bill's mom and dad. Francis and Nora died
in that horrible snow storm on Armistice
Day. The lodge seems so big and empty now,
with just the three of us. Bill and Art are
taking it real hard. Nora was just 55, and
Francis was 58. Too young to die. The boys
are so angry. They drink and they swear,
and then they go off by themselves and brood.
They can't find peace. I wonder sometimes
what this family has done to deserve such
suffering. Were we too proud? Too happy?
Did we need to be humbled? Didn't the death
of William Paul humble us enough?*

*I hope all is well with you, my dear Ruth,
and that heaven is shining more favorably
on you than it is on us.*

Your sister at heart,
Joyce

. . .

August 14, 1942
Dear Ruth,

It hasn't even been two years since we lost
Bill's parents, and now Helen, one of his
sisters, is dead. You might remember me
talking about her. She lived in town with her
little boy, Robert. She died of cancer, about
a week ago. How she suffered! Ruth, I will
never forget this. When I go I hope it's quick.

Poor Robert, he seems so lost. His mother
meant everything to him! We have taken
him in with us. Bill and I are going to adopt
him. He has no one else in the world, except
that father of his who disappeared years
ago. We'll never be able to take Helen's place,
but we can certainly give him love and try
to help him through some of the hard times
ahead.

Art was given leave to come home for a
week. He seemed just crushed when he first
got here, but after four days, and just two
days after the funeral, he was ready to leave.
We couldn't find Bill's other sister. Last we
knew she was out West somewhere.

Bill and I are just exhausted. You can
imagine what it's like trying to manage
the lodge and the resort and outfit campers
without Art. And then spending hours on
end at the hospital the last few days Helen
was alive. Bill seems really blue. I can't
get through to him. Robert has taken to
following me around the house and helping
me in any way he can. He's such an angel! I
pray God to look after him.

To top everything off, I think I'm pregnant. My period is late and my breasts feel tender. Normally I'd be happy, but with Bill going through such pain and Robert grieving and moping and needing every bit of love he can get, and so much work to do, I just don't have time to even know how I feel about having another baby.

Your loving friend,
Joyce

• • •

June 3, 1950
Dear Ruth,

You've been gone for just a week, and it already seems a year has passed. It was so wonderful to have you here. I don't know how I would have gotten by these last two weeks without you. I'm so tired. Can't get enough sleep. I feed Paul when I go to bed. Then he usually wakes up in the middle of the night and I bring him into bed with us, and he wakes up again about 5:00 ready to eat. You saw the way he eats during the day. Every two or three hours he wants my breast. It shows, he's such a little butterball. I don't think I've ever seen a happier baby. His happiness feeds me every bit as much as my milk feeds him. I certainly need every ounce of strength I can get with the tourist season having just started.
It's been wonderful to see Bill with the

*baby. I remember you saying that Paul has
such beautiful eyes, they sparkle like water
on a sunny day. I think Paul has his own
sunshine, and it's enough to light up Bill's
face. I haven't seen him happy like this in
years. I know you think I'm wrong, but I'm
sure Paul will help bring Bill and me back
together. I have no doubt children can do
that. And I've never lost hope as far as Bill
is concerned. He's had a hard life, and he's
had to give up a lot. I know that he wanted
to go back to the U someday. He had dreams
he wanted to live, and then he got saddled
with all this responsibility. But we all have
dreams that we have to give up as we grow
older. I'm sure that having such a beautiful
baby will help Bill forget what he can't have.*

*Little Paul is crying and that can only
mean one of two things—change me or feed
me! And right now! Patience is the first
virtue I will try to teach this child.*

*Goodbye, Ruth, my dear, dear friend.
You're an angel.*

Your loving friend,
Joyce

• • •

September 8, 1951
Dear Ruth,

*I keep on thinking about what you said on
the phone. That you weren't surprised. I
wonder why I couldn't see it, when it went*

*on right before my eyes. Why am I the last
to learn, when it's my husband? And to
have to learn this from Robert! He has seen
everything that's gone on. The girl who quit
this summer without giving notice. I was
so angry with her, and here she was flying
somewhere to get an abortion, all because of
Bill! And all the other girls! Some of them,
Ruth, were just sixteen! Can you imagine?
He's old enough to be their father! He could
go to prison for what he's done. If it wasn't
for the children, that's where I'd send him.
It's where he belongs.*

    *I confronted him. He wasn't surprised
by what I knew. Didn't seem to care much,
either. He said if I wanted a divorce, he'd
leave and give me everything—the kids, the
lodge, the resort. I almost told him to go, but
I'm not ready for that. It's so humiliating, to
go through something like this, and still not
be able to tell him to get out.*

    *I'm so worried about the children. After
all it was Robert who told me everything.
He's incapable of lying to me. Whenever he
tries he blushes and grins and looks away
and shuffles his feet, and anyone can see he's
lying. When I asked him if he knew why that
girl left without giving notice, he turned red
as a beet and shuffled his feet and looked
away, so I said Robert I can see you know
why she left. I said look at me, and he did.
And I said I want the truth. You tell me
everything you know. And he did. If Robert
knows, you can bet Fran and Christine know
too. It's one thing for a father to behave the*

*way Bill does, but what a horrible thing for
children to have to know. If I could keep all
this from them, the pain would be so much
easier to bear.*

*Thank God I can talk with you. What
would I do without you?*

*Yours truly,
Joyce*

• • •

*April 16, 1954
Dear Ruth,*

*Fran and Christine are in school, Robert
went into town to pick up groceries for the
week, and Paul is napping. It's quiet as a
tomb. So quiet I can hear the snow melting
and dripping from the eaves. And my
thoughts ticking away in my head. You're the
only person I can write to about them.*

*It's been almost four months since Bill
disappeared. I know he's dead, and yet I
find myself dropping whatever I'm doing
and looking at the door, or at a window, half
expecting to see him. I see his clothes in the
morning, hanging in our closet, waiting for
him to put them on. And at night I feel his
arm around me as I sleep. I wake up and
realize he's gone, and I don't want to get out
of bed ever again.*

*The sheriff is going to do another search
for his body in about two weeks. The snow
will be pretty much all gone by then. I'll be*

real happy when he and his men are done and gone.

Last Sunday I was going through Bill's things and came across two packets of letters, wrapped together with a rubber band. It was in the very back of his desk drawer. The handwriting on the first envelope was mine. I started to pull the rubber band off, but was so old it broke to pieces, and some of them stuck to the paper. The envelopes contained all the letters I'd written to him. The ones I wrote to him after the first summer I spent with my aunt and uncle at the resort. And the ones after that second summer. I was surprised at the things I said to him. I sure hope he didn't show the letters to anyone. There were some that brought back painful memories. Like the letters I wrote to Bill after William Paul died, when I was staying with Mom and Dad. You know if he was alive today he would have just turned fourteen. He'd be the man of the house.

Ruth, I don't know what I would do without you. No matter how much time passes between our letters and our phone calls, I know you're as close to me as a sister—even closer. I'll call you soon. The sun is shining a little more each day. I know your heart beats time with mine.

Your loving soul sister,
Joyce

• • •

August 23, 1989
Dear Ruth,

It's been such a long time since I wrote to you.
So much has happened since, I hardly know
where to begin. So I'll just blurt it out. I'm
dying of cancer of the pancreas. There. Now
I've said it. My doctor told me months ago I
have anywhere from a month to six months
to live. I can't be far from the end.

I'm quite a sight! The cancer is affecting
my liver and it's given me a really sickly
yellow color. And I've lost so much weight!
My arms and legs look like toothpicks and
my stomach is so bloated it looks like a
watermelon standing on end. The doctor—
he's the pill doctor, the one who gave me
the Librium and Valium and all the other
drugs. He told me they could operate on me,
but my chances of surviving would only be
about 15%. And the chances of getting all
the cancer out wouldn't even be that good. I
asked what he would do if he was in my
shoes. He said he'd probably get a case of
scotch and move to his cabin and try to enjoy
what was left of his life. I said that sounds
like a good idea for you, but I can't stand
whiskey. Makes me sick. And I reminded
him that he of all people should know that.
Well Ruth, I'm just about as good as dead.

I would love to see you again before I go.
I hope you can come and visit me just one
more time.

Your loving Joyce

. . .

September 19, 1989
Dear Ruth,

*Fran whispered the good news in my ear this
morning. I thought I was dreaming at first.
With all the painkillers I'm taking, I sometimes
don't know if I'm awake or asleep. I'm so happy
you're coming, even if for just a few days. That's
probably all you'll be able to stand of me!*

*I don't do much anymore. Either I lie in
bed, or Fran helps me sit in the chair in front
of the window so I can look out. I read or I
sleep, I remember and I dream. When I wake
up I'm not sure if a day has gone by or a week.
Or maybe just a few minutes. I spend so much
time reading and remembering, sometimes I
have the feeling that what I think I remember
is something I remember from a novel. It's so
hard to keep it all straight. The other day—
or was it this morning?—I remembered my
little Christine being kidnapped, and I was
so afraid she would be killed that I started to
cry. But then later I was reading a book and
realized that what I was reading was what I'd
remembered. So I must've read it before, and
just forgot.*

*There is so much I've forgotten. So
many holes in my life. Sometimes I dream
things that seem to fill in the holes, but
they disappear. It's kind of like watching
mist on the lake in the early morning. You
think you see ghosts or something, but the
mist clears and there's nothing but the lake.*

Sometimes I find myself crying, and I don't know exactly why. I think it's probably because I've remembered something, but I've already forgotten what I remembered. And I think I'm crying as much because I can't remember as I am because of what I've remembered.

A lot of my memories lead back to Bill. I loved him so much. Words could never say how much I love him. All these years I've laid here

Words have been crossed out with a pen to the point of being unrecognizable.

thinking of the place where he lies, until I can see it all in my dreams. It's night. There's snow. So much snow. It must have been a blizzard. A whiteout, as they say. And the shouting. But the shouting is all inside me. The snow must have silenced it. Must have filled its mouth so the shouting was silent. We were pulling him across the snow on a sled. Robert was helping me. Fran just stood there at the top of the hill crying. He didn't know what to do. We were almost down to the bottom, and then I heard someone else crying. It got louder. I ran back up the hill. And there was Paul, coming out of the white, walking on the snow, like a little Jesus walking on water. I ran to him. He was crying and shouting Mama, Mama. He seemed to fly into my arms. I opened my coat and pulled his face into my bosom and took him into the house and held him with his face pressed against my chest and wrapped a blanket around us. He nestled his face between my breasts and trembled in my arms beneath

*the blanket for several minutes. I prayed God
to help me and make him forget what he might
have seen that night. I needed to be strong,
and I needed Paul to forget.*

*I was tempted sometimes to start a new life,
but I chose to stay right here, so I could see the
place where he lies. I know I'm an old woman,
but I feel young. I've never been older than 32,
and he's never gone beyond 34. He's still alive
in me.*

*The pain is getting bad, so I'm going to
take my pills and sleep a while. Writing this
letter has been my biggest accomplishment in
months. I can't wait until you're here.*

*Love,
Joyce*

Paul rereads the letter, then reads again the fourth paragraph about the whiteout and the shouting silenced by the snow. And about himself walking on the snow, walking on water. He remembers the boy in his dream walking on the plane of snow. And then flying. It feels like what she described. It's different, but ... He feels cool and sweaty and queasy, as if he were going to faint. He continues rereading the paragraph, trying to keep his mind clear and focused, struggling to understand this uncanny feeling that somehow he knows the experience she dreamed. And remembered. He looks at the paragraph. Yes, she implies that her memories feed her dreams. For the life of him he can't remember what she wanted him to forget.

The road lies before Paul like a train of thought he pursues by driving as fast as he can. Fragments. His trip has netted him more fragments. Bits and pieces of his life, scattered among pictures, letters, and newspaper articles. But one name seems to come up over and over—Stone. It was Stone who was helping Mother pull someone on a sled in her dream. Stone who told his mother about the girl who'd had the abortion, and apparently about the other girls as well. Stone who worked with his father and listened to him talk about women being flypaper. Stone who discovered Mother when she tried to commit suicide. Stone who called the hospital, and Stone who brought her home from the hospital. Stone, who seemed so insignificant, almost invisible when he was growing up, is now ubiquitous. He remembers the day when he went to Stone's shack to find out why Mother had thrown him out and kept his relationship to him a secret. Stone talked for a couple hours without answering his question. That'll be for another time, he said. Well, now is that time.

15

PAUL TURNS OFF THE BLACKTOP ONTO THE winding, gravel road, bordered by three-foot walls of plowed snow. A three-quarter moon lights up the snow at the edge of the dense wood. He makes a turn and sees a gray flute of smoke rising from Stone's shack. He parks next to the old Ford pickup and gets out. Jason is already barking loud enough to wake the dead from the last century. The door opens, a shaft of light cuts through the night, and Stone, in blue jeans and a brown and green flannel shirt, stands in the doorway, holding Jason by the scruff of his neck.

"Who's there? Who's there?" His voice sounds angry. He sees Paul walking toward him out of the night. "Ah, Paulie, it's you. What the hell are you doing out at this time of night? Quiet, Jason. Come on, boy, it's just Paulie. Come to visit. At a strange hour."

Paul enters the shack and stands in the glare of the naked light bulb dangling by an electrical cord from the kitchen ceiling. Jason lets off barking and takes to dancing around him, leaping on his belly, licking his hands, then dropping to the floor and almost tripping him as he squeezes between his legs.

"Jesus Christ, Jason, go lie down over there by the stove. Go on! Get the hell out of the way!" Stone looks up at Paul. "What the hell are you doing out so late?"

"Late? It's not even ten." Hanging up his coat and kicking off his boots, Paul breathes the fetid odor of the kitchen area and feels an intimacy with Stone's life that repulses him.

Stone leans against the counter next to the sink and crosses his arms. "Well, some of us have got to get to bed so we can get up with the sun."

"Last time I was here you had to leave before we got a chance to finish our conversation."

Paul walks past him toward the wood stove in the middle of the living room and faces the fire, spreading his hands above the stove and letting the heat penetrate his pants and warm his legs.

"That so?"

Paul turns to face Stone. "Yeah."

Stone looks at him for a while, then says, "I think I'll have a drink. Want one?"

"What have you got?"

"Whiskey. And water."

"I'll take whiskey."

"That makes two of us."

Stone gets down a bottle of Jim Beam from the cupboard next to the sink, pulls the string to turn off the light, and carries the bottle and two juice glasses over to the table. A small lamp casts an arc of light across most of the table—the only light in the shack, aside from the glow emanating from the air vents in the wood stove.

"Want some water with your whiskey?"

Paul shakes his head no and sits down with his back to the hot stove.

Stone nods and asks, as he sits down across from him,

"What did those ol' farts used to say when you'd ask 'em that?"

"I'm thirsty, not dirty."

"Yep. Course they were probably just as goddamn dirty as they were thirsty. And then some. Filthy sons o' bitches."

Paul watches Stone pour a couple of ounces of whiskey in each glass. He takes his glass, clinks Stone's, and tosses half of it down. He leans back in his chair, beyond the arc of light, and watches Stone rotate his glass on the edge of its base and gaze at the amber-colored liquor. The huge bony hand, with the big knuckles and the thick hair on the fingers, looks as if it could easily crush the glass. Finally Stone looks up at him, his brown eyes gazing back at him with an animal inquisitiveness. Long, greasy strands of wolf-gray hair hang over his right temple and shaggy eye brow, and his dense, rough beard of the same color covers his jaws and neck.

"So?"

"So, I went down to St. Paul to visit Mother's friend Ruth. You remember her?"

"No. Should I?"

"We talked about her last time I was here."

Stone leans back in his chair, beyond the arc of light, his face obscured by the dark. "I don't remember."

"Well, it's been a while. She came to stay at the lodge to help out about the time I was born."

"Oh, yeah."

"Ruth showed me a scrapbook full of old newspaper articles and pictures and letters. Some of the letters came from Mother. They talk about a lot of things—her life when she was a kid growing up on the farm; Ruth's visit, after I was born; my father paying for an abortion for one of the waitresses he'd fucked. Now the abortion, that's something Mother learned about from you." Paul pauses for a minute to see if Stone will respond.

Stone says nothing, and his face reveals nothing.

"You know, the last few months I've gotten a lot of interesting pieces of information about my mother and father, but I couldn't quite put them together. It's strange. So much information, so little understanding."

"Can't see the woods for the trees, huh?" Stone empties his glass, leans forward, pours himself another, then settles back in the darkness.

"Yeah, I guess that's as good a way as any to sum things up. So I'm driving from St. Paul back to Mirer and I'm going nuts because I've got all these atoms of information bouncing around in my head and it's all I can do just to keep enough of my mind on the road so I don't go in the ditch. Which is just what I did."

Paul pauses, trying to read Stone's face.

"Hope you're all right."

"I'm okay," Paul answers, nodding his head, thinking about the absence of sincerity in Stone's voice. "So, I'm driving back and I'm wondering, how can I put all the pieces together so they make sense? I need someone to help me. Someone who's been around here the last forty, fifty years, and has seen what's gone on. One name keeps coming up over and over: Stone. You were there when my brother and sister and I were born, you told Mother about that girl's abortion, you discovered Mother when she nearly died from that suicide attempt, and you walked out of the hospital with her after she recovered. You were in her life—in our lives—all the time. Never left. Not even when she threw you out and told Fran and Christine not to tell me you were my adopted brother. Why did she do that?"

"That's a long story. And it's already late." Stone finishes his whiskey and is about to stand up.

"Oh no, I let you off the hook once before. I'm not moving until you tell me what the fuck went on there. Why did she throw you out?"

Stone stares at him.

"Did she catch you stealing money out of the till?"

Stone smiles broadly and then laughs, shaking his head. "It sure in hell wasn't anything like that."

"In trouble with the police?"

"No, never."

"Were you sleeping with any of the girls who worked there?"

Stone smirks. "No, nothing could be further from the truth."

"So what the fuck was it?"

Stone leans back into the dark.

"I'm not leaving until you tell me."

"You really wanna know?"

"Yeah, I really wanna know."

"Have another drink, Paulie. You're gonna need it."

Paul pours another couple of ounces into his glass, takes a sip, and sets it down. "Shoot."

"Your mother ... our mother ... threw me out because she'd been sleeping with me."

"What the fuck are you talking about?"

"Hey! You said you wanna know why she threw me out. I start telling you, and you get your ass in an uproar." He smiles. "Joyce threw me out because she loved me."

"You're not making sense, Stone."

"There is no way to make sense."

"Try."

"Maybe I'd better have another drink." Stone pours himself a couple more ounces of whiskey, downs nearly half of it, and lets out a deep sigh. He sets his glass on the table and stares at it for a while, then begins speaking. "I was only eight when my mother died. Eight. You know how young that is? I didn't even realize there could be someone else in my life besides her. I was in paradise. Nothing was missing. As long as she was alive."

"What does this have to do with my Mother throwing

you out?"

Stone chuckles. "Always eager to learn. Well, once you learn what I'm gonna tell you, you'll never be able to forget it, no matter how much you want to."

"Go on."

"You know, I've never told anyone this. Now, by God, I want to."

Stone gets up and walks around the table and behind Paul's chair and disappears in the bedroom. Paul wonders what the hell he's doing in the dark. What's he looking for? He can't see a thing in there. Then Stone emerges, carrying his 30 Ot 6 rifle. He sits down and lays the rifle across his lap. In one fluid movement he lifts the lever and pulls the bolt back.

"What's with the gun?"

Stone loads one bullet in the magazine, then a second, and then a third. He pushes the bolt forward with his thumb and pulls the lever down with that same fluid movement culminating with a metallic click and a bullet locked in the chamber. Paul feels that click puncture his sense of safety as if it were a balloon. Stone lays the rifle on the table, his right hand resting on the stock near the trigger and the barrel pointing toward Paul.

"I thought you'd give up, go back to Paris, forget all about us poor dumb fucks. But you didn't. And you're not going to. Eventually you'll find out. So, I'm gonna tell you everything. This is my show. Don't ask me any of your fucking questions. By the time I get done talking, you'll wish you'd never stuck around."

"What's with the gun?"

"The gun? Oh, that. It does make you wonder, don't it? Like, what am I gonna do with it? Am I just gonna hold it, kind of play with it a little bit. I might do that. I've spent a lot of time cleaning and polishing this ol' girl. I got a special feel for her."

Paul glances at Stone's right hand and his splayed fingers stroking the bolt and trigger guard. The son of a bitch is enjoying his little drama.

"Or maybe I'm gonna use it. Maybe I'm gonna shoot Jason." Stone leans to his left so he can peer over the edge of the table at Jason, who has raised his head from his paws at the sound of his name and gazes at Stone with a forlorn look. Stone cocks his head to the side and imitates the dog's woeful expression. "Shoot Jason? Just for the hell of it?" He shakes his head, "Naw. Jason's a good dog."

"Cut the histrionics. What's with the gun?"

"Careful, Paulie, this is my show. You don't tell me to do nothing and you don't ask no questions."

Paul pulls back on his anger. He'll have to be careful.

Stone seems to be smiling. "We were talking about what I might do with this gun." He pretends to wonder, a puzzled look on his face. "I might just shoot myself. Now there's an idea. But, is it an idea whose time has come?" He chuckles and shrugs his shoulders. "Maybe I'm gonna tell you everything I know, and then shoot you. Like in those spy novels, you know? You learn too much, you gotta die."

Paul wonders what Stone could possibly know that had to be kept secret. He's got to be putting him on.

"You read spy novels?"

Paul shakes his head no.

"Don't like 'em, huh?"

Paul sees himself grabbing the gun out of Stone's hands and hitting him over the head. His whole body tenses for a few seconds, as if he were actually going to attack.

Stone takes a drink, sets his glass on the table, looks at Paul again and smiles. "Maybe I'm not gonna do a damn thing. Who knows? I guess you'll just have to wait and see."

Paul would like to shake whatever Stone knows right out of him. Who does he think he is?

"You really should've left after Joyce's funeral." Stone

slowly shakes his head. "Not a good idea to stick around." He shrugs his shoulders. "But the show must go on. Right?"

"I'd be happier if the show went on without that gun pointing in my direction."

A flash, a metallic crack, and Paul feels what must have been a bullet whiz by his left arm. He opens his eyes to see Stone hovering over the table, his face flushed red, screaming at him. "This is my fucking show! Shut the fuck up, you asshole! Don't think I wouldn't put a fucking bullet right between your eyes."

Paul's whole body feels as if it's shivering. He might never leave the shack alive. He looks in the direction of the door, the only escape. No way he could get that far before Stone killed him.

Stone settles back in his chair, lays the rifle down on the table, and fixes him with his eyes as he measures out his words with controlled rage. "There are two bullets left, Paulie. It only takes one. You understand?"

Paul nods his head.

"Good. I wanna have two bullets in this rifle when you leave."

Stone finishes his whiskey, refills the two glasses, leans back again beyond the arc of light, sighs, as if he were about to take on an ordeal, and after what seems a long time, begins talking in a monotone.

"My mother was an angel. My angel." He takes another sip of whiskey and reflects a minute before continuing. "Those last few weeks, people were coming by to take care of her. They were pushing me aside and taking her away. When I could, I'd put my face close to hers, listen to her breathe. Touch her neck, feel her pulse. Bill took her to the hospital. I wasn't even with her when she died. Joyce drove me to the hospital. It was dark. I laid my face on her stomach, put her hand on my head. It was already cold. It still feels cold."

"Look, Stone, you don't need to go through all this. I just wanted to find out—"

Stone lunges forward. "Shut up!" Leveling the rifle at Paul. "I said this is my show. You're listening, I'm talking, and you're not leaving until I've said what I have to say."

Stone's dark eyes burn. Rage has turned his face red.

At the sight of it, Paul pulls back inside himself. Patience, he thinks. Be still. Get out alive.

"You're testing my patience real bad. Now, sit back, relax, drink your whiskey, and listen." Stone leans back, his face obscured. After a while he starts talking. "My mother's death left a hole in me big enough to drive a truck through. I was sort of ... what's the word? Cama ... coma ... What the fuck is the word? You're the word guy, what the fuck is it?"

"Comatose?"

"Comatose. Yeah. Like I was almost dead. Joyce ... she was so ..." Stone slowly shakes his head, as if at a loss for words.. "She had this way of looking into my eyes, like she could see all the way inside, all the way to the bottom. And when she'd try to get me to talk, she'd give me that look, and she'd say, 'You can tell me,' and I'd tell her whatever she wanted to know. Something about her made me trust her. It might've had to do with her being pregnant and all."

"Pregnant? How in the hell could that ... "

"Paulie!" Stone fingers the trigger. "I'll tell you when I want something from you." Stone reflects for a few seconds, then continues. "She must've been about five months along with Fran when I moved there. Maybe six. A month or two later she started getting really big. We all kind of turned around her, like planets. People who worked there ... customers ... Bill ... me. We were all in orbit around her ... around her belly. She'd put her hands on it and hold it, like all her happiness was there, and she wanted to feel it. We were always thinking about her."

"We? Or you?"

"I was with her more than anyone else, so maybe I felt it more. I gravitated toward her because she was so happy. Real happy. It was like she had this little stove inside her that was always stoked with love and burning hot. And burning hotter all the time. You could see it in her cheeks."

"You talk as if my father wasn't even around."

"This isn't about him. Okay? He doesn't count for shit in all this. It's all about her."

"What do you mean?"

"I loved her."

Paul's stunned. He looks at Stone's face in the dark. What is this? Is he joking? Just playing with him? Part of this "show" he talks about?

"She was beautiful. More than just beautiful. There was no one else like her. I used to watch her ... I was afraid he'd get rid of me if he saw me staring at her, the way I did. But I couldn't help it. It was like I had a sixth sense about being someplace where I could see her, without being seen. I used to watch her rock Fran, sing to him, nurse him. She'd lean her head back, close her eyes, and all her happiness would spread across her lips. He'd fall asleep, and keep right on sucking. Stop, then start again. Her breasts were so white ... they looked so soft ... I wanted to touch them, lay my cheek on them. She'd remove her nipple from his mouth and it was so red, so big, and sometimes there'd still be milk oozing from it. My lips would almost reach for her nipple. Sometimes she'd open her eyes and see me looking at her, and she'd cover her breast, close her eyes, and go to sleep.

"Years went by. And still everything she did brought a lump to my throat. The way she breathed. Talked. Ate. Walked. Combed her hair. Looked at herself in the mirror, like she was seeing someone new, someone so happy. The way she'd stare out at the lake when she was nursing Christine. Every little detail, right down to the beads of sweat that trickled down her cheeks on hot days, the way her hair curled from the humidity, her chest rose and fell as she breathed. Everything. Absolutely everything. If I could've seen her shit in a toilet I would've gawked like she was performing a miracle ... turning bread into the body of Christ, or something like that."

Paul listens, stunned, speechless. Is Stone really saying what he's saying? How could Mother possibly have loved him, this ... this nephew. An adopted son, for Christ's sake.

"What do you think of that, Paulie?"

Paul looks at Stone. Looks at him for a very long time, stupefied by what he's heard. "What can I say with that fucking gun pointing at me?"

"I told you, I wanna have two bullets left when you leave."

"Yeah, well ... What do I think? I think you were obsessed with my mother."

"Obsessed, huh? She was everything to me—my mother, my aunt, my guardian angel. Everything. So ..."

"So I think that qualifies as obsession, yeah."

"Well, it's not like she didn't encourage it. When she was pregnant with you, she'd hold my hand against her belly, or my head, with my ear pressed against her. I'd hear the heart beat, feel the feet kicking, and I'd tell her everything I was going to do to help her take care of that baby. Like I was the father. It's only logical, don't you think, I'd want everything the father could have?"

"Maybe you assumed too much."

"Hmm." Stone smiles. "One night I walked by her room. The door was open. Just enough for me to get a peek. The lamp on the table next to her bed was turned on. She was lying on her side, asleep, facing the door, and you were lying on your back next to her. Her robe was spread open and the flaps of her maternity bra were undone. Her breasts were just as white as cream. They almost glowed in the dim light.

Both nipples were so red. I felt a tingling all through my body, like pin pricks, or electrical charges bursting in my veins. I felt dizzy, just looking.

"Bill had gone to take one of the waitresses home. She was probably sixteen—my age. I knew he wouldn't be back until midnight. At least. And it was only about eleven. I walked over ..." Stone seems to look into the distance beyond Paul as if he were seeing what he saw that night. "Walked over to the edge of the bed and got on my knees, like I was going to pray." He sits forward and places his hands palm down on the table. "I put my hands on the bed, leaned forward, shaking with fear, and took a nipple in my mouth and began to suck. Her milk was sweet as honey, and after I tasted it, and let it flow through me, I wanted nothing more than to suck forever from her breast. And then ... then she really surprised me. I'd been expecting her to wake up and scream or hit me, but instead I felt her fingers on the back of my head, and then her hand, and I knew she knew. I kept on sucking until the milk stopped flowing from one breast, and then I tried to take the other, but your face was in the way. She laid back, so I could get at the nipple. She never opened her eyes, but all the while I was sucking I felt her hand on the back of my head, and her fingertips stroking my hair. When there was nothing left, she pulled her hand away. I stood up to leave. She looked like she was sleeping. On my way out I stopped in the doorway. She'd pulled her robe shut. Her eyes still closed. This was our secret."

Stone leans back into the darkness.

Paul can't even breathe. How could she? After a few minutes, he mumbles, "Lots of secrets in this family."

Stone nods his head. "More than you'll ever know."

"And my father?"

"Ha! By the time he came back I was asleep. Even though it took me a couple hours." Stone leans forward to reach his glass, settles back in the shadow, and drinks.

"Go on."

"Paulie, I'll keep on going, regardless of what you want."

"I know. This is your show."

"During the day, she treated me the same as always. But any time he left at night, I'd walk by her room to see if the door was open. She'd always put her hand on my head. I knew, if I kept quiet about this, it would continue as long as she was nursing you." He leans forward into the light, smiling as he laughs gently, his brown eyes warming to the thought. "I never said a word. Not 'till now."

Stone sets his empty glass on the table and is about to pour himself another drink when he stops, looks at Paul, and holds the bottle toward him. "You want another?" Paul pushes his glass forward. Stone fills both glasses, leans back in the shadow, takes a sip, and stares at Paul.

"Tell me, Paulie, don't you wish you never came back?"

"I want to get this over."

Stone appears to grin. "Doesn't it just fucking kill you, I was sucking the same tit at sixteen you were sucking when you were in diapers?"

"On a shock scale of one to ten, we're talking maybe a three."

"Well, Paulie, that's just the beginning. So don't lose that shock scale." He laughs. "You remember Joyce found out Bill paid for one of his girlfriends to get an abortion."

"She found out from you."

"Yeah, you betcha. I wanted her to know, and I wanted her to know I knew. I knew she knew Bill was cheating on her with those girls. We all knew it. She wouldn't've let me do what I'd been doing if she didn't know. As long as no one talked to her about it, it didn't exist. But once I told her, everything changed. Her face turned red, she started crying. She wanted to be alone. A few days later, he was gone one night, and I found the door open a few inches.

Only there wasn't a light on. I went in, closed the door partway, and waited until I could see everything. She was in bed, as usual—her robe was open, she seemed asleep. But she was alone. I guessed she'd put you in your bassinet, a few feet from the bed. I closed the door. Once my eyes grew used to the dark, I walked over to the bed. This time, when I started sucking her breast, her hand took me by the shoulder and pulled me toward her. I understood. I got in bed with her. I was so excited I came as soon as I was in her. Pow, it was over. How does the song go? Wam bam thank you ma'am!"

"Yeah." Paul sits, unable to move, depression weighing down on him.

"Or Mom." Stone chuckles. "Well, she calmed me down. We did it a second time. She climbed on top and bent over so I could nurse while she rode me. I was drinking her milk, my hands were on her ass, and then my fingers were touching the lips of her pussy and my wet prick, and she rose and fell on me. Hard. And then I was coming in her, and she was coming in me. Like one fluid was flowing through us, and my cum would turn into her milk, and her milk into my cum. Like a miracle. Like water into wine. Only better." Stone laughs, and then continues in a nostalgic tone. "It felt like it lasted for hours." He sips his whiskey, holding the glass just below his mouth where he can breathe the fumes. He appears in the darkness to look at a distant point above and beyond Paul's head, a smile barely visible on his lips. Then he looks at Paul. "Got a hard-on?"

"No."

"I bet you do."

Paul clenches his jaws.

"Hmm. You remember the taste of your mother's milk?"

"Fuck off, Stone."

"Well, it tastes—"

"Sweet as honey. You've already told me."

"Yeah, I did, didn't I. Well, I guess I'm repeating myself in my old age! Or maybe I just like thinking about it so much." Nods his head. "I thought I'd get a reward for telling her about the abortion, but I never dreamed I'd get that. Never dreamed she'd love me like that. And I've never stopped dreaming. Never wanted another woman since."

Stone pauses for a few seconds. Then he raises his glass toward Paul, saluting him, and takes another sip.

"You know, brother, I've always felt a kind of special connection to you. You'd just come out of that body I so much wanted to be in. If I could've, I would've pushed my head right up her pussy. I would've pushed my whole body into her, so I would've been in her body." Stone takes another sip. "Weird, huh?"

Paul nods his head.

"How does that register on your shock scale?"

"Fuck the shock scale."

"I'd much prefer to fuck our mother, but she's dead." He remains silent for a few seconds. "I'm not going to get a rise out of you with that?"

"I won't jump for it."

"I shouldn't have even tried."

"You just wanted to remind me, it's your show."

"Yeah. Well, where was I?"

"You were fucking my mother and sucking her tit."

"Right. The next couple three years were the best of my life. And the worst. After a couple months of making love, she stopped leaving her door open. He started hanging around the lodge at night. And the next thing I know she's sweet as sugar to him, and I'm off in my room howling inside and whimpering to myself, like some fucking dog. Winter comes. Then spring. She's still cool toward me. I don't know what the hell's going on.

"Summer finally comes, and bam, he's at it again. But

she suspects something. One night I hear them shouting. Then he's gone. He comes back the next morning. But from then on, he's gone a lot at night. After a few nights of crying, she starts to leave the door open. I sneak in. She uses her hands to show me what to do in the dark. One night she guides my head down to her belly and thighs, and then pulls my face into her pussy. From then on, that's how we did it. I wondered if that's how they made love. But I never asked. Fall came. The girls left—by then she suspected every girl who worked there. And the two of 'em start getting back together again.

"Another summer, more girlfriends. Joyce leaves the door open. Same thing. But this time, in the fall, he goes out looking for women in bars. The door is open for me. She takes more chances. Keeps me in her bed longer, so he nearly walks in on us a few times. I'm sure he suspected his adopted son might be sleeping with his wife, because that's about the time he begins making Christine his little princess. Or queen. That's when we all start calling her Queenie. Remember?"

"I don't remember when it started."

"Little Queenie this, little Queenie that. Little Queenie can do whatever little Queenie wants. She can stomp her feet and have temper tantrums if she doesn't get her way, even shout at her daddy. If me or Fran had done that he would've beat the shit out of us. But little Queenie gets whatever little Queenie wants. She gets presents ... lots of 'em. But he doesn't give any to Joyce. She tries to get back at him. She goes on and on about me. How handsome she thinks I am, how I remind her of the way he looked when they first met, how some woman will be very lucky to have me for a husband. She brings you into the act. Her little prince, and all the cute things you do and what a beautiful baby you are. Shit, she even tries to use Fran. Talks about how he helps her around the lodge. Nothing worked, and that was fine with me. Because at night, when he'd go out, it was my turn.

"One night I fell asleep and didn't wake up until morning. He didn't come home. She woke up a little after I did. Lay real still ... with her head turned toward the window. I tried to kiss her. She pushed me away. I put my hand on her hip. She picked up my hand and pushed it back. I couldn't figure out what was going on. I got up and left. He came home later that morning. Didn't offer any explanations. Spent part of the afternoon sleeping. He left for a while that night. I tried to talk with her, but she wouldn't say a word. I couldn't figure out what the hell was going on. It should've been obvious, but you know how it is when you really don't wanna see something—it's right in front of your nose, so close it could take a fucking bite out of you, and still, you just can't see it. From then on, about once a week, he'd just disappear."

"Where was he going?"

"I don't know. But he was drinking a lot. Sometimes I'd go downstairs in the morning and find him asleep on the couch. Smelling of booze." Stone sips some whiskey, reflecting in the dark. "Things started to change then in ways I still can't understand. Some nights she'd leave the door open and I'd go in. She'd pull me in, like she couldn't wait, and then she'd send me off. I felt like what she wanted wasn't me, it was just what I did for her. Like ... maybe she should've paid for it. Other nights, the door never opened. Some days she talked to me, other days she didn't. Still, I thought she loved me, and I could make her love me more and want me and only me. Pretty crazy, huh?"

"I wouldn't know where to begin."

"Everything was crazy. And getting crazier. Bill didn't give a shit about her, but he was really into the game they were playing. He upped the ante. Gave Queenie even more presents—dolls, perfume, jewelry, clothes. Nothing was too good for Queenie. There might've been money too. But as time went by, things changed with Queenie, and she seemed real uncomfortable around him. Joyce watched 'em like an eagle. God, the tension in that house! There was so much electricity flickering around it felt like the place could blow up anytime. And it just got worse." Stone stares at Paul for a while in silence, then says, "But you're so smart. I bet if you'd been just a little older, you would've figured it all out."

"What do you know about Christine and my father?"

"Well, I know our dear father was doing something with our queen sister, but I don't know exactly what. Was he fucking her? And if so, was he using his dick or his finger? Or maybe his tongue. Maybe he was just feeling her up. Or maybe when he sat her on his lap to give her presents he gave her a bonus at the same time. Ask her sometime." He chuckles. "I bet that would make her oil boil."

"Poor Christine."

"Hmm." Stone laughs. "Yeah. Poor Christine."

"You think she and Fran knew what was going on?"

"I don't know. I really don't. Those two three years, we were all caught up in a game. We were all somehow players, and every player was being played. Even if I'd wanted to, I couldn't've gotten out. And the biggest problem was I couldn't want to get out. My head was so fucked up. I think we were all fucked up."

Paul nods in agreement.

"The next summer—"

"Which summer?"

"The last summer the asshole was alive. Things really changed. He didn't hide anything from Joyce. Didn't even try. She wanted to hire boys to wait on tables that summer, but, no way." Stone snickers. "He did the hiring. And played around with every girl he hired. He had a way of talking like a man of experience, and making it sound like, if they really got to know him, he'd give them something they could never get any other way. It worked most times. I thought sure he'd get in trouble with some girl's parents and the police, but he was always one lucky son of a bitch when it came to not getting caught. From that summer on he didn't pay any attention to any of us anymore. Not even Queenie. First few weeks of the summer Joyce was having me come to bed two three times a week with her. Then it stopped. And about the same time, a new player entered the game, and all the rules changed."

"Valery Night."

"Bingo!" Stone tips his glass toward Paul, then takes a sip of whiskey.

"The woman whose name you couldn't remember when I asked you about her."

"Did I forget her name? How could I've done that?" He extends his raised hands in front of him as if hoping the answer might fall like a football from the sky, then slowly shakes his head. "Just goes to show, you can forget almost anything—given the right situation."

"Yeah. I should've known you knew more than you were letting on."

"As soon as she came on the scene, he stopped playing around. She'd show up, have a drink at the bar, and leave. He'd close ten minutes later. After a while, he'd close before she'd even left, follow her right out the door, and we'd see him tail her out of the parking lot. Right on her ass. Every once in a while one of my buddies would say something about his father having seen my old man in a bar with 'that teacher.' The one who had us read those 'dirty books.'"

"Us?"

"Us? Yeah! I had Miss Night for English my senior year."

"No!"

"Yeah."

"What was she like?

Stone shakes his head. "She made Joyce frantic. When Bill was around, Joyce would still talk about how I reminded her of the way he looked when they first met, and how some lucky woman was going to have me someday, but she also started doing ... physical things. Like running her fingers through my hair, or across my shoulders. Touching me a lot, smiling, you know, suggesting stuff." He slowly shakes his head and mumbles, "I always thought there was a real chance for something to happen between us. Why not? It had already happened for me! Besides, there wasn't that much difference in age. Twelve, thirteen years. When I looked at her, I didn't see my mother. I saw this beautiful woman I was in love with."

After a long silence, he leans forward, pours another couple of ounces of whiskey into his glass, and holds the bottle up toward Paul, who shakes his head no. Stone takes a drink, stares into his glass for a couple of minutes, sighs, leans away from the light, and starts talking again. "I wanted him gone. Just fucking gone." He pauses, then continues. "I really thought we could go on being lovers. Forever." He pauses again. "That was weird, wasn't it?"

Paul nods his head.

"It was like living in a dream. Kind of dream you never wanna tell anyone, cause it's just too weird."

Paul feels the crushing weight of depression on his chest.

"You're not saying much."

"What do you want me to say? She was my mother."

Stone seems to reflect as he takes another sip of whiskey, then continues. "I used to have this fantasy that we would get married someday. I would marry my aunt-mother, and there'd be no problem, because there was no direct blood line."

"You really were nuts!"

"Out of my fucking gourd."

"Didn't Fran or Christine suspect anything?"

"Probably. They might've figured it all out. Might've known all along. There were lots of things we didn't talk about."

"Why not?"

"Once you talk about it, it's pretty hard to go on living as if ... well, as if your cousin and adopted brother wasn't screwing your mother. Or your father wasn't cheating on your mother. Or doing something kind o' slippery with your sister." He takes a sip of whiskey. "We were all scared. They were our parents. They were supposed to protect us ... I guess. Isn't that what parents are supposed to do?"

"I never really had parents, so it's hard for me to say. But I would guess you're right."

"Yeah, in a normal family—"

"A normal family? Is there such a thing?"

"I wouldn't know. The only one I've ever known was this one. If it was normal, I pity the fucking world. Huh! We were all so fucked up! Above all the two of them. They sucked us in. Like a whirlpool. Everything was spinning around inside. Inside and outside. You knew that some really nasty shit was going on, and people were getting hurt, you among 'em, but you couldn't get out of it." He takes another sip of whiskey. "He did, though. Ol' Valery, she was his lifeline. Once he started seeing her, he started acting like, you know, he had something he was gonna do. And he changed. Like at Christmas that year ... "

"What year?"

"The last year. Christmas Eve. Went real good. Presents for all the kids. I felt like a kid myself. Both Mom and Dad seemed happy. Things were like they were before all this started. When he must've still loved her. Around midnight all of us except Dad went upstairs. A little later I was in bed wondering why he'd been so nice to her and to the rest of us, when I thought I heard a car. I looked out my window and saw headlights flashing across the snow through the trees ... and the tail lights of his car. I waited for a few minutes and then went to Mom's bedroom door. It was open a few inches. I went in. Laid down next to her. She just whispered, 'Go back to bed.' I touched her cheek. It was all wet. After I got back to my room I realized she might've left the door open because he hadn't come to bed yet, and not because she wanted me.

"But he did come back the next day. Even helped fix Christmas dinner. I don't know what he was trying to do. Maybe he thought he could be papa and husband and have his mistress too. Maybe he was like me. Thought you could add things up without having to subtract anything. I don't know. This time, though, no one really warmed up to him. We had dinner in the afternoon, and an hour later he was gone.

"That night Mom left her door open. I went in and lay down. She asked me if I'd promise to do whatever she told me. I said yes. Then she climbed on top of me. Later, she told me to go to my room and wait for her to come and get me. I was lying in bed thinking about what she might want me to do, when I heard the door open downstairs and I knew he was home. He didn't come upstairs right away, so I suspected he was down in the bar, having a drink. She never came. I finally fell asleep.

"The next day things went pretty much the same. He left in the late afternoon. It started to snow. Big, lazy snow flakes that came down real slow. He didn't come home for dinner. No one said anything. I kept on looking out the windows. The snow was getting real heavy, and the wind had picked up. Last time I looked, all I could see was snow blowing around. We all went to bed. Or at least to our rooms. The wind was howling so loud I couldn't sleep. After a while I heard the door downstairs open and slam shut. He was home. I waited. Listened. He didn't come upstairs right away. I was sure the others were listening too. A few minutes later I heard his bedroom door close. And then voices. Angry voices. Loud, but not loud enough to hear what they were saying. After about twenty minutes it got quiet again, and I dozed off.

"I was asleep when I felt her hand grabbing my shoulder and shaking me. She told me to get up and go with her. I followed her back to her room. There he was, lying on his back, in his undershirt and underpants. The covers were pulled down to his knees. There was something sticking straight up out of his chest. I went over to the bed. I recognized it right away. The handle of a knife. A fillet knife. I'd used it a lot. I knew how easily it could cut through meat and cartilage and skin."

"Oh, no. No." Tears stream down Paul's cheeks. How could she kill him? How could she? He shakes his head. "Oh, God, no!"

"Hard to believe, isn't it? I never dreamed she'd do it. I had this feeling that maybe, if I just pulled the knife out and put it away, everything would be okay. It just didn't make sense that this man, who had always seemed so large and so powerful ... who could've broken me like a twig ... there he was, lying on the bed, dead, like some animal carcass. Dead meat. I could still see him, talking and alive, and there he was, dead. A fillet knife sticking out of him. I could've carved him up like a deer."

"Oh, God! God!" Paul shakes his head, the tears continuing to flow.

"Next thing I know she's telling me I should go down to the boat house. I couldn't understand her at first. She had to get in my face and tell me all over again: go to the boat house, get the auger and ax, and a rope and anchor, and carry everything—everything, do you hear me?—everything to the Black Hole, and make a hole in the ice. Make it in the middle of the ice. And then come back." Stone takes a sip of whiskey. "She looked at me, and I understood."

Paul closes his eyes. It's all beginning to make sense, the way a nightmare makes sense.

"You know what it's like to try to walk in a blizzard?"

Paul nods his head, not really hearing him. Why did she have to kill him?

"Can't see a fucking thing with all that snow blowing. And sure as hell not the boathouse. But I know if I go downhill, I'll find it. No time to think about why I want to make a hole in the ice, why I want an anchor and rope. I get everything together and load it all onto the toboggan and head back. My footsteps are already full of snow. I get to the side of the lodge and I'm sheltered from the wind, but as soon as I get past the lodge the wind's howling again, screaming ... blowing snow into my eyes. It stings. I break through the crust on the snow and sink almost to my knees. At the bottom of the hill I start stumbling where the reeds and cattails are bent under the snow, so I know I'm on the edge of the Black Hole. And then it's smooth and firm. I'm on ice. I walk far enough so I know I'm near the center, and then I shovel, drill, and chop until I've got a hole big enough.

"I get back to the house and go upstairs. She's thrown a sheet over him. It looks like a tent, pointing up in the middle where the knife is still stuck in his chest. She's sitting in a chair, looking at him. I start pulling back the sheet, but I stop as soon as I see his face. I feel her hand on my elbow. She tells me to throw the sheet on the floor. She has to tell me again. I do it. But I can't stop looking at the knife. When I try to push his body through the hole, the knife'll get stuck. I grab hold of the handle, and pull. The knife comes out easy enough. Some thick dark blood bubbles out of the wound. I look at the knife and the blood for a long time, and then I realize Mom is shouting, 'Take his ankles, take his ankles!' I saw she was holding him by his wrists, and then I got it. We pulled him off the bed, onto the sheet. He falls like a sack of potatoes.

"She takes the sheet at one end and I take it at the other. We haul him out. Partway down the stairs I trip. We drop him. A huge racket. I'm going crazy and swearing, fucking goddamn fucking body, and just going nuts, and finally I grab him by the feet and pull him down the rest of the stairs. His head bumps on the steps, and each time it bumps I think, you deserve it you asshole, and then I remember he's dead and can't feel it anyhow. I finally get him around the landing to the bottom of the stairs and we start to wrap him up in the sheet again so we can carry him out and next thing I know there's Fran and Christine on the landing, looking down at us, and they're both crying and screaming, and Mom's shouting at them to get back to bed, and I'm swearing about one fucking thing after another.

"We get him near the door, and she's putting on a parka and boots and shouting at Christine to go take care of you because all of a sudden you're screaming and crying. Everyone's going nuts. Except Fran. He just stands and watches, like we're not real. I look at him and wonder, what the hell am I doing? But I know what I'm doing, and if I stop ... but I can't. Once we get Bill outside, we pick him up and drag him onto the toboggan. Fran follows us. We haul Bill down the slope toward the Black Hole. The fucking wind's blowing snow in my face, stinging my eyes, raging through the trees like a god damn firestorm, and I'm going nuts. I've got so goddamn much snow stuck to my eyelashes, my eyes start to freeze shut. I try to follow my footsteps from before, but they're almost completely filled in with snow, and half the time while I'm pulling him down the hill I can't see a fucking thing. Then all of a sudden the toboggan's just as light as air, and I realize, shit, he rolled off. I can barely see Mom's form a few feet away. Everything's white. I shout at her, but she doesn't hear me. I can't see him, so I follow the toboggan back and start groping around till I find him in the snow and roll him back on. I get to the bottom of the hill and look around for the hole in the ice.

"Then it happens. There's been all this racket, the wind howling and us screaming, but now I hear something else. It's like a baby crying. I look back and I can just barely see Mom running up the slope and shouting 'Paul.' I follow her. Pretty soon I see, just barely see something moving. It's you, walking on the snow. You're shouting, 'Mama,' with your arms out in front like you're blind. She picks you up and wraps her arms around you, and almost immediately you stop crying. Mom grabs a blanket out of Christine's hands and carries you into the lodge. I pull Bill over toward the hole, where I'd left everything. I tie the anchor to his neck and drop it into the hole, but it doesn't fall into the water because the hole's already started to ice over. So I drop the anchor in the hole, over and over, smashing it into that fucking hole, until it goes through. I pick him up by the feet and try to push him in, but the hole's not big enough. So I take the fucking ax and chop that fucking hole like I was killing every goddamn thing I've ever hated, killing God for taking my mother and my old man for having dumped us and Bill for having hurt Mom. I try pushing him in again, and this time he slides into that black water like a big seal ... like he belongs there.

"By the time I finish hauling the toboggan with the augur and ax to the boat house and make it back to the lodge, you're in bed, asleep. Fran, Christine, and Mom are sitting around the kitchen table. They're drinking hot milk. She pours me a cup. Talks about how the hot milk will settle our nerves and help us get to sleep. About how we've been through a lot, but now everything will be fine. Huh," he laughs. "Those two kids just saw their dead father hauled out like an animal carcass and dumped through a hole in the ice, and she tells them everything'll be just fine. We just need a little hot milk. We didn't say a word. We didn't even look at one another. I felt like I was in a dream. Then she starts talking about how we gotta stick together and help one another. That's what a family does. Everyone sticks together, no matter what. We're all safe, as long as the family's safe. No matter how serious any of our wrongs might be, they're forgiven here.

"After Mom stopped talking, we just sat there for a while, not saying a word, keeping it all to ourselves. I was scared shitless. We all were. Scared of what we'd done. What might happen to us. And what we didn't know. Without saying a word, we all agreed we'd keep that night secret from the world. We'd keep the sickness inside.

"Fran and Christine went upstairs to bed. I was gonna go too, when Joyce remembered Bill's car. I drove it out onto the main road, and then backed up as far as I could. I had to stop all the time to make sure I was still on the road. Then I'd back up some more. Didn't stop until I got so far I was afraid I wouldn't be able to make it back. I put it in first and drove the car into the ditch. Then I put it in second to make it look like Bill had been driving slowly. I followed the car tracks back to the lodge. By the time I got there, they were gone. The snow gave us all the cover we needed."

Paul feels broken. "I think I'll go back to the lodge. I'm tired. I want to go to sleep, and never think of this again."

Paul begins to stand up.

"Sit down, you piece of shit, or I'll put you down."

Paul sees that Stone is pointing the gun at his chest. Would it be so bad to die?

"I mean it, Paulie. Sit down. Or I'll blow a fucking hole right through you."

Paul sits. How could they have done this to one another? She loved him so much, she wanted him—even after she'd killed him—to take her in his arms and hold her at night as she lay in bed. And him, he might have dreamed of a different life, but he kept coming back to her. Why? He must've loved her, still. In spite of everything. Paul looks at Stone.

"The only thing I don't get is this: why did he drive home in a blizzard? Above all when his mom and dad froze to death in a blizzard on the same road?"

"Don't know. Maybe he wanted to be dead."

"And why would he want that?"

"Only way he could escape."

"That doesn't add up. Not if he was so enamored of Valery. I think he was a lot more interested in living than dying." Paul reflects, then adds, "What if there was something very powerful drawing him back? Maybe he realized he loved Mother after all."

"Oh!" Stone laughs. "Paulie, you just can't stop thinking, can you? The wheels never stop turning. You should've been a detective. You're a real Sherlock." Stone pauses, then adds, "You know what I think?"

"Not a clue."

"I think he didn't give a fuck. He just didn't know there was going to be a total whiteout. That's all. But, in the end, it doesn't make any difference, does it? Once he got there, Joyce made damn sure he'd never leave her again. She spent the rest of her life looking out her bedroom window at the place where he was buried. In the muck, in the shit at the bottom of the Black Hole."

Paul bites his lip. The pain helps him focus, helps him listen, and forget about what he's feeling. Later, he thinks. Later.

"You know, Paulie, if you want to understand our family, you've gotta understand this: there was a lot of love. A lot of love. Your mother spends thirty-five years sitting in her bedroom window looking out at the place where your father's buried. Because she's so in love with him. And I spend thirty-five years looking at your mother, watching her sit in the window." Stone pauses, then adds, "You look like you don't believe me."

Paul shakes his head. "I believe you. It's just ... I didn't know."

"Thirty-five fucking years, Paulie. I don't know what I meant to her, but she meant everything to me. When I was on the inside, there was no more difference between her and me than between the skin and the flesh of a peach. It was too good to see the light of day. Too good to last. Once Bill was dead, everything changed. I don't know why. Guilt, maybe. Or maybe she just didn't need me anymore. He wasn't going anywhere. Or she might've been afraid people would find out about us and—"

"Yeah, she had a lot to be afraid of, didn't she—aunt, mother, and mistress, all in one."

"Huh! Mistress is the wrong word. Unless by that you mean master. She held me curled up in the palm of her hand. And when she was done, she threw me away. Bought me this shack and the land it sits on, and told me to never set foot in the lodge again. And I didn't. Not until the day of her funeral."

Stone takes a sip of whiskey and coughs. "This isn't puttin' enough fire in my belly to keep me warm. You shiverin' over there?"

"It's getting cold."

"Not scared, just cold, eh? Jesus, man, gotta speak up. How does that song go? 'Put another log on the fire,'" he sings with a twang, imitating Waylon Jennings. He stands up. "Now, if I leave this ol' girl on my chair," he nods toward the rifle he laid on the seat as he stood up, "you wouldn't try to do anything with her, would you?"

Paul's tempted, but he feels he's got a better chance of getting out alive if he humors Stone.

"Not gonna say, huh? Well, that's okay. I don't think you've got the balls."

"Maybe I've got the balls not to panic and do something stupid."

"Always the smart guy. The smart one who got away ... but was dumb enough to come back." Stone shakes his head as he walks around the table, passing within inches of Paul.

Paul feels his presence as he passes behind him and watches him as he gets an armful of logs from a pile behind the stove and, nudging Jason aside with his foot, squats in front of the glowing coals. He's about to toss in a birch log the width of his forearm when he stops and, holding the log up as if it were a club, says, "One of these could do a fuck of a lot of damage to a guy's head."

"I don't get it. Why do you hate me so much?"

Stone tosses the log onto the coals, creating an explosion of red hot embers.

"Maybe 'cause you got a life. Maybe 'cause you think you're too good. Lots of reasons."

The birch bark smokes, then bursts into a small flame that grows within seconds to a real fire.

Paul shakes his head. How could he have not seen all these years that the one person he trusted from his past might actually hate him?

Stone tosses another birch log onto the flames, then a couple more logs of pine or oak, and stares into the fire, his face aglow with the flames. He shuts the stove door and heads back to his chair. Paul follows Stone with his eyes. He could be carrying a log in the hand he can't see. Stone finally plops into his chair, empty handed, and leaning back into the darkness mumbles, "Now it's going to get so fucking hot in here we'll probably have to strip down to nothing."

"Can't get that hot."

"It can get hot as hell in no time." Stone sticks his index finger in the glass and then smears whiskey across his cheek, as if he were putting on invisible war paint. He does the other cheek. "You ever lose someone who meant everything to you? Someone ..." He looks mystified by his own thought and incapable of finishing the question, but finally adds, "... Someone you really couldn't live without?"

Paul tries to read his face, wondering where this is going.

"I mean someone who, once she's gone, you're dead on the inside. Completely dead." He draws out his words as if he has to think of each one individually.

"I know what you're talking about."

"No ... I don't think you do. Because you're still ... you're still alive inside. I can sense it. The walking dead know one another. I recognize ... I recognize my kind. We're a whole different breed. You might've suffered a little, but you're not dead. You're not feeding a corpse when you eat."

"I think everyone's been there, Stone. Everyone's felt that, at one time or another. Maybe not as much as you, but—"

"But that's kind of the whole fucking point, isn't it? How much? How fucking much? I was sixteen when we started. Nineteen when it ended. I could never want another woman. Not really. Not with that craving in my gut that was so strong it made me sick."

Paul feels sympathetic, and then catches himself: Stone is talking about making love to his mother. He should want to kill him.

"I tried. I'd go to the bars in Mirer. Get drunk with some woman. We'd go home, fuck, and fall asleep. The women were okay. We got it on. But I couldn't," he shakes his head slowly, "I couldn't stop thinking of her. I'd fuck them and think of her." He looks at Paul. "One of 'em you might've known. Lived in the woods, down by Moose Lake. Drank like she had a fire to put out. Tall woman. Pretty once, I could tell. She knew you. Did she ever! There was a song, she said, made you think of her. Something about a woman named Suzanne."

"Molly!"

Stone sings, off-key and out of time, "You know that she's half crazy, but that's why you want to be there. She played it for me several times. More than I wanted to hear. You sure made an impression." He nods his head. "But, I remembered—way too late, I guess—it's not a smart thing to drink with someone when you can't stop thinking about something you can't talk about. I couldn't take a chance. She might've talked."

"You killed her?"

"Had to."

"You son of a bitch!" Paul lunges toward Stone.

The gun flashes.

"Oh! Aiee! Shit!" Paul collapses in his chair.

"Shut up, asshole!"

A burning sensation. Blood runs through his fingers and down his neck. Paul draws his hand away from his neck and looks at the blood. "Oh, God! You shot me, you son of a bitch!"

"You're lucky. Next time I'll aim for your chest." Stone stares at him for a while. "You wanna drink?"

"Oh, God! It hurts!" He presses his bloody fingers against the wound in his neck.

"You're not gonna die, for Christ's sake." Stone stands up, pours some whiskey into Paul's glass, then fills his own, pulls a blue bandanna out of his pants pocket, tosses it across the table to Paul, and sits down. "It's just got some sweat on it."

Paul crams the bandana into his glass, with one hand wrings out most of the whiskey, and applies the improvised bandage to his neck. "Ah!" he grimaces with pain.

Stone watches him, smiling. "Well, here's to Molly. May the bitch rest in peace."

Paul feels as if he's going to vomit.

"Don't wanna drink to Molly?"

He spits the words out. "Let's just get this over with."

"Don't even wanna know how I killed her?"

Paul maintains the pressure on the wound. Just a little more patience, and maybe Stone will let him go.

"Amazing how hard someone'll fight to live. They'll scratch and claw, eyes popping out of their heads. Makes you wonder what they're living for, to put up a fight like that. Molly didn't seem to have a great life, but she sure struggled to hang on to it. Course, maybe she was just afraid of what comes after."

Paul sees her, her big dark eyes bulging, panic, and he starts to cry again. Molly, you had so much life. He lets his hand with the bandage fall to the table. Blood slowly trickles down from the wound.

"I didn't enjoy killing her. I liked her. But you can't let people know some things, and go on living."

Paul glares at Stone. Molly didn't deserve that.

"With that goddamn sheriff—what's his name? Swenson. That was different. He just had to play detective every chance he got. Another fucking Sherlock. The thought of that old fart drinking a whole fucking pint of whiskey and driving his car out on thin ice just breaks your heart. Makes you wonder, when the fuck are people gonna learn not to drive on thin ice?" He shakes his head. "Happens every year."

He's been here all these years, always ready to help out. So quiet, so much a part of the background, who would've guessed. He may as well have been invisible.

"And Valery, I'll be goddamn if she didn't come back that spring, you know, when the sheriff and his cronies searched the woods again for Bill. She probably shouldn't have stopped to pick up that hitchhiker on the way out of town, 'cause wouldn't you know, he went and bashed her fucking brains in with a lug wrench. But, around here, you can't drive by someone you know who's got a flat tire in the middle of nowhere. She did the right thing." He shakes his head. "So many lakes and marshes that can just swallow up a whole car. And that water, with all the muck and the iron, you can't see more than a foot down. You look at those books in the stores, with all the pretty pictures of trees on the water, like in a mirror—they're so pretty, but who knows what's underneath? We got enough water around here to hide an army."

"Who else, Stone?"

"I don't know. I don't keep track. You gotta learn how to let go."

"Who else?"

"Hey! I was just keepin' things quiet, protecting Mother, so I could hang around. Like some poor, fucking, mangy dog, hopin' for a bone. Trotting back and forth, waiting for my chance. Coming in as close as I dared, staying just far enough away. Down by the Black Hole, in the dark, I'd watch her sitting in the window. She seemed to be looking right at the place where I pushed him down through the ice. Years went by, and I'd see her sitting in the dark, looking out at that same place." Stone shakes his head. "She was never gonna let go of him. Never. She didn't give a fuck about me. I shoulda just stayed away. Gone away for good. But I kept on coming back. I needed to see her. Needed to feel she was looking at me."

"How could she be looking at you if she was looking at the place where he was ... buried."

"'Buried' is the right word. He's down at the bottom in all that loose muck. You know, the kind of stuff you step in and it just starts to float. Kind of like shit."

"How could you think she was looking at you?"

"Because if she looked at the place where I buried him, she'd see me. She'd see me at night, in the canoe. Or on the far side of the Hole, standing just beyond the reeds. She knew I was there. It became another secret between us. Kind of like in the beginning, when I first used to go into her room, and she'd put her hand on the back of my head. Now we had another secret, and as long as I didn't say anything to anyone, she'd keep on coming to the window at night. Even if she was looking at him, I was there, and she was looking at me, and I could watch her looking at me."

"You put yourself in the place of a corpse."

"The place was as much mine as his. And all her love was in that place."

"How do you know?"

"There was never another man in her life. Not even her children counted as much as what was there. Not even you. And she loved you. But you weighed nothing in the balance."

"Nor did you, apparently."

"But I was in his place. And she knew that."

"How do you know?"

"I know."

"This makes no sense."

"It makes perfect sense."

Paul stares at him, baffled by the absurdity of it all.

"Or it did."

"And now?"

"She's dead." Stone pauses for what seems a long time, and then says, "You know, when you're a kid, and you're growing up, and you're dreaming about what you wanna be—a cowboy, a pilot, a fireman, whatever. I had those dreams. The other day I started remembering them. It made me sad. Because, once I started going into Joyce's room at night, I started dreaming about her. And I never stopped. The other day, when I was remembering those growing-up dreams, I realized something. It almost made me sick."

"And what's that?"

"I realized I'd died." He looks at Paul. "Ever seen a fly that's been wrapped up for a while in a spider's web? It's just a dry, dead hulk. Crumbles to dust in your fingers."

"Who's the spider?"

"Oh, she was."

Paul shakes his head. "No. You were the spider. The spider, the web, and the fly. You did it to yourself."

Stone stares at him for a long time. Suddenly he laughs. "The funny thing is, my eyesight's gotten so fucking bad these last few years, it could've been a dummy I saw in the window. You ever seen that movie *Psycho?*"

Paul nods his head yes.

"There were times I'd be looking up there seeing her in the window and wondering if she was still alive, or if that asshole Fran—you know, he's just as fucking weird as they come—I've wondered if he's not carrying his dead mother around the house."

"It doesn't make any difference if she was alive or dead."

"Oh, you're right, Paulie. You're right so much it just pisses me off! But think about this. There always seemed to be so much love in this family, and yet everyone felt starved for it. How can that be? You're so fucking smart, explain that."

"I don't profess to—"

"No," Stone laughs. "You'd be smart not to profess to too fucking much of anything."

"Okay, I won't."

"Maybe each one of us is the spider, the web, and the fly. After all, what made you stay?"

Paul's eyes wander from the rifle on the table to the bottle and the glasses, then back to the rifle and Stone staring at him with a smile or a smirk on his face. Paul nods his head.

Stone chuckles. "Now you're one of us, Paulie. You know just about everything. You poor son of a bitch." He laughs.

"Good luck." Stone lifts his glass in a toast, takes a drink, and sets it down. His head rolls a little, just enough to make Paul wonder if he might pass out.

He tosses the bloody handkerchief on the table. "I think I've learned all I'm gonna learn tonight. I'm taking off." He pushes his chair back and starts to stand.

Stone snaps, "Sit down!" He points the gun at Paul's chest, finger on the trigger. "You make one more fucking move and I'll blow you away."

Paul sits.

"I'm not done with you yet. Besides, I can't let you leave if your neck's still bleeding. Wouldn't be polite."

"It's stopped." Paul gingerly touches the open wound. "Aiee!" The hot, dry air burns his raw flesh. Sweat drips down his back. He glances over at the stove—a little inferno with dancing flames.

"Stone. Always sinks to the bottom. What a loser. Lot of pain in losing." His eyes burrow into Paul. "You always get your ass in an uproar if I don't tell you everything you wanna know. Now I wanna know." He smiles. "So, we're gonna play a little game."

"Not interested."

Stone rests the 30 Ot 6 on the table so it's pointing again at Paul. "Your interest don't count for shit." He pauses, then continues. "I wanna give you a chance to show me you know this pain I've been talking about. So, we play the game. Here's the rules. If you really know what I've been talking about, then for some time now you've been feeding a corpse every time you eat, so it'd be a blessing if I was to put this last bullet right through your heart. If you know, don't say anything, and I'll put you out of your misery."

Paul looks at the barrel of the 30 Ot 6 eyeing him.

"If you don't know, you can tell me what kind of pain you're thinking of, and if I think you're almost dead, but still got a chance to live, I'll let you walk out of here. If you haven't got a clue, and you try to flat-out bullshit me, I pull the trigger. You understand the game?"

Paul has been thinking of his father driving through snow, through a whiteout, trying—he wants to believe this—trying to reach his mother, trying to save their love. And of his mother, holding onto her love until the very end. If he can get out of this mess … He knows what's important.

"Paulie!"

He looks at Stone.

"Do you understand the game?"

"I'm too tired. I didn't get it."

Stone explains the game all over again. "You get it now?"

"Let's see. If I know exactly what you're talking about, I'm already dead. I'm feeding a corpse when I eat. I don't say anything and you do me the favor of putting me out of my misery. If I'm not dead, and I have some knowledge of your pain, I tell you what I know, and you let me go—if you're convinced I'm telling the truth. And if I don't have a clue, and I try to bullshit you, you shoot me."

"That's it." Stone grins and nods his head.

"Okay. Let's play." Paul pauses for a few seconds and then starts talking. "I used to see a psychoanalyst. One day I was lying on the couch …"

"Lying on a couch? You gotta be kidding!"

"No. I was lying on a couch."

"Holy shit. It's a weird world."

"So I'm learning. To get on with my story … I 'd been really depressed, having a hard time sleeping. And while I was lying there, in a stupor, I blurted out something about love being like grace. It was a gift. And either you received it, or you didn't. If you didn't, you were out of luck, because you couldn't earn it. And without it, you were nothing."

"Oh, Jesus, Paulie, you better come up with something better than this bullshit."

"Just a beggar, looking through a window at a feast, and everyone on the other side is part of one big happy family … that gets to eat. You devour the feast with your eyes, you imagine how it would taste, how it would feel in your mouth, but you can't eat it. You're hungry. Always hungry. As long as I could remember, I've hungered … I've performed some of the stupidest antics, just to get past the window and eat my fill."

"This better be going somewhere." Stone again repositions the rifle, which has slid to the side.

"And then I told him about the night I tried to spy on a woman. On Claire."

"Claire … Claire … That name's familiar."

"I've talked about her." He pauses for a minute, takes a deep breath. "We'd broken up. I was a real mess. I'd go for long walks at night, trying not to think of her, and I'd find myself looking up at her windows. One night, late, I was walking by her place. No lights. I assumed she was in bed. A car drove by, stopped about a hundred feet away, and backed into a parking place. A woman got out. I recognized Claire's laugh. The driver, a man, got out too. I crossed the street and ducked into the shadow of a doorway. They entered her building. A couple minutes later the lights went on in the living room. She approached the window and drew the curtains shut. I watched as one and then the other silhouette came into view; the silhouettes merged, separated, disappeared, and the lights went off.

"I crossed the street, buzzed the front door of the building, and walked through the entry into the courtyard. Right before you entered the courtyard there was a button that you pressed to turn on the lights in the yard so you could find your way to a staircase at the back. Obviously, I didn't push the button. I hid in one of the corners in the yard. In total darkness. I could see Claire's two bedroom windows, the curtains drawn. Two shadows moved about, merging and separating, but I couldn't tell what they were doing. Suddenly the lights went on in the courtyard, and two couples entered. They saw me in the corner and stopped. One of the men asked if I had lost something. The other asked if I was looking for someone. 'In the corner?' one of the women asked, laughing. My mind was racing, trying to find an answer, but all I could do was mumble no several times, and then I said something about just getting some air. I walked by them as fast as I could. I felt so ashamed. They laughed at me."

"That's the best you can do?" Stone studies his face.

Paul shrugs. "I've had a little taste of your daily dose of pain."

A long silence. Stone leans back in his chair, out of the light.

"You'd better get your ass out of here, before I blow it away."

Paul tries to see the expression on Stone's face, but it remains inscrutable in the dark. He stands up, hesitates while trying to think of something to say, walks over to the doorway, puts on his boots and coat, and stops for one last look. Stone's head now seems just a dark, featureless form; the fire glows red through the joint between the hinges of the stove door; and Jason, lifting his head, gives him one last look and then settles his head on his paws and closes his eyes.

The voice from the darkness says, "You're one of us now, Paulie. You may not be that dead, dried out fly, ready to crumble into dust, but you've been caught."

Paul nods, turns toward the door.

"One last thing, Paulie. Why did Bill decide to drive back to the lodge in a whiteout? It'd be interesting to know."

16

THE NEXT MORNING PAUL SITS ON THE EDGE OF
his bed, elbows on his knees, face in his hands. The night
still weighs on him. "You're one of us now, Paulie." To go
on living is just to have all this history churning in him,
forever. It'll never stop. Never. He knows that. And life
will never be anything but a temporary distraction. A
diversion from what he can never forget. Like Stone, he'll
be feeding a corpse when he eats. Maybe he should've let
Stone kill him.

The whole day he broods over the conversation with
Stone.

That night, in deep, black water, he sees a huge shape,
like submerged crystal or ice, in the distance. He moves
toward it, and then around it, as easily as if he were
walking on land. He notices something dark embedded
in the ice. As he comes closer he sees his father, dressed
in black, beneath several inches of ice. His father, but his
brother in age, his twin. He moves closer still. His father's
eyes wide open, staring at something beyond Paul. He

thinks, what are you looking at? His father doesn't answer. What do you want? He hears his father's thought just as clearly as if it were his own. My future. What I dream myself to be. Paul wants to tell him it's too late, he's already dead. There is no future. Then he realizes he is becoming part of the ice. He will remain frozen, forever staring at his dead father. He breaks through the ice and finds himself sitting in bed, gasping for air.

First thing that morning, Paul buys a plane ticket to Paris.

He has to get out of here. What if Stone were to come after him? But why would he, if he already let him go? Paul touches the bandage on his neck; the wound still burns. Fran stared at the bandage when Paul made his call, but didn't say a thing. Paul wouldn't have responded if he had. They can't talk. Stone and Fran were both right. He should have never stayed after his mother's funeral. He doesn't belong here.

In the late afternoon, Paul sits near the fire, a book on his lap. His last day in the lodge (he looks around at the mounted animals—the bear, the bobcat, the moose and deer heads—so stoic in the silent gloom) and he's gone. For good. Never coming back. One night at a hotel in Minneapolis, right next to the airport, and then he flies out for the last time. No return trips. Ever.

Someone knocks at the front door. Paul walks into the light of the outer dining room and opens the door. It's a policeman. Paul doesn't know him, but he has seen him in Mirer. A quiet guy. In his forties. Solidly built, with a square jaw, brown hair, and a mustache. The man introduces himself as Sheriff Janovich. He needs to talk with him. Paul leads him back into the lodge; they sit down near the fire. Janovich announces that Robert Bauer is dead. Paul nods his head. The news seems consistent with the gloom he feels.

He notices the sheriff is staring at him. Janovich adds, "It looks to be a suicide. Maybe three days ago."

Paul admits that's when he saw Stone last.

"Stone?"

"His nickname."

"Ah. And what was the purpose of your visit?"

"Just to ... get caught up with an old friend."

"A cousin, actually. He is your cousin, isn't he?"

"Yes. My cousin. And my brother, by adoption. At times, almost a father."

Janovich looks at him and nods his head, as if he understood. "And he lived in that cabin, separate from the rest of the family?"

"Yes."

"What did you talk about?"

"I just ... just stopped in to say good-bye. I'm leaving for France tomorrow morning."

"Hmm." Janovich seems to be studying him. "What happened to your neck?"

"My neck?"

"Yeah, your neck. You've got that bandage there."

"Oh, that. I, uh ... I was walking in the woods and uh ... a branch broke off from a white pine. It fell right on my neck."

Janovich stares at him and nods. He doesn't look convinced.

"Hurt like hell."

"I guess." Janovich's eyes drift around the room, as if he were looking for something.

"That's awful, about Stone. I mean, Robert."

Janovich's eyes lock onto him again and grip him so tight he can't move. "How did he seem when you left?"

"Fine."

"Not sad, or depressed? Or unusually happy?"

"No. He seemed fine."

"Did you see a 30 Ot 6 rifle?"

Paul shakes his head, no.

"Any spent rifle casings?"

Paul again shakes his head no.

"Smell of gunpowder?"

He shakes his head a third time.

Janovich's eyes finally let him go.

He lets Janovich know he'll be staying now for a few days, until they can have a funeral and bury Stone. He stands in the doorway after Janovich has left, looking down at the boathouse, remembering Stone's description of that night. He should hate him, but he can't. Stone was just a boy.

Three days later Robert "Stone" Bauer is buried next to his mother. He loved her so much, that seemed the best place for him. The priest battles the wind as he intones from the missal and announces the reunion with Christ after death. Paul looks across the open grave and the casket. Fran, gaunt, angular, impassive, his long black hair streaked with gray flagellating in the wind, glares at a point just above Paul's head, as if he can see some transgression that requires retribution. He seems to be in one of his old testament moods, when he could say that the slaughter of thousands of innocents was right and just, if it were God's will—or the will of God's chosen. Christine, standing next to him, the tight curls of her hair fluttering in the wind, wears the dark glasses that conceal her eyes, thoughts, and feelings. A few people from town: a tall old man, bent over, white hair and gray, ashen skin; another man, middle-aged, short, paunched, and bearded, with thick dark brown eyebrows that meet above his nose; a couple of women in their fifties or sixties, their heads scarved, their blurry eyes fixed on the casket; and a few more mourners standing behind them. Aside from Fran, Christine, and the bearded man, who works in one of the bait and tackle shops, Paul doesn't recognize any of them.

He wonders, as he scans their faces, what they might know and are keeping to themselves.

After the service he leaves alone. Driving slowly, paying no attention to where he's going, he sees Stone stepping out of darkness. "Paulie, there was so much love." Stone shakes his head and fades into the night. The voice continues whispering. "My mother was an angel. I lived in paradise. Nothing was missing, as long as she was alive." He lost a part of himself. And was never whole again. Except, maybe, with Mother. "Oh, Paulie, she was everything to me—my mother, my aunt, my guardian angel. Her milk was sweet as honey. I felt her fingers on the back of my head, and then her hand, and I knew she knew." So much love found and lost so early, how could he not feel he'd already died? "You sleep in a dead man's bed, gives you a different look on life." He began sleeping in that bed as soon as he made love to his aunt-mother. Maybe that's why black humor came so easily to him. It was so much like him to say, "Before long someone's gonna find me frozen, haul me out like a big ol' log, and throw me in the rear end of a pickup. Kindling for the devil." He knew more than he should have ever known, and he paid a price in having to carry it all with him. "Let go of the past, Paulie. There's nothing you can learn will do you any good." Paul nods his head and thinks, you knew how to keep things in the dark, my friend. But I have to live with those things in the light.

Paul becomes aware the car has stopped. He's reached the summit of a hill on a blacktop road. The road ahead descends a slope and climbs to a higher summit; on the right, scattered pine trees, uneven mounds of snow through which dead vegetation pokes its elbows, and flat rocks and scattered boulders wet from melting snow; on the left, below, a deep valley, white studded with trees, and the smooth white surface of a lake. Shit, he's completely lost.

*
* *

Paul watches Fran carve thin slices from a roast of beef; they curl and then slump to the platter. He stares at the left hand holding the fork in the roast, at the stubs with puckered skin where the fingers used to be. Christine, sitting next to a window, still wearing her glasses, shivers and complains of not being able to warm up. She pulls her unbuttoned sweater tight and clasps it with her left hand while with her right she picks up a mug of coffee, holds it close to her lips, and inhales the steam, occasionally sipping the hot brew. Fran finishes slicing the meat and lays the butcher knife across the edge of the platter. They buried Stone just a few hours ago, and now they're sitting at a table in the outer dining room eating lunch, hoping the sun, which has reappeared today, will warm their cold spirits. Paul picks at the radishes and green onions in the yellow sauce of the potato salad, then sets his fork down and looks up at Fran, who is eating with absent-minded, mechanical determination. Paul gazes outside at the lake ablaze in the sun while listening to the monotonous dripping of melting snow. The warming weather has triggered a thaw.

Christine says, out of the blue, "You saw Stone just before he killed himself."

Fran stops chewing his sandwich and looks at Paul. "Yeah."

"Why do you think he did it?"

"Probably because of what he told me."

"And what was that?"

"He was Mother's lover. She killed our father. Stone tied an anchor to his neck and sank him to the bottom of the Black Hole."

The room falls silent.

Fran looks up, then down again at his plate. "It can be

dangerous—"

"Fran!" Christine's voice cuts off his thought.

It cuts through Paul too. He flinches, looks at her. Her dark glasses make her look like a third-world general.

She looks at Paul and smiles. "Just think, in two days you'll be back in Paris. I bet you're happy!"

"That's right."

"I never understood why you decided to stay on here with Fran." She looks around. "This place just isn't you."

Paul stares at the black lenses.

"Fran told me you were interested in knowing why Mother threw Stone out."

"Yeah, I was."

"Stone had some rather strange … ideas. Ideas that existed only in his mind. He thought Mother was in love with him." She shakes her head and laughs. "Ludicrous! And that's what Mother thought too. But she was concerned that if he stayed here, and started talking, sooner or later he'd find someone who might believe him. So she decided to send him away." She pauses, then adds, "He was very unstable. You knew that, didn't you?"

"No, I didn't."

"Well, no wonder you seemed to have … allowed yourself to be influenced by him."

"Influenced?"

"You know what I mean."

"No, I don't."

"At any rate, Mother was so afraid of what might happen if he started wandering around, she bought him the land and the cabin and got him all set up."

"And shut up?"

"He was happy as a clam in its own juice."

Paul stays focused on Christine's glasses. "If he was as happy as a clam, why do you think he killed himself?"

"Who knows? With someone like Stone, there could

be any number of reasons. When I think of all the crazy things he talked about over the years!"

"Like what?"

"Oh, I don't know. Just crazy things. The kind of things you prefer to forget."

"Things like sleeping with his aunt-mother, and getting rid of his uncle-father's corpse?"

"Yes, as examples, those will do. And he might have believed those things. He probably told himself so many times Mother was in love with him, and she killed Dad ... I'm sure he believed what he was saying. And he probably acted on that belief. With Stone, that kind of thing was entirely possible." She pauses, then adds, "You know, I think what Fran was going to say, when I cut him off a few minutes ago," she looks at Fran and smiles sweetly, "is that it can be very dangerous for your health to live up here year 'round, alone, in a cabin, with so little to do and so much time. People get a little crazy, and after many years, they can get very crazy."

"I know how people can get up here."

"In spite of his ideas, he was pretty harmless. I don't think anyone paid attention to him. Do you, Fran?"

"He was a joke. People just laughed at him."

"It's not a good idea to repeat Stone's stories. People who knew him would probably just ignore you. But there are those who didn't, and they might wonder. Besides, it's embarrassing to have someone talking about your parents that way. Mirer's a small town. First thing you know, people will be gossiping and pointing, there'll be articles about us in the papers, and we'll be on the news. You don't want that, do you?"

"I won't be here."

"Fran will. And I come back here."

"I'm not interested in telling anyone."

"Good. Because we wouldn't want any of Stone's crazy

stories getting people to open up an investigation. One that was closed long ago."

"I just want to know for myself. I want you to take off those glasses, look at me, and tell me if what Stone said is true or not."

Christine keeps her glasses on and taps the table top with her fingernails. "Stone probably believed what he said, but believing something doesn't make it true."

Fran adds, "If he believed those stories, he shouldn't 've ever told them to a stranger."

"A stranger? Fran, I'm your brother!"

"You're not one of us."

"Ah, there it is. Finally, out in the open! What does it mean to be one of us? Tell me, what does that mean?"

"Fran only meant we see you so seldom, it's almost like you're a stranger."

"Bullshit! There's more to it than that. So, Fran, what do you mean by 'us'? Do you mean the people who know what really happened the night our father 'disappeared'? That's the right euphemism, isn't it?"

Fran's eyes fix his anger on Paul. "Go to hell! And keep Stone company."

Fran looks down at his plate. He reaches toward the middle of the table for the butcher knife on the meat platter and begins tracing lines with the knife point in the large smear of yellow potato salad dressing on his plate. Then he starts moving bread crumbs around on his plate with the tip of the knife. "Stone got exactly what he deserved. I hope he does burn in hell!" Fran's hand stops. He looks up at Paul and says, "You remember what the priest said? To know what hell is, light a match and hold it to your finger. Feel the pain. Imagine your entire body held to a flame for all eternity. Then you can begin to know the horror of hell." Hell burns in Fran's eyes—or maybe it's just the late afternoon sun.

"You seem to like thinking of Stone burning for eternity."

"He'll be paid the wages he's earned."

Paul's eyes target Fran's. "And how about you, Fran, are you being paid the wages you've earned?"

Christine abruptly turns the conversation to practical matters: there's the cost of the funeral that needs to be settled, and the liquidation of Stone's estate—if you can call that shack an estate. She laughs.

Finally the last red glow of the sun fades out. Christine and Fran begin to take on the gray shades of dusk. She removes her sunglasses and looks at Fran.

"I think we need to remember the good things about Stone. He helped out when Mother was dying. He ran the resort and didn't ask for a thing. We should pray that God forgives him." She looks across the table at Paul. "We need to leave the past in the past and get on with our lives."

As the shadows darken, the fiery, manic Fran metamorphoses into the Lincolnesque Fran, stone quiet, with a long nose, pointed jaw, deep-set eyes, and a shock of black, gray-streaked hair. Gazing at that stony figure, Paul wonders what happened to the brother whom he'd started to get to know, before he disrupted things by going to the library and digging up articles, reading his parents' letters, and talking to Stone and Ruth.

"Fran, I don't know exactly what happened thirty-five years ago, but whatever it was, you've paid a huge price. I feel sorry for what you've been through. I'd like us to be able to—"

Fran's right arm strikes like a cobra, and Christine screams. The butcher knife sticks in the table, where a second before Paul's hand had been resting. Fran thrusts himself into Paul's face.

"You have no right to feel sorry for me. I've spent my whole life with the person I loved most."

Paul's shaking. He feels cold, sick. He can't take his

eyes off the knife.

Fran is standing straight now. He leans on his left hand, the thumb and two fingers splayed across the table, and with his right grabs the knife and works it back and forth so he can pull it out of the wood.

Paul's eyes move from the knife to the stubs where the fingers had been. His eyes remain fixed on the mutilated hand that continues to rest on the table as Fran lays down the knife and sinks back into his chair.

"How did you lose those fingers?"

Fran's head snaps up, as if it were a reflex. He looks down at the stubs and then back up at Paul. Christine looks at Fran, her eyes boring into him.

Paul asks again, "Fran, how did you lose your fingers?"

Fran hesitates, then answers in an apologetic tone, "I screwed up." He looks into Paul's eyes as if seeking forgiveness. "I meant to cut off my hand."

"Why?"

"I don't know. I went out in the woods and did it. I guess because I hurt. I wanted to get rid of the hurt."

"What was it that hurt, Fran?"

Fran closes his eyes and slowly shakes his head no. He looks as if he might burst into tears.

"What made you hurt so much you would chop off two fingers to get rid of the hurt?"

No response.

Paul reaches out and touches the back of Fran's left hand and repeats slowly, almost in a whisper, "Why did it hurt, Fran?"

"Because he hurt."

"Who?"

Fran doesn't answer.

"Who, Fran?"

"Dad. I wanted to feel ..." Fran closes his eyes and clenches his jaw in an effort to dam the feelings that well up inside, but the tears start to flow and stream down his cheeks. "I wanted to feel his pain. I wanted him to take me by the hand the way he always did when I was little. I wanted to hold on to him. So I held his pain."

"Fran," Paul whispers, overwhelmed with sorrow.

Fran looks at him through his tears. "It hurt so much. I wanted to scream how much it hurt, but I couldn't. So I tried to cut off my hand. I'm such a ... such a loser. I couldn't even do that."

Christine says, "We were just children. She told us we must never tell anyone, or the police would take her away and we'd be all alone. We'd be orphans. They'd split us up. We were so afraid."

Fran continues talking. "I cut myself off from him. From everyone. My hand screamed with pain. I hurt. Mother hurt. I hurt with her. I held onto that hurt and to her, so I could hold on to him." Fran bows his head. Paul strokes his hand until the tears stop. Fran leans back in his chair, lets his head roll back as he stares at the ceiling, then leans forward, resting his face in his hands, his elbows on the table.

Paul has nothing to say. He has no words. He knew his own pain growing up; he didn't know the pain Fran and Christine had to live with.

Night fills the room. Fran and Christine become dark forms, like penitents on the other side of the veil. Guilty only of knowing. In the dark they speak without shame.

Fran describes the horrible sight and ripe-melon sound of Dad's head bouncing on the steps as his body was dragged from the landing to the bottom of the stairway; Christine talks about the body being dragged out of the house into the blizzard and her fright upon discovering that he, Paul, not even four years old, had been awakened by all the screaming, had come downstairs, and had followed them into the storm; and Paul remembers—so vaguely he would have questioned the reality of the memory if it had not felt so true—a whiteout in which he groped in the snow-filled, suffocating air, trying to touch a figure reduced to a blur, an intangible form in the absolute whiteness that seemed to move just beyond the reach of his outstretched arms.

Another long silence. Something has changed. He can feel it. Ping! Like a crack fracturing the invisible wall that has always separated them.

Christine talks about the days, weeks, and months following the murder, when she and Fran lived in constant fear the secret might be discovered and the family destroyed. The longer they concealed the murder, the more guilt they felt, as if they too had participated in the crime, and the greater the need to conceal it. Over the years the obsession with silence and secrecy so consumed their attention and bound them—all three of them, Mother too—bound them so tightly together they could hardly communicate with anyone outside their little society. "Not even you," Christine adds, as she looks in Paul's direction. Since his arrival, she confesses, she has called the lodge at times she and Fran would agree upon so she could find out if Paul had learned anything about the murder.

"What would you've done if the two of you decided I'd learned too much, or I was going to talk to the police?"

Neither Christine nor Fran replies. He stares at them, their faces inscrutable in the darkness. He's still on the outside, looking in. What are they thinking? What would they have done? Would they have killed him?

"I never would have repeated to anyone, above all the police, anything I'd learned."

Silence.

Then Fran begins talking. He recalls memories of Dad playing with him in the lake, swimming like a fish with Fran on his back, blowing water like a walrus, tossing him in the air and letting him plunge into the water in explosions of laughter; holding his hand as they followed animal trails through the woods, looking for signs of deer, moose, and bear; taking him canoeing, the thrill of running the small rapids on the Kawishiwi River and portaging to lakes where they never saw another human being. And he remembers too how Dad would put his arm around his shoulder and give him a hug or tousle his hair when he would come running back from an errand, and wink at him as he listened yet again to the old farts tell stories about the Normandy invasion, the African campaign, and the Battle of the Bulge. Fran would move behind the bar and stand tall with his dad.

Then things changed. His ninth year—the year he received a pair of skis for his birthday in October—Dad started teaching him how to ski. He promised the following winter they'd go skiing together and explore the wilderness from here to Canada. But the next winter came, and the one after that, and all Fran got were more promises. He tossed the skis in his closet. The same with the rifle he got another year and the promises of going hunting. And when he'd return to the bar from running an errand, Dad would either nod to acknowledge his return, or simply ignore him, as he did with the regulars, who still came in the afternoons and told their war stories.

Fran remembers too something happening with the young waitresses, and he recalls very clearly Valery Night, with her long dark hair and dark eyes, her low-cut blouses and dresses, the long earrings, and above all the perfume he smelled the one time he got close to her.

"The whore. God knows the flesh is weak. But only God can judge. And give eternal life. I can feel Dad's presence, like the breath of life on the water and through the leaves. He's here, in this house."

Christine says, "If God judged him, he had to forgive a lot."

"They should've never let Stone in this house. He fed off of her, like a vampire. Like the ones in the movies. I saw them together. Saw him bending over her."

Christine mumbles, "I didn't want to see. But I couldn't stay away." A brief silence. "Poor Mother. After Dad died, she went crazy."

Fran says, "She broke up her room real bad. Then she tried to kill herself."

"When she was in the hospital, we went in her room." Christine shakes her head. "Broken picture frames, glass everywhere, clothes torn and thrown every which way, pictures ripped out of albums."

"I taped some of 'em back together. I bought two new albums, so all the pictures could be put together again. Someday she'd want to look at 'em. Someday she'd heal." Fran remains silent for a minute, and then adds, "There was a time when we were all happy together."

Paul looks in Christine's direction. He remembers Stone's challenge: ask her about her relationship to Dad.

"If God were to judge Dad, why would he have to forgive a lot?"

Christine doesn't answer.

"Does it have something to do with Queenie?"

Christine flinches, as if he touched her with a hot poker. "Don't ever call me by that name again."

"All right."

After a brief silence she says, "He was the first man I loved. He left his mark."

Paul watches her as she gazes out the window into the night.

"Dad created Queenie. He named her. He made that little girl think she was loved. Loved more than anyone else ... Even more than her mother." She looks at Paul and says, "I know what you're thinking. I've known since you started snooping around, talking to that creep Stone.

Daddy never had sex with me. He never fucked me. Never."

"I never thought—"

"But he used me. And he hurt me."

She turns her gaze back toward the window.

"He'd give so much to Queenie, so much more than to his wife, Queenie's head was in the clouds. She reigned from the top of the mountain."

"We all felt it," Fran mumbles, hunched over, his elbows on the table.

Paul notices the trace of bitterness. She was Queenie for him too when he was growing up. He always thought Mother had put her in that position.

"I thought he would never hurt me. But he did. He was only interested in Mom. He didn't love me more. He just used me to hurt her. I don't know if he loved me at all."

She opens her purse, fumbles around inside, and suddenly a flame illuminates her face as she lights a cigarette. Tears have pooled in her eyes and wet her cheeks.

"Sooner or later, Queenie always got dumped. She'd fall off the mountain, and a landslide of pain would hit her chest." She looks at Paul. "You were too young to know the war fought in this house." She stops to look around the dining room and the barroom. "And we—all of us kids, even Stone—we were the weapons."

She takes a drag off the cigarette, stubs it out in her plate, then squeezes one hand with the other, as if a tight grasp could stifle her emotions.

"If he'd been really strong ..."

Fran interjects, "He was strong."

"... he would've left her ... long before Valery. But he couldn't do it. He couldn't let go. And maybe ... maybe there was something more."

"Of course there was. He loved her."

"If he did, he hated her for it."

"No. No." Fran shakes his head, as if he could shake

away her version of the past.

Christine continues, "He just played at leaving. He didn't do anything to change his life. He had affairs with little girls. Impressed them. And broke their hearts. A cheap trick. He was good at that."

Fran continues shaking his head.

She looks at him. "You have wonderful memories of Daddy. I do too. I remember him holding me on his lap and reading to me. I remember the funny stories he used to tell. I remember the feeling of his whiskers against my lips when I kissed him goodnight. I also remember, when I was older, how it felt for Queenie to be forgotten. And how it felt when he wanted me to feel loved—the way he touched me and looked at me. I was lucky he had those girls. And Valery."

Silence.

"What a horrible thing to do to a child, to make her a little queen. To put her in that place." She shakes her head. "I'd do anything, with every man who came after him, no matter how degrading, just to be Queenie. Twenty years of therapy, trying to understand her. " She pauses, and then adds, "Queenie doesn't exist anymore." Another pause. Then she reflects, "For a long time I didn't want to have children. I'm so happy I never had a daughter."

Hunched over his elbows, Fran has listened in silence. He shakes his head and looks at her. "You done? You just about done saying your evil things? He might've strayed. And maybe he didn't always love us the way we would've liked. But he was a good man. That night, he was coming back to her. To us. He'd found his way. If Stone hadn't whispered in her ear—"

"Fran, Mother did it. No matter how hard that is to accept, it's true. He couldn't keep his hands off other women. He couldn't tell the difference between his path in life and the next pretty woman who showed up."

"Stone thought it all up. He's the one who called Dad, he's the one who told him Mother was acting hysterical, and he was afraid of what she might do."

"But she could've very well—"

"Wait, wait, just a minute," Paul interjects. "Stone called Father and asked him to come home?"

Christine and Fran nod their heads, yes.

"But why would he ... ?" Suddenly everything falls into place. Stone had a vested interest in Father driving home in a blizzard. Stone, who was in love with his aunt-mother. Stone, who was crazy enough to believe one day she might marry him. "There was no direct bloodline," he said, as if blood would've been the only obstacle. Stone was jealous of his uncle-father and wanted his aunt-mother all to himself, and that could never be as long as his uncle-father was alive.

Stone wasn't just a victim. Yeah, he was being played, but he was a player too. Mother didn't murder Father all alone. Stone had a hand in it—to what extent, Paul thinks, I'll never know. But this much is certain: Stone was playing his aunt and uncle as much as they were playing him. He'd learned the game. And maybe Stone was playing me too. Of course. He was taunting me when he asked me why Bill decided to drive back to the lodge in a whiteout. "'It'd be interesting to know.'" It sure would. Swenson, the sheriff, would've liked to've known. In one of those *Mirer Times* articles, he wondered why Bill Bauer would risk driving in a blizzard on the same road on which his parents had frozen to death in a blizzard thirteen years before. What Swenson didn't know was that Father was responding to a call from home. But the sheriff must've known about that call; Valery Night would've told him. And that's probably one of the reasons why both were suspicious, and Stone killed them.

Paul shakes his head as he realizes the person he

trusted more than his brother and sister, even more than his mother, had a hand in killing his father. And Christine and Fran knew. No wonder. No wonder he almost never saw them with Stone. It was Paul, a teenager, who would visit Stone at his shack. Paul to whom Stone would talk when he worked around the resort. Oh, sometimes he'd see Fran and Stone together—like the time Stone dressed the carcass of that buck in the woods, and humiliated Fran, and Fran screamed at him. But otherwise, he remembers snide remarks, tension. Stone's a creep, a vampire. It was all there, right in front of him, but because he didn't know, he couldn't see, and he couldn't understand. He's seen so much so quickly, he almost feels dizzy, drunk dizzy.

Christine and Fran are looking at him, probably wondering what's the matter with him.

"I didn't understand. I just didn't understand."

Christine replies, "You weren't supposed to."

"I've been unfair to both of you."

"We've all had to pay for that night. You didn't understand; we understood too much—more than children should ever have to understand. My God, we were just children!" Christine shakes her head, takes a deep breath, and talks through her tears. "We felt so much shame and guilt, but we did nothing wrong. We committed no sin."

Paul looks at Christine's hands folded on the table in front of her. He reaches across the table and takes her hands in his, and then he takes Fran's mutilated hand in his other hand. Time passes. He holds their hands. Her crying stops. She draws one hand out from under his and then covers that hand, so she is holding his hand just as he is holding hers. Eventually Fran places his unmutilated hand on top of Paul's other hand. They remain like this for a long time. It's taken so long for them to let go of the past, to hold one another.

He begins to think about what will happen when they

do let go. They can't continue keeping the secret about the murder to themselves. And the survivors of the sheriff, of Valery Night, of Molly—if there are any—they deserve to know.

"I think we need to talk"

Christine asks, "What?"

"We need to talk to the sheriff about Dad, and Stone, and the other people Stone said he killed. We need to put all this behind us, once and for all."

Christine and Fran stare at him for a long time, and Paul wonders if he has just put up a wall again. But it's too late. They might not ever completely tear down the wall of silence, but they aren't going to rebuild it either.

Christine nods her head. "All right."

Fran nods his head.

Paul releases their hands. "I'll call him in the morning."

Paul invites Janovich to the lodge and tells him everything that happened the night he talked with Stone. When he describes Stone wounding him, the sheriff looks up from his notes and nods his head; he knew all along the story about the branch falling on his neck wasn't true. Christine and Fran confirm that Stone might have played a role in murdering their father and that he sank the body to the bottom of the Black Hole. After the three siblings finish, Janovich looks over his notes.

"There's no way," he tells them, "to corroborate Robert's claim he murdered Sheriff Swenson or Valery Night. No one ever found any clues that could be tied to a murderer in the case of Swenson, and as for Night, she and the car could be in any of a thousand places. Robert was right about that—there's enough black water around here to hide an army.

"Now, his story about Molly, that kind of surprises me. You see, we got good evidence suggests a guy who was executed in a prison in Texas just a few weeks ago, he killed Molly. He told another prisoner about it not long before he got his last meal. We let the *Mirer Times* know and they published an article. Funny thing is, Robert talked to me about it one day when I ran into him in town. Probably the last day he was alive. He asked me if I thought we'd solved the case. Had kind of a funny look in his eye." The sheriff shook his head. "Robert was a strange bird. Hard to figure out."

"That's a bit of an understatement, Sheriff," Paul says, wondering why Stone would have lied to him.

Janovich nods his head, then pauses, appearing to weigh his words. "As for your father, that hole you talked about has been his grave all this time, and your mother's ashes have come to rest with his remains. I don't see any reason to disturb their peace."

That night, dead tired, Paul falls into a deep sleep, a sleep that feels deep even to his unconscious mind, as if he were thousands of feet beneath the surface of an ocean. He's standing in a room illuminated somehow in the center, shadows all around. There's a bed in the middle of the room. He moves closer. Mother is lying on her back, her eyes staring at the ceiling. She's wearing a white gown, perhaps a wedding dress. He stands above her, looking down at her face, her dark brown hair. There's something like star dust beneath her beautiful dark eyes and across the bridge of her nose. He bends over her face and blows the star dust away, but all the features of her face blow away as well. Where her eyes were, there's now just the smooth, unblemished surface of skin. He becomes aware of a heap in a corner of the room; he knows that heap is his mother's corpse.

*
*   *

The next morning, everything's packed. In less than an hour, he and Christine will leave for Minneapolis. He calls Claire. After the fourth ring, someone picks up. He hears Claire's voice.

"*Allô.*"

"Claire."

"Paul?"

"*Je rentre.* I'm coming home."

ACKNOWLEDGEMENTS

Writing a book manuscript is a solitary project, but transforming that manuscript into a book that people will read requires a team effort. I was very fortunate to have Amy Cutler, my production editor at Beaver's Pond Press, head up a team that included Jennifer Manion, my astute editor, and Jay Monroe, the gifted designer who created a visually stunning book.

Many people have helped me grow over the years and become the writer I am today. I want to thank those whose names come to mind.

- Bharati Mukherjee, Helen Schulman, and the writers at two Bread Loaf Writers Conferences, as well as Julie Schumacher and the graduate students in her class of Advanced Fiction Writing, who critiqued early drafts of chapters from Whiteout.

- Alison McGhee and Mary Logue, who provided me with excellent critiques of the entire manuscript.

- My writers group: Amy McCumber, Angela Henriksen, Claudia Kelly, Laura Waxman, Reva Rasmussen, Teresa Chandler, and Victoria Tirrel, who critique all my work.

- My friends who have sustained me in good times and bad: Serge and Barbara Guérout, Barry Woodward, and Tod Sloan, as well as Paul Bergh and Jill Barnum, who died much too young.

- My parents, Dorothy and Edwin Duren, both deceased, and my brother and sisters Gary, Sharon, Deborah, and Deanna, who have all influenced me in ways too complex to enumerate here.

- Laurie Cherry, my niece, who is always supportive.

- Marie Kirchner Stone, one of my high school English teachers, who turned my life around, and Hélène Cixous, my mentor at the University of Paris, who inspired me to redefine my course once again.

- Marie-Hélène Estrade and Laurie Ingram, who will always have a place in my heart.

- My sons Neil, Michael, and Daniel, who have taught me so much about love. I understand things today that I could have never understood without them.

- And Jane Basssuk, my partner in all things, one of the kindest people I have ever known, who understands that we live for dreams and love, to give and receive, to nurture and grow.